Sons of Osiris

Book I

The Sword of Kings

For Devin

MICHAEL WESTMORELAND

Sons of Osiris: The Sword of Kings by Michael Westmoreland

First Edition: March 2022

Copyright © 2022 by Michael Westmoreland

www.michaelwestmoreland.com

All rights reserved. No portion of this book may be reproduced in any form without permission from the publisher, except as permitted by U.S. copyright law. For permissions contact Michael Westmoreland at
westofthemores@gmail.com

This novel is entirely a work of fiction. The names, characters and incidents portrayed in it are the work of the author's imagination. Any resemblance to actual persons, living or dead, events or localities is entirely coincidental.

Michael Westmoreland asserts the moral right to be identified as the author of this work.

Michael Westmoreland has no responsibility for the persistence or accuracy of URLs for external or third-party Internet Websites referred to in this publication and does not guarantee that any content on such Websites is, or will remain, accurate or appropriate.

Cover Art design © Graphic Soul Art
Internal Map design © Graphic Soul Art
https://www.instagram.com/graphicsoulart/
https://www.graphicsoulart.com/

Edited by Dan Larsen and Kris McCormick
https://www.greenpeneditorial.com/

For Nikki

OSIRIAN KINGDOMS
EHTHILIA
MONSCARREN
KORZEG
DAECE
VOLUUTIA
SKULPOS
HOSTELLUS
MERRININE
THE ORLESTIAN SEA
Nuuthracia River
Vekroa River
Hylonen River
Myladacee River
Aeno Langdem River

The Sword of Kings

Book I

- Prologue -

In an era of swords and spears, where maps are drawn with the blood of soldiers, the Old World stood upon the brink of collapse as war and pestilence rampaged across the landscapes. Uncaged, these omens of annihilation slaughtered at will. They destroyed entire populations in a matter of days.

Cavernous mountains separate the tribes of rivaling nations, and vast forests spread through the valleys like blankets of green. Barons and lords have scattered to the far corners of their territories, leaving nothing but mud and muck between them. With each year, the battlegrounds grow larger and pressure the local settlements to abandon their roots. Rusting blades, rotting corpses, and desolate encampments fill the valleys in oceans of ruin.

The Age of Kings had been long forgotten, creating a period of darkness for all of mankind. Any who dared reach for the crown never lasted long; the gallows became their final homes in less than a month. The world craved a savior; it called for its ruler to rise from the ashes and pave a way to a new dawn. The darkened times persisted, however, casting shadows of death and doubt to everything it touched. Doomed lie the world, and as so it remained.

But, amidst the chaos tearing at the seams, a new challenger appeared. Armies of brutishly skilled men poured over the western mountains in droves, forcing all in their wake into submission. Those who resisted were sent to the dirt without hesitation. The clans of the Old World panicked. They decided to band together for the first time in hundreds of years to rise against these invaders. However, no matter their numbers or tactics, they stood no chance in defeating the wicked nature of the men from the mountains. Natives of the dying lands fled like rats as red flags flickered in the distant winds. They all came to fear this new tribe.

The tribe of the Aznogs.

Unsatisfied, legions of Aznogsi warriors descended into the valleys seeking plunder with their engines of war to fuel the campaigns they launched against the native clans for complete control of the known territories. They grew hungry for the Old World, preferring it greatly over the uninhabitable mountain chains they ventured from. And so, they conquered all they wandered upon and restored a sense of order to the native clans.

The Aznogs operated without strict leadership; their way of life dictated that no one man could ever hold influence over the entire civilization. Instead, strength became the law for their tribe. Aggression was rewarded and cowardice punished. Those born into the tribe unworthy of the armies were slain to weed out the weaker breeds, leaving those who remained the fiercest any army could offer. The young and ravenous replaced the old and frail, and this cycle repeated without mercy, without warning, and without failure.

The Old World transformed into a system of classes with the Aznogsi warlords at the top. Common soldiers and the women and children of their tribe sat just below. All else remained under their heels, either as slaves or the lucky few who managed to prove their worth as tradesmen. Years passed, and the Aznogs scoured the lands of all they could take. They grew stronger with each captured village and felled enemy. The tribe became unstoppable – until they reached the sea.

Finally, the almighty Aznogs stretched themselves to the limits of their empire, the world growing smaller the more they advanced. Without a neighboring civilization to defeat, the warlords grew restless. They turned their eyes to one another. The standard rule, the only rule, that the Aznogs abided by-to never war with each other-faded like stones sinking in a murky abyss. Soon enough, the darkened times returned. Brother turned against brother, friend against friend, and the law of strength shifted to savagery among the tribe. The curse of the Old World had returned.

The gods watched the earth burn once more. Neshka, ruler of the spiritual planes and creator of man, wept as her children tore at one another like untamed beasts. To combat their inevitable extinction, she bestowed upon them a gift, hoping a worthy redeemer would arise to restore true order and enter in an era of peace.

Atop the highest peak of the central mountain chain that divided the Old World, a beam of light scorched the earth. A hint of gold trickled down from the whirling clouds, and all peoples within eyeshot flocked to it, curious as to what phenomenon had occurred. As the first tribesmen climbed over the rocks, their eyes beheld a glorious sight. A golden sword floated down and hovered above the ground. The Aznogs had never seen such a design of blade before, for three edges sprung from the hilt in a corkscrew to the tip. Mesmerized, they raced for it. Their greed for a new weapon of war blinded them to the dangers that came wrapped around it.

One by one, the Aznogsi men and women made their attempt to pry the sword from the shimmering aura of light it rested within. The sword weighed their sins and past misdeeds, eager to find its true wielder among the masses. Any tainted soul that approached angered it. The aura around the blade rose to life and burned the hearts of the undeserving, carving holes in their chests with bolts of holy fire. Eventually, the hopeful faces of the tribe's youth fled in terror and never climbed the mountain again. Until, one day, a young boy from the farthest outreach of the Aznogsi empire ascended the cliffs to test his worth.

Hands covered in blood and body near collapse, the slave boy staggered toward the beam of light with weary eyes, and the protective aura gathered in his direction and stretched out to him. He planted his shaky feet in the earth, stiffened his posture, and held a prideful chin to the light. Neshka saw the purity deep within the young boy and pitied him. The strength of a bear and courage of a lion sang out from his heart. Shortly after, the sword hovered out from its ethereal shell and presented itself.

"*Talos gad, (Take it,)*" a heavenly voice said to him from the passing winds.

He touched the jeweled hilt with his forefinger, sliding his palm across the grooves molded from gold shortly after. As soon as the slave boy strengthened his grip on the sword, the energy of a thousand suns exploded into his body. A red shine coursed through his veins, up through his gasping mouth, pointed toward the sky.

"*Zo hollos zura, primuus torrosa, (I bless thee, chosen redeemer,)*" the heavenly voice said. "*Shezek sen glask, rueunesk sen mars ... carasang gaz luciden ig healang rast cin ... zot ifantas, zot vellentoz, zot ... Osiris. (Broken to sand, weathered to stone ... born in light and raised from ash ... my child, my creation, my ... Osiris.)*"

The slave boy screamed at the intense pain of Neshka's gift infusing into the very fiber of his being. Armed with the power of the gods in his blood, Osiris stood atop the mountain a new man. A hulking figure replaced the weak and beaten body that stood before the sword. Osiris studied the glow in his veins and the golden blade in his hand. He surveyed the lands below, sneering upon the filth of the Aznogsi nations, and vowed to bring forth a new order.

Osiris trekked through the territories of the Aznogsi warlords and unleashed the same cruelty they had rendered unto the Old World. Some saw his divinity as his right to rule, gathering under the banner of the gilded eagle. The rest required ... persuasion.

Within a year, Osiris had amassed an army fit enough to march upon all others. He wrangled the anarchy of the Aznogsi ways, bringing true law wherever he roamed. Like the native clans of the Old World, the Aznogsi warlords decided to gather in unison to devise a plan of retaliation. A meeting was summoned, and the warlords received grand invitations. When they arrived, however, they quickly realized they had been deceived.

There, before them, stood the Holy Uniter, wielding the blessed sword in one hand and sorcery in the other. Osiris swiftly put an end to the nine Aznogsi warlords and declared his supremacy. He tore the corpses into a dozen pieces each, tied them to the masterless horses, and sent a message to every man and woman still following the rule of savagery that all who dared oppose him would meet the same fate.

With peace declared, the clans of the Old World and the Aznogsi tribe merged seamlessly; two civilizations became one and more advanced foundations of infrastructure strengthened the roots of these kingdoms. Cities expanded in all directions, weapons of war developed for defensive purposes, and wealth amassed as the people harvested the bounties of the land around them. The caste system that separated the two peoples melted away. Common currency arose, languages integrated with one another, and knowledge was shared. The Age of Steel followed the darkened times, and the Old World was reborn by the Holy Uniter's hand. All who rallied under his banner hailed the great King Osiris, the first king to establish a sustainable government since the feudal era. The earth healed, villages grew to towns teeming with life, and a sense of order laid the foundation for the scientific and industrial revolutions to follow.

The years ticked by, and Osiris grew weary trying to manage thousands of square miles of territory from the eastern seas to the western mountains. Though the golden sword he carried granted him a lengthened life, he knew his empire would not last after his death. And so, Osiris fathered eight children with his chosen queen. The power bestowed upon him only allowed male heirs to enter the New World, an unmovable tradition that carries on till this day. Each son that Osiris raised was given a portion of his kingdom to rule, creating eight separate nations that formed the territory called Osiria.

Ehthilia, a land of roving hills and green fields, acted as the frontline for all travelers who wished to enter from the mountains beyond the known world. Hostellus, the kingdom in the crater, rested between the natural borders of the hills and stony peaks with a handful of entrances, isolating it from the rest. Monscarren, the land of red mountains, invited the land's finest stonemasons and architects to thrive among the brick and clay. Korzeg, the known world's most northern kingdom, saw fierce winters and forced the inhabitants to live buried in the snow. Voluutia, home of the horse lords, allowed its people to build their cities upon the mesas, giving them invaluable defenses against invaders. Merrinine, the endless grasslands, stretched far and wide across the southern border, twice as large as any other kingdom; the great river that ran through its heart gave life to all the cities and towns on its banks. Skulpos, the coastal kingdom, exported oceanic goods for all its neighbors and brought forth exotic fishes from the sea. And, finally, Daece, a series of fortresses clustered together, utilized the natural defenses of the towering forests to keep its people safe and to preserve many of the original manuscripts written by Osiris and his closest disciples in grand libraries guarded by the woodland gods themselves.

The eight kingdoms of Osiria entered a pact by force of Osiris's decree. War would never come to them from another, and they were to unite as one nation should foreign invaders lay claim to their lands.

Osiris's sons ruled his nations as he overlooked them all, acting as the final magistrate should conflict arise for any reason. He roamed with vigor, but the spirit of a god could not live within a physical body forever. To cement his legacy on the world, Osiris called for his children and assembled an eternal brotherhood, a guild of his descendants to pass down the divine right to rule to all who held Osirian blood in their veins. The Holy Uniter engraved his mark on the world, creating the Order of Sons to carry out his will until the end of time.

Each heir spawned from his blood became a Son of Osiris upon birth, and, in his waning years, Osiris ensured that all living members of his Order came to follow the creeds he had created. The day when his spiritual entity outpaced his physical body came swiftly. After nearly two-hundred years of reign, Osiris ordered the priests of his temples to bring forth his ascension ceremony. From light he had been created, and to the light he returned. The soul of the Holy Uniter flew across the winds and settled in every major temple that had been erected for his tribute, fading back and forth between this world and the spiritual planes.

But, of course, amidst his absence, peace did not last. His direct children, The Eight Sons, gnashed their teeth at one another as their father's holy relic rested in a monastery without a declared inheritor. They dared not break their father's code, but the creed they swore failed to hold back the bickering that led to violence among the Sons on plentiful occasions. Some argued that the sword be kept where it lay: dormant and away from the world, as it was not needed. Others claimed that it should be used as it was meant to be and that neighboring, unexplored lands should be colonized.

Tensions rose but the armies of The Eight Sons remained caged behind the walls of their cities. An entirely different type of war broke out across the kingdoms: one of information, of espionage. All the Sons waited patiently for one to overreach so they could justify a campaign for the Sword of Kings. Eventually, one of them snapped. The sword was taken, and eight nations plunged into civil war. The wielder battled against all other kings, marching toward the eastern sea for reasons unknown. As quickly as he took the relic from its cradle, the sword carrier met his grisly demise at the hands of his brothers. They cursed his soul, blackening his shade for all eternity, and damning him to the darkest depths of the afterlife. In doing so, though, the sword slipped through their fingers. It became lost to the world for centuries along with its limitless power.

The search for Osiris's blade became an obsession for the Sons, and on many such occasions, neighboring kingdoms entered partnerships to find it. They scoured every inch of the known world, but their father's relic was nowhere to be found. One after the other, the Sons abandoned their quest altogether. The golden sword faded into a myth. There are some, though, who cater to the legend of the mighty Sword of Kings and seek it in secrecy.

It is now the nine-hundred and seventy-third year in the Age of Steel, ten centuries after Osiris was crowned by Neshka. Clues of the sword's whereabouts have surfaced, and one king is determined to find it at any cost. He must be careful, though, for where there are lions ... lie hyenas.

Chapter 1
The Black Prince

Day 12 in the Month of Snow, Year 973 in the Age of Steel

Darkness circled over the village in the form of endless storm clouds. Lightning cracked the sky in a rainless onslaught. A man, trembling with exhaustion and covered in ash, stood in the town center and aimed his bloodied longsword at every movement in the alleyways and streets branching off from the main road. Eyes darting back and forth, he watched for the demons stalking him from afar, waiting for him to lower his guard. A hundred corpses littered the courtyard, most of them bearing shoddily made garments of animal skins. The others wore decorative, black armor and dual-horned helmets. Though their eyes hid behind the thick steel protection, the man sensed their gaze upon him.

"We're waiting ... Zededia," a ghostly voice said, calling from the void.

Zededia shifted back and forth, unsure of where his attackers would come from next, and time slowed to half-speed. He looked to his right and saw one of his last remaining soldiers fall to his knees as an axe cleaved its way through his neck. Another shouted in pain as an enemy warrior hacked his arm off. A third man under his command sprinted over the bodies armed with a one-handed sword. Zededia beckoned for the survivor to join him and pivoted together, back-to-back.

In his peripheral vision, several distorted figures raced between the city buildings, laughing and clanging their weapons against the ground. Paranoia usurped control. The fear of death and desolation stunned him. As Zededia looked on, more of his soldiers fell lifeless to the earth.

"You ... cannot ... save ... them...," a low, more wicked voice said. "You ... will ... die!"

The phantoms pursuing him poured from every crevice of the village, wailed like the damned, and surrounded him in black shadows.

~ ~ ~

Then, suddenly, everything ground to a halt. The horridness of the vision faded as the man woke from his nightmare in a slithery, cold sweat. He flinched at the dream, hiding from the shame of that day earlier in his life when he had let his rage roam unchallenged. Heart pounding, his eyes dashed back and forth. He tried his damnedest to regain mental balance, but his solitude ended as quickly as it began. The illusion melted from memory as a loud knocking from the chamber doors shook his confusion away and brought the man's attention to another issue. Sitting upright in his bed of wolf pelts and delicate silk, he pushed his hands across his face, eventually forcing himself up on quivering legs.

He stumbled across his room, illuminated by the dim moonlight that glistened across the marble floors. A large bay window in the tower of his fortress allowed the white light to clearly shine through. The man gathered his cloth tunic from an old table across the room. He eyed a large map of the surrounding area and observed the markings on the coarse parchment, including a small dagger stabbed into the table through the left-center portion. Running his fingers across the crude map, he circled the dagger point around the white symbol scripted underneath the blade along with the name of the castle he focused on: Vaedor Sellos, the City of Victors, written in an ancient language of the kingdom's founders. The thoughts of his older brother, the king of the Hostellus, angered him.

Zededia placed his palm on his forehead, which throbbed and felt warm to the touch. He ran his hands over his shaven face and his short, chestnut brown hair to drive out the fatigue. As the knocking continued, he proceeded to dress in the rest of his usual attire: a tunic covering him from shoulder to mid-thigh, a black cloth undershirt that reached his wrists, and a large ring that held a bright blue gemstone on his left forefinger. He brushed a patch of pale skin on his left wrist where a bracelet once was, and he struggled to remember where he had left it. Next, he slid his slender legs through a pair of thick cotton pants. Stumbling in the darkness, he attempted to lace his leather boots. The click from his shoes against the floor rolled in his ears and overwhelmed the knocking and muffled words from beyond the wooden doors.

"Oh, for shit's sake," he said. "I'm coming."

He threw a long, dark cape over his shoulder and then pulled the hood over his head. The torn cloak barely reached the floor behind his heels. His aggravated thoughts stirred, and he cursed the early summoning.

The concern and confusion from his dream remained distant. Faltering once more, he moved toward the visitor at the door. The prince loosened his shoulders, stiff from the night, and cracked the bones in his neck. Iron hinges and handles jolted against the cedarwood, causing an echo to bounce against the chamber walls. After a moment, he sighed under his breath and raised his dry eyes to the man outside his chamber.

"What is it, Caedus?" the tall prince said in a dull tone.

His cerulean irises pierced the lantern-lit hall's darkness as he looked to his summoner.

"My prince, a caravan is entering the Blackwood from the Merrinine checkpoint high in the mountains," the shorter man dressed similarly to him answered with a deep voice that hummed.

"And?" the prince said as he started to place disbelief in the importance of his summons. "Caravans pass through our lands daily."

"A Vaedorian escort surrounded it, Zededia. Two dozen soldiers at least. A bit unusual, no?"

The muddled Prince Zededia paused for a moment. He rubbed the bridge of his nose as he thought of the circumstances that could revolve around his soldier's news.

"Why is Matticus sending such an armed garrison through my lands at this time of night?" Zededia said with closed eyes. "They must know that the torches would be spotted from a great distance. And why are they coming from Merrinine?"

"Some sort of assault?" Caedus asked.

"No," Zededia said, a hand covering his face. "Matticus hasn't even been able to march within two miles of the tower in daylight, much less in the dead of night. He gave up chasing after us a long time ago. However, if he thinks that a horribly disguised attack from the mountains above will differ from the past, he's descended into a deeper madness than what plagues him."

Zededia paused to consider his older brother's bold tactics.

"He's transporting something," he said with a tired sigh.

"Hmm?" Caedus said.

"Something he deems the lives of thirty men a worthy price for its deliverance."

"Do you think he's found the sword?" Captain Caedus asked.

The fabled weapon of his ancestor hadn't passed through his brain in months. However, he hadn't forgotten his family's obsession with the artifact. The thought of holding it for himself infected his brain much like it did his father.

"Unlikely," he replied. "If Matticus learned of the sword's location, he'd send every man in Vaedor Sellos to find it."

"Should we let them pass, then?"

Zededia slowly shook his head. He thought for a moment about what Matticus could be transporting that was so valuable other than the Sword of Kings.

"No. Whatever they're doing here, it rises above normal trade. Take Seether with you. Intercept them. Bring me the survivors."

"Yes, my prince," the loyal captain said.

Zededia dismissed Caedus with a flick of his wrist and heard his footsteps fade in the distant stone staircase. The prince then exhaled and walked back into his chamber. To dissolve his exhaustion for good, he took a handful of chilled water from a silver bowl nearby and splashed it on his face. Fully awake, the prince paced over to his bay window and observed the early morning darkness with the moon arched high in the sky. His eyes swayed over the vast, dense forest that surrounded his fortress, and he noticed a thick fog that concealed his brother's castle on the other side of the crater that encircled Hostellus.

Several minutes later, as the prince surveyed the foothills, he heard his castle's iron gates rise. He looked down below his chamber and listened to the metallic gallops of his men riding off from the great stronghold submerged into the mountainside.

Satisfied with Caedus's swiftness, Zededia turned away from the window and inhaled once more. Releasing his frosted breath, he paused to align his priorities and decided to seek spiritual aid for his troubling dream and the haunting memory that it brought back.

The prince departed from his chambers and navigated his way through the central tower. Widespread and open, the grounds behind the sturdy walls of his fortress separated them from hundreds of merged buildings built from stone and thatch and soothed his eyes. The sight of his home warmed him. His castle remained silent, save a light rainfall that swept over the forest. He eyed the massive barracks where half of his army slept while the other half took posts on the walls. The night guard patrolled thoroughly, wandering between the paved streets, crenelated walkways, and entrances of every major building or sector of the city.

Zededia nodded to greet them as he passed, and when he traversed beyond the soldiers' district, he looked upon the grand temple entrance embedded into the mountain. Large, round columns stood tall from the peristyle outside the archway to the sanctuary. The rain highlighted the moonlight across their impressions as droplets trickled down.

The prince approached the temple with crossed arms and a hooded head to conceal himself from the rain. He scanned the insides of the circular interior and saw a woman in decorative robes kneeling in front of a large, godlike statue. As Zededia explored, he sensed the priestess rise in his peripheral vision while his primary focus lingered on the marvelous marble figure. Pacing around the deep reflecting pool, he stared into the water and felt the soothing warmth of a lit altar nearby.

He crept lightly to leave the priestess at ease. His eyes drifted to the large tapestries that displayed religious symbols before he shifted his attention to the priestess.

"Welcome, young Zededia," she said while turning to face him. "How may I be of service to one of Neshka's children?"

The prince continued toward the woman and kept his arms hidden. He approached the edge of the reflecting pool and looked into the shining water. The priestess softly gripped his forearm shortly after.

"What ails you, sire?" the oracle asked. "Seldom do you visit me without a burden."

He hesitated, reliving the nightmare through his thoughts while the matronly woman moved her hand to his shoulder.

"My sleep evades me," the prince said with a hazy voice. "I am troubled by a recurring vision."

"I see," the priestess said quietly. "Your mother often found distress in her sleep as you do. What do you see in these dreams?"

Pausing once more, Zededia looked to the pool to escape the answer.

"Death," the prince said, "at my hands."

"Hmm."

Zededia understood the vagueness of her answer but hesitated still. He tightened his lips and replaced his focus.

"I'm ... back at the territory of Konkour ... back when we initiated our invasion. I walked through the moments of that day as clear as they occurred."

"Ah, yes. Konkour has haunted you for many years now. A dark day of your past."

"Yes," the prince said. "I can't seem to shake its hold on me."

Zededia heard a chuckle rise from his counselor.

"And why do you want to forget such a day? Mistakes are only valuable if we learn from them, not forget them."

"I have learned; I am reminded every day," Zededia said as he started to raise his voice. "My past stalks me like a shadow. There is no removing it from memory."

He shamefully looked back at the priestess after she lifted her hand from his arm.

"Then you still have learning to do."

The prince shifted his lips to one corner after hearing what he didn't want to.

"Your journey to peace begins here," the woman said as she placed a finger on his chest. "Face your mistakes and ask for forgiveness. If you don't know who to ask, then ask yourself. Perhaps you can find it in your meditation, my prince. It is a powerful tool for you."

Zededia nodded, thanked the wise woman, and turned to leave.

"Neshka watches over all her creations, especially Osirians. It would be wise to seek her."

The prince emptied his lungs, having left any thought of Neshka and divinity sunken in the dirt.

"I don't need help from the gods," Zededia said as he walked away from the priestess. "I can solve this myself."

The thought of succumbing to the help of the divine caused conflict within him. While his travels led him to many encounters with the old gods in the spiritual plane, many of them proved too constricting to make his efforts worth the trouble.

Leaving the temple grounds in the misty rain, Zededia longed for an alternate route of alleviation. The prince wandered around the inner sector of his castle and saw the emptiness of the darkened morning. By day, his home would be teeming with life and commerce, but he enjoyed the quiet brought by nightfall. To avoid the cold drizzle, he stepped toward the shelter of the buildings in the town center. He eyeballed a small cave-like entrance in the rocky cliffside across the courtyard and stirred his courage to brave the rain once again.

As a perk to his home, Anzagaar Nostir, a natural hot spring flowed from the mountains that surrounded the Hostellian territory. A sheltered stone building had been built inside the cave and over the spring to domesticate it, and the warm waters had given him relief from winter's bite in previous years.

Upon his arrival at the springs, Zededia's facial expression returned to its normal state: blank and emotionless. He wiped the water from his chin and turned his attention to the ceiling of the bathhouse. Over the rectangular pool that centered the room, hundreds of gems and rocks shone like stars in the sky. Zededia remembered stories of how his ancestors built these Illumination Chambers to channel their spiritual energy. He pictured the same type of place that lay deep within the Hostellian Mountains directly behind Vaedor Sellos on the other side of the crater in a similar cave.

The prince removed his damp clothing piece by piece and laid them on a natural shelf nearby. He twisted his torso to loosen his spine, and his dense, plentiful muscles shifted under his skin. As he moved closer, he looked up to the illusionistic auras above, and the white dots seemed to follow his eyes. They soothed him, removing the weight of time on his mind. Slowly, the naked prince placed his feet on the first step of the spring. Hot coals kept the water warm, and the spring's source ran deep into the earth. Zededia stepped onto the second step and let the bath melt the frost in his bones.

After allowing his lower legs to acclimate to the temperature, the prince fully submerged himself into the calming pool. He surfaced, wiped the blurriness from his face, leaned against the wall with his arms along the bank, and rested his head with closed eyes. The spring's humidity kissed his bare skin and covered him in a film of condensation. His body smiled at the relaxing sensation. As Zededia began to unwind, he started to slip into the void.

He allowed his mind to detach from his body as the priestess had suggested. His senses departed from the material world, and the prince sank farther into the meditative state as the conciliating current of water surrounded him.

Warring within him, the harrowing illusions from Zededia's dream battled with his will to drive them away. He concentrated with all his self-discipline to force his brain to sharpen in focus. His physical body flinched when moments of tension arose. Completely gone from the material plane, Zededia wandered through trials of meditative practices for nearly two hours.

Finally, after a grueling process of concentration, the dissociated prince found the center of his composure. His mind ceased to fire as violently as it did before, and peace flowed like a calm stream. Once Zededia found balance, he released a deep exhale and, with it, all his stress. The tranquility didn't last for much longer, though, as heavy, wet footsteps stomped against the floor of the bathhouse.

"Commander," Captain Caedus said as he jogged into the humid cave.

The Black Prince clenched his eyes as he fell back into reality. He tensed his shoulders to release the stiffness in his torso.

"We've returned."

"Your timing is impeccable, Caedus," Zededia said in a teasing manner as he remained in his relaxed position with closed eyes.

His body fought against his need to leave the pool with muscles drained from the overexposure to the hot waters.

"Shall I let the Vaedorians make themselves at home, then? Maybe brew them a cup of tea?"

Zededia mustered the strength to pull himself out of the spring and walked toward where his apparel lay. As the prince shivered away from the pool, he gazed out of the cave entrance and discovered that the light spray of rain had shifted into a violent storm.

"No, I suppose not," he said.

A flash of light illuminated the dark bathhouse for a split second, and the deep roar of thunder followed shortly behind. The prince sighed.

"Let's go."

Zededia tightened the strings that held his tunic together and put a firm hand on his captain's shoulder as he exited the spring. The freezing rain covered his face and chilled his skin, snapping his focus back to the matter at hand.

Before scaling the main tower of his castle where his prisoners remained, Zededia entered his chambers to grab his weapon that had made a name for itself across Hostellus and the surrounding lands. The prince walked over to the east wall, where a marble shrine jutted from the floor to meet his waist. Upon the shiny, minuscule mesa, Zededia's great longsword rested within a bundle of silk. He removed the fabric cover layer by layer, and the white-silver edge of the blade glowed in the prince's eyes from the candlelight behind him.

As Zededia took a firm grip of the lethal steel, the sinister nature that came along with carrying it coursed through him. Memories of the victories won by the razor-thin sword in his hand flooded back to him. With hell to deliver, the prince set off to greet the invaders in his home.

Once he had climbed to the top of his towering fortress, Zededia barged through the wooden door that opened to the roof. He stepped into the thundering rain and turned his head to observe the Vaedorian soldiers with glowing red eyes that appeared from the sorcery in his divine blood. Each guarded by a soldier of the Legonae, Zededia's elite army, four souls from Matticus's transport remained. Fear poured out from them as the Black Prince approached. He gazed upon their white gilded eagle insignia on their chests and sneered.

Zededia held a stone-cold facial expression with his hands behind his back. His hood, along with the darkness of winter's morning rain, covered his face in a clouded shade.

"I had never imagined myself within the walls of Anzagaar Nostir," the lead knight said. "Much less in the presence of a man so damned his own family didn't even want him."

Glancing over the prisoners, Zededia remained unmoved and reserved.

"Courageous words for a dead man," Zededia shouted over the barrage of water. "You should know by now that Vaedorians don't last long in my territory."

The prince flicked his wrist and watched the paladin fall forward after his soldier kneed him to the floor. Zededia's piercing gaze broke through the knight's bravery, but he received no response.

"Why is Vaedor Sellos sending a column of soldiers through my lands from Merrinine?" he asked. "What were you transporting?"

"Eat shit," the knight said. "Just kill me and get it over with."

The prince then raised his eyes to his soldier standing behind the captive and clenched his lips.

"As you wish."

Once the Legonae soldier took a step back from the kneeling Vaedorian, Zededia furiously drew his sword, heaved his arms at the man, and decapitated him as a bolt of lightning exploded in the near distance, thundering over the prince's bellow that followed the strike. The veins in his arm and neck bulged and glowed the famous, bright red color that he and his relatives carried. After watching the blood-spewing corpse fall to the puddles of water on the roof, the prince covered his gritted teeth and recomposed himself.

The crimson splatter from the Vaedorian knight painted each of the other men. Zededia took great delight in the terror he inserted in the other three prisoners. He wiped the blood off his chin, sneered, and washed his coarse hand in the heavy rain.

Zededia jerked his longsword into his left hand and flicked it clean. As he stared at his villainous blade, he ordered his men to dispose of the corpse. They tossed the headless knight over the tower's edge, and Zededia returned to his neutral state.

"You're a monster!" another captured soldier shouted out of panic.

Zededia met the fearful gaze of the second man.

"A monster?" the prince said in a quiet voice.

His blood began to boil once more with vicious anger, and he exploded an open hand toward the second man's throat, crushing his windpipe. Zededia lifted the Vaedorian soldier above his eye level, squeezed the man's esophagus, and glared with hell in his eyes. The longer he held the prisoner, the more he enjoyed the squirming. He drew in the helpless plea from his crying victim, savored the surge of power, and smiled through the storm overhead.

"If you're so loyal to your fellow knight, why don't you join him!" the enraged prince roared as he hurled the chained man toward the jagged mountainside below.

Once Zededia regained his balance from such a violent throw, he heard screams of horror from the Vaedorian he had sent to a shattering fate. Shortly after, the cries ceased as the man splattered against the rocks like a sack of rotten meat.

"There are no monsters here, soldiers of Vaedor Sellos!" Zededia shouted in ecstasy toward the last two survivors.

The veins in his neck and face glowed with a bright red hue once more. He descended from the excitement to regroup.

"Only the damned."

Zededia caught the frightened eyes of a young soldier looking back at him with a shaky gaze. Curiously, he stepped closer to observe the third prisoner.

"You," the prince said as he raised the soaked tip of his sword toward his target. "You're barely of age to fight. What are you doing amongst this lot?"

The stunned prince watched as his present company struggled to mutter a response. For a moment, Zededia found a small sense of remorse growing in his bitter soul.

"I–I am Eros," the small soldier said to the Black Prince. "Son of Eridos. I was– was sent here on my father's behalf."

"Sent on your father's behalf?" Zededia asked in confusion. "What kind of man would send his son to die at the hands of the Black Prince rather than go himself?"

Almost insulted that Matticus would send a boy barely able to speak among men into his territory, Zededia scoffed. His patience withered.

"Speak, boy, while your tongue still wriggles in your mouth."

"My father is ill and cannot serve the crown. By law under King Matticus, an able heir must take the place of the incapable until said person is fit to serve once more."

"And where did good King Matticus send you, hmm?" the Black Prince inquired, sharpening his eyes on the boy.

"S-Skulpos," Eros said.

"Skulpos?" Zededia asked. "What the bloody fuck is he doing there? King Neptabyss is no friend of his. What were you transporting?"

In an instant, the boy's glance twitched over to the fourth prisoner. Zededia widened his eyes and turned his attention as well. When he studied him, the prince noticed that his remaining prisoner differed entirely from the previous. It was then that Zededia noticed that *he* was actually a *she*.

"Take him away," Zededia said to Captain Caedus with his eyes locked onto the girl. "We may have a use for him yet."

As quickly as the prince's order left his mouth, Caedus nodded and pushed the boy forward. Zededia paused in confusion. He studied the poor girl further and noticed her fresh cuts, bruises, and torn clothing.

"Matticus found you in Skulpos, didn't he?" Zededia said to himself. "And he was bringing you ... back to Vaedor Sellos? Why?"

He only received a spiteful gaze in return. Nevertheless, Zededia leaned in.

"He needs you alive," he said, "but he obviously didn't care for your wellbeing beyond that."

The prince reached for her bruised arm, but she squirmed away and denied him. She struck his hand with her elbow, forcing him to retreat. The sharp sound of his soldier unsheathing a sword rang in his ears. Zededia raised his hand to order him to cease.

"It's all right," he said. "She's been through quite a journey for it to end here."

Zededia met eyes with the girl as he knelt on one knee.

"What need does Matticus have for you?" the Black Prince asked.

To his expectation, no answer came from the girl.

"Why was he looking for you?"

She remained silent. Zededia sighed as he stood upright.

"Fine. I suppose I'll do it my way."

The Black Prince opened his left hand and stepped toward the girl. His eyes glowed with a green hue in place of the red one from before. As much as she resisted, she could not deny Zededia his desire for information. He reached toward the girl and firmly placed his hand on her right temple with his thumb over the bridge of her nose. The prince closed his eyes and concentrated on the dark magics from his ancestors. He took a deep breath, cleared his mind, and allowed his spiritual gift to shine.

"Sel kar zant mythraedos, (Show me your mind,)" the Black Prince said in Aznogsi, the language of his ancestors, while staring into the tattered girl's panicking eyes.

As he exhaled, a green aura covered his shoulders and flowed along his forearm toward the girl's head. Like a phantasmal force, the essence seeped into her skull and ejected itself back into its summoner's arm after a few moments. Zededia staggered as the parasitic mist returned. He fought to catch his breath, coughed, and blinked several times as his brain attempted to decipher the reaped imagery. The pale green aura then dug its way into his veins, and his eyes shifted as it coursed through him.

He captured the sight of an ancient temple that sent him into an intoxicated frenzy. Matticus's desperately desired secret bounced through his thoughts. At last, the Sword of Kings revealed itself to another Osirian.

A devious smile grew on his face, and the pale greenness in his eyes faded. As he returned to a normal state, the prince turned to his soldiers and broke out in a burst of subtle, sinister laughter.

"Finally," the Black Prince whispered. "I've found you."

Chapter 2

Rats

Day 12 in the Month of Snow

In the glorious capital city of Hostellus, the mighty King Matticus, eldest son of the deceased King Matias, paced through the throne room of his fortified keep. Nervous, he fiddled with his hands behind his back as he walked, and the leather boots that covered his feet and shins clicked across the floor. After several passes in front of his father's marble statue, Matticus developed a sullen expression and rubbed his fingers across his lower jaw and over his chin's dense, rough hairs.

"Sire," an elderly, gray-bearded man in bright white robes splattered with blood said from the nearby staircase. "The child is here."

The king shifted and jogged to the stone staircase toward his chambers. His white and blue robes that signified royalty flowed against his body as he ascended the keep's levels.

Once at his quarters, he heard a muffled, high-pitched cry from the other side of the wall. Matticus placed his palm on the large wooden door and gently pried it open. He scanned the room and saw several young women around his bed. Looking behind them, he moved toward the soft cry to gaze at the newest member of his family.

Matticus made his way through the small crowd until his queen came into view. With a tender touch, he placed his hand on her forearm as she held the newborn. He brushed her messy hair aside and focused on her beauty and the child they had brought into the world. The Vaedorian king flushed his anxiety and sighed a breath of relief.

After a few moments, he knelt beside the bed and held the queen's hand in his own. Matticus then felt a firm grip on his shoulder.

"A perfectly healthy young prince, Your Majesty," the physician said as he turned his attention to the queen.

Matticus embraced his wife and child as the healer inquired about the queen's health.

"What shall his name be, Livia?" he asked with a joyous voice of honey.

A pause emerged as the queen attempted to catch her breath. Meanwhile, Matticus's pride peaked as he observed the squealing child who would strengthen his legacy.

"En ... Ender," Queen Livia said with the little amount of strength she retained.

"Ender," the king said to himself as he took his child into his hands. "And so, a new Son of Osiris is born."

Matticus's attention broke once he heard the doors of his chambers creaking. He turned to find his first son peering through the opening.

"Come, Mattox, don't be shy," Livia said.

Matticus handed Ender back to the queen and beckoned for his eldest. He brushed the toddler boy's head with his hand as he scurried by. At home with his family, the king relaxed in the euphoria of the moment.

"My king," a young squire said from the doorway. "The Hostellian lords have gathered in the council room. They request your immediate presence."

Frustrated, King Matticus exhaled and shook his head, and a stern look overthrew the jovial expression on his squared face.

"When do they not?" he said to himself.

Matticus looked to the queen for approval of a sudden disappearance, and he received a gentle nod. In return for her understanding, he gave a remorseful bow before setting a course for the government hall connected to the keep by a stone walkway on the second floor. Forced to suppress the warm emotions in his heart, he replaced them with more sovereign and mature thoughts. He had never enjoyed the council meetings, but they proved to be a necessary aspect of his rule.

As the king trudged along the stone sky bridge, he prepared himself for the argumentative atmosphere that consumed these types of gatherings. From the outer balcony, he could already hear the various lords and clergies bickering among themselves. Matticus placed his palm on the council chamber's doors and took a moment to rally his strength.

He stepped inside, ignored his shouting subjects, and noticed a hooded figure in a blue cloak leaning in the dark corner near the entrance. A subtle wave flew his way as he passed.

Matticus took his place at the head of the table and raised his open right hand out of bewilderment toward the leaning figure in the corner.

What the hell is going on? Matticus mouthed to Prince Lucien, his brother and third son of Matias.

His gesture of annoyed confusion received a slight shrug from his brother. The tension elevated, causing his ears head to throb.

"Enough!" the king shouted over the other men as he rubbed the bridge of his nose.

Effectively silenced, the troubled men around the council room turned their attention to Matticus and, once he sensed their eyes upon him, he brushed his face with his hand.

"Why am I here, Boaros?" Matticus asked the corpulent military man to his right.

"My liege, there is trouble brewing among the people of Hostellus. Lord Cerevel has spotted several riders from Anzagaar Nostir near his lands," the armored man said.

"And in addition to that, sire," an older gentleman dressed in white, religious robes said in an interruption. "The caravan you dispatched to Skulpos to intercept the raiding party survivors is at least a week behind schedule. We received a letter from the crater checkpoint three days ago, yes, but that means they should have arrived by now."

"We are five hundred miles from the cliffs of Skulpos, Monselles. Not to mention over half of that journey is through nearly impassable mountains, *and* they had to venture south away from Zededia's lands to avoid being seen," another man said. "It could take them *another* week to return if they need to venture farther south.

"This was a doomed mission from the start. We should be focusing our efforts on strengthening our garrisons around the border."

And then, like clockwork, Matticus watched the remaining councilmen in the chamber erupt once more. He dropped his head, pressing his chin to his large chest.

"Be quiet! All of you!" King Matticus shouted as he slammed his palm on the wooden table. "For the gods' sake, you're going to drive me to murder."

Matticus released a deep breath.

"Now," he said. "Explain to me what's so damn important that it's keeping me from my wife and sons."

After a few moments of collected silence, Matticus sighed.

"Sire," the cleric said. "The people outside of our walls are losing faith in us. Zededia's influence is spreading. Our scouts have reported that some of the outlying towns are already giving him their support."

Matticus squeezed his chin with his thumb and forefinger. The king thought of his exiled brother to the east; his dormant anger toward him rose. He then looked back to Monselles once he broke free from his trance.

"We must regain control of the people, Your Majesty," Monselles said. "If they do not trust that we can protect them with Hostellian knights and sturdy shields, our infrastructure will crumble."

"Then we will burn those villages to the ground. Show all who dare show support for Zededia what is to become of them."

"I would advise against that, my king," one of his military strategists said. "If we are to show hostility to the towns on the outskirts of Hostellus, we risk turning them into martyrs. Additionally, the Black Legion may come to their aid. We are spread too thin already. Until the Hostellae return, we would struggle to overcome Zededia's forces so far from the city's walls."

It had been almost three years since the Hostellae, the primary armies of his kingdom, had embarked to Korzeg to aid King Holthiem in a defensive war against the northern raiders, and Matticus felt the pressure of their absence more so than ever.

"Then what do you propose?" the king asked.

The men at the table around him turned to one another and conversed. Matticus's patience drained, but he found himself in a difficult position.

"There are those within our walls, sire," one of the lords said.

Matticus raised an eyebrow.

"Defectors?" another said.

"It's likely," Spymaster Rachtus said. "Word is spreading across Hostellus of the Black Prince's resistance to Vaedorian rule. He has allies here to carry out his message when our dead return from the battlefield."

"Then we start there," Matticus said, chiming in. "If we are to keep our people in line, we need to regain control on what information is spread among them."

"What would you have us do, sire?" Rachtus asked.

Matticus met the dark, scarred eyes of his Spymaster. After years of learning from his father in the political fields of his home, Matticus thought carefully on how to proceed. His men looked to him for an answer as the pause continued.

"The remnants of Zededia's Order linger in the city," Matticus said. "They hide ... like rats."

The king tapped his finger on the arm of his chair.

"They have evaded our attention for long enough," he said. "If we are to snuff Zededia's influence out from our home, then we are to seize every man, woman, and child who even resembles support for him. Any who harbor members of his Order, any who carry his insignia in their possession, any who so much as speak his name in good will ... they are to be in chains."

Prince Lucien's frown of disapproval caught his attention in his peripheral vision, but he ignored it. The councilmen in front of him nodded one after another.

"There will be one voice in Vaedor Sellos," he said.

"As you command, my liege," Spymaster Rachtus said.

"Good. Now, go."

Matticus flicked his hand forward and dismissed his men. As they stood and stepped away from the table, they each paid him a respectful bow. He kept his eyes glued to the light shining from outside as the door opened, and once the council had left, he brought his palm to his face and pressed his fingers into his eyes. Soft footsteps echoed in the meeting chamber shortly after.

"Well done, Matticus," his brother said with a sardonic tone. "You've effectively turned Vaedor Sellos into a regime."

"Spare me your cynicism, Lucien," he said while pulling his hand away and allowing his eyes to adjust. "Perhaps that's what our kingdom needs right now."

Matticus eyed his brother as he took a seat at the council table and rested his feet on top of it.

"Hostellus needs more sovereignty?" Lucien said with crossed arms. "Two Osirians fighting for control isn't enough?"

"That's precisely what I'm trying to undo, Lucien," the king said in anger.

Lucien glared at him and remained unmoved.

"Hostellus has *one* ruler. *One* king," Matticus said, lifting his forefinger up. "I will protect my kingdom against all threats, regardless of their nature."

"Our brother is not a threat—"

"He is every threat!" Matticus shouted. "Zededia is an enemy of the state! A criminal, a murderer! He threatens everything our father and his father built for us! The Black Legion and the Legonae represent all that is evil in this world!"

Noticing the rage in his voice and the faint glow in his hand from the adrenaline pumping through his system, Matticus leaned back in his chair and released a deep breath to calm himself.

"He is a scourge, Lucien...," Matticus said.

"Do you hold that opinion for Hostellus's benefit?" Lucien asked. "Or for yours?"

Matticus glanced at his brother from the corner of his eye. His brother stood from the table.

"Zededia will never cease to resist you," Lucien said. "You can imprison every man who walks under his flag ... and he will still challenge you for what you did to him."

Without a response, King Matticus sank into his chair. Lucien cast him a discouraged expression, and he watched him turn away to the door of the council chamber.

"You should be with your family, brother," Lucien said over his shoulder.

Matticus's guilt replaced his fading aggression. His scowl disappeared as his brother looked back at him.

"While your humanity is still intact."

~ ~ ~

Uneasy about Matticus's plan of action, Prince Lucien exited the council chamber with a heavy heart. The feud between his brothers further rampaged toward a finale with each passing event. No matter how he approached the situation in his thoughts, he struggled to find any position that would both unite his siblings and offer him sanction from treason. Standing on the balcony that overlooked the inner courtyard below, the prince inhaled the cold, damp air. His lungs awoke from the frigidness, and he released his breath before pulling the hood of his royal blue cloak tighter over his head.

A drink sounded rather appealing to him, and he knew the perfect place to find one while avoiding the attention of the townsfolk.

Unlike his brothers, Lucien despised the spotlight that followed his Osirian name. He found the publicity and attention of the royal family overwhelming on nearly all occasions. After watching Zededia for many years before his exile, the youngest son of Matias had mastered the ability to blend in with the citizens of Vaedor Sellos and vanish from one district to another.

Lucien walked across the balcony and into the keep's main chamber where Matticus's throne lay on a raised floor. The white marble softened his footsteps as he descended the exterior staircase, stepping past the guards of the palace before they recognized him under his cloak. High, dense walls encircled the inner section of his home, and the sun of winter's midday barely topped them to reach his bright green eyes.

The prince effortlessly slipped by a garrison of the Vaedorian Guard, Matticus's personal soldiers that rarely left the upper city. Whenever Matticus ventured through and outside the city, however, they circled him like a moving wall. The white feather plumes on each side of their helmet announced their presence from a mile away, and the massive blue shields they carried could withstand a mangonel strike. Lucien strolled by, keeping a watch for them from the corner of his eye, and he soon reached the towering steel gates that separated the inner sanction of the city from the common grounds on the other side. Lucien walked alongside the rampart until a portion of the mountain jutted from the earth like a pillar to form a natural barrier and broke the wall into segments. He glanced over his shoulder to ensure his solitude, pressed firmly on a loose section of the mountain, and moved it aside.

A small, secretive passageway appeared from behind the makeshift door. Lucien slithered through the tunnel and found himself on a rocky ledge above an alleyway of the city's Mercantile District. Quickly, he hopped down to the paved road, tightened his cloak around his shoulders, and set a course for the teeming street ahead. The shadows of the corridor shielded him from view, but Lucien paused before stepping out into the open, looking for a gap in the sea of scurrying citizens.

When the right moment arrived, the prince meshed into the crowd. Save his towering height, Lucien blended in with the craftsmen of Vaedor Sellos by covering the emblem on his chest and lowering his chin to conceal his face. Though he remained undetected in plain sight, the prince met the eyes of a young boy walking through town with his mother. Lucien presented a half-grin, winked, and pressed on. The clanging of hammers, shouting of merchants, and echoes of conversations filled his ears. Despite the lackluster appearance compared to his life in the palace, the prince enjoyed the aroma of the common areas.

Lucien wove his way down the hilly street until he came upon a clearing near the mountain's base. He eyed a shoddy tavern from under his low hood. Walking carefully toward the alehouse, he searched around, hoping to see someone he expected to meet. However, to his disappointment, the prince found no sign of his company. Deciding to enter the pub nonetheless, he passed through the weathered, creaking doors.

Inside, Lucien glanced at the barkeep and signaled for a drink. Years of sneaking down to the lower city had granted him a few friends among the commoners, and he appreciated their willingness to conceal his identity from the public. Lucien sat in a far corner of the tavern out of sight and placed two gold coins upon the table as the barkeep took them as payment for a tall beverage. He nodded in silence before taking a mouthful of the potent brew. He flinched from the bitter, burning taste. Although he had become quite familiar with the taste of alcohol in his mid-twenties, it stung his throat just the same.

After an hour and through half of Lucien's third ale, the prince watched an old, gray-bearded man enter the pub. As the elder walked toward him after a shared glance, the prince pushed aside a chair for his company and raised an eyebrow.

"I was beginning to think you had finally smoked yourself into a coma," Lucien said with a laugh.

"Forgive me, my prince," the man said as he sat down. "I was delayed with the queen."

"Hmm. Am I an uncle once more, then?" he said.

"Yes, you now have *two* nephews to look after."

"You know, I never imagined you lasting this long as the royal physician," Lucien said with a smile. "Surely, I thought you had grown tired of serving my family shortly after I was born."

The prince chuckled to himself before taking another swig.

"I have been stitching and healing your family since your father was a boy, Prince Lucien. I know no other life."

As he polished off another pint, Lucien smiled and cleared his throat.

"It's good to see you, Thancred."

"And it is always a pleasure to see you, my young prince," the bearded man said in return.

Lucien signaled for his fourth drink and shook his head to stave off the buzz in the back of his skull.

"So," the prince said as his voice began to lose its edge, "I suppose you have news from the east?"

Lucien received a subtle nod from the herbalist, and a small pause fell between the two men when the barkeep brought their drinks.

"It seems that what we had predicted is now a reality," Thancred said with raised eyebrows. "Zededia has intercepted the transport from Skulpos."

Lucien squinted.

"Why on earth would Matticus send a month-long expedition to Skulpos when he knows the Legonae patrol the entire eastern sector of Hostellus?"

"For a girl," Thancred said, sipping his drink.

"A girl?"

The prince leaned back against the wall, crossed his arms, and looked at his old friend with a confused expression.

"That's right," Thancred said. "According to Matticus, she's the key to finding *Osirisigniros*."

Stories of the ancient Aznogsi artifact flooded back to him.

"The sword?" Lucien asked. "The Sword of Kings? I thought it was destroyed? Its pieces scattered after Osinian's defeat at Nazkigaad?"

Thancred leaned over the table; Lucien did the same.

"Apparently not," Thancred said. "The first Son of Osiris may have sent his father's sword into hiding before his death, and Matticus may have found the one person who has seen it and is still alive."

"What do you mean, still alive?" Lucien asked in a louder voice.

The prince retreated as he caught the attention of the other patrons in the inn.

"What do you mean still alive?" he asked again in a whisper.

His patience grew thin as he sat on the edge of his chair while Thancred paused to take another drink.

"It is rumored that one of the other kings hired a team of thieves to retrieve an artifact deep within the mountains between Hostellus and Voluutia," the doctor quietly said. "Though my information might be a bit dated from my contacts outside the city, I'll bet you Matticus figured out that the artifact in question is the holy sword of your ancestor."

Lucien blinked as he processed what Thancred had told him. Imagining either one of his brothers armed with the Sword of Kings struck.

"If Matticus finds the sword ...," Lucien said in the middle of thought. "Zededia may not be long for this world."

"This campaign spreads further than your brothers, I fear," Thancred said. "Ever since he took the throne, the lords of Hostellus have pushed Matticus to lay claim to the lesser kingdoms around. If he agrees to march upon Ehthilia as they desire, I doubt he will stop there."

Lucien's eyes widened as he realized the devastation his brother was capable of.

"We've held peace among the other kingdoms for two-hundred years, Thancred. If Matticus finds the sword, war will break loose among all eight kings. And if Zededia lays his hands on it, he'll use it to level Vaedor Sellos and seek his revenge for his exile."

"Regardless, we cannot intervene. Your brothers must solve this dispute themselves, and we must hope that the sword is never found," Thancred said. "If the Sword of Kings reaches the hands of the wrong Osirian, the world will fall to chaos yet again."

A pause overcame the two men, and Lucien tightened his lips after he came to the uneasy conclusion that following Thancred's advice would lead to the best outcome. He fought hard to convince his heart to remain neutral.

"If given the choice, I would prefer Zededia to find it first. While I can't say he won't use its power for *something*, I doubt he would attack Vaedor Sellos outright. The sword would grant him great power, but his armies are still outnumbered ten to one."

Lucien took a moment to calm his racing mind.

"You are to do nothing about this, Lucien. There is no place for our actions here. Not yet. There are too many people in the city we would be putting at risk, not to mention ourselves."

Begrudgingly, Lucien agreed, and his friend stood from the low stool to make an exit.

"When will I see you next?" Lucien asked.

Thancred gave him a worried, over-the-shoulder glance.

"Soon. Your brothers are venturing near the end of their feud. I may have need for you in the coming days should an opportunity arise. Farewell, my prince."

Lucien waved goodbye to his mentor and sat in thought. Alone again, he beckoned for another drink. As the prince drained his glass, he heard some sort of ruckus outside. Muffled shouting and rattling chains alerted him and drew him to the door of the inn.

Stepping outside to a small gathering, Lucien frowned as he saw the panicked faces of a handful of citizens in the middle. The white and blue armor of Vaedorian soldiers shined through the gaps of the crowd. Those on the outskirts stood silent as the soldiers barged their way through. Lucien slipped to a shaded clearing in the alley next to the pub and hopped up on the low stone wall that guarded it. Curious, the prince watched the commotion from the shadows.

"Please!" an elderly man said. "Leave us be! We've done nothing wrong!"

His curiosity shifting to frustration, Lucien saw two guardsmen shackle the old man after picking him up from the ground. They herded the others in the man's company and restrained them as well. The crowd started to murmur in hushed tones.

"We are loyal to the crown! Please, spare us these chains!" another man said, holding his bound hands in front of his chest to plead.

What now? Lucien thought.

The crowd dispersed as a mounted soldier strolled through the street carrying a small scroll. Lucien squinted as he studied the scroll and recognized it as a declaration of law the enforcers of Vaedor Sellos carried whenever they arrested someone. Powerless, the prince remained hidden, but an urge to pardon the detained citizens nearly edged him forward.

"By law under King Matticus Osiris," the knight said, reading from the unraveled scroll, "all persons suspected of aiding an enemy of the state through evidence of treason, slander of the crown, or otherwise unlawful actions deemed by His Majesty are in breach of the Vaedorian Charter and are hereby sentenced to imprisonment until the royal court releases a statement of innocence and pardons the persons in question."

The murmurs of the crowd elevated to shock.

"Those before you in chains," the knight said, "are accused of showing allegiance to Anzagaar Nostir and the Black Prince. Their capture will ensure that the true loyalists of Vaedor Sellos are kept safe from those who seek to undermine our glorious kingdom."

Lucien jumped down from the low wall and moved to the corner of the pub. A low-pitched horn sounded from the group of soldiers, and the knight pulled a whip out of the saddle on his horse. The crack of the leather caused Lucien to jolt as the knight slashed it in the air to motivate the prisoners to move. Some of the bystanders fled from the street; others remained to watch and cheer.

A heavy sigh escaped through Lucien's nostrils.

"Thancred is right," he said to himself. "Matticus is going to force Zededia's hand faster than either is prepared for."

The soldiers escorted the arrested citizens away, leaving Lucien to question his neutral position between his brothers.

Chapter 3

Preparations

Day 13 in the Month of Snow

In the training pits of his fortress, Zededia Osiris studied the young recruits learning about warfare with sharp eyes. He kept a stern face with crossed arms as he walked through the grounds. His elite warriors of the Legonae produced nothing less than excellence; failure or weakness led to intense punishment. Enforcing them as the highest standards of a soldier, Zededia ensured that discipline and honor were beaten into every man that carried a sword under his flag. The pain and suffering he inflicted upon his men in their training stages translated to perfection on the battlefield, the same path he had followed from childhood.

He heard the dull swords of sparring matches clang against each other and the shouts of encouragement from the bystanders around the sand pits. Eyeing the headmaster of his academy, Zededia walked toward Captain Caedus as he gathered the rising officers of the Legonae around a large, stone podium. Each of the captains in training looked to the Black Prince in awe, but he upheld his cold, calculated expression.

"Today, we are going to continue our sessions with the war game," Caedus said as he spread a crude map across the squared platform.

The captain then grabbed a large sack from the ground that jingled with metal pieces inside. Zededia grinned at the old game he had studied intently as a young soldier. Gathering each unit together to form an army had acted as a puzzle to him, and he had become obsessed with the challenge of figuring out how they best fit. He remembered playing the game with his father and brothers for hours at a time, mastering the art of war and learning how to become one of the most lethal commanders to ever hail from the Osirian lands. As Caedus spread the game pieces across the board, the prince watched as each player took his respective game pieces that represented the type of unit he deployed.

"The Legonae consists of six different units," Caedus said. "Each with their unique role, responsibility, and placement on the battlefield.

Zededia scanned over the figurines that Caedus poured onto the map. He stared at the gleam reflecting off one with a large, pointed spike jutting from the crest of the helmet.

"First: the defenders," Caedus said. "Heavily armored soldiers wielding one-handed swords and a massive shield to protect his fellow man. They are the front line of our army and are experts in close combat. Second: the halberdiers. They are broken into two segments with the first standing directly behind the defenders and the second in front of the longbowmen. Both are present to counter a cavalry advance."

Caedus placed the poleaxe bearing figure with a row of ascending spikes from the back of the helmet and down the middle like a metallic plume, and Zededia reminisced over the battles he had won thanks to their defensive capabilities.

"Our heavy cavalry rests at the center of our army," Caedus said as he removed more metallic pieces from the pouch on the table. "Ready to charge at any moment, Captain Ursa's battalion specializes in dispatching large crowds and breaking stalemates."

Prince Zededia nodded along with his captain's explanation as he spread the mounted units over the table. He glanced over their helmets with a flat plume of feathers sprouting out from the back like a fan.

"Longbowmen in the rear, protected by the cavalry and frontline that pick off the enemy from afar."

As his ranged units stuck out in Caedus's hands, Zededia thought of Captain Seether and his band of expert marksmen distinguished by a sharp point rising straight up at the back of the helmet with the sides arching to meet it like the edges of an arrow.

"Captain Redding and Captain Corso lead a team of light cavalry," Caedus said. "They rarely see direct conflict and wait to chase down enemy archers and siege engineers."

Zededia's light cavalry appeared less daunting than his heavy knights. They carried four small spikes on their helmets with one on each rounded corner.

"And now," the captain said.

Caedus then pulled out a sinister looking unit; a hint of excitement coursed through Zededia as he eyed the straight-standing figurine with two spikes on its helmet rising just above each eyehole.

"The Slayers," the Black Prince said with a smile.

All the young officers turned and stared at him as his dark voice caught their attention.

"Commander Zededia created the Slayer Guild in our youth," Caedus said. "Perhaps he should have the honor of introducing them."

The prince stepped forward, his cape flowing behind him.

"The Slayers," he said, "are fearless. Unbreakable; unstoppable. I personally break them down to their lowest point, and, when they come out on the other side, they are ready to be molded into the finest soldiers the world has ever seen. More lethal than even the mighty Aznogs. They surpass the highest levels of warfare."

A silence fell over the crowd of eager war students as Zededia caught a nod from his captain.

"When the soul is willing, the body is ready. The Slayers operate in a unique fashion. Given their use of a two-handed sword, their battalion is broken into lines of five men each. When a line dispatches the approaching wave of enemies, the next replaces them, and then the next line replaces them, and so on and so on. They are artists on the battlefield, and the masterpieces they create are the severed bodies left strewn across the ground in their wake."

Bright eyes focused on him. Zededia let a faint grin appear on his face.

"Carry on, Lord Redstone," he said to Caedus, addressing him by his formal name.

"Of course, Commander," Caedus said as the students turned their attention to the podium.

Zededia stood by his captain while Caedus began to explain the boundaries of the war game. He scattered the rocky dust near his feet, recrossed his arms, and watched Caedus lay each piece of the strategy-building exercise in a precise position.

"Before you is a recreation of the Battle of Novalos in Year 546," Caedus said. "When the Hiiti invaded Ehthilia, their endless armies of slaves poured through the gaps in the Northwestern mountains on foot and rampaged across the kingdom faster than the Ehthilians could repel them. Outnumbered, they found themselves surrounded by a fast, regenerative army. If we were in their place, how could we defeat them?"

"Use the defenders, my lord," one of the boys said. "Place them on the outside while our longbowmen fire at them from a distance. Should they break through the line, send the heavy cavalry through to alleviate the pressure."

Zededia's grin grew.

"Very good," Caedus said, moving the figurines on the table in accordance with the student's suggestion. "In this case, proper tactics and synergy would allow us to overcome their numbers; the Ehthilians did so to great effect."

"This is our approach to the Vaedorians, as well," Zededia said.

"That's right," Caedus said, shifting the pieces once again.

The prince observed several cavalry units lined on the opponent's side.

"Here," Caedus said, "we have the Battle of Moas in Year 317."

As his captain reset the allied pieces, Zededia looked around at the students and watched their eager eyes glance at the game.

"After the eight Osirian kingdoms were solidified on a map, many resisted the idea of succumbing to another king. A band of riders from Voluutia rebelled against their king and launched an attack on the territory's largest ore mine. Against an all-cavalry opponent, how should you proceed?"

"The halberdiers, Captain," a different student than the first said. "They'll need to lead the counterattack."

"Good suggestion," Caedus said, "but the Voluutians did that and only that. The bandits realized this and dismounted, charged on foot, and slaughtered the pikemen with ease. What should we do differently?"

Zededia looked around among the recruits.

"Supplement the army with a garrison of Slayers," one of them said. "They should be able to handle the bandits in close combat. Or we can send in our cavalry at that time. They won't be able to react quickly enough for it to matter."

"Good," Caedus said. "Your ability to adapt and mold your armies to the situation is a key component to victory."

Next, the prince scanned over the board as Caedus removed all the ally pieces except for one and placed the rest on the opponent's side in a large circle around the edges of the map. His grin started to fade as he recognized the scenario his captain had arranged. Without moving a muscle, Zededia glanced at his soldier.

"Now," Caedus said, "this one is challenging."

The echo from the metal base of the lone figure rang in Zededia's ears. Memories of the battle he had taken part in nine years prior haunted him.

"The Siege of Appostal," Captain Redstone said. "Year 964."

Feeling a tingle on his hand, Zededia looked down at it. He expected a glaze of blood on his skin, but his palm was bare. The prince blinked, moved his hand back behind him, and returned his attention to the game.

"Before the Legonae laid waste to Konkour, the greatest stronghold of the Northern Raiders, we marched to a town called Appostal. Mainly a trading town, Appostal remained neutral throughout the duration of our war with King Imperion's forces. Until, that is, our enemy decided to ambush us in the dead of night, cutting us off at every escape."

While Caedus explained the battle like a poet reciting an epic tale, the prince felt his heartbeat in his chest and neck.

"A handful of us were sent to scout out the neighboring lands in search of a foothold deep within Imperion's lands. Outdated information led us to believe that the Imperalites had vacated the area to strengthen their numbers at the capital. But we were wrong."

Zededia slipped into a trance. For a moment, Caedus's weathered face morphed to a younger version when the two of them stood among the ruined buildings of Appostal. Sounds of shouting, clanging steel, and tearing flesh filled his ears.

"The Imperalites screeched from the hills all around, ringing the call to arms. No escape; no retreat."

Caedus looked at him for a moment.

"How can we win?" he said.

Quiet and still, Zededia did all he could to keep his breath under control. The aggression he carried while marching through Imperion's territory returned in the form of clenched fists. Each of the students around the podium fell silent, and the Slayer figurine stared at the prince with a dead, hollow gaze. Zededia hadn't thought of Appostal in years. The far more harrowing events of Konkour a month later blocked out everything from that time. He hadn't forgotten the scars he came out with, though. Or the faces of the men he lost. His heart pounded as if the Imperalites were closing in. The rising tension reached his throat, the fire burning within him raged, and the centers of his eyes started to glow red. Seconds later, Zededia opened his constricting hands and reached for his longsword.

"We cannot win, my lord," a younger blond boy said from the middle of the pack.

Returning to reality, Zededia shifted his focus to him and lightly frowned as he didn't expect such an answer.

"In this instance, with the odds stacked against us so, our efforts to defeat our enemy wouldn't amount to anything. We should look to do something else?"

"And what is that?" Caedus asked.

Zededia intently listened. The boy hesitated.

"To survive."

"Brilliant, Nyalis," Prince Zededia said in a dark voice after a brief pause.

He stared at the smaller boy with a stoic yet proud face.

"Victory takes many forms in war," he said. "Sometimes, all you have to do is not lose."

He shifted his attention from Nyalis to his captain.

"Isn't that right, Lord Redstone?"

"More now than ever, my prince," Caedus said before looking back at his students. "That's enough for today. Back to the pits."

The recruits scurried off passed the prince toward the sparring grounds for combat training. Zededia shared an awkward moment of silence with Caedus as he knew the haunting memory of Appostal afflicted him just the same.

"Forgive me, Commander," Caedus said. "Perhaps they are too young to learn of that war. I'll teach them another way if you desire."

"No," Zededia shortly said as he turned to watch the youth of his army jog to their next assignment. "They need to understand our failures. *My* failures. If we prepare them now, they won't repeat our mistakes."

The pebbles crunching underneath Caedus's boots alerted him.

"You need something of me?" the captain asked.

"Yes. Summon the others and meet back at the tower before dinner. We have matters to discuss. Recall Captain Corso from Rosen," he said. "We'll need his riders."

"Yes, my prince."

Slipping back into his memory of war in his past, Zededia stared off into the distance. His vision fell out of focus, he tightened his fists, and the cold of the passing breeze chilled his skin.

"We didn't fail at Appostal, Zededia," Caedus said. "We did what we were ordered to."

Zededia took a deep breath and released it through his nose.

"There are twenty men who would disagree with you," he said in a quiet, deep voice as he continued to allow his sight to blur.

He then turned his head and looked at Caedus with a blank face.

"If they could."

Weighed with the burden of his past, the Black Prince stepped away from his friend. He neared the stone archway that separated the training pits from the rest of his fortress, his footfalls crushing the gravel as he went.

"What did you see?" Caedus asked from a good distance away.

The prince froze in place.

"In the girl?" Caedus said, prying further.

Looking over his shoulder, he glared at his captain.

"Our future."

~ ~ ~

Later that day, Zededia walked through the main hall in the tower of his castle. The torches on the walls battled against the yellow sunlight. Servants scurried about, preparing to cook and serve dinner to the prince and his captains.

Nearing the grand table that centered the hall, Zededia deeply concentrated on the schemes running through his mind. He pulled his decorated wooden chair out from the table, sat down, and removed the hood that hid his face. The prince replayed the vision he reaped from the thief girl repeatedly, the Sword of Kings shimmering with a golden hue. As he waited for his soldiers to appear, he panned his gaze over the hall. His eyes passed over the elegant gothic architecture and grand oil paintings that captured the glory of his victories in battle. After reflecting for a moment surrounded by his castle's beauty, the arched doors cracked open and allowed the dim light of the sunset to spread across the marble floor.

Zededia eyed Captain Redstone followed by a few others: Ammon, a massive, hulking man with a dark skin complexion and bald head who leads the defenders; Seether, a mysteriously cloaked man wielding a formidable longbow; and Ursa, the next in line to take Zededia's position as commander of the Legonae. Behind them a few paces walked Captains Redding and Corso, the light cavalry captains, and Captain Sykas, leader of the halberdiers.

The seven officers of the Black Legion approached the table and bowed to the prince. Once they took their seats, he calmed his racing thoughts, collected himself, and exhaled.

"Gentlemen," he said, "our time of action has come upon us."

Silence overcame the room as he met the eyes of his men.

"We have been gifted with an opportunity that no man has had in six hundred years."

Zededia held his captains' attention with a firm grasp. The torchlight flickered in his eyes.

"*Osirisigniros* has returned to the realm of man," the Black Prince said. "Ripe for the plucking."

"Where is it, sire?" Captain Ursa said.

"It has been returned to the Greater Temple of Osiris," Zededia said. "The girl knows where it is."

"The girl from the caravan?" Caedus said.

Zededia nodded.

"She's seen it. Or knows someone who has."

All the captains at the table murmured to one another.

"There's a problem, however," he said as his men conversed.

They paused and looked back at him.

"And what is that?" Captain Redstone asked.

Shifting his lips, Zededia sank into his chair.

"We can't take it," he said with a sigh. "Not easily, that is."

"What stands in our way, sire?" Captain Redding asked.

The prince tapped his chin with his forefinger.

"Matticus," he said. "As always. He has eyes in every city, settlement, and shack in Hostellus. If we were to make an attempt for the sword, he would know of it before we could ever reach it."

"Why would that be such an issue?" Captain Sykas said.

"Because," Captain Redstone said, "if Matticus knew the Sword of Kings was within reach, he'd send every able-bodied man in Hostellus to find it."

"That's right," Zededia said. "The only reason he hasn't done so yet to drive us from Anzagaar Nostir is that it's a waste of time. Despite his blind hatred for me, we don't pose a large enough threat for an all-out siege. But, with *Osirisigniros* in the picture, the game changes. Matticus would sacrifice his own flesh and blood for that sword; that is why we cannot allow him to have it. Osiria would plunge into a civil war yet again fueled by his greed for power."

The beams of light shining through the stained-glass windows of the meeting hall scaled the pillars lining the room as the sun began to set. Zededia took a moment to clear the muddied thoughts from his mind and pinched the bridge of his nose.

"The only way to ensure my brother never sees the Sword of Kings is to obtain it ourselves. And to do so, we must blind him from our movements," the prince said.

He paused for a moment, the solution to the dilemma at hand weighing heavily upon him.

"We must march to the Hostellian plains," Zededia said, "and I will draw him out from Vaedor Sellos."

Looking to Caedus as his closest advisor, the prince received a worried glance from his captain.

"Matticus would never decline an opportunity to run his sword through me. With him occupied, taking *Osirisigniros* from its cradle carries negligible risk."

"If you are to face Matticus, my prince," Captain Ammon said, "who is to claim the Sword of Kings?"

Zededia opened his mouth to speak, but he mustered no reply. All the captains at his table looked around at one another ... all but one.

"I will," Captain Caedus said.

The prince darted his eyes at his greatest friend, conflicted whether to send him on such a perilous journey. However, a suitable replacement whom he trusted as much as Caedus failed to present himself, even among the other officers.

"Very well," Zededia said. "Lord Redstone will ride out to find the Sword of Kings. The rest of us will lead the Legonae to the Hostellian plains to occupy the Vaedorians until he returns."

"And then?" Captain Seether asked.

Feeling Caedus's glare beaming at him, Zededia hesitated.

"And then," he said, "we will go from there."

Though vague, his answer seemed to satisfy his captains.

"How many soldiers can Vaedor Sellos produce to fight against us?" Captain Ursa said.

"Not many," Captain Redding said. "The Hostellae still reside north of Korzeg where they've been for years now. It would take them weeks to return if King Matticus called them back now."

Zededia completed simple mathematics in his head, estimating how many Vaedorians lingered behind after his brother sent the bulk of Hostellus's armies to defend their cousin's land.

"Even still," the prince said, "four thousand strong will pour from the city. The Vaedorians will always outnumber us."

The prince waved a finger in the air and motioned toward the table. Seconds later, the kitchen staff emerged from the swinging doors behind him, and the scents of freshly cooked chicken, potatoes, and greens filled his nose.

"That is why this will be a war of attrition," Zededia said.

One servant placed a hearty plate of food in front of him and another filled his goblet with dry, red wine. The prince lifted his cup and inhaled the bitter aroma of the drink.

"We do not have to beat the Vaedorians," he said before taking a sip. "We must simply outlast them. With less than a thousand troops ourselves, we'll need to plan our advances carefully."

Zededia leaned forward, beginning to eat, and his company followed suit. He eyed Caedus's glance from the corner of his eye, as if his captain expected him to say something more. The prince kept quiet, though, and chewed a mouthful of chicken to ignore him.

Half an hour passed, and the shine of empty plates replaced the savory meals devoured by Zededia's men. Low conversations continued among the captains as the prince subconsciously whirled his wine goblet. The pieces of his plan started to fit together in his head, the variables decreasing the more he thought. Something stuck out to him, however; a thorn to be pruned remained.

"There is one last matter to discuss," the prince said before taking the last sip of his wine.

The eyes of his men returned to him. Zededia nodded to the guards posted near the main doors of the tower, and they quickly heaved on the iron handles, prying them open. Three Legonae soldiers walked inside, the sounds of rattling chains clicking against one another echoed behind. As they stepped to the side, a worn and filthy face appeared above the gilded eagle emblem that bounced on a white-silver cuirass. Zededia dismissed his servants from the hall. His fierce eyes locked onto Eros as his guards escorted the boy forward.

"The Vaedorian," he said.

Eros's panicked eyes and ragged breath provoked no sympathy; Zededia looked on with a steeled gaze.

"What is there to discuss, sire?" Captain Seether said. "Kill him and be done with it."

A shrill gasp left the boy's quivering lips.

"That's not necessary," Captain Corso said. "What harm has he done to us?"

"He's a Vaedorian," Captain Ursa said.

"We could leave him imprisoned," Captain Redding said. "He's of no threat in a cell."

"I don't like the idea of keeping a soldier from Vaedor Sellos within our walls if we are to depart from them. We'll need every sword possible when we march to the plains. We can't afford to keep men behind just to guard a prisoner," Captain Ammon said.

Zededia darted his eyes back and forth between his officers as they debated the fate of the Vaedorian boy.

"We could let him go," Captain Sykas said. "He wouldn't reach the city for days."

"We've never let Vaedorians go free before," Captain Redding said. "He'd be the first to set foot in Anzagaar Nostir and tell the tale."

"Ammon is right," Zededia said. "We cannot release him."

The prince stared at Eros, who quivered so much the chains on his wrist started rattling.

"Then, what?" Corso said. "We execute him?"

"Perhaps," the Black Prince said in a dark voice.

After he spoke, the guard nearest to Eros drew his sword, the steel scraping against its sheath and echoing through the tower.

"No! Please!" Eros said with tears in his eyes.

Though the Vaedorian boy squired away, the Legonae soldiers held him firmly in place.

"Please! I-I won't tell a soul I was captured!"

Zededia's blank expression deflected any sentiment. The cries for mercy from his enemy showed weakness, a trait he hated more than any. Standing from his chair, the prince moved his gaze to each of his captains.

"We are in agreement, then?" he said. "The boy cannot stay."

None of the men at his table muttered a word. Zededia stepped away from the table and held a hand up to motion his guard to sheath his sword. Tears and mucus streamed down the Vaedorian's face as the prince approached. Wriggling his fingers to loosen them, he glared at the boy and walked behind him. Eros shook with fear; Zededia stopped right behind him. He closed his eyes, slightly lowered his head, and brought his hands to the boy's shoulders.

"Shhh," the prince said to calm the terrifying boy. "It's all right."

An eerie look filled Zededia's eyes. With one hand, he moved Eros's lengthy brown hair to behind his neck, and with the other, he wiped a tear from his cheek.

"P-please," Eros said between stuttered breaths.

Zededia pressed his fingers into the boy's shoulders.

"Everything ... is all ... right."

Taking a deep inhale, the prince unfocused his eyes and stared forward through the back of the boy's skull as he whimpered. In one fluid motion, Zededia shot his hands to Eros's chin and forehead, ripped his hands apart with all his strength, and snapped the boy's neck like a twig.

The Vaedorian flopped to the floor, limp and lifeless; Zededia kept his eyes fixed on the distant wall. After a moment, he looked back at his officers with a cold stare.

"Prepare the Legonae," he said. "We march for Vaedor Sellos."

Chapter 4
A Grimm Accord

Day 13 in the Month of Snow

King Matticus scanned his majestic throne room as the members of the court scurried around. Lords and ladies he had handpicked to lead Hostellus's economy and military mingled with one another, teeming with laughter and excitement. The queen sat to his right, and he reached his calloused hand to cover hers. Matticus dropped his eyes to his eldest son peeking over into Ender's crib at his feet as Mattox toyed with the infant.

The commotion of the court buzzed in Matticus's ears while he met the looks of his tenants. Tables of fresh, cool vegetables from the city's gardens surrounded buffets of roasted pork and poultry. Scents of a tender stag caught Matticus's attention, growing ravenous as the day progressed.

Every few minutes the elite guards patrolled by, their deep blue capes flowing behind them, and the meaningless flirtation of the lords amused him amidst the agonizing boredom of sitting on his throne for hours on end. Occasionally, he glanced at the grand painting of his father dressed in shining silver armor that hung over the main doors to the keep. Under King Matias's superior gaze, three small boys stood with their heads held high. Matticus looked at the portrait of himself in the painting as he stood barely taller than Zededia. Lucien's toddler height created a valley between the two older brothers. The king's youth taunted him, reminding him of happier days in the Osirian family.

"You should try to be happier, Matticus," Queen Livia soothingly said in his ear. "Your court is full, your sons are healthy, and the day is bright."

His stern face sprouted a small grin.

"I suppose," he said under his breath.

Though he curved his lips in a fake smile, the king's mind raced with heavy thoughts. Moments from the council meeting he had attended yesterday and the events surrounding his brother to the east troubled him. Matticus's paranoia grew as he sat motionless, gnawing at him like a rabid dog.

"Shadows dance around us, Livia," he muttered. "Waiting for us to falter."

"You worry too much," the queen said. "Relax and enjoy one day of being a king."

Matticus groaned. He couldn't help but look for trouble. Something seemed off in his court. Unexpectedly, the armored guards next to the keep's entrance broke free from their stagnant stance and pulled the doors to the keep open. The king frowned as he eyed a familiar figure enter his home.

"I was unaware we were expecting visitors this shortly before dinner," Livia mentioned with a soft voice.

"We aren't ..." Matticus said.

He focused on the strangely dressed man. Pelts and worn armor stuck out like a sore thumb against the colorful robes and dresses of the lords at court. A gleam shined off the silver wolf's mask hiding a scarred face behind. Matticus hadn't seen that metal sneer in almost a year. He clenched his teeth as the knot in his stomach rose to his throat. The citizens of the court didn't seem to pay much attention to the approaching man, but the king kept a firm eye on him.

"Who is that?" Livia asked.

"Someone who does not belong here."

The helmeted man wrapped in animal skins neared and knelt before the king.

"My liege," the man said through his helmet. "I humbly request an audience with you to discuss some ... personal matters."

The frown on Matticus's face deepened.

"There is no place for you in my home," he said. "Leave us at once."

"I can assure you, my good king, this conversation demands your attention."

"Enough."

Matticus started to raise his hand for the guards.

"Perhaps I should take my mask off, then? Show everyone my pretty face?" Grimm said with a subtle laugh.

The king's eyes widened.

"Wait," he said.

Grimm's involvement in anything at this time of day puzzled him. Darkened moods crept over him and threatened the jovial atmosphere of the party. He looked down at his sons and their innocent faces.

"Let's discuss this ... elsewhere."

The pauldrons on Matticus's shoulders scraped as he stood from his throne. He waved off his men that started to mobilize toward his position.

"Come with me," he said with a harsh tone.

Livia's hand slipped away from his grasp as he stepped away. The laughter and happy conversations faded behind him. As the king ascended the marble staircase, he looked back at the statue of his father, an acidic sense of guilt glaring at him from the stone eyes.

On the fifth floor of the keep, Matticus pushed his way into a small chamber with a rounded table stationed in the center. The warped wood of the door creaked, and the iron hinges squealed. He walked over to the window that overlooked his city and held his hands behind his back, waiting for his company to enter.

"You are not to visit the city while the sun is still in the sky," the king said. "This was the deal."

Footsteps ceased near the table, and the stunned silence that followed suffocated Matticus's patience.

"Why are you here, Grimm?" he asked.

Matticus looked down to the courtyard below where his citizens bustled about in their daily lives. A sudden, metallic thud boomed throughout the room, and he assumed that Grimm had removed his mask and slammed it on the table. However, when Matticus turned around, he noticed a different helmet covered in dried blood rested on the table. Matticus frowned, stepped toward Grimm, and analyzed what had been laid before him. A large eagle emblem crowned the helmet. His focus shifted to Grimm's crude fingers tapping on the bloodied steel.

"This ... interesting piece of armor made its way to me this morning," Grimm said.

The tapping continued.

"So," the bandit said, "are you going to tell me?"

The king tensed his shoulders.

"Tell you what?"

"Where are you sending your scouts, Matticus?" Grimm asked. "The last time I checked, the other kings don't take too kindly to espionage."

"My soldiers lie in Hostellus," the king said. "Aside from those I sent to Korzeg, none of my men venture into the other kingdoms."

A deep, ragged laughter forced the king to curl his ears. Grimm removed his mask and threw down his hood. Nearly flinching, Matticus observed the horribly disfigured face and the white, milky eye with a deep scar running through it from his forehead to lips. The bandit picked up the Vaedorian helmet and held it up to him.

"This tells a different story," Grimm said.

Matticus sneered as Grimm dropped the helmet, sending it tumbling across the stone floor. He traced its bounces with his eyes while subtly clenching his fists.

"What are you doing in Skulpos, Matticus?" Grimm asked, his sly smile shifting to a sinister expression.

"Why do you care?" he said.

"Because the delicacy of our relationship demands a certain sense of ... trust," the bandit said while raising his hand to the king.

Matticus stared at the dirty finger pointed to his face and nearly tore it from Grimm's hand. The pits of his eyes started to glow.

"You're quite brave to raise a finger to an Osirian."

"And you are foolish to think I would do so without a little leverage."

Matticus calmed himself at Grimm's threat. He paced back toward the window then pivoted to face his visitor.

"Everything I've given you," the king said, his voice darkening, "can vanish in minutes. What could possibly do to me?"

Grimm chuckled with a hoarse throat.

"Didn't your father ever tell you to not bite the hand that feeds you?" he asked.

Matticus squinted.

"What are you talking about?"

"I know you long for Ehthilia," Grimm said. "And you've forgotten who you hired to weaken it for you. If the other Osirian kings discovered that Hostellian gold is fueling the Ehthilian insurgency, you'll be swept off this earth faster than you can draw your blade. You know better than I do. Your cousins are waiting for an excuse to war with you. Should they find out you broke the treaty, I'd imagine they'd call for your head."

Facing a situation he had never predicted, King Matticus squirmed as a chill crawled up his spine. He walked over to a shelf hanging from the wall and uncorked a decorative decanter. From it, he poured a dark amber liquid into a cup. Grimm took a seat at the table in the center of the room, and Matticus walked over, took a sip of his liquor, and sat across from the bandit in a leisurely fashion.

"So," the king said, "what exactly is it that you want?"

"I want an answer to my question. What the fuck are your dogs doing in Skulpos?"

"I don't see how that's relevant to you."

Grimm leaned over the table on his elbows.

"Because," he said, "the group of thieves your soldiers so callously slaughtered were *my* men."

Matticus took another sip of his strong drink.

"Then I suppose I could ask you the same question," he said. "What are *you* doing in Skulpos?"

"Let's call it ... business," Grimm said. "I'm not usually an errand boy, but my client pays well."

A slow sigh left Matticus's nostrils.

"We were both after the Sword of Kings," Grimm said. "And while I'm not too peachy about you poaching my only source to the largest payday of my life, I don't really care. I want a bigger prize."

"A bigger prize?" Matticus asked. "What could possibly be worth more than that? Why, just mentioning the Sword of Kings to the other Osirians could give you more power than any other man possesses."

"Trust me," Grimm said, "you don't want that to happen. *I* don't want that to happen. If word spread to all kings that their ancestor's sword had magically reappeared, we could collapse into total war. No one would come out on top, not even you."

Matticus nodded in agreement, remembering the lessons of the Aznogsi tribes who nearly sent themselves into extinction. The cool air wisping through the windows chilled his skin as he sat in thought.

"That's why he hired me to find it. So that none of the other kings would know what he's planning before it's too late."

"*Who* hired you?" Matticus asked.

Grimm's devious smile appeared once more.

"That information isn't for free, even for a king."

With a deep sigh, Matticus closed his eyes and pinched the bridge of his nose.

"What else do you want? Hostellus has provided you with enough kors to fill your pockets for three lifetimes, and your men roam free and unchallenged."

"Material treasures don't interest me anymore. Not even the Sword of Kings," Grimm said with a snarl. "Like I said, I want a bigger prize."

Matticus raised his cup and finished his drink.

"Indulge me, then," he said, surrendering.

A haunted silence trickled from Grimm's half-open mouth behind rotting teeth.

"The legends of Osiris's magics are able to frighten the fiercest of men, to break their will," Grimm said. "That's ... that's real power. The kind that won't ever depreciate or fade."

"And?"

"And ... your line has endured a thousand years of famine, disease, and war. What other family holds such a reputation?" Grimm said. "Osirians are the most influential, most feared individuals across all kingdoms and in territories you've never even heard of. That's why I want ... to become one, and I need another Osirian to do it."

The ritual to turn an ordinary man into a demigod was an outlawed practice, taught to Matticus at an early age that it was to never be performed under any circumstance.

"You're delusional," Matticus said. "You can't seriously be talking about a blood transfusion. That was a horribly unsuccessful and incredibly gruesome process that only ever worked one time, and he died shortly after, coughing up the same blood that the priests of old put into him."

"A man has his desires, Matticus. When they reach high enough levels, the consequences don't look so bad. We both know you've experienced the greed I speak of."

A hint of claustrophobia crowded Matticus as he scanned the room. He wobbled his cup on the table between his fingers, pondering Grimm's insanity.

"Even if it could work, the texts that describe such a sorcery have been eradicated from this world. None exist anymore."

"You don't know your cousins like you think you do, then," Grimm said in protest.

Matticus sat upright in his chair.

"What do you mean?"

"Well," Grimm said, "if there's anyone alive today who still has access to a fully intact grimoire from Osiris's time, it's your brother."

The forbidden texts that his brother favored brought memories of his childhood. As the king walked through the years, though, he remembered the hatred that Zededia's unfiltered use of magic sparked in him.

"So," Grimm said, "if you agree to get me the book, I'll tell you who hired me. I'll even give you the details of the job if you want them."

Though Grimm's sly face could easily conceal a lie, something told Matticus that the thief told the truth.

"Fine, I'll get you the text," the king said. "Now, on with it."

Grimm leaned back and put his heels on the table.

"Three months ago," the bandit said, "an emissary from an Osirian king approached me about a job somewhere in the middle of the Lunendar Mountains—somewhere in between Hostellus, Merrinine, and Voluutia. Said his master would pay out twenty thousand gold kors upon completion."

"Go on," Matticus said after a pause.

"Well, naturally, he held my curiosity until he told me what he was after: Osiris's great weapon, the Sword of Kings. So, I laughed at him and sent him on his way with one less tongue than he arrived with."

Matticus smirked in disapproval.

"Then, a little later, the same Osirian king met with me himself. Paid a thousand silver kors just for a simple consultation."

Without so much as a name, Matticus already began to guess the culprit in Grimm's tale.

"Upped the ante to thirty thousand gold kors and asked me to reconsider. So, I did."

Matticus rolled his eyes.

"Mythian hired you," the king said with a sigh. "No one else would so foolishly spend his kingdom's money."

A wet laughter resonated from the bandit.

"That's right. Mythian funded my crew to fetch his bloody sword," Grimm said. "But he said he'd only speak of further details with the man I would send to retrieve it."

"Why not go after it yourself?" Matticus asked.

"I've got better things to do than hunt down a relic whose evidence of return is sketchy at best," Grimm said with a laugh. "I didn't trust Mythian. Even if I did, there's a reason no one travels through the Lunendar Mountains anymore. Too dangerous. Old legends of evils before your people's time lurk between those cavernous abysses."

Matticus looked down to the floor, his father on his mind.

"I know of Matias's obsession with the sword, how it nearly drove him mad."

A death stare pulsed from the Matticus's face; Grimm nodded in respect of the late King Matias.

"So, I was happy to send someone off to find it," the bandit said. "Didn't expect one of my boys to actually find it, though."

"Who did you send to fetch it?" Matticus said.

"My brother."

Scoffing, the king shook his head.

"Where is your brother now?"

A sour look overtook Grimm's face.

"I don't know," he said. "He sent me a letter saying he made a discovery and that he was going to search some temple. That was the last thing I heard from him."

Though few places fit the description, Matticus struggled to pinpoint the exact temple Grimm spoke of.

"Half of his team split off to resupply in Merrinine and pick up Mythian's payment. They were supposed to contact me once they made it to Skulpos, but ... well, you know the rest."

"Hmph."

"That was weeks ago," Grimm said. "So, I'll assume my brother didn't make it out with the Sword of Kings, and I'll also assume your men brought back the rest of his crew."

"Meaning what?"

"Meaning the only people across all Osiria who might have seen the sword's resting place are in your possession."

Curling his lips inward, Matticus shifted in his chair and tapped the table.

"No, they aren't," he said. "My men haven't returned yet."

"Well, that's just brilliant," Grimm said with a snarky tone. "If you hadn't gone and muddied everything up—"

"Then Mythian would have *Osirisigniros* by now, and you would find yourself out of a contract, out of options, and in a ditch somewhere."

The bandit grimaced.

"Be that as it may," Grimm said, "things just got a lot more complicated. I'm not sending another crew on a wild chase after this sword, so my bargain with Mythian now falls to you however you want to handle it. And if you want Ehthilia, you're going to uphold his end of the deal in his stead."

Without much room to negotiate, Matticus nodded.

"So be it," he said.

Grimm reached his filthy hand across the table toward him. Hesitantly, Matticus shook it and struck an accord with him.

"Now, go back to your snake hole," Matticus said. "Once the Sword of Kings is mine and I march upon Ehthilia, you will have your ritual and I will have my war."

The bandit stood up from the table.

"It is always a pleasure when our paths cross," Grimm said with a loose grin as he placed his mask back on after taking a half-hearted bow. "Until we meet again ... sire."

Matticus heard his company's footsteps resonate toward the door. The iron handle bounced against the thick oak after it shut, and an intense ache started to pound in his head.

Echoes from the party downstairs hummed through the floor and lured him back to his family. Eventually, Matticus stood himself and walked back over to the shelf for another drink.

The king then proceeded back to the throne room, meandered down the grand staircase as his guests came into view below, and paused to take in the atmosphere. None in his keep knew of his plans at hand, not even the queen. Matticus met Livia's gaze over her shoulder; guilt coursed through him as she gave him a half-smile. The excitement and carefree nature of his tenants made him nauseous, the dark thoughts in his mind dampening his mood.

Matticus sauntered through the party as his blue cape kissed the marble floor. A stone-cold expression glossed over his face. After retaking his place on his throne, he shifted his eyes between the colorful decorations without much care. The razor edge he walked upon loomed over him like a rain cloud.

"Is everything all right, Matticus?" he faintly heard Livia say.

"Everything is fine, dear," he said quietly. "Just a bit of business."

The party continued, and Matticus glared at Grimm's ragged cloak exiting the keep. As the day waned, he grew anxious about the coming events. Years of scheming barreled toward a climax with the finish line in sight.

Chapter 5

Shades of the Past

Day 14 in the Month of Snow

Snow trickled down from the purple sky as the Black Prince stood watch over his fortress from the third story balcony outside his keep. He leaned against the stone crenellations and watched his armies prepare for their march to the Hostellian plains. His nose, frozen and pinkish, sniffed the damp air. Though his master plan neared fruition, one final act remained before he could leave the safety of his walls. As he scanned over the battalions of black-armored soldiers, soft footsteps rolled against the platform behind him.

"Good morning, Commander," Caedus said.

"Good morning, Captain Redstone," Zededia said. "Something brings you to me?"

He traced Caedus's glare into the courtyard.

"The Legonae will be mobile by the day's end," Caedus said. "Captain Corso rode out this morning to scout out a forward camp near the edge of the forest."

"Excellent. We should be ready ourselves soon enough."

Commander Zededia placed a firm hand on his friend's shoulder to usher him out of the cold, but Caedus remained in his position.

"Something else, Captain?"

"You haven't told them what you're really planning?" Caedus said. "The others?"

Zededia paused and stared at Caedus with a tense expression.

"No," he said after a moment, "and I won't."

Turning to the warmth of the tower, Zededia stepped away from the wall.

"You don't think they should know?" Captain Caedus said. "They've served you for eight years, Zededia. Some, more. They're more loyal to you than most men are to their wives."

"That's precisely why they *shouldn't* know," the prince said, halting in his tracks and elevating his voice. "I have already dealt with you trying to stop me. I don't need them to do so as well."

Zededia continued on, leaving shallow footprints in the snow. He entered the tower with Caedus following behind and remained silent. Flustered, the prince leaned over the railing that overlooked the dining hall by his hands, closed his eyes, and calmed his racing mind. When he opened his eyes, he glanced at the table below and fell into a mild trance. Caedus approached and rested against the railing as well.

"We're so close, Caedus," Zededia softly said. "I can almost taste our freedom."

No response came from his captain.

"Are you prepared to make your journey?" the prince asked.

"Yes, Commander."

"Good. There's one more thing you need, however," Zededia said as he pushed himself from the railing and made his way to the staircase leading down to the rest of the main hall.

"And what's that?" Caedus asked.

"A guide."

Zededia's footfalls echoed deeply through his empty keep as he walked.

"The thief girl isn't enough?" he heard Caedus say.

"Once you're inside the temple, maybe," Zededia said.

The guards standing in front of the arched doors opened them as the prince neared. A cold gust of wind wisped inside and gave life to the cape of his cloak. Crossing his arms, Zededia stopped on the top steps outside the tower.

"But you need to get there first," he said. "You need someone who knows the way."

"I doubt there's anyone here who fits that description other than you," Caedus said.

Zededia released an icy breath from his nostrils.

"I know. I'm going to have to search ... elsewhere."

He looked at his friend out of the corner of his eye. Caedus's emotionless face glared back in concern of what he alluded to.

"Are you sure that's a good idea?" the captain said.

"No," Zededia said. "But there's no better option."

Platoons of soldiers marched by in the street carrying massive shields in one hand and their helmets in the other, the shining emblem of the Black Legion showing on their chests.

"Gather your things, Captain Redstone," the prince said. "I'll summon you once I have your guide."

~ ~ ~

Half an hour later, the Black Prince brushed the large columns outside Anzagaar Nostir's holy temple with his fingers, feeling the groves in the weathered marble. He walked near the reflecting pool where he had sought the priestess for counsel and eyed the large, decorative door that concealed the underground chamber away from the rest of the building. Removing his hood out of respect, the prince proceeded. Zededia crossed the temple floor in the cover of darkness, pushed it open, and scanned the staircase that dropped into a black abyss.

He descended the straight stone staircase, and midday's light faded behind him. An unlit torch stuck out to him from the left; he removed it from its holder and placed his right around the thatch end with his fingers, caging it on all sides.

"Iluundi, (Illuminate,)" Zededia said, fueling a sorcery in his ancestors' mother tongue.

Immediately, the torch lit with a bright orange light and cast shadows across the prince's lightly unshaven face. Runic symbols lined the columns, symbols he recognized from a witch long before Zededia's time who performed similar dark magics. He thought of the old necromancer that dwelled in his home before Osiris's time and how her controversial experiments with the afterlife laid the foundation of Osirian sorcery.

Once he reached the base of the stairwell, Zededia studied the eerie atmosphere that had seen hundreds of supernatural rituals. Although the prince found comfort in the darkness, here, the black air carried an additional sense of dread. Zededia's unease strengthened and writhed against his spinal cord, but his bravery pushed him forward.

A small chest lay in the most remote section of the chamber. From underneath his robe, Zededia pulled out a key attached to his necklace. The iron key warmed his hand after resting against his skin. When he opened the chest, the prince eyed a leather tome depicting sigils of ancient magic on the cover. He brushed it with his hand and then grabbed a pouch and a short knife. The altar lay behind. Zededia heard it calling to him, the runes singing from his ancestral line of mages and sending deep vibrations through his bones.

Stepping into the circular pit where a pattern of lines carved their way across the floor, he studied the runes in each different section and removed the cork of the pouch with his teeth. The scents of mold from the cold, damp floor and oil from the pouch stung his nostrils. Zededia knelt near an opening in the center where the carved lines met and poured the oil into the tiny trenches. He watched the viscous liquid flow through the cracks lined with copper before bringing the flame from his torch to ignite it.

The oil lit ablaze with a bright green hue. He stood back from the ritual pit and watched the spiritual pattern softly burn. Zededia then reattached the torch to a column nearby while keeping his eyes focused on the seal before him. Stepping over the low flames, he sat himself in the center of the circle. The heat soothed his cold skin while he knelt and removed a crude knife from his belt. A moment of hesitation shot through the prince as he hovered his hand over the concave depression in the floor that acted as a place of offering. Zededia slid the knife lightly across his palm, allowing a few drops of his empowered blood to drip into the altar.

The prince concentrated heavily. He purged his mind of all thoughts of the tangible world around him and focused on the void. As he breathed, an illusionistic trance wrapped around him. His breath slowed while he detached, an ancient energy coursed through his veins, and he succumbed to the afterlife waiting in the shadows. An otherworldly presence overcame him, bonding with the fiber of his soul and pulling him into a deep meditative state.

With the ritual complete, Zededia connected with the phantasmal forces he sought. His spirit escaped his physical body and landed in a shallow pool of water. The prince opened his eyes to observe the cosmic landscape: blotches of violet, maroon, and black streaking across the sky with mystic entities floating by in the distance. He stood from the water that stretched as far as his sight could reach. A dark purple wisp of light danced across the opaque darkness above and scattered tiny blots of white that resembled stars in the ethereal plane.

Zededia smiled as he took in the beauty of the spiritual realm. He churned the chilled water with his feet and watched the ripples fade. With the ailments of the physical world gone, he felt free and weightless. The cloud of anxiety in his mind dispersed as the soothing silence brought him peace.

As the prince scanned the cosmos above, the ground shook, causing ripples to transform into waves a few meters away from him. The surface of the pool erupted into an explosion of mist after brewing for a few moments, and the prince raised his arm to shield himself from the spray. Zededia waited patiently for the water to settle, and once it did, he lowered his hand and grinned.

A massive, hunched-over humanoid figure stood before him with a ragged cloak over its torso and head. It turned, moving slowly like a tree swaying in the wind. The prince blinked as a decrepit, rotting hand stretched toward him holding an iron lantern with a green flame. The towering entity kept its face hidden under the torn cloak, but a pair of eyes matching the color of the lantern peered through the darkness under the hood.

"Zededia ...," the ancient being said in a thunderous, sedated voice. "Son ... of Osiris ... I thought I felt your presence emerge...."

"Hello, Bogrikrash," Zededia said.

"It ... is good to see you ...," Bogrikrash said. "But you were here ... yesterday ... were you not?"

"No, my old friend, I haven't been to Elysia in some time now," the prince said, referring to his ancestors' name for the spiritual plane.

The lumbering guardian groaned, filling the prince's ears with a deep hum.

"Hmm ... time moves so ... so strangely in your realm.... Nevertheless ... what brings an Osirian ... back to my home?" the watcher asked.

Zededia lifted his chin and stood firm.

"I am here for the dead," the Black Prince said. "There is one whom I seek."

"Osinian ... yes ...," the deity said. "Your spirit speaks loudly.... Easy ... to hear."

Something stunned Zededia for a moment before he stepped closer to Bogrikrash. He let his grin fade as a thought overcame him that stabbed at his heart.

"There is another I seek first," the prince said.

"Oh?" the spirit said. "Where ... would they be?"

Zededia hesitated and glared at the ancient guide.

"The gardens."

Bogrikrash retracted the lantern, and Zededia heard him whisper into it in a foreign tongue. The orange flame behind iron turned bright blue. An open palm then reached out to him.

As payment for the voyage, the prince removed a small pouch from his belt. From it, he removed several smooth, shiny gems and placed them into the rotting hand. Bogrikrash pulled them up to his hooded face, dumped them in his mouth, and ground them to dust.

Zededia stood back as his guide summoned a whirlpool between them. The lantern stretched back out, and the prince brought his fingertips to the flame. As soon as he did, Zededia's spirit phased into fluid state and quickly spiraled through the center of the whirlpool. He warped through the network of the cosmic plane, bouncing between his memories and the faces of the dead that popped up as he traveled.

The swirling stream spit Zededia out onto a soft field. Thick, dull blades of grass brushed against his boots. As he looked around, the water that soaked him seeped out his clothes and fell to the earth. A sea of green spread out as far as he could see, and, in front of him, a hill rose across the horizon.

Zededia walked forward, a sense of dread filling his heart. He knew what lay ahead; the agony of the memory haunted him each day. His feet became heavy and his legs weak. Normal breaths quickened to shorter ones. The Black Prince had avoided this part of his life for years, afraid to face his pain. He started to ascend the low hill, and smells of spring flowers floated by through the breezes and filled his nose. The euphoria of the scents he familiarized with the gardens battled with the shame and guilt that suffocated him.

Atop the hill, Zededia glared upon the scenery with watery eyes. Glorious fields of flora took his breath away; he paused to behold their magnificence. Flowers of all colors and species waved at him in the winds, and a grand pavilion stood tall in the center of the garden. The peaceful atmosphere did all it could to soothe him, but the prince remained in place, his feet cemented to the earth and refusing to step onward. He scanned across the fields, looking for her.

Then, wading through an aisle between rows of purple tulips, she appeared. A woman, young and graceful, sauntered by without a care in the world. Her smile eased him better than any medicine. Zededia waited, watching her flawless brown hair bounce and fall over her shoulders. She carried a small child, no more than two years old. He squirmed and laughed as she twirled him around. A grin broke through the prince's stone expression in one corner of his mouth. The bright green eyes of the toddler boy shined under black, curly hair.

Tiny footsteps alerted him to his right. Zededia turned his gaze away from the woman and saw two boys running up the hill around four and six years old. The older boy outran the younger by a good amount, and neither seemed to pay his spirit any attention.

"Matticus, wait!" the younger boy yelled.

The older boy pressed on. Zededia watched the child version of his older brother barrel over the crest of the hill and sprint toward the woman. She beckoned for Matticus with one hand and the toddler in the other. He buried his head in her side in a warm hug. Not having seen his brother in such a happy state since their youth, Zededia almost remembered what it felt like to love Matticus.

"Wait!" the younger boy yelled again, this time from the top of the hill, and Zededia looked back at him right after.

The boy stood frozen and stared directly at him. For a moment, Zededia thought that the pair of bright blue eyes just yards away actually recognized him. The prince's mouth fell slightly open.

"Zededia!" he heard the woman in the fields call. "Come on! What are you doing up there?"

Breaking the trance, the boy continued down the hill. Something inside the prince yearned for a moment to speak to his younger self, but he couldn't, not in a memory. Once his younger self reached the rows of flowers, the pebbles underneath shot into the air behind him. Zededia watched the woman hand the toddler to Matticus, pointed at the pavilion, and the two walked away as instructed.

Alone with her four-year-old son, the woman opened both arms. The boy giggled and jumped in his mother's embrace, and she swept him up and spun around. A single tear leaked from the outer corner of Zededia's eye as he watched.

"Momma, momma," the boy said. "I got you this."

Pulling out a crumpled yet beautiful flower, the boy handed it to her. She looked at it for a moment, smiled, and pulled the boy into her chest and shoulder as tight as she could. Zededia sniffed to clear the moisture from his nostrils as he saw his child self wrap his arms around her neck. Time lulled for a moment; the prince lingered in the memory of that day for as long as he could, savoring each passing second as if they elevated him like the most potent hallucinogen.

The boy leaned away, and the woman kept her wide smile. After a moment, she started to step toward the pavilion to join her other sons, but she paused. Zededia's entire body seized as she turned and looked at him. Heart pounding, he fought every instinct to chase her. The woman glared in confusion as if she were searching for something. She looked away after a moment with young Prince Zededia in her arms. As he stood on the hill while his mother carried him to the pavilion, he hardened himself and flushed his vulnerability away.

"She knows when you visit her," a voice said from his left.

Zededia turned, slightly startled. The spirit of his father, pure and free of the injuries he sustained in battle, appeared before him. Keeping silent, the prince cast his eyes back to the fields.

"She may not see you," Matias said, "but she knows you're here."

"As did you, so it seems," Zededia said in a hoarse voice.

"I am always vigilant for you, Zededia, in this world and yours."

The prince crossed his arms and refused to look at his father.

"Then you know why I am here," he said.

"Yes ... though, I must say, I am concerned for you."

Zededia softly chuckled and cracked a sarcastic grin.

"Well, don't be," he said. "There's no cause for concern."

He sealed his lips once more and looked away. In his side view, he sensed his father turn to him.

"Have I not always expressed my concern for you?" Matias said.

The prince stalled.

"I suppose," he said. "But your concern took the form of punishment. Discipline. I never had..."

As he trailed off, Zededia found himself unable to complete his thought. He sighed, closed his eyes, and shifted his feet.

"I could not give you what your mother could," Matias said, "and I fear your desires in life are a result of that."

"What do you want, Father?" Zededia said in a darker voice.

Expecting a quick reply but hearing nothing, he turned to look at Matias. The former King of Hostellus stood with arms behind his back. Zededia slightly lowered his defenses as he saw his father's sullen expression.

"I know the end you seek," Matias said with his broken gaze cast toward the fields of flowers.

Zededia's eyes wandered in thought before returning to the garden.

"Are you going to stop me?" he said.

"There is nothing I *can* do to stop you, son," Matias said. "I can only ask you to reconsider."

A breeze rolled by, whispering in the prince's ears. The tension between he and his father rose.

"I will not stray from my path," he said after a moment.

"I cannot allow you to continue down this road—"

"Why?" Zededia said with a hint of anger in his voice and while twisting to his father. "Because it's the same path you sought?"

"Yes," Matias said with a pained voice.

Zededia took a long moment to reflect over the decline of his father's sanity after his mother's passing.

"I have made my decision," the prince said.

A sour taste filled his mouth.

"Bogrikrash," he said loudly. "I'm done here. I've grown tired of this place."

In the air behind him, a portal started to form out of churning rays of light. Zededia stepped off the hill and started to descend it with the ghost of Matias behind him. The scents of the flowers withered away, and he resealed the wound caused by the heart-rending bliss that came with the memory of the gardens.

"We worry for you, my son, your mother and I," he heard his father say.

He paused.

"It pains us to see so much darkness inside you."

Zededia had nothing further to say to his father. Keeping his back turned, he looked up to the portal.

"To the Seal of Elohiir," he said.

A second later, Zededia's spirit phased through with the aid of his guide. The same transition as before played out, and the prince forced all thoughts of his parents out of his mind.

Upon arrival at his second destination, the prince staggered on a surface that paled in comparison to the soft grasses of the meadow. He dropped feet-first onto a massive circular platform floating above a seemingly endless abyss. Similar runes to the ritual chamber in his home lined the outskirts of the platform. Once his eyes adjusted, he glanced over the side and saw a faint reflection of water hundreds of feet down. A door emerged from the blackness of the void and rested at the edge of one side of the seal. He eyed the stone gateway and bolstered his courage, for he stood at the heart of hell.

A dull red flame flickered from a torch on the archway. Though Zededia feared the great spirits beyond the gates, he placed one foot in front of the other and kept his stance firm.

"Zo naztakag Osinian Osiris. (I summon Osinian Osiris,)" the Black Prince said in powerful voice. *"Zomed hastesteg ell lett Elohiir Sokos sen bolgeg zot mesk. (He is bound by the Seal of Elohiir to answer my call.)"*

Suddenly, the stone doors cracked, swung toward him, and scratched against the surface of the platform like fingernails on a ceramic plate.

An entirely new level of murkiness escaped from the chamber, and a black and gray mist covered the ground. Zededia struggled to see any sort of shape or object as the thick fog crept toward him. Two faint sources of red light shone through the haze and moved toward the prince. Soft footsteps rolled against the floor inside the doorway, the mist started to wisp around him, and ghostly wails screeched from the void. The Black Prince braced himself. Blighted shadows poured from the gates, and the two red dots grew closer together to form a pair of sinister eyes.

Zededia stood silent with a blank face. As the fog faded, a silhouette of a man stepped from the darkness. The black clouds of the mist gathered to form the resemblance of a man. The prince recognized the soul before him as one that lived in torment. Thinking back to the stories of old when the first children of Osiris bound together to defeat their brother, Zededia knew the spirit before him carried a damning curse.

The shade approached him, but the prince held his ground. Prior experiences with the dead fueled his courage. Stopping a few feet from him, the spirit glared at Zededia with a fierce gaze.

"Ozlent naztakag kar rast Ozek Monns sen lett Elohiir Sokos? (Who summons me from Ozek Monns to the Seal of Elohiir?)" the spirit asked, its voice deep and echoing across the platform.

"Zoam Zededia, Osirisantir, (I am Zededia, Son of Osiris,)" the prince said. *"Ene zant lett aenas Osirisantir? (Are you the first Son?)"*

Though the prince presented courage in his stance against a banished spirit, his heartbeat elevated.

"Sett, (Yes,)" it said.

A subtle grin stretched across the prince's face.

"Ozno voned gad? (What year is it?)"

Osinian's curse affected him more than Zededia thought.

"Gaded lett desnikaetis pour gaz lett Saleros Maentra, (It is the fourteenth day in the Month of Snow,)" he said. *"Za enve kros direst lett noen-seer-sectiri-zorois Uslansinezlentos. (We have just entered the nine-hundred-seventy-third year in the Age of Steel.)"*

Zededia's tongue started to ache after speaking the harsh -r and -z sounds of the ancient dialect. Few in his world possessed the knowledge to communicate in the language of his ancestor; Aznogsi rarely appeared outside of the rituals and magic the Black Prince performed.

"Oldeki enve zant agnos sont, Zededia, Osirisantir? (Why have you come here, Zededia, Son of Osiris?)"

For a moment, the prince found himself at a loss for a response. He spent years crafting his plan for the sword. Now, speaking to its last carrier, Zededia struggled to form his argument to sway Osinian into giving him his aid.

"Osiria ti mosa rok, (Osiria is at great risk,)" Zededia said. *"Aeno ir zigna draze lethnied lett Osirisigniros. Zomeg brozno gad sen konkour lett antgae toraes. (One of our own seeks the Sword of Osiris. He will use it to conquer the other kingdoms.)"*

Seeing that the spirit remained unmoved from the dire explanation, Zededia waited for any kind of reply. He eventually understood that his vague warning kept the Osirian shade unmoved.

"*Zo ishkenag zanto grazeki sen dask gad ullagen zom roak. (I need your help to find it before he does.)*"

The shade squinted its red eyes.

"*Da zo grazeki dask lett Osirisigniros, ozno sen porz zant rast tsenag cod lett gall boroenz? (If I help you find the Sword of Osiris, what's to stop you from using it for the same purpose?)*"

The test of Zededia's heart came swiftly. Osinian grew in stature as he absorbed the mist that crept over the seal.

"*Lozesk zo daskag lett signiros, (Should I find the sword,)*" Zededia said, "*Zo ozesk prozem gad. (I would destroy it.)*"

Osinian's hostile gaze shifted to curiosity.

"*Kros osi zant ozesk. (Just as you would.)*"

Returning to its normal size, the shade gave the prince a skeptical look.

"*Zant neoll lett kaasi saalas nozos, toa? (You know the truth behind my curse, then?)*" it asked.

"*Sett (Yes.)*"

Zededia relaxed his tense muscles. The shadow appeared much more friendly than before.

"*Nossek nox noell lett xeszk ir zot gaar, (Not many know the nature of my death,)*" Osinian said.

"*Tallosett ti rakaskeg ell dorzsett ozlent konkour, (History is written by those who conquer,)*" Zededia said proudly. "*Gad maeas stregzen dorzsett ozlent folst. (It rarely favors those who fall.)*"

Osinian fell silent for a moment, seemingly lost in a trance of his own. Zededia held out his hand.

"*Ohtherat sen kar, (Bind to me,)*" he said, "*ish zoag feshrirag zant gaszen lett luciden mar'aerie. (and I will carry you into the light once more.)*"

The prince took a step closer.

"*Grazeki kar amerag zanto pekra slilezigir cod burron. (Help me protect your father's dream of freedom.)*"

The fog ceased flowing from the crypt behind. Osinian took longer than Zededia liked to decide.

After a moment, the shade condensed itself into an orb of black mist, stunning the prince and luring him closer. Zededia neared, and a tentacle erupted from the orb and viciously burrowed into the prince's chest. Gasping for air, Zededia lost control of his body as an intense pain shot through him. The blackness of Osinian's spirit surged through his veins much like the red glow that appeared from his conjured sorceries. Osinian meshed with every fiber of Zededia's soul; the entirety of his eyes shined like two obsidian rocks as he shook and stared into the sky. The prince's lungs screamed for air, but he remained locked in place, legs trembling and hands twitching. Flashes of white light exploded behind the veil of clouds above like lightning, thunderous roars shattered the sky, and Zededia crashed to his knees.

"*Ell lett tlesa Elohiir, ozlentas soko zant jeshirang ullagen, (By the name Elohiir, whose seal you stand before,)*" Zededia heard the shadow say through the chaos ritual, "*zaam aalezakages gaz threshna, lor zaenag gaz vozoc. (we are separate in flesh, but tethered by heart.)*"

A storm raged around him, sending streams of fog racing in all directions.

"*Zo kelenirag mensh zant, Osirisantir. Zignos pyri ... at aeno. (I walk with you, Son of Osiris. Our souls ... are one.)*"

The binding ritual brought forth its conclusion and the fabric of Elysia started to break in Zededia's eyes. His vision faded, the storm clouds overhead closing in all around. He fell to his back moments later. Like a blackhole, the trails of shadows screeching through the air around him collapsed on his chest. The void swallowed him, and he vanished completely from the spiritual plane.

Zededia awoke from his meditation and crashed to his back, his heart pounding and forehead sweating. The green flames of the summoning circle extinguished in unison. Unsure if he had returned to the physical world, the prince tested his motor control by waving his hand in front of his face. He sat upright, tried to calm his panicking mind, and wrapped his arms around his knees. When he looked at the back of his hand,

Zededia noticed that his veins had slightly darkened. The prince slowly stood to his feet, his body desperately trying to recover from the exhausting journey to Elysia.

After a moment, the Black Prince froze, paralyzed from the neck down, when the rock-like feeling in his abdomen erupted and forced him to vomit all over the floor. Rather than spewing stomach bile across the runic circle, the black cloud from the gate of the spirit world poured over his teeth like water through a broken dam.

Zededia groaned as the parasitic mist sent his body into a mild shock. He hunched on his knees and hacked up his lungs as his throat clawed for air.

Once upright for the second time, the Black Prince blinked to clear the haze from his sight. Before him stood the silhouette of Osinian, Osiris's firstborn. He locked eyes with the shadow and watched it take its first steps in the physical world for the first time in centuries. After it examined its hands and arms, it conjured a long blade made from the same mist.

"*Horros ti maar, (Free at last,)*" Osinian said.

Zededia called the shade back to him by raising his hand, and the spirit retracted itself back into him through his open palm. A new realm of sorcery opened itself to him with the harnessed power of the shadows. The flesh of his fingers shifted to the mist on command. His senses reached the darkest corners of the ritual chamber as the shadows acted as extensions of his arms.

The temple above shook as his armies paraded through the fortress. Orders from his captains rang down through the opening in the ceiling, and the time for the Legonae's march to war approached. Zededia walked toward the staircase with steps as light as air and a deep, sinister laugh behind his lips. Osinian's spiritual form overtook the upper right corner of his head, the prince's right eye shining bright red over a devious smile. The Black Prince had claimed his formidable ally. A dark power filled him as the essence of Osinian wove its way into his soul.

Chapter 6
Eighteen Lashes

Day 14 in the Month of Snow

Prince Lucien stood atop the keep of Vaedor Sellos and leaned against one of the squared merlons. The bright sky shined with the sun's stinging light as it cast golden rays over the stone buildings of the city, each sector laid before his eyes—from the Merchant's District where he had met Thancred in the lowly pub to the grand academy that housed over a thousand young recruits learning to become a Vaedorian soldier.

He spent the entire morning in solitude hidden away from the party on the keep's main floor. Whenever Matticus invited Hostellus's nobles to the city, he aimed to steer clear.

The dark forest that surrounded Zededia's fortress toyed with his vision from miles away. Though the dead fields below surrounded the high walls of the city, the dense Blackwood stretched closer with every year, leaving only an hour's ride between the two.

With a dry breath, Lucien hummed in the back of his throat. He mimicked a tune from his childhood, one that his mother sang to him. The roofs of the city's buildings reflected the sunlight and illuminated the beautiful architecture. While the prince admired the marvelous structures of Vaedor Sellos, the endless streets and alleys seemed like a prison at times. He secretly longed to join one of the clandestine gangs in the underworld of the city where thieves, outlaws, and spies alike made their living. Something about the life of a man without attachments pleased him. His spirit craved an opportunity to wander, and he often found himself jealous of Zededia's experiences across Osiria before his banishment.

As a cold breeze wisped by, Lucien heard the trapdoor to the keep open behind him. He remained still, keeping his focus on the scenery below.

"Tired of playing nice with the members of the court?" Lucien said loudly over his shoulder.

Heavy footsteps followed his question.

"How did you know it was me?" King Matticus said.

Lucien rubbed his chin.

"Who else besides you or I ever wander up here?"

As his older brother approached, Lucien crossed his arms. The prince spat his mouthful of saliva off the roof to the ground below, wiped his lips, and refocused his gaze upon a vast forest in the distance.

"So, what's worrying you?" Matticus asked.

With a raised eyebrow, Lucien twisted his neck toward the king.

"Does something have to worry me for me to be here?"

"The only reason an Osirian seeks solitude atop his keep is when something is plaguing him."

Disliking how right his brother's statement proved to be, the prince lightly shook his head.

"It's ... nothing," he said. "Little sick of home, that's all."

"Hmm."

Lucien turned his attention to a group of boys playing in the street below. Their carefree nature warmed him.

"Do you ever wish you could roam away from Vaedor Sellos?" he asked.

Matticus shifted beside him, grinding the loose rubble under his boots.

"Sometimes," he said. "Though, I rarely have the energy, much less the time, to leave the city. I am burdened by my affairs here."

The prince started to chuckle.

"You're the king," he said with a grin. "You can do whatever you like."

"If only it were that simple," Matticus said with a sigh.

"Is it not?"

Lucien noticed the frustration boil under his brother's skin.

"There isn't a moment of my time where I can relax, Lucien. The lords of the outer cities need constant supervision, Zededia threatens us at every corner, and I can never tell the intentions of the politicians on my council. I don't have the luxury of your lack of responsibilities."

"Perhaps that's because you haven't appointed me any," Lucien said.

"And it'll damn sure stay that way," Matticus said. "I'm saving you from a life of torment. Being a royal is far more trouble than it's worth."

"You could delegate, you know," Lucien said. "Give me command of an army. I'll be to you what you were to father."

"No," Matticus said immediately.

Lucien lightly frowned.

"Why not?" he said.

He waited for an answer, but the king gave none while staring out over the city.

"Because," Matticus said, "I will not make our father's mistake."

Annoyed at the cage his brother placed around him, the prince's attitude shifted sour.

"Afraid I'll level a civilization like Zededia?" he said after reflecting on his brother's allusion.

"His descent ... was more than that," Matticus said. "After he destroyed the Raoans and left their empire a pile of ash, he became ... darker. His military tactics grew more savage, his obsession for dominance more vibrant. Dismantling an entire civilization made him realize nothing and no one could stand in his way. The lashes he received did nothing to sate his craving for war."

Lucien hadn't seen Zededia since the night of his exile. While Matticus skirted the line of defamation of his brother's name, the prince only remembered the fond memories of the three of them in their youth.

"He's a monster, Lucien," Matticus said.

"He wasn't always."

He glared at Matticus in defense of Zededia. Matticus glared back with a side glance.

"Maybe," the king said, "but the past doesn't change how things are now."

Matticus stepped closer to him.

"The Zededia you knew no longer exists. He is a different man. A villain."

Lucien absorbed his brother's perspective, but he struggled to support it.

"Mother's death broke him," he said in a muffled voice.

He heard Matticus release a deep breath.

"It broke us all," the king said.

A flock of birds flew by overhead from the gray mountains behind Vaedor Sellos. Lucien looked back to their peaks and traced the ridgeline across the northern side of the crater.

"So, you have all the power in the world yet are suffocated by a monarch's obligations," he said, "and I am stuck in this city with no influence on our people's lives. Not even yours."

He sensed Matticus turn to face him directly in his peripheral vision.

"You have the greatest power of all, Lucien."

"Oh? Enlighten me."

His brother looked him sincerely in the eyes.

"Of all the councilmen, priests, soldiers, everyone, you are the only man I can trust. You're the only one who doesn't greet me with a knife held behind their back."

Sentiment between him and the king rarely appeared. Lucien's heart believed his brother's kind words, but it took him a moment to accept them as Matticus had closed himself off from emotion years ago. A strange feeling alerted the prince, his astute perception detecting a change in his brother's stance. Desperation for an ally, perhaps.

"You've never needed my support before," he said. "What's changed?"

"The war with Zededia draws closer to its end each day," Matticus said. "As it does, the diplomatic situation of Hostellus becomes more volatile. I fear I may need your aid on more than one occasion."

Matticus stepped away from the crenellation in Lucien's side view. A heavy hand rested on the prince's shoulder.

"You are all I have left," Matticus said. "Can I depend on you to be there when I need you? To do what needs to be done to protect our people, our home?"

Anxious, Lucien hesitated.

"Yes," he softly said.

His brother patted his shoulder.

"Good," Matticus said.

Lucien questioned his ability to choose a side between his brothers. He struggled to tell if he'd lied to Matticus to simply end the conversation or truly meant his support. The king walked away after giving him a nod, leaving him alone with the silent landscape in front of him. Longing for something to ease his scattered mind, Lucien thought of ways to entertain himself, but none seemed overly appealing.

The doors to the keep's interior opened once more. Lucien glanced behind, confused why Matticus had come back outside. When he looked, though, he saw one of the servants from the party instead jogging in his direction.

"Your Highness," the servant said, "your presence is requested by the royal physician."

"Hmm? What for?"

"I'm unsure, sire. He asked me to tell you to meet him in the wine cellar beneath the keep."

Strange, Lucien thought. *Since when does Thancred call for me so urgently? He must have news about Zededia.*

"Thank you," the prince said, dismissing the servant.

His curiosity raced, and he had something to apply his attention to at last. Lucien reentered the keep with haste and wondered what his old friend needed from him on such an abrupt notice.

~ ~ ~

The musty aroma of the wine cellar surrounded the prince as he stepped down the old wooden stairs. Moisture clung to the walls and bits of moss grew in the crevices between them. Lucien scanned through the shelves of stored goods with the assistance of a lit torch on the distant doorway. Making his way through the cellar and kicking dust under his boots, he thought back to the times when he and his brothers would hide from the guards responsible for watching them in various places around the castle. The dark, cluttered basement proved to be an acceptable place for secret missions their mother would send them on. As the joy from nostalgia distracted him, he heard a thud followed by a light grunt behind the iron gate that separated the wine storage from the rest of the chamber.

"Thancred?" Lucien said.

"Ah, Prince Lucien," the old man said. "I'm glad you're here. I thought I was going to have to do this alone."

"What is 'this' exactly?" the prince asked.

As he stepped closer, he saw Thancred hunched over in the shadows of the doorway. Lucien then noticed a large stone on the ground and the gaping hole in the wall where it had been as the doctor pushed a copper crate across the ground that smelled of a familiar fragrance.

"King's Leaf?" Lucien said. "What the hell are you doing with a crate of King's Leaf?"

"What else does one do with forbidden items in the city?" Thancred said with a smirk. "Selling it of course."

Lucien sighed.

"What makes you think I would want to partake in your illegal trade?"

A bright smile peered through Thancred's gray beard.

"Why, because I am asking you to," his friend said.

"I'm sure one of your other associates could have helped you. Is there a reason you sought me particularly?"

After seeing Thancred struggle to move the heavy container, Lucien walked over and shoved it with his foot in the proper direction.

"An old man can't spend time with someone he holds dear to him?" Thancred said.

"While I've always enjoyed our adventures together, I seem to recall you telling me that you'd send for me once you caught word from Zededia."

The smile on Thancred's face faded slightly.

"Yes," he said. "Well, I will soon. I thought you'd like to accompany me so you can hear for yourself."

Lucien kicked the box farther into the next room and noticed a small hatch nearby.

"Besides," Thancred continued, "You seemed like you needed a little excitement."

"I do, old friend," the prince said as he sat on the crate. "I do indeed."

He waited for a moment while Thancred gathered a few belongings from the hole in the wall in the previous room.

"How did you recognize this as King's Leaf so quickly?" the doctor said, looking at his order parchment. "It doesn't give off a strong odor. Makes it easy to hide."

Lucien associated the faint, tobacco-like scent with his youth. Though Thancred was right about its low odor, he frequently smelled it in his father's study.

"Father smoked King's Leaf quite often. So much so that Mother wouldn't go near him for hours after. I'll never forget the smell."

"Ah, yes," Thancred said. "I remember, now. Your father always favored the Merrin's supply over ours. More potent, I suppose."

"He would have gathered it himself had it not been made highly illegal by the priests during my grandfather's time. Never understood why such a law was passed. Not like King's Leaf does much harm."

"Eh, there are a dozen laws of Hostellus made from religious beliefs, my prince. I've learned to not question them."

Thancred heaved on the metal hatch that creaked in its hinges while Lucien stood to move the crate. The tunnel down below reeked of dirt and mildew.

"Down you go," Thancred said.

"Smuggler tunnels?" the prince asked. "What I would have given to know these were here when I was a boy."

"That's precisely why your father made me swear I'd never tell you."

The prince grinned and placed his feet on the top rung of a wooden ladder. Dropping into the darkness, he coughed to clear the dust from his mouth. Lucien squinted and peered down the long corridor. After his eyes adjusted, he realized it stretched much farther than he would have guessed.

"These used to be old escape tunnels in case of a fire," Thancred said while climbing down the ladder. "But Vaedor Sellos hasn't suffered a fire in a hundred years.

Those who remember their construction still use them to traverse throughout the city without drawing attention to themselves."

"Sounds like an outlaw's paradise."

"They do provide excellent cover for unconventional merchants, yes."

The prince held onto a torch that Thancred handed him. Dimly lit, the tunnel walls flickered with shadows.

Lucien wandered through the underground of the city for several minutes, trusting that Thancred knew where he was going. A clearing appeared ahead after half a mile of walking and caught his attention.

"Where are we now?" the prince asked.

As he stepped into the clearing, he glanced at the pattern of light cast upon the ground. Tracing the sunlight, Lucien observed a squared grate above. Citizens walked over the grate from time to time twenty feet above his head.

"This is a supply drop," Thancred said.

"A what?"

"Couriers will drop their packages down from the grate above at night."

Lucien traced Thancred's pointed finger to an adjacent hallway to the left that led to a steep drop off.

"Crime lords and other denizens of the tunnels retrieve them in a bit of underworld dealing."

"Hmm."

Another long silence came about as Lucien walked with Thancred down the seemingly endless tunnel. With time to think, he allowed the thoughts of his subconscious to spring back up. He couldn't help but ponder over what Matticus said to him earlier. The feud between his brothers became more intense, and he heavily disliked the idea of something horrible occurring to either one. His face hosted a sullen expression the longer he reflected.

"Something the matter, Prince Lucien?" Thancred asked.

He snapped from his trance, he lightly shook his head, and heaved on the rope that pulled the cart of King's Leaf.

"I'm fine. Just something Matticus reminded me of this morning. Zededia came about in our conversation, and he mentioned something that I had nearly forgotten."

"Oh, and what is that?"

Lucien nudged the rope higher on his shoulder.

"Do you remember when Zededia was lashed for his aggression against the Raoans? About nine years ago?"

"I am afraid I cannot forget. Why do you ask?"

Staring into the darkness ahead, he handed Thancred the torch and gripped the rope with both hands.

"Even after all this time, Matticus seems to think that it wasn't enough for Zededia, that he should have received more."

"Zededia couldn't stand for three days afterward," Thancred said with a light scoff. "What more could Matticus want?"

"I don't know," Lucien said in agreement. "But Father was never the same after that day."

Lucien's echoing footsteps kicked the dirt and dust and sent small clouds circling through the air around his ankles.

"What parent doesn't feel guilty for punishing their child?" Thancred said.

"I know. But it broke him," Lucien said, thinking of how Matias's depression increased over his last years as king. "I think Matticus became angry at my father's guilt, as if remorse should never have been shown to Zededia at all, by any means."

A dryness swept through the prince's mouth and he rolled his tongue around to remove the discomfort.

"I didn't even get to attend the event and it still haunts me."

"That's right," Thancred said. "Your father kept you away so that you wouldn't see what he did."

"So, he *did* deliver the lashes himself, didn't he?" Lucien asked, looking at the old man. "Matticus told me that he did, but I never believed him. I didn't have the heart to ask about it. No one spoke of that day after it happened, not even Zededia."

His friend released a deep breath. Lucien waited for the doctor to answer, but he only heard the grinding of the cart's wooden wheels across the earthy floor.

"Yes, Lucien," Thancred said. "Your father lashed Zededia until his back was more blood than skin. Tore the flesh from his spine with the serrated whip."

Lucien cowered at the image placed in his head.

"Your father ... held back tear-welled eyes the entire time ... but that didn't stop him from beating your brother until he collapsed to the ground."

For a moment, Lucien's skin crawled as if Matias were there to punish him as well. His father carried discipline everywhere he went, wielding it like a sword against mediocrity.

"I never understood why he chose to give eighteen. Seems like an unusual number," Lucien said.

"That was your eldest brother's idea," Thancred said. "One lash for every village Zededia razed in retribution for Appostal."

"Appostal?" Lucien said. "What is that?"

Again, Thancred hesitated.

"Appostal was your brother's only defeat in combat since he took the position of commander of the Legonae," the physician said. "I'm not surprised your father had it erased from record and from memory from all who knew about it. The Legonae's reputation as unbeatable is still upheld."

"Then, how do you know about?" the prince said.

"Some still remember," Thancred said. "Those close to Zededia."

The doctor's information gave new light to the war in the north when he was fifteen, too young to march with the Hostellae.

"I suppose you were closer to him than I realized."

"Who do you think sutured Zededia's wounds?" Thancred said with a laugh.

A faint light shone from around the bend in the tunnel. Lucien fixated upon it as the claustrophobia started to settle in.

"I know you're longing to wet your blade with the blood of our enemies, but your task holds the greatest importance of all."

His friend kept the same blank expression as always, but the prince knew Caedus's silence meant more than his words. Zededia hated goodbyes; he gave the captain a firm nod of understanding.

"You will lead the Slayers, then?" Caedus asked.

"Yes," Zededia said. "I'll march to the gates of Vaedor Sellos if I must; if that's what it takes to keep Matticus occupied. Our first priority is keeping his attention on us so he doesn't send an entire fucking army after you."

"As you command, sire," Caedus said. "Do you have my guide?"

Zededia hesitated for a moment and took a deep breath. He whistled and, out of thin air, the shade of Osinian Osiris appeared in front of the gathered riders. Caedus's soldiers jolted.

"Calm yourselves," Zededia said. "He will lead you to the temple through the mountains. Once inside, the girl should be able to take you to the sword."

The Black Prince bowed his head to the shadow of the ancient Osirian king.

"Osinian is your lifeline. He will serve you until you return to me."

Zededia motioned for the shade to move near Captain Redstone.

"You have eight days, Caedus," the prince explained. "Retrieve the sword and return to me where we agreed. I should be able to buy you enough time to grant you safe passage, but Matticus's spies are likely to spot you, so stay vigilant."

The prince noticed his captain taking a long look at Osinian.

"How can I be sure this ... thing ... will lead me to the correct place?"

"At worerst ir zanto statzan, rueno, (Be wary of your words, pawn,)" the shade said in a defensive tone with squinted eyes pointed at the captain.

Zededia stretched an arm out to Osinian to diffuse the tension.

"It would be in your best interest to respect him, Captain Redstone," he said. "He once sought the same goal as we do now; he is an ally we can trust."

Urging the remaining soldiers forward, Zededia sat alone with Caedus. A dead-serious stare stabbed at him from his peripheral vision. The prince's patience started to wear thin, for he knew that look and what it meant.

"You're not going to sway me," he said.

Caedus rode closer. Zededia saw his mouth open to speak, but the captain remained silent.

"My path is set," the prince said.

"I know."

His captain strolled forward to meet with the rest of his crew; Zededia's stomach knotted from his guilt.

"Caedus," he said.

Lord Redstone turned his horse and looked back. The prince then spurred his horse and caught up with him.

"I know this is not the end you wanted for us," Zededia said. "But it is the best end for all."

"If you insist," Caedus said with disapproval.

Reaching out his hand, Zededia placed his hand on his friend's shoulder.

"I'm counting on you," he said. "Without you, our efforts will fall by the wayside."

After a second of hesitation, he received a concurring nod from his captain. Zededia rebalanced himself on his horse.

"Good," he said. "Then I will see you when your task is complete."

He tightened the slack from the reins of his horse and held on with a firm grip.

"Farewell, Captain Redstone," he said.

Without another moment to waste, the Black Prince galloped on away from the safety of the fortress, the plans he had put into action too far along to stop now.

~ ~ ~

Caedus watched intently as Zededia departed Anzagaar Nostir.

"Farewell, Commander Osiris," he said with a heavy heart. "May your fate be prolonged until I return."

Anxiety started to creep over the emotionless captain, but he knew his strong-willed friend had already made his decision. With the delicate scheme at hand, Caedus was forced to accept his role and carry on for the sword. He exhaled a deep, icy sigh as his view of Zededia faded.

The beating war drums shook the ground in the distance as Caedus descended the ramp for the open gate ahead. Before he could look to the shade bestowed upon him by his commander, it dissipated into the air. Caedus clenched his lips and remained skeptical of its intentions. The rest of the party waited for his lead close by.

"Are we ready to take our leave, sir?" one of the soldiers asked, breaking his trance.

"Yes," Caedus said.

He glanced at the thief girl bound to the horse's saddle by a thick rope. Her glare of daggers pierced through the cracks in her hair covering her face.

"Do we have a destination in mind, my lord?" the soldier said.

Caedus concentrated for a moment, the sparse details of Zededia's description struggling to fit together.

"Vaguely," he said. "We'll find out soon enough."

With all preparations made and company gathered, Caedus signaled toward the dense forest outside the fortress, secured his belongings for the journey in the packs next to him, and pulled his winter garment closer to cover the bare skin of his neck.

The five mounted travelers waved to the townsfolk of Anzagaar Nostir as they strolled by, and the captain turned his head to gaze upon the safety of the tower once more as he rode under the gatehouse. Home now lay behind him once more.

A lesser-traveled path branched off from the main road to the city a few hundred feet out. Caedus eyed the trail that led deeper into the mountains behind the tower and veered off in its direction. As he wove his way through the thickets of the wooded terrain, he lost sight of the fortified walls. The quiet murmurs of the woods overcame the drumbeats from the marching Legonae. Creaking oak, crunching leaves, and the occasional caw of the regional crow flocks toyed with his ears.

The farther away from civilization the captain rode, the more warped the trees became. Caedus's frustration from the interfering twigs heightened and he grasped several and tore them from the branch they sprouted from. None of his soldiers spoke a sound as they rode, keeping quiet as soldiers of the Black Legion usually do. As a quality that he had adopted from Zededia, the captain remained a man of few words and preferred the silence. The natural sounds of the Blackwood entertained Caedus well enough and soothed his frosted ears.

After a few hours of traveling, the first day of his journey neared an end as the sun withered behind the mountains. Caedus knew that he could easily traverse the forest through the darkness, but as he drew close to Hostellus's border, wrong turns awaited in every direction. Time already aligned against him; he steered his company to the next clearing and ordered for his men to arrange a temporary settlement.

The captain dismounted his horse and wiped the dampness from his nose. One of his soldiers then handed him a pack of food to distribute, and he caught another glance of the girl on her horse.

"Get her down," Captain Caedus said with a deep voice.

Returning to the pack, Caedus grabbed a bundle of bread and handed it to his second soldier while the third attempted to lift the girl from the horse. He heard sounds of a struggle, and when he turned, she had wrestled her hands away, twisted her torso, and spat in the soldier's face. The Legonae soldier drew a sword, but the captain held his palm in the air to cease any further aggression. Walking toward his prisoner with a face of stone, Caedus maintained fierce eye contact with her the entire way. He removed a small, curved dagger from his belt and brought it toward her, moving his eyes toward the rope around her wrists. She smacked his advance away, and he shot a darting glare back at her frightened face.

"Give me your hands," Caedus said in a commanding tone with unflinching eyes.

He grasped her forearms, pulled them toward him, and cut the thick ropes with his dagger.

"Get yourself down if you insist."

After Caedus placed his tool back in his belt, he noticed the confused look on the girl's face. He walked back to his horse and grabbed another wrapped chunk of bread from the lot to toss to the closest rider. Caedus took a piece for himself, securing it with his elbow against his side, and moved a log near the freshly sparked fire his men prepared. The captain sat to rest and unraveled his meal. Moments later, he returned his attention to the thief girl, who staggered her way down to the ground.

"Come. Eat," he said bluntly.

The girl ignored his invitation.

"You can either eat what we provide," he said, holding up a piece of bread, "or starve. I don't really care."

Hearing slow footsteps crunch the dead leaves on the ground, Caedus waited as she stepped closer. He gnawed on the tough starch and looked up at her. The girl limped and showed aged bruises on her arms. For a moment, he pitied her. Caedus observed her ragged clothes and how her eyes darted from him to the food in his hand. He offered some for a second time, and the girl snatched it up faster than he expected. From the looks of her, Caedus guessed she hadn't eaten in days. Watching her tear into the bread like a savage, he slightly lowered his defensive attitude toward her. Her abused appearance struck a chord in the captain, and he continued with his meal in silence as his men settled in their spots for the night.

The fire in the hearth flickered and warmed his hands in the wintry night. As the charred wood of the fire crackled and cast shadows against the dimming forest, Captain Caedus cleared his throat and grabbed a leather flagon of wine.

"So," he said while uncorking it, "what are you called where you are from?"

To his expectation, no response followed. He took a gulp of wine and wiped his mouth.

"How did you end up in Skulpos? Did the Vaedorians chase you there?"

This time, a pair of sharp eyes beamed from the bread in her hands to his curious face. He grunted and turned his head away to watch his three soldiers talk among themselves.

"I was trying to reach the sea," she said, breaking the silence.

Twisting back to her, the captain opened his ears.

"I was trying to get away from here."

Caedus tossed his flagon of wine to one of his men that started cooking over the fire.

"Where are you from before, then?"

"I was born in Ehthilia, but my parents were taken by the bandit lords when our home was invaded and forced to evacuate...."

The captain recognized the day she spoke of as when Grimm and his army of criminals overthrew King Ambrose and renamed the capital city Beggar's Keep. He always wondered why Matticus refused to send forces to Ehthilia's aid.

"I was thrown into a crew who robbed and killed whoever they ran across ... until a new contract took us toward Merrinine."

As Caedus took a bowl filled with soup from the party's chef, he glanced over to her. The orange light of the fire glimmered in her luminous eyes, and his heart moved at her beauty hidden under the scars of her travels. Sensing a troubling topic, he felt it best to not pry any further. He stirred his food, churning a piece of potato around the outer edge of the bowl. The silence returned while he ate, and Caedus paid her little attention after that.

"What about you?" she asked, reengaging. "You're no friends of the king in this land. Who are you, then?"

Hesitating to answer, Caedus lowered his bowl. He glanced off through the darkness of the forest and reanalyzed his beginnings and the path that led him to his current position.

"I am Caedus, son of Caed, and a lord in House Redstone. I serve as a captain of the Legonae, the army of the Black Legion. My commander, Prince Zededia Osiris, leads us in exile from our fortress, Anzagaar Nostir."

"Osiris?" the girl said as she looked up in confusion.

Caedus raised an eyebrow.

"Yes, he is an Osirian. What do you know of them?"

"The men I belonged to were hired by an Osirian king to find something. We were sent deep into the mountains after a temple."

News of a mercenary team after the Sword of Kings passed through Caedus's mind without surprise. He paused, slurping more of his dinner from the spoon.

"Was it Mythian?"

"I don't know," she said. "I didn't get much information about the job."

The captain cleaned his bowl.

"If there's one Osirian who hires others for his dirty work, it's Mythian."

Caedus held a distasteful tone while referring to the king of Merrinine. He despised Zededia's cousin, having only met him on one occasion. Once was enough.

"Have you always been a soldier, Lord of House Redstone?" the girl asked, moving closer to him as the moon breached the mountains that towered behind.

Caedus thought deeply of his youth, recollecting his journeys across Osiria.

"No," he said. "I was born into a different profession. Only by my luck did I have the chance to prove my worth as one."

"What were you, then?"

The earthy scents of his home flooded back to him as he remembered his parents.

"I was a stonemason," Caedus said, looking into the flames of the campfire. "I was born into a family of master craftsmen, the finest in all of Monscarren."

"Monscarren? That's days away from here. How did you manage to end up here? Wherever we are...."

Caedus realized how disoriented his guest had become after her journey.

"You are in Hostellus now, home of the conquerors," Caedus said to enlighten her. "But when I was a boy, around nine years old, all the great stonemasons of Monscarren were called to action. A wall had been commissioned by the late King Matias in Vaedor Sellos. So, my father took me with him to see the city."

"Seeking builders from so far away ... seems unusual," she said.

"Not entirely," Caedus said. "Monscarren masons are highly sought after, our skills with a hammer and chisel unmatched. The Vaedorians paid double what others would to construct an outer wall as quickly as we could."

"Why?"

"Shortly before, Hostellus fell under attack from a clan known as the Raoans, a fierce tribe of savages who settled in the valleys north of Korzeg. When they reached Vaedor Sellos, King Matias was unprepared. Vaedor Sellos suffered minimal losses, but, um...."

"But what?"

Caedus rolled the end of his thought on the tip of his tongue, the pain of the memory shared by his commander afflicting him even though he hadn't been present.

"They lost someone rather important. Important enough to merit the construction of the largest defensive structure I've ever seen. Matias wanted to make sure he'd never lose one of his own ever again."

His train of thought wandered off and focused on the rage that erupted from Hostellus following the invasion. Zededia's bloodied sneer over streets of corpses in Raoan territory became visible to his mind as clear as the fire in front of him.

"As I was saying," he said, "my father brought me to the capital when I was nine, about twenty years ago. We spent three years building Matias's wall, living in the city the whole time. When we finished, my father wanted to take me back to Monscarren, but another path had been set for me."

"And what was that?" the girl asked.

Caedus grinned.

"Our work on the wall had eventually granted us a reputation. Matias invited some of the builders, my father among them, to the keep during our first year, and that is when I met the man, or boy at the time, who inspired be to become a soldier."

"Your commander?"

The captain nodded.

"Yes, Prince Zededia and I became lifelong friends before the day had ended. He taught me swordsmanship skills in secret. That was all I did in my spare time, staying out all night on some occasions. Whatever it took to become a knight."

The trip of memories distracted Caedus for a moment, the first time he saw Zededia replaying over and over. His eyes wandered from the decaying fire to the earthy ground and then to his fingers.

"Eventually, my father gave me the choice of returning to the Red Hills or staying behind to chase a dream. So, I stayed. Joined the Vaedorian military academy, progressed as one of the most elite swordsmen in my class, and graduated at the same time as the present king, Matticus Osiris."

"Did your father disapprove of your choice to stay?"

A chuckle left Caedus's nostrils. While Monscarren earth ran through his blood, he couldn't imagine a life without a blade at his side. Nature's call toyed with his ears, the white stars ahead piercing the dead canopies.

"No. My father proudly left me to my wishes, to serve as knight, and my mother understood. I wanted a different life than the one set before me. So, I seized it at the first opportunity. Over the years, I was able to claim a stake of land back home and built my own army to serve under Zededia when he formed the Black Legion."

A calm tone shadowed the camp of travelers after the captain finished his narrative. The fire dimmed from the lack of fresh fuel, and the girl brought her knees to her chest to sleep. Lord Redstone picked at the callus on his thumb that formed from gripping his weapon as everyone around him fell asleep, and he scanned the camp one last time before dozing off himself. Caedus moved to the ground, rested his head on a log, and wrestled with his teeming nostalgia.

Tomorrow crept over the mountains; the journey continued.

~ ~ ~

In the comfort of his homeland, Prince Zededia Osiris led his armies over the roving foothills of Hostellus for two days. Day sixteen in the Month of Snow appeared, and the prince grew eager to set eyes on the wheat fields around Vaedor Sellos once more. Hundreds of armored soldiers shook the forest, the leafless trees swaying with their footsteps. He eyed a handful of standards among the lot from his captains' flag-bearers. The torches carried by some of his men provided adequate light, but the moon of the morning outshone them in every direction. Clanging armor and creaks from the tree branches bounced across the forest. Zededia smiled at the sounds, the sounds of war.

Captain Redding rode beside him heading a group of horsemen behind. Zededia glanced over the Slayer battalion on his right, their sinister helmets bobbing like waves of an ocean.

Eventually, as the moon started to disappear, the terrain smoothened. Tangled roots and jagged rocks shifted to softer earth. Dead grasses sprang up around his horse's hooves, and the prince focused his keen eyes on the gradual decline of the fields leading to Vaedor Sellos.

The Black Prince emerged from the forest with his armies like ants out of the ground. Stopping on the ridge barely out from under the branches, he held his fist in the air. The war drums ceased their relentless beating, and a thousand men halted in their place. Zededia took a moment to savor the scenery and basked in the calming atmosphere. He knew the sweeping silence before battle all too well. It chilled his skin like the scarce snow on the ground. He could already taste blood in his mouth, the copper flavor burning his tongue. Like a twisted artist, he used these preludes of war to channel his motivation.

The Black Prince filled his lungs through his nostrils, taking extreme pleasure in every scent of steel, wood, and sweat. A shiver of pure, frenzied ecstasy slithered along his spine. The conquering mindset of his youth closed in. Zededia curved the corners of his mouth under his hood, knowing that he would have the chance once again to display his immaculate skills as a warlord.

Suddenly, to his great surprise, something caught his attention across the plains near the northern road leading to Ehthilia. Zededia squinted, and he soon heard a faint rumble. The tiny light of a lantern shined miles away. More started to spring up and gradually moved toward the white city on the other side of the crater. Shortly, Zededia's eyes had adjusted enough to scan over a slow-moving mass. Horror struck him as he realized what it was.

"What is that, commander?" Captain Redding asked.

Zededia sat stunned with his mouth agape.

"The Hostellae," he said quietly. "They've returned."

Chapter 8
The Armies

Day 16 in the Month of Snow

Low lantern light illuminated the empty halls of the keep in Vaedor Sellos. King Matticus watched the orange sunlight creep over the mountains to the east from the perch of the secret intelligence chamber on the top floor of his castle. Several bookshelves lined the walls, and a massive map draped down from the ceiling like a tapestry between them. Behind him, Spymaster Rachtus stood at the map and studied the markings drawn that all pointed toward Ehthilia. Matticus turned to face his officer.

"Ambrose's forces are withdrawing from Torrant," Rachtus said. "I suspect they will retreat to Maelensis by the end of the month."

The king glanced at the map his spy referred to.

"The fact that Grimm has been able to match an Osirian army with a band of lawless fiends is proof enough that Ehthilia is in need of a cleanse," Rachtus said.

"Have you received word from the Hostellae?" Matticus asked. "When should we expect their return from Korzeg?"

"Soon," Rachtus said. "They've gone dark for a few months, but the last message the commander sent me said the end of war would come before the first snowfall. They are to depart from King Holthiem's command once they've liberated Korzeg's outlying villages from foreign control."

Matticus traced the long route from Osiria's most northern territory to his home across hundreds of miles of mountains, rivers, and forests.

"It will take them a month to make the voyage home," he said. "Perhaps we should call them back now."

"If we recall the Hostellae before our end of the deal is complete, Holthiem may decline to complete his," Rachtus said. "We will need Korzeg's forces if we are to challenge Voluutia."

"Hmm."

Matticus moved over to the table in the center of the room with a similar map to the wall laid upon it. He scanned the small figurines spread about that represented Hostellus's battalions. Several stood atop Vaedor Sellos with a few others near the outskirts of the kingdom. Rachtus's footsteps sounded off behind.

"We are spread too thin," the king said. "If we move against Ehthilia, Zededia will use that as an opportunity to strike. We don't have enough men to defend from his raids and take control of an entire kingdom."

"We must be patient, my king," Rachtus said. "My warboys have plotted out every inch of Ehthilia. With the proper forces, our conquest will be unmatched."

Exhaustion started to overcome him. Matticus hadn't found the comfort of his bed in two nights. Washing the fatigue from his face with his hands, he took a deep breath.

"I'm tired of waiting," Matticus said with a hint of frustration. "Tired of politics and playing nice with the other kings. *Osirisigniros* is in play once again, and with its deliverance, I will suffer their mediocracies no more."

Matticus leaned over the table on his hands.

"The sword is here, Rachtus," the king said as he scoured his eyes over the kingdoms of Osiria. "Somewhere on this map. Still no word from our caravan?"

"No," Rachtus said. "No word since their message from the border checkpoint in Merrinine."

The more time passed, the more Matticus's fear for his caravan grew.

"We can't depend on them anymore," he said. "We need to—"

Suddenly a loud horn bellowed from a distant part of the city, cutting Matticus off. He rushed to the nearby window and peered out. A dim light drew his attention far away, and he recognized it as the signal fire burning bright and tall at the main gate to the city; it only lit when foreign armies approached the city.

"We must reach the gates," Matticus said. "Someone is here."

~ ~ ~

Lucien sprang awake in the bed of his chambers. He flailed his arms and jerked the cloth sheets aside. A blaring horn rang in his ears and startled him to the core.

The prince sat up, darted his eyes around, and brushed his hand through his thick, curly hair as he attempted to regain his senses.

After Lucien stood up, he quickly grabbed his tunic hanging from the bedpost and dressed himself. Several rushing footsteps echoed in his doorway. When he peered out into the hall, the guards passed by, and he eyed his brother marching toward the staircase.

"Matticus!" he yelled. "What's going on?"

"Stay here," the king said. "Do not leave the keep."

Still just as confused, the prince froze. He looked down at the other end of the hall at his brother's chamber. Lucien then grabbed his boots from the ground beside him and slid them on before scurrying onward.

Before the prince reached the royal chambers, Queen Livia stepped out.

"Lucien?" Livia said with Prince Ender tucked against her chest. "What on earth is going on?"

Lucien glanced down at the weary eyes of his eldest nephew standing at the queen's feet and holding onto her nightgown.

"I don't know," he said. "Matticus told me to remain here before departing to investigate."

Livia's panicked face concerned him.

"I'm sure it's nothing. Matticus will be fine."

"It ... it's not Matticus I'm worried about."

The prince raised an eyebrow.

"What do you mean?"

"I saw the signal fire, Lucien," the queen said. "I know what it means. Zededia is marching upon the city, isn't he?"

Given the information he gained from Thancred and the smugglers from Anzagaar Nostir, Lucien started to think Livia was right.

"It's possible," he said. "But why would he? He knows he can't assault Vaedor Sellos with his forces and win. Why now?"

"There is always a game with Zededia's actions, and he's always the better player."

Lucien thought carefully about his brother's cunning reputation. He glanced around to ensure that none of the remaining guards of the keep lingered to eavesdrop.

"Perhaps," he said.

"Lucien...."

The prince raised an eyebrow.

"I ... I'm distraught. All this talk of Zededia and the rumors I've heard of his return...."

"Why are you so intrigued with Zededia?"

Queen Livia hesitated for a moment; Lucien noticed her eyes started to well.

"Because I love him."

Taken aback, the prince allowed his mouth to fall open. Realizing the depth of the situation and the news he just received, he struggled to figure out what to do.

"We should ... talk elsewhere," he said.

The queen nodded and turned to hand her sons over to her servants lingering near the bed. Lucien watched her kiss them both, which only heightened his curiosity. The dynamic between her and his brothers puzzled him greatly. When she returned, he stepped aside so she could walk out of earshot of the young princes.

"The library is usually vacant at this hour," Lucien said. "Shall we go there?"

Livia agreed. He escorted her through the keep with a close eye, but the guards were preoccupied with the stirring commotion outside the city. Hostellus's grand library sat adjacent to the keep on the side opposite to the council hall where Matticus had discussed his kingdom's future plans a few days before. The walkway that connected the two buildings stretched over the gardens of the upper level. Lucien peered down and saw faint blankets of color in the morning darkness as the sun started to surface. The section of purple tulips caught his attention the most.

Once at the doorway to the library, Lucien glanced at the beautiful stained glass walls that arched up to a point as if he stood inside a globe. All the scholars and intellectuals of Vaedor Sellos logged countless hours in the observatory-like building. Memories of studying ancient military tactics with both his brothers flooded back to him; Lucien eyed the exact table he sat at almost every time. He led Livia to a secluded part of the library surrounded by towering shelves of books, scrolls, and other sacred texts. Lucien grabbed a lantern from one of the shelves and set it on the table before sitting down. Across from him, Queen Livia rested her elbows on the stained wood and held her hands together. Lucien kept quiet to allow her to speak, but she seemed worried.

"You've become anxious for Zededia over the last few days, haven't you?" he said.

Livia sighed.

"Yes," she said. "Every time I think of him, my heart races. The thought of him coming to harm in this feud with Matticus brings me much ... pain."

Still as confused as before, he tried to connect the pieces of the love triangle together.

"I can't bear to be away from him any longer, Lucien."

"But my queen," he said, "what about Matticus?"

Livia sniffed as tears started to form in her eyes.

"Matticus does not care for me," she said. "Nor I him. I birthed his children, yes; I love them very much, but my love lies in Zededia. Matticus simply married me to take me from him."

The months leading up to Zededia's exile blurred together in Lucien's head. He began to recollect his eldest brother's swift decision for a queen, though, when Matias fell ill before his passing. Everything started to make sense; the evidence behind Matticus's plot against Zededia continued to grow.

"I knew they've hated each other for years," Lucien said, "but I never suspected it ran that deep. How long were you and Zededia involved before Matticus wed you?"

Livia grew a wide smile.

"Zededia and I met when we were thirteen," she said, wiping her eye. "My father was a gardener for the very fields outside these windows. I was privileged enough to live in the upper ring. Your brother came out to the gardens frequently. I watched him for months and he never even noticed. He seemed so ... so quiet. Just wandering through the rows of flowers with a blank look on his face."

Zededia's emotionless face popped into Lucien's head; he nodded in agreement.

"He never knew I existed until I saw him drop one of the flowers he had picked. I followed him after picking it up, and he bumped into me with it in my hand."

Livia started to subtly laugh.

"He stared at me for ten seconds before he said a word. But, um ... after that, we were inseparable. We've been in love ever since."

"And Matticus knew?"

"Of course," Livia said with a scoff. "Matticus pursued me at a young age too, but he learned of my love for Zededia. He wanted to punish him so desperately that he didn't realize he was punishing me."

Unsure of how to console the queen, Lucien shifted his eyes around the library. The early morning light passed through the colored glass of the windows and cast beautiful rays across the marble floor. Livia pulled something out from the inside of her dress and fiddled with it; Lucien glanced back and studied it.

"Zededia used to write to me," she said, "every week shortly after his exile. He hasn't written to me in months, though. I fear he has forgotten me."

"Well, if it comforts you, he hasn't written to me at all," Lucien said with a half-smile.

"Yes, well ... I doubt Zededia would write love letters to you the way he does me."

The prince laughed.

"No, I suppose not."

The queen's smile faded after a moment. She stood up from the table and disappeared behind one of the distant bookshelves, leaving Lucien to wonder what she was doing. Returning with something in her hands, Livia sat back down. Lucien read the title of the book she carried and recognized it as an anthology of poems his father had forced him to memorize as a part of his education.

"Zededia would read to me for hours," Livia said, eyes glued to the lines of perfectly crafted phrases. "Stories of love or war; I didn't care. I listened to every word."

"Anastesian was my mother's favorite poet," the prince said. "The great tales of King Onodaur's affairs in Daece with all of his maidens ... she loved to read about them."

Livia closed the book after reading a few pages.

"This is all I have to remain close to him," she said. "This and the flowers outside. They rarely help, though. I long to be with him; these are just cruel memories."

Her saddened sigh pained Lucien. The goodness of his heart searched for ways to help and unite her with Zededia, but treason against Matticus and his authority as king followed close behind.

"I need a way to be close to him again ... even for just a moment."

As the prince sat stunned, the weight of the rivalry between his brother's pressed on him in yet another way. He thought hard, the loss in Livia's eyes stabbing at him.

Suddenly, inspiration struck and he sat upright in his chair.

"Come with me," the prince said. "I know of a place I can take you."

~ ~ ~

The horns continued to boom through Vaedor Sellos as the king galloped down the city streets with his entourage of guards and officers behind him. Flags waved furiously atop their standards in the hands of his men, and Matticus readied himself for war. Zededia hadn't marched upon the plains outside his castle in three years, but with the pattern of escalating events over the winter, he didn't question his brother's movements for a second.

He rode into the courtyard adjacent to the main gatehouse, eyeing the yellow plains outside as the iron doors cracked open. Hundreds of soldiers poured from every alley and building nearby. The darkness of the night cowered away at the sun's presence as Matticus led a charge across the stone road that split the wheat fields in half. Roars of his men and thundering hooves rattled through the air. The outer wall protecting the city's fields and agriculture district grew larger as he rode closer. Some of the workers tending their crops turned their attention to him and raised their tools in support of the king's valiant strides. Matticus led his rallied men out into the open plains that surrounded Vaedor Sellos. Like a trickle of water breaking off from a stream, the Vaedorian riders shifted their course at his command. He quickly eyed a massive army in the distance, but he couldn't distinguish their armor to discover their origin. Nonetheless, the king galloped on, ready to defend his home.

Matticus ripped his sword from its sheath and held it high, the group of intruders aimed in his direction. The horns of battle blared over the charging horses and clanging metal.

However, as King Matticus and his army of knights barreled over the plains, a flag sprang up amidst the invading army. Fluttering a vibrant blue color, the flag hosted the unmistakable insignia of the white eagle, the symbol of Hostellus. Matticus frowned in confusion and lowered his blade. He slowed his horse from a gallop to a trot over the next several seconds, each of his men behind slowing as well. At first, Matticus assumed that Zededia had stolen a Vaedorian standard and meant to use it to trick up, but upon further inspection white armor and blue capes coated the men in the distance. Matticus's eyes widened with shock. His armies had come home.

The hostility in Matticus's heart shifted to excitement. Riders of the Hostellae broke off from the pack and mingled with the rest as they approached. Matticus came to a stop and removed his helmet, searching for the Hostellae's commander among the bunch. Soon he spotted the decorative plume of blue and white feathers that pointed out from his warlord's helmet. Matticus cracked a faint grin, encouraged his horse forward, and placed his fist on his chest to symbol a welcome to his soldier.

"Hostellus seems darker than when I left it," the warlord said. "It seems things have worsened in my absence."

Matticus's grin widened at his soldier's playful taunt.

"It's better than six feet of snow, no doubt."

The man removed his helmet, revealing his blond hair and pale blue eyes.

"No doubt at all," he said.

After stopping his horse adjacent to the soldier's, Matticus extended an open hand to him, grasped his forearm, and shook it heartily.

"Welcome home, Commander Nysis," the king said.

"Thank you, Your Majesty," Nysis said. "The Hostellae are eager for service."

Suddenly, shouting erupted from the mass of knights gathered on the plains. Matticus broke his attention from the conversation and searched around. Several Vaedorians pointed to the ridgeline far away next to the edge of the forest. Smoke trails spiraled toward the sky from the trees. The king's heart sank. Commander Nysis removed a looking glass from his saddle and extended it; Matticus stared to study the black flag that rose over all else on the ridge.

"It appears our rest will have to wait," Nysis said.

Matticus took the looking glass and peered through it. A band of knights bearing black armor and spiked helmets sat tall on sturdy horses while foot soldiers scurried about behind them to set up an encampment. Matticus lowered the glass from his eyes. As the anticipation of battle crawled over his skin, his breathing increased in pace. The Black Prince emerged from exile to make an appearance, and the Legonae had come for war.

Chapter 9
Setting the Stage

Day 16 in the Month of Snow

Commander Zededia rested upon the top of the hill that dipped into the Hostellian plains below. Eyes keen, he watched over his soldiers as they prepared a base camp for their occupation. They pitched tents, distributed supplies, and began to dig trenches around the base of the hill to place palisade spikes in. The Black Prince turned his hooded head toward the castle across the battlefield on occasion, the faint trickle of snow from above blurring it in the distance. Throughout the day, he watched his brother's armies move into the safety of the outer wall that surrounded the dozens of farmhouses. Vaedor Sellos tripled in strength over the course of one morning, but Zededia had come too far to abandon his campaign. The prince stared at the Hostellae gathered behind the wall, and he longed to test them with the entirety of his might. Six feet of stone and mortar were all that separated him from his enemy; that, and miles of open fields ready to bathe in the blood of men.

"Sire," Captain Ursa said as he approached.

Zededia shifted his attention to his soldier.

"Our encampment will soon be ready," Ursa said. "We are fortified by the forest behind and the trench below. The Vaedorians won't be able to drive us out so easily."

"Good," Zededia said. "They've surely taken notice of us, but I doubt they'll do anything about it tonight. They're tired from the journey home; they'll need to rest, which is fine since that places time on our side. Lord Redstone will have the advantage from here on out."

"Seether's men are on watch until we advance in case they decide to try anything."

Zededia nodded. He continued his silent study of the snow-dusted grounds after looking away from his captain, motionless in a trance.

"Are you all right, my liege?"

The prince hesitated. Gaze locked on the road to his former home, he sank into a subtle frenzy. His dream of warfare on his brother's lands neared fruition, and the sight of Vaedor Sellos after four years of banishment gnawed at him like worms under his skin.

"Yes," he said darkly. "It's just ... good to be home."

Having taken in all he could stomach, Zededia spurred his horse and rode with Ursa through the camp. His captain informed him of other statuses of the army, including food, cloth, and armament distribution. Zededia listened along as Ursa started to discuss battle plans next.

"We should form a defensive front parallel to the ridgeline when we advance. That way, we'll force the Vaedorians to fight uphill should they push us back," Ursa said.

Concurring with each statement, Zededia allowed his focus to wander. Something drew his eyes and alarmed him. A peculiar looking soldier tried to blend in with a marching patrol, but his head barely reached their elbows. Zededia steered his horse away from Ursa to investigate.

"Sire?" the captain said.

The prince followed the bobbing helmet until the small soldier separated from the rest and made his way to a terribly pitched tent hidden behind a wide oak tree. Zededia watched him disappear around the tree and then parked his horse in front of the tent to await its owner. Seconds later, the soldier emerged from the tent, looked up through the black helmet that poorly aligned with his eyes, and jumped in startlement.

"C-commander," the small soldier said, fumbling with his gear.

"Nyalis?" Zededia said as he recognized the voice. "Is that you?"

The boy sheepishly removed the helmet and revealed a frightened face to him. Confused and irate, Zededia dismounted, walked over to the boy, and knelt on one knee.

"What on earth are you doing here?" he said with a scowl. "Recruits are forbidden to partake in warfare; you are not a soldier of the Legonae yet. The battlefield is too dangerous for you."

"I-I just wanted to be a part of the army," the boy said. "There's no one at home to stay with. The other recruits don't like me."

Zededia sighed as Nyalis looked at him with a shameful, saddened face. Sending a man to escort Nyalis back to Anzagaar Nostir meant taking an able body away from the war effort. Additionally, the oath he made to Nyalis's father before his death on the night of the Legonae's exile from Vaedor Sellos to keep him safe shot forward from the back of his mind. The prince felt for the boy. An orphan, Nyalis truly had nowhere else to go. Zededia stood to his feet and rested his hand on the boy's shoulder. He looked around, met eyes with Ursa, who gave him a light shrug, and shook his head as he faced a difficult decision.

"You ... you may stay," Zededia with a defeated voice. "But you are to cause no trouble. You are to remain in my sight at all times, is that clear?"

"Yes, commander," the boy said, an eager smile appearing on his face.

"All right ... now, come with me," he said, turning back to his horse.

"Where are we going?" Nyalis asked.

"A war meeting," Zededia said over his shoulder. "As a future officer of the Legonae, perhaps you have something to gain from attending."

~ ~ ~

In the command tent of his camp, Commander Zededia stood with each of his captains around a table with a large piece of parchment splayed out upon it. He held a thick piece of charcoal used for marking and began to draw the outline of the battlefield down the hill. On one end, he marked the Vaedorian front line, and on the other, he drew the Legonae's position. Next, he drew a thin, curved line next to the symbol of his camp to resemble the start of the decline down into the plains.

"Our perimeter is set here," Zededia said. "With the Blackwood to our backs and protection from the ridgeline, we are able to maintain a foothold here."

Zededia drew arrows originating from the enemy's side.

"The Vaedorians," he said, marking the parchment, "will attempt to approach from here, here, and here. They outnumber us greatly, so they'll try to surround us if they can."

The prince moved on to the center of the parchment.

"We need to keep their attention drawn to us here, on this basin. There is a second ridge, barely noticeable, that separates the incline of the valley from the plains. Any charge the Vaedorians send toward us will falter in momentum. They'll be forced to meet us on foot if they wish to fight at full strength, and the basin is far enough away from the outer wall that any ranged battalion will have to step out into the open should they utilize it."

After a moment, Zededia drew a rectangle around the basin he referred to.

"This is the killing box," he said. "We keep the fight here and withdraw to the command post, is that understood?"

"Yes, Commander," the captains said in unison.

"We'll create a front in an arch at the edge of the ridge with the defenders, and we'll save the cavalry to intercept flanking units."

Zededia created two smaller lines between the killing box and his camp facing inward.

"Seether, split your longbowmen into two segments aimed toward the middle of the box, and send your crossbowmen near the front line to soften enemy infantry. Everyone else, stay in formation to await further orders. This is how we'll open, and we'll adjust in accordance with the Vaedorians' approach."

With a solid strategy in motion, Zededia stepped away from the table to allow his captains to make any appeals. He glanced over at Nyalis sitting in the corner of a tent and gave him a wink.

"The plains spread wide, sire," Captain Ammon said, pointing to the box. "How are we to funnel the Hostellae to such a narrow target?"

"We'll have contain on the edges with Seether's longbowmen," Zededia said. "With focused fire, we can pinch them in. The light cavalry can linger near the perimeter as well to encourage them to stay inside. Matticus also relies heavily on his strategy of a frontal assault. He'll send in wave after wave of infantry until we are tired and surrounded by corpses before sending in his knights. That's why we're not to stray from formation. If the defenders' wall is broken, the day is lost."

"Yes, sire," Ammon said.

Zededia crossed his arms and glanced out of the command tent as a gust of wind blew the flaps open. Trickles of snow covered the ground in a thick blanket.

"Luckily, the weather is on our side," the prince said. "The Hostellae will struggle to mobilize in cohesion over a sheet of ice. We'll force them to come to us, play by our lead, and surrender control of the fight altogether."

A calm silence fell over the men in the tent.

"Our victory condition lies within the time we can give Caedus," the prince said with crossed arms. "Be smart. Be vigilant. Be disciplined. I am counting on each of you to do your job. Do it well."

Zededia dismissed his captains with a wave of his hand. After they left, he turned his attention to Nyalis, who sat with eager eyes and a bright attitude.

"Well?" Zededia said. "What do you think?"

"What do I think of what?" the boy said.

"What do you think of the nature of a war meeting? Doesn't seem too complicated, does it?"

Nyalis gave him a wondering look.

"I suppose," he said. "Though, I don't understand why you're so—"

"Meticulous?"

"What does that mean?" the boy asked.

Zededia grinned.

"It means thorough," he said, "and we are that way to prepare as best we can."

Walking over to his ward, Zededia sat down on a crate next to him.

"The Legonae are the greatest army in the world," Nyalis said. "No one can beat them."

A soft chuckle bounced through the prince's throat.

"Nyalis," he said, "many of the battles we've won are over before they begin. Preparedness, strategy, adjustments, these are the keys to victory, not your skill with a sword. Despite the legends around the Legonae, there is nothing special about them—nothing superhuman or advanced. Just ordinary men trained to perfection. That is why my officers are as carefully chosen as the disciples of Osiris. Greatness breeds greatness. It passes through generations."

"Am I to find such greatness?" Nyalis asked.

Zededia placed his hand on the boy's nape.

"You are destined to be the greatest."

He shared a fond moment with Nyalis, the beam of hope in the boy's eyes lighting the path to the future of his people and strengthening his confidence in his decision to pass him the torch of command in the distant years.

"Now," Zededia said, standing from the crate. "We should be going."

"Where, Commander?"

"To find you a sword, of course," he said over his shoulder. "Just because Captain Redstone is away doesn't mean you're allowed to stray from your training."

Zededia emerged from his command tent and marched through his camp with young Nyalis behind him, the white carpet under his boots crunching with each step. In the center of the encampment, several of his soldiers erected an armory for surplus and masterless weaponry. Rows of gleaming silver blades hung from the back wall, and Zededia reached for one that suited his apprentice. He then handed the short sword to Nyalis hilt first.

"Every sword in my army meets the standard of perfection," Zededia said. "Crafted from the finest metals Osiria has to offer, they are unbreakable and capable of shredding through the thickest of armor."

Nyalis's face lit up with a grin.

"But," Zededia said, "it is merely a tool. It is the swordsman who gives the blade its full potential."

His apprentice nodded and whirled it around from side to side.

"All right," the prince said. "Let's put it to use."

Zededia entered the training ground his soldiers had cleared off to sharpen their skills on the eve of battle. A cold, stoic expression washed over his face, the expression of an instructor. With a firm hand, the Black Prince slowly unsheathed his fearsome longsword, held the blade up near his nose, and twirled it down to his side.

"I am sure Lord Redstone has taught you well," Zededia said. "How well, I wonder?"

He slid his right foot back behind his left.

"Take your position, Nyalis, and present your weapon."

The boy mimicked his stance and held his sword out in front with two hands.

"Good," Zededia said. "Before we begin to spar, you must first understand *how* to fight. Caedus has given you the basic knowledge to be a sufficient soldier; I will teach you to be superior."

"Yes, Commander," Nyalis said.

Taking a deep breath, the prince's mind opened to the years of militaristic training he endured.

"There are many fighting styles the warriors of Osiria use," he said, "but Hostellus primarily recognizes two."

Zededia held his sword horizontal with shoulders cocked and the hilt near his chin while pointing the blade at Nyalis.

"*Igni*, or 'the warmonger' as some call it, is an aggressive fighting stance that focuses on brutal, powerful attacks aimed at the opponent's torso. An *Igni* swordsman keeps his blade high to hold the height advantage and strikes across the body with channeled strength from the back foot. Strong, assertive, and effective for engaging multiple enemies, *Igni* fighters are initiators; they strike first and fast, apply constant pressure, and strive to overpower their target with sheer force. This is the style of nearly all Hostellus's swordsmen, including my brother, Matticus."

After Nyalis nodded in an understanding, the prince shifted the hilt of his blade to his right hip and held it at an upward angle.

"*Promaast*, or 'the retaliator,' is a defensive fighting stance that opposes *Igni* in many ways. Instead of relying on power and an ability to beat an opponent into submission, the *Promaast* style seeks advantages in positioning, maneuverability, and reactive strikes."

Zededia moved his sword in a cone with the point barely moving and the hilt revolving in a wide circle in front of him.

"In this stance, you are working from the inside out. Deflect any and every strike away from the body, and, when your opponent falters from their failed attacks, use the openings in their defense against them. This style is used by the elite guards of the palace of Vaedor Sellos along with the majority of the Legonae on most occasions."

"What do you mean most occasions?"

Returning to a neutral stance, the prince grinned.

"A swordsman truly gifted in the art of war is capable of shifting between multiple stances," he said. "Some situations merit different styles for offense or defense, strength or elusiveness, or other factors. That is why it is important to master one yet understand all."

"What fighting style do you use, Commander?" Nyalis said.

A pause arose as Zededia elegantly waved his sword around like a painter would move his brush.

"*Virtuo*," he said. "Or 'the danseur.'"

He advanced toward Nyalis, putting his elite skills with a blade on display by pivoting on his feet, swinging his sword in vertical strides with incredible fluidity.

"A mixture of *Promaast* and *Serrast*, Lord Redstone's favored stance with a one-handed weapon, the *Virtuo* stance is one of the most difficult to master."

Light as a feather, the prince practiced his move set at half speed to show Nyalis the intricate steps. He flicked his sword over the backs of his hands multiple times, switching between normal and reverse grip, and slid back and forth from the right and left sides of the boy as he stepped closer.

"My movements mimic those of a serpent. Fast, slippery, and impossible to counter without proper knowledge, this stance prioritizes strikes from my opponent's peripherals, forcing them to balance their attention in two directions. *Virtuo* fighters favor dodging and deflecting over parrying and use their target's energy against them. Confuse them with deceptive strikes, pressure them to hastily answer, and find the weak spot once they've sacrificed their footing. This style is what I personally teach to every Slayer under my command."

Zededia continued to move his arms as he spoke, his sword controlled and disciplined as if it were an extension of his hand. Once a few feet away from Nyalis, he sank to a low stance with a wide base, held his sword with one hand near his chin like the *Igni* stance, and balanced the blade along the forearm of his other. He smiled at the boy from under his hood and relaxed from his poised position after a moment.

"It takes years to master a fighting style, and many more to master that one," Zededia said. "So, that's why you're going to focus on the others for now."

"Yes, Commander."

"Good," the prince said, returning to his original spot across from Nyalis on the other end of the training area. "Watch me; pay attention to my sword placement. If you're anything like your father, you'll advance at a far faster rate than most."

Zededia proceeded to fill the rest of the day with young Nyalis by his side to learn the ways of Hostellian warfare. As the afternoon progressed, the prince took pride in his apprentice as he saw results after every teaching. A great soldier in the making, Nyalis started to form the necessary foundation of an officer of the Legonae.

The snow continued to float down in dense clumps, covering the plains in nearly a foot of powdery ice. Zededia found himself sitting near a large fire on the outskirts of the training grounds, knees close to his chest and hands reached out to the hot flames. Captains Ursa and Ammon sat around the fire as well with empty bowls of stew. The black pot hovering over the charred wood emitted pleasant scents of beef and potato. From behind, Zededia heard faint grunting and the churning of snow. He looked over his shoulder and eyed Nyalis still hard at work, sparring against the air.

"He's a dedicated one to be sure," Captain Ursa said.

"Yes," Zededia said, watching the boy still. "Yes, he his."

Nyalis's grunts of exasperation from his awkward movements amused him.

"He's going to work himself to death, though," the prince said.

Zededia picked up an empty clay bowl.

"Nyalis!" he called.

His apprentice ceased in his tracks and looked at him.

"That's enough for today. Come, grab your dinner while the fire still flickers."

Holding out the bowl to the boy as he trotted over, he slid over on the freshly cut wooden log he used as a seat. Nyalis poured a healthy serving of stew and held it in his shaky hands, fighting off frostbite. The prince pulled his cloak tight over his shoulders. Night fell over the camp, and the snow deepened with each passing hour.

Zededia listened to his captains converse with one another as Nyalis slurped his food.

"Not quite as good as food prepared at the tower, huh?" the prince said.

"It's still good," Nyalis said with a full mouth.

The cinders of the fire began to crumble.

"It's important to rest," Zededia said. "Training wears on the body. You need to allow it to recover before you can expect to advance."

"I need to be the best," the boy said. "I can't do that if I'm resting. I'll only improve while I train."

"You cannot rush your experience as a soldier. You are always training, always learning. There are no shortcuts."

The boy set his empty bowl in the snow.

"I'm not training right now," he said.

Zededia scoffed with a smile.

"When your body trains, your mind rests. When your body rests, your mind trains. Both are equal and complementary to each other. You need both to reach greatness."

"I ... that doesn't make much sense."

"What are you thinking about right now?" the prince asked.

The boy paused.

"Well ... my swordsmanship skills, I guess."

"What about them?"

Zededia looked at Nyalis with an inviting expression, waiting for the epiphany to arrive.

"What I should do differently."

"Exactly," he said.

Pointing to his temple, the prince tapped it.

"You are thinking of how to become better, how to improve. It's near impossible to do so in physical training. Only through rest and reflection can you prepare yourself for the next opportunity. Put together a string of days where you learn from the last and make better, quicker decisions, and you'll see yourself advance at a far faster rate. That, Nyalis, is how you progress."

The boy nodded. Zededia looked at him for another moment and heard his teeth chattering. Unraveling his cloak, the prince raised his arm over Nyalis's head to shield him from the cold. A moment passed, and the boy inched closer and leaned his head against the inside of Zededia's chest. Warmth washed through the prince. The father-son type of relationship he kindled with young Nyalis strengthened. Zededia held onto his dream for an heir, but with love and the possibility of such with the woman he craved so far away, it dwindled with each passing year. Raising Nyalis with the promise he made with the boy's father provided him with an adequate substitution, though.

Zededia sat near the fire for another hour with his captains. He traded strategies and battleplans with them, aiming to tie up all the loose ends and eliminate as many variables as he could. Eventually, the flame died down to just cinders. The prince's men stood from the log circle shortly after, leaving him alone with the boy barely awake under his arm.

"Master Zededia?" Nyalis said with a hazy voice.

"Yes?"

The boy adjusted and opened his eyes.

"Will I ever be as good of a soldier as my father?"

Zededia grinned and looked down.

"I'm sure of it," he said.

"Was my father a great man like everyone said?"

Harsh memories pained the prince. The loss of his friend years ago still stung like a fresh wound. A familiar face echoed through the scenes of battle and triumph.

"Your father was one of the greatest men I've ever commanded, both in heart and with a sword."

Zededia's hoarse throat darkened his voice.

"It would be highly commendable should you follow in his strides."

One of the singed twigs in the fire cracked, drawing his attention. Despite his efforts, Zededia couldn't purge the night of his exile from his mind. Flashes of burning buildings flew by; the faces of the men he lost glared at him from beyond the sealed gates of Vaedor Sellos.

"I can't remember my father's face," Nyalis said. "I've tried, but all I can think about is the night we left the capital."

"What do you remember from that night?" Zededia asked.

The boy hesitated.

"Momma woke me up in the middle of the night. She said we had to leave. My father was gone, with his men, probably. We left our home before grabbing anything, and I don't remember much after that ... just ... the gate."

Zededia knew exactly what Nyalis referred to. The sense of guilt weighing in his stomach sank like a rock.

"I remember you carrying me," Nyalis said, "before giving me to Captain Ursa. My parents were locked inside the gate. He told me not to look, but I wanted to."

With a flushed face, the prince battled with the emotion behind his exile. Hearing Nyalis's pain and knowing that he ultimately caused it forced pooled tears in the corners of his eyes.

"The last time I saw my parents' faces was ... when they slipped me between the bars of the gate."

Nyalis quietly sniffed, and Zededia squeezed his shoulder with his hand.

"What do *you* remember?"

Heavy eyes stared off into the charred embers in the hearth.

"I was ... in the keep at the time. King Matias, my father, had been ill for months. Too weak to move. Matticus and I took turns watching over him as best we could. After he came to relieve me, I retired to my chambers to sleep. But I was awoken by the sounds of clanking metal bouncing off the walls outside my door. The guards rushed down the hall to my father's room. I followed in a panic. When I got there, after nearly trampling the men in front of me ... Matticus was there. I couldn't hear what he said in that moment; I became deaf with fear. Soon after, though, the guards turned toward me ... and drew their swords."

Zededia briefly paused.

"I ran as fast as I could into the courtyard outside, and a war broke out. My soldiers, soldiers of the Black Legion, were under attack. The Vaedorians ... our friends ... started to execute them. I was branded a villain, and because I sat as head of the Legonae, so were they."

"Why?" Nyalis asked.

A deep sigh escaped from the prince's nostrils.

"Matticus betrayed me. He claimed that I had killed our father and plotted to kill him next to take control of the throne. The guards had no choice but to obey the new king, and he ripped the opportunity to prove my innocence away before I could speak. I grabbed the nearest horse from the stables, galloped through the streets of my home, and gathered my men to make an escape. Your father was selfless enough to aid me. We stayed and fought for our survival as all Vaedor Sellos turned against us. We saved as many as many as we could, but our time was cut short."

Taking a controlled breath to steady himself, Zededia lingered on the final moments of his memory.

"When you and your mother approached the gates," he said, "we lost control of them. Matticus's men broke the chains and they screeched to the ground until they crashed into the road with enough force to split the stones in half. I was lucky enough to jump under as they fell, but your parents were ... further behind. I heaved on the gate with all my strength even though I knew it was futile. Your father on the other side, he rushed up and looked at me with a fearful gaze. I saw the light in his eyes fade. He trusted me to get his family out safely, and I failed. I kept trying to pry the gate open and kept trying to cling to hope. Next thing I know, he's squeezing you through this little square hole between the bars and you're in my arms. At that point, I realized he had made his choice. He made me swear to protect you. I handed you to Ursa, and when I turned around, he held his hand up. Told me to go."

Zededia lowered his head in defeat.

"And so, I did."

Nyalis sniffed again, and a pained silence followed.

"I miss my father," the boy said.

Zededia clung tighter to Nyalis.

"So do I."

The calls of the nocturnal forest creatures sang out throughout the camp. Nyalis kept quiet at Zededia's side. Nudging the boy, the prince started to emerge from his cocoon. He stood up from the log, shook the frost out of his legs, and dusted the snow off his pants.

"Best you get some sleep, Nyalis," he said after ushering the boy up. "We'll resume in the morning. Oh, and place your things in my tent. You'll stay with me for now or at least until you learn how to pitch a better tent."

"Yes, Commander," the boy said after sleepily wandering off.

Alone with his thoughts, Zededia collected himself and pressed all notions of guilt and remorse aside. Glaring off into the distance, he shifted gears toward the enemy across the fields. The battle-hardened ferocity that fueled his legacy retook control of his thoughts. War neared, and he needed all his strength and focus to come out on the other side with a victory in hand. The Vaedorians awaited. Matticus awaited.

Chapter 10
Clandestine

Day 16 in the Month of Snow

In the dead of night, after escorting Queen Livia through the empty upper city, Prince Lucien took her to a forgotten part of the keep. The city rested deeply wedged into the western mountains of the Hostellian crater that provided ample hidden passageways and secret chambers. Lucien walked into a darkened room accessible only through a concealed door that mimicked the stone patterns of the throne room adjacent to it. He took a moment to allow his vision to adjust, eyed the next door in the center of the wall of the mountain, and stepped toward it. Livia held tightly to his hand as he searched through the room carefully to not crash into something at his feet. Eventually, Lucien approached the doorway that stood out from the light gray shade of the earthy limestone and moved his fingers across the hardwood until he made contact with a heavy iron lock. The prince then took hold of the chain around his neck and pulled it out from under his gambeson. A small key dangled at the bottom and jostled as he brought it to the door.

"What's that?" Livia asked.

"The key to my mother's room," Lucien said, "and her sanctum."

The door opened; a faint, colorful light blurred through suffocating shadows. Lucien stood aside and allowed Livia to enter first. When he stepped inside, he stood next to her and marveled at the beautiful sight before him. A perfectly circular mosaic of luminescent stones glowed like a bright star. Blue runic symbols lined the perimeter of the circle surrounded by a background of white gems. In the center, deep brown and light green gems formed a majestic willow tree with flowing branches. Lucien's eyes sparkled as a half-grin appeared on his face. He heard Livia softly gasp.

"Just wait," he said.

Lucien walked over to the vibrant mosaic and placed his palm on a loose portion of it in the middle of the tree. The disk sank into the wall after he pressed it. Suddenly, a deep click shook the wall and the mosaic cracked open. Livia stepped near, and he pried it away to reveal a massive hall that towered stories over his head.

Columns lined the hall to support the mountain above; it spread out to form the chambers of a mausoleum. The ceiling above glowed with similar luminescent stones high above that dimly lit the room. In the distance, a bridge connected a gap in the floor, and the rippling reflections of water danced on the banks.

"Is that—"

"The Nekroa," Lucien said. "It flows from deep in the Hostellian mountains, and transport ships sail it all the way to the Orlestian. Few know it runs this deep into the capital, though. Many think it stops at the underground lake about a quarter mile to our right beyond that wall."

"This ... this is marvelous," Livia said.

"My forefathers lie here," the prince said. "The burial ceremonies are kept secret from the public, though. Only a select few know this place exists."

Between each of the columns, long blue carpets created paths to the tombs embedded in the walls of the mausoleum, and statues of the deceased stood on each side. Lucien made eye contact with a few of the figures, some of which he recognized from his family history.

Over the bridge, Lucien led Livia into small hallway, and a similar light as the mosaic highlighted a grand archway. The prince's heart started to beat faster, for he clung to the sentiment of the approaching chamber in a tight grasp.

"Mother's meditation room used to frighten me as a child," Prince Lucien said, "but as I grew older, it became a soothing presence."

The prince stopped just before the marble archway.

"I've lived in Vaedor Sellos for twenty-six years, yet I have never known of such a place. Neither of your brothers ever spoke of it," the queen said.

"Matticus I would not have expected to bring it up. He never liked the dark. He used to be jealous of the time my mother would spend here with Zededia."

Lucien stepped over to the white arch and grazed his fingers on the damp symbols carved into them.

"I'm surprised that Zededia never took you here, though," he said. "He loved this place. Would spend days here after Mother's passing. I suppose it made him feel connected to her in some way."

Feeling a tug on his sleeve, he turned to meet Livia's saddened gaze.

"He never talked to me about your mother much," the queen said.

Lucien looked to the floor as memories of mourning, both his and his brothers', passed by him.

"My mother's death broke him," he said. "I hadn't seen such a loss in happiness in any person, and I don't think he has fully recovered, nor ever will."

As he turned back to peer inside the meditation chamber, Prince Lucien moved inside to show the queen the powerful connection to the spirit world. A dome like natural structure covered the top of the room, and thousands of tiny, shining gems sparkled toward the floor like those in the previous hall. Lucien paced near the center of the rounded cave where a raised, circular platform held a wide array of silk blankets and cushions. He looked over his shoulder at the star-stricken queen as she absorbed the astronomical sight. Her wondrous gaze forced him to smile, and he stepped closer to the inviting area below the cosmic scenery.

"Oh, by the gods," Queen Livia gasped. "The stars above our heads could not produce such beauty."

After kneeling next to the blankets, the prince felt the fine silk in his right hand and reminisced in the faint memories of his time here as a boy. He noticed a lack of dust around the room and how tidy the meditation platform seemed.

"Perhaps Matticus travels here more often than I realized," he said.

"Why do you say that?" the queen asked as she sat on the edge of the comfort-filled area.

After studying the room, Lucien deduced that someone else had been here to keep things clean and in order. On one of the pillows, he picked up a small bracelet with a blue gemstone sewn into the middle.

"Nothing...." he said. "It doesn't matter."

The queen sank into the softness of the bed-like platform as he moved about.

"If Zed wasn't training with Father's private guards, practicing his necromancy, reading, or causing mischief with his friends, he was here," Lucien said.

Sensing that Livia had found a euphoric moment of her own, the prince deemed his task complete. He scanned the rock formations above and moved his eyes between the streaks of shine and glimmer.

"I don't know what he did in here aside from staring into the ceiling," he said, "but at least it's an occupying view."

Studying the twinkling ceiling once again, Lucien's soul became connected to the spirits of his family line. The energy of the meditation chamber linked him with all his forefathers.

"My father originally discovered this place while his miners dug for gems after digging through the edge of the underground chambers, but once my mother wandered in, she refused to let him continue."

The prince glanced over to see if Livia had understood, but she lay mesmerized in a trance.

"I can feel him here, Lucien," she said. "It's like he's here with me."

"Shall I leave you here, then, my queen?" Lucien asked.

A light smile appeared through the silk fabric over the edge of the platform that thanked the prince for sharing his family secret.

"If you are needed elsewhere, please, attend to whatever calls you," Livia said with a smooth voice. "I'm sure you have better interests than lounging with a love-deprived matriarch."

She fell back into the cushions.

"Oh, just leave me here," she said. "I'll find my way out eventually."

Lucien gave a half-grin to the queen before bowing, and then he turned to make his path back toward the keep. As he stood under the marble arches, he glanced over his shoulder. A sense of selflessness warmed him after leading Queen Livia to a cathartic connection that could ease her longing. Lucien quietly left the chamber to not disturb her peace. A dark trip across the mausoleum stood between him and the rest of his day. More pressing matters were at hand, forged by the curiosity of his brother's whereabouts.

After navigating the tombs under the mountain back into the keep, Prince Lucien slid his way back into the throne room, expecting to find someone to inform him on why the entire city seemed to stir. None of the guards stood in his sight, nor any of the servants.

"Matticus!" he called.

The silence puzzled him. With a subtle shake, the floor started to move under his feet, adding to the confusion. He hadn't felt that sensation in years, but it was one he recognized. The Hostellae began to mobilize. Fearing the evidence of Zededia's return, the prince darted for the stables. As he exited the keep, he ran into Thancred on the portico.

"Ah, my prince," the doctor said after Lucien nearly crashed into him, "I have been looking everywhere for you."

Lucien regained his balance and cleared his throat.

"I-I've been with the queen," he said. "She came to me for help, and I took her somewhere to alleviate her stress."

"Perhaps that is best for Her Majesty."

The prince squinted.

"Why? Also, where the hell is Matticus? Where the hell is anyone?"

Thancred gave him a worried look.

"King Matticus has deployed his armies to the Hostellian fields. The Legonae have marched upon Vaedor Sellos. Zededia has returned."

Lucien's surprise turned into shock. Zededia hadn't directly challenged the Vaedorian armies in two years.

"They're ... here for war?" he asked.

"It appears so," Thancred said. "But the timing of such war is quite disadvantageous. For both your brothers."

"What do you mean?"

The doctor leaned closer.

"We cannot speak here," he whispered. "Matticus's paranoia of internal support for Zededia has peaked."

Struggling for the next move, Lucien's mind played a nightmare of his brothers battling against one another, the same that had been plaguing him since Zededia's exile.

"What now?" he asked.

"I'm going to meet with a contact from Anzagaar Nostir at Blackbriar's Pub in the Merchant District tonight. Come with me. Hopefully, we'll know more then."

"All right."

Lucien started to take his leave, but Thancred placed a hand on his shoulder.

"Be sure you are not followed, my prince. The Order cannot reveal its presence within Vaedor Sellos just yet. Our secrecy is our only protection."

Though he nodded in an understanding, Lucien became snared on Thancred's mention of 'the Order.' He had heard rumors of Zededia's followers surviving in the city after they were expelled along with him. The elements of the entire situation drowned him in questions; something else was at play. Lucien kindly saluted Thancred before eyeing the main gates ahead, stepped off the stone porch of the keep, and attempted to fathom the brewing events on a course for a massive collision. Matticus had already launched his armies toward action, and Lucien could only wonder what Zededia had in store.

~ ~ ~

On the opposite side of the city, King Matticus stood watchful over his marching armies from atop the central gatehouse as the darkest part of night swept the land. Over a dozen monstrously armored soldiers surrounded the king while he gave commands. Matticus shifted in his stance while the snow covered his short hair. The cold penetrated his broad muscles, but he had grown used to the chilling weather over his twenty-nine years in the temperamental climate of Hostellus.

The king studied the thousands of foot soldiers departing into the wheat fields below. Their synchronous footsteps beat in his ears. Muffled shouts from his military leaders below followed the pounding steps, and Matticus once again witnessed his father's analogy of "March of the Giants," a war term that referred to the thunderous strides of warriors on their way to fight for their glorious kingdom. The glimmers and shines of Hostellian steel caught his eye from the reflections of torches.

Turning his gaze farther away, Matticus eyed the regiment of cavalry leading the march toward the Blackwood in the distance. The rows of horsemen bobbed up and down as they rode, blurring together like river currents.

"How many could we muster?" he asked the commander of the Hostellae.

Shuffled footsteps moved toward the king's position.

"Six hundred paladins follow General Komm," Nysis said from underneath his decorated helmet. "Eight hundred longbowmen under Captain Hiran."

"How many infantry?" Matticus asked.

He heard Nysis remove his helmet. The king lowered his vision to right below his position to watch row after row of shield-and-sword-wielding soldiers trudge through the snow into the fields.

"Four thousand, my liege," Commander Nysis said, breaking his concentration. "Oloyor will lead them to meet the Legonae tomorrow morning."

"Will we have enough to defend the city?" the king said, looking up at the white flecks floating down from the night sky.

"Zededia won't reach the city," Nysis said to reassure him with a cocky tone. "But we have thousands more ready to defend her. Many are in need of recovery."

"Then let's hope you're right," Matticus said.

Matticus's confidence strengthened in the vastness of his forces, but his face remained cold and fierce. He glanced up from his uniformed soldiers to the horizon ahead where flickers of orange light outlined the forward post. Torchlights from Zededia's camp gleamed into view through the heavy snowfall. The king could nearly taste the death of his hated brother. The hour to dive his sword through Zededia's flesh drew near.

He longed for the Black Prince's demise and savored the opportunity to bring it by his hand, but the mortal reminder from previous duels revamped their severity across his right forearm. The scar tissue pulsed under his armor.

"Should I face Zededia in the fields," King Matticus said with piercing eyes toward his enemy in the distance, "you are to not aid me in his defeat."

A subtle silence fell over the king and his commander. The ice thickened in Matticus's hair as Nysis stepped closer to his right.

"Are you sure, sire?" Nysis said.

"Yes," he said, looking down at the spot on his arm where Zededia injured him almost a decade ago. "I will face him alone, and I will rid him from this earth for good."

As Matticus's brain surged over the memory of the last time he had fought Zededia in a true match, the duel to decide who held the title of Champion of Hostellus, the king's smaller scar above his lip vibrated as well. While the younger Matticus ranked high in a pool of the city's most elite soldiers, he hated second place. He licked the rough mark on his lip from where Zededia had left his eternal brand. An unquenchable thirst for revenge sent him to a trance.

"Sire?" Commander Nysis said. "Are you alright?"

Matticus blinked the frost out of his eyes.

"What do you remember from my duel with Zededia in nine-sixty-three? In the Tournament of Champions?" the king asked to see if his defeat left an impression on his soldier.

"If my memory serves me right, that was the only year you and Zededia faced each other, wasn't it, my liege?" Nysis said.

Matticus nodded while the image of his exiled brother appeared during the memory where the two dueled. The loss taunted him.

"Do you remember how it ended?"

Hearing Nysis clear his throat before the answer, the king inhaled to calm his brewing frustration.

"I believe your brother won, sire," the commander said, hesitating. "A near perfect match, save the busted lip and gash on your arm."

"Right," Matticus said in agreement, "but Zededia did not win because he bloodied my face or tore my skin."

The king then twisted his head to where his chin brushed the thick armor on his shoulder. Memories burning in his thoughts, he beamed at Nysis with a boiling anger that stemmed from his failure ten years prior.

"Zededia cheated. He used magic when it was forbidden. No one else could see it, but I could. And from that moment on, Father chose him over me."

With a fierce malice, Matticus gripped the waist-high wall on the edge of the gatehouse with such strength that the stone vibrated and the king's veins glowed with the bright red blood of his ancestor in his hands, fingers, and eyes.

"I wanted to peel the skin from his flesh," he snarled through his teeth. "And I'll savor the day when I finally can."

Once all his battalions stood in formation outside the massive walls, Matticus dissolved his tension through a controlled exhale. He glared at columns of soldiers dressed in heavy winter gear under shining metal armor. Returning his sight to the treeline in the far distance, the Vaedorian king felt his skin crawl with anger. The war he had wanted four years ago rested on the cusp of this day. His brother had finally crawled out of the snake hole into the open. An ecstatic sensation took the reins of his thoughts and catalyzed the desire to clash against the Legonae with all the hate he could rally.

"Forgive me, sire, but I'm not following your connection to your duel with Zededia to now," Commander Nysis said.

"I've thought deeply of that day in my father's presence," Matticus said, dark inflections in his tone. "I remember the disappointment in his eyes; the praise he gave Zededia. I remember the agony of my right as king slipping through my hands. For ten years, I've reflected over that moment, the moment when Zededia stole the last of my father's favor from me."

The true motivation behind Matticus's hatred emerged from the crevices of his heart, urging his aggression and poisoning his reason.

"I have plotted Zededia's demise for a long time, and now that he appears here, right before me, the anger I felt for him in that moment is as fresh as the snow on the ground."

"And what of the sword, my liege?"

Matticus had nearly forgotten about his ancestor's great weapon. His quest for the blade crept second to killing Zededia, and now that the Black Prince marched to challenge him, many doors opened to the future.

"After I kill that fucking snake, the sword will be my hammer used to forge my empire. Osiria will know one king yet again."

"Many will oppose us, sire," Nysis said. "We need to plan our conquest carefully."

Matticus's blistering mind fell victim to the greed of his commander's introduction of all eight kingdoms serving under his rule.

"Yes, Rachtus and I have been planning for a while now," the king said. "With you at my side and the Sword of Kings in my grasp, nothing will stand in my way. Holthiem will join us to the north, and we will choke Voluutia on multiple fronts. None of the others stand a chance."

In the midst of restating his scheme, Matticus's withered love for his youngest brother rose to combat the totalitarian plan. The king's face loosened, he released his grip, and a pleasant memory from his childhood pressed through and fought against his bloodlust. For a moment, Matticus thought of Lucien and his kind wisdom. An advisor to him for many years, Lucien occupied much of his thoughts. He knew he'd never agree to such a war.

The last strand of peace in the Vaedorian king fought with all its strength to preserve the good-natured heart buried in jealousy. Nausea overcame him shortly after.

"Where is Prince Lucien?" King Matticus asked, in need of his peacekeeper.

"I've not seen him, my king," Nysis said to deter him. "Perhaps we should descend to the armies below."

Matticus thought he had seen his youngest brother with the queen earlier in the day with his sons, but he struggled to remember.

"Yes," the king said softly. "They will need our presence to face Zededia's legions."

He turned for the left tower of the gatehouse that held the ramp system within and signaled for his bulwark-like guards to follow. The king's mind battled with an internal conflict; the anger of his past raged against the forgiving nature that his father had instilled in him and that Lucien supported. His head throbbed and his cheek twitched. For the first time in a while, a sense of loneliness washed through him. His family lay elsewhere and he rejected the anger trying to take control.

"Wherever he is," Matticus said with a sigh. "I hope he is all right."

~ ~ ~

"Come quickly, my prince," Thancred yelled over the weather while standing in the doorway of the back room inside the pub he told Lucien to meet him at.

The hooded prince hunched his shoulders as the dense frost on his cloak weighed heavily on his head. Barely able to recognize Thancred through the darkness of night and the thick ice raining from above, Lucien struggled to step in the doctor's direction. Once he reached the stockroom Thancred stood near, he scuffed his boots on the stone outside. Ducking to enter the candlelit room attached to the pub, he noticed another man inside.

"Prince Lucien, this is Baeno. He is our contact from Anzagaar Nostir," Thancred said. "He's come to inform us of the situation."

"A warm hand extends to you, Lucien Osiris, courtesy of your brother to the east," the shorter, bearded man said.

Lucien shook hands with Zededia's agent as Thancred pulled three stools over near a table.

"Baeno is the head runner for the Black Legion in Vaedor Sellos," the doctor said. "Stealing supplies and information from within the city wherever he can."

Lucien raised an eyebrow to his older friend.

"To what efficiency? Matticus has all but *tripled* the guards at every major point in each district. How in the world you manage to steal a crumb with the new laws in place is beyond me," the prince said. "I'm still unsure how the first caravan went through."

Baeno and Thancred shared a sly smile between themselves as Lucien sat clueless to the mischief.

"A little bribery goes a long way," the spy said with a grin, "and there are more of us in Matticus's ranks than he's aware of."

"How frequently do you supply the Legonae?" Lucien asked.

"You'll have to forgive me, Your Highness," Baeno said, "but I'm not at liberty to discuss logistics with anyone outside the Order."

Lucien frowned as he surely thought his prestige as a member of the Royal Family granted him enough clearance to know such things.

"Do not linger on Baeno's discretion, my friend," Thancred said to soothe him. "I am also unaware of what they do under Matticus's nose."

"The fewer who know, the less likely we are to be caught," the spy said, elaborating.

With a firmer understanding, the prince respected the secrecy, even if he disliked the exclusion.

"I suppose that is best for you," Lucien said with a soft sigh. "So, why have you summoned us here tonight, Master Runner?"

Zededia's inside man grabbed a stool from Thancred and seated himself as Lucien removed his winter cloak. The prince brushed the ice from his nose and eyebrow before taking a seat himself. He heard Thancred strike a piece of flint near another candle and saw him place the flaming wick in the center of the table, shadows fluttering across his face.

"Plans are in motion, gentlemen," Baeno said. "Plans that will revolutionize the future of Hostellus."

The prince paused.

"That's awfully bold. I'll assume that has something to do with Zededia's sudden appearance across the plains," Lucien said, visualizing the pieces of Baeno's allusion aided by his understanding of his exiled brother. "He's found the sword, hasn't he?"

A soft quiet fell over the table.

"That's right," the spy said to concur. "That's extremely sensitive information, however, and we want it to stay that way."

"You have our discretion," Thancred said.

Baeno leaned toward the prince, and Lucien opened his ears.

"My liege, Zededia, has already dispatched a team to fetch the Sword of Kings."

Realizing that the sword was not only within reach but in close enough proximity for Zededia to send someone to retrieve it, Lucien began to catch onto his brother's game.

"And so, Zed marches upon the Hostellian Plains to what? Distract Matticus?"

"Precisely," Thancred said, answering for the Black Prince's spy. "But what we don't know, Baeno, is what is needed of the Order here in the city."

Lucien raised a hand to put a pause on the conversation.

"What exactly is this 'Order?'" Lucien asked. "You've mentioned it several times now."

He watched the doctor turn to Baeno for approval. The runner nodded.

"Three years ago," Thancred said after clearing his throat, "a group of men from all eight Osirian kingdoms combined to create a secret community responsible for ensuring the balance and safety of Osiris's descendant territories. Nine men formed a pact with each other to serve the greater good of humanity; one man from each kingdom represented their respective lands and recruited whomever they could to act in the favor of the order."

"But there are only eight territories that Osiris laid claim to?" Lucien queried after a moment. "Osiria contains no other lands?"

"Eight founders from the eight lands," Thancred said, clarifying, "and one to govern them as the grandmaster."

The list of possible candidates shortened in a hurry. Any royal would have great difficulty hiding their involvement in such an organization. They would have to operate outside the rule of law.

"Zededia?" Lucien said as the clear answer came to mind.

The two men across from him nodded simultaneously.

"So, are you the representative for Hostellus?" Lucien said toward Thancred, thinking how the doctor had acted on Zededia's behalf on several occasions and defended him more than anyone he had met.

"Indeed, I am, my prince," his gray-haired mentor replied. "I am the high master of Hostellus, ranking second to your brother in the Order of the Black Legion."

An entire world of secrecy flooded Lucien's naive mind. Not once had he realized such a system of governing existed within the strictly regulated walls of Vaedor Sellos.

"That answers more than I thought," Lucien said. "Does my status as a prince grant me any sort of leverage in this Order?"

His friend awkwardly remained silent.

"Thancred?" Lucien said.

"Erm, perhaps we shouldn't waste Baeno's time any further," the doctor said.

"Right," Lucien said with disappointed curiosity.

He turned back to Baeno.

"How can we be of service?" Thancred said.

"There is something we need from you, High Master," Baeno said.

Lucien's dismay faded as he returned to the conversation.

"Zededia has already emptied half the city," Lucien said. "He's making a move for the Sword of Kings. What else could he need?"

"King Matticus is extremely affluent in allies, Prince Lucien. His influence stretches much farther than we can challenge," the Black Prince's runner said. "Caedus's discovery is almost assured."

"Caedus..." Thancred pondered as the cogs of his old mind churned. "Caedus Redstone?"

"Zededia's right hand man," Lucien said. "Is he who was sent to retrieve the sword?"

Lucien leaned back on his stool and crossed his arms.

"That doesn't surprise me," he said. "And you want us to help prevent his discovery? How?"

The thunderous sound of the Vaedorian gates closing echoed in the tavern. Militaristic shouts bellowed outside. Lucien knew that Matticus had readied himself for battle and would grow more eager to seek the holy weapon in play.

"We need you to be our ears," Baeno said. "We have difficulty operating in the keep; we are blind there in many ways. Matticus selects his guards rather ... infuriatingly.

We've tried on several occasions to place an agent at his side, but the king rarely accepts those he doesn't personally know."

Lucien leaned forward again.

"So you're asking me to *spy* on King Matticus?" he asked.

"Essentially," Baeno said. "We need you present in Matticus's inner circle to filter out any news of Lord Redstone or the sword."

Pondering the immense amount of treason asked of him, the prince sat stunned.

"And if I come across someone who possesses said news, what am I to do with them?"

He heard a soft chuckle from the spy across the table.

"I'm sure a man of your talents can ... dispose of them however you choose," Baeno said.

Having never killed another man before, Prince Lucien hesitated with a knot writhing in his stomach.

"I'll see what I can do," Lucien said after a moment.

"Good," Baeno said with a smile. "My commander will engage the Hostellae as soon as the sun creeps over the mountains. Be smart as you act in his stead."

Lucien thought of the endless march of soldiers he had avoided all day.

"Matticus has rallied thousands to fight for him. How can the Legonae possibly challenge them? How can Zededia prepare them for such a war?"

From a devious grin on Baeno's face, Lucien heard the spy's rib cage rattle once more with a deep laugh.

"Don't worry, Your Highness," Baeno said. "We've been waiting for a chance to kill your soldiers for a long time. We're ready."

The tension in Lucien's abdomen doubled. His road ahead lay submerged in the unknown. Baeno stood from the table, bowed, and left him with Thancred, and the prince forced himself to swallow his fear with an uncertain gaze toward tomorrow.

Chapter 11
The Red Snow

Day 17 in the Month of Snow

In the early morning on the third day of his voyage, Captain Caedus Redstone ushered his team of companions through the pitch-black darkness under a massive snowstorm high in the Lunendar Mountains. The horses struggled to travel in such weather, but the vigorous captain pressed forward with courage and strength. Caedus attempted to spark a torch from his pack; the harsh, icy wind foiled his actions with a swift strike.

"Shit," Caedus said to himself in the howling wind. "Damn storm."

He turned to see if he could identify the outline of his four team members behind. Through the blackness, his adjusted eyes scattered over the moving blobs and his ears twitched at the sloshing snow from the horses' hooves.

"Captain!" one of his soldiers shouted. "We need to rest! The horses cannot travel in these conditions for much longer!"

Caedus disliked the idea of slowing his pace, but he realized the only time the group had stopped to restore their strength was on the first night of their travels when the captain sparked a conversation with the girl. He frowned, scanned the neighboring areas for any settlement along the far eastern border of Hostellus, and found no sign of any light in the cold, narrow valley he trudged in.

"Fine," Captain Redstone said with a grunt. "There had better be a town wedged somewhere these frozen rocks. This road leads to the border checkpoint to Merrinine, so something should be close."

Moving forward, Caedus buckled down on his saddle and slowly carved a path through the terrain. After half an hour of gradual progression deeper into the steep mountain chain, a faint glimmer caught the captain's watchful eye. Like a vagabond reaching an oasis, Caedus widened his eyes and focused on the target. As his strength faded, he agreed with his soldier's suggestion to seek shelter. Barely able to feel his feet inside his damp boots, Caedus spurred his steed toward the hope of safety in the distance.

"There," he said. "We may find a place to rest after all."

"What is that place, my lord?" one of his soldiers asked.

Caedus stopped to study the light, but no major buildings stood out to his careful eyes.

"I don't care," the captain yelled, disgruntled from the painful chill in his bones. "As far as I'm concerned, it's Anzagaar Nostir."

Captain Redstone steered his company toward the yellow glow off the trail of his mission. Upon closer inspection, the one distant light shifted into several, and Caedus found comfort in discovering a settlement of some kind. Whether the inhabitants would accept him or not fell short of his worries; he needed a place to rest no matter how welcoming they would be.

A tall wooden wall held hanging lamps outside of the town as Caedus approached. Shoddy, the fortifications revealed how little governance the settlement had seen. Caedus thought it unlikely that either Hostellian or Merrin rule reached this far.

From under the several layers of his hoods, Captain Redstone blinked to search the wall for a gate. His tired eyes read a sign hanging from a post nearby that held "Tollmuc" inscribed on it. As if on cue, a sliding panel on the wall opened and an old, withered face stuck out as Caedus tapped the snow off the marker.

"Who are ye?" the old man shouted through the breeze. "Why have ye come to Tollmuc?"

The thick pronunciation from the man caught the captain off guard, having been used to the prim and proper environment of a professional army. Understanding his current position, Caedus found himself without any room to argue or lie.

"I am a captain of the Legonae, army of the Black Legion. I serve an Osirian," Caedus said. "The soldiers under my command, along with myself, simply seek shelter from the snow."

"From Hostellus, are ye?" the gatekeeper asked with a low tone. "Or Merrinine?"

Caedus found the question interesting as if its owner preferred one answer over the other.

"Eastern Hostellus," the captain responded.

A slight sneer peered through the opening in the wall toward Caedus. The keeper paused for a moment and picked his teeth with his tongue, causing a hint of anxiety to clog the captain's throat.

"Not from the capital, then?" the scruffy man asked.

"Used to be," Redstone said. "Not anymore."

Caedus heard a low chuckle from the man on the other side of the wall.

"Don't take too kindly to Vaedorians these days," the man said with a mouth full of rotting teeth. "But you don't look the sort to like 'em either."

Shortly after, a crude snap sounded from the wall. The captain pulled his horse back as the shaky gates opened toward him with two spear-wielding peasants to provide an escort. Once Captain Redstone moved his team in the gateway, the keeper stopped him with a trembling hand.

"You can stow your horsies in the stables here to the left. Inn's just down the road if ye need a drink," the old man said with a lantern in his other hand. "Don't cause no trouble, master rider, and none will come lookin' for ye."

Caedus peered at the man for a moment and deemed the shifty warning valuable. As the captain scanned the township, crooked buildings and jagged roads hurt his eyes at their sight. He twisted his torso to dismount his horse while maintaining a watchful gaze on the crumbling landscape. Before the guards took his steed to the stables, Caedus grabbed his sheathed sword and the empty food pack from the saddle.

Muffled laughter shouted off from the distance, and the captain motioned his team forward toward the tavern. Through inches of snow, Caedus marched with the three soldiers and the freezing girl behind him. He turned to check on her status, having sealed himself off from her questions for the last day. The captain stopped for a moment, instructed his men to walk ahead, and allowed her to catch up.

Her inviting eyes melted the frost chilling his bones. For a moment, Caedus found his emotional side rising in an unwanted fashion. He looked upon her beautifully symmetrical face that birthed a narrow jawline and perked cheeks. The slightly darker skin tone caught his attention for the first time, and he realized that the girl had likely spent much time in warmer locations.

"Are you all right?" Caedus muttered, attempting to hide the sudden realizations of her attractiveness.

"I-I'm not too fond of the snow."

An extreme rarity, Caedus flexed the muscles in the right half of his face to produce a subtle grin. He focused on her dark hair flickering in the light wind before ushering her forward.

"Come then," Captain Caedus said as an invitation. "Let's see if we can find something strong to drink."

Redstone followed the thief girl, and he realized that she stood only a few inches shorter than his six-foot stature. Daunted for a moment, Caedus shook off his distractions and kicked the ice on his way to the tavern. Once he reached the doors outlined with the light inside, the raucous laughter filled his ears to the brim. Caedus pushed the door open for the girl and, to his expectation, several pairs of eyes fell upon him. He saw his soldiers in the corner waiting for their purchased drinks.

Once the attention dripped away, the captain passed by several townsfolk, some too drunk to see him properly. He gripped the hilt of his short sword, his trust for the locals as weak as the fences outside. Caedus sat himself down at the table next to his soldiers' along the back wall of the pub. The bones in his neck creaked with every movement, so he swiftly jolted his jaw to the left and right with his hands to crack them. After, he received a concerned expression from the girl across from him.

"How do you not just ... off yourself by doing that?" she asked.

Caedus chuckled softly at her concern.

"You'd be surprised how far the human spine can twist before breaking," he said.

The barkeep approached just as he finished his sentence and a frightened face stared back at him.

"Erm ... what can I pour you, Master Rider?" the large man asked.

"Brandy," Caedus said.

He reached into the pack and grabbed a bag that clinked as he gripped it. After opening the pouch, Caedus plucked a shining gold kor from it.

"I also need to resupply," the captain explained. "Are kors an acceptable currency here?"

"Aye, my lord," the barkeep said after noticing the prestigious emblem that signified Caedus's status as an honored noble. "But I'm afraid we're a bit scarce on food these days. Won't be able to surrender much. Winter's been harsh this year."

Captain Caedus grunted out of disappointment.

"I'll take what you can spare," he said while pouring out five more gold pieces from the lot of his money. "Four for enough food for three days, two for the drinks and dinner for two us."

He plucked one more from the pouch.

"One to feed the horses."

The server happily accepted Caedus's generous payment, and the captain turned to the hungry girl to his right as the larger man walked away to fetch their meal.

"What?" Caedus asked after her perplexed eyes caught him off guard. "Are you not hungry?"

"No, it just sounds like you've had some experience with ... snapping necks," she said.

Caedus looked around as he tried to wiggle around her statement. However, the assumption rang true in his memories of battle.

"Perhaps," he said.

Struggling to meet her eyes after admitting the lethality of his past, Caedus pulled his short pipe, a wrapped portion of tobacco, and a match from his satchel. He packed the pipe and lit the bitter plant before exhaling a hazy puff of smoke. After avoiding the question for a moment, Caedus looked back at the girl without moving his head.

"What?" the captain said in defense. "I'm a soldier. Soldiers kill."

"And how many men have you killed, Captain Redstone?" the girl asked.

Scanning over years' worth of war during his service in the Hostellae against the Northern Tribes that plagued Osiria throughout his teens and early-twenties, Captain Caedus calculated his kill count.

"Hundred," he bluntly said. "Maybe more."

Though the faces of his slain opponents branded his soul, he refused to reveal his remorse, for it dwindled when he remembered the purpose of their deaths.

"Enough to keep me alive," Caedus said as he held the pipe in the corner of his lips.

The answer trailed off as it left his tongue. Caedus darkened his last statement to insinuate a change of topic. To his relief, the thief girl fell silent. The pause created an awkward tension between the two, and the captain disliked the distance he had created. He shifted the pipe across his mouth once more.

"You never told me your name," Caedus said to light a spark once again.

He looked at the girl and saw her defeated expression.

"You have a name, don't you?" he said, prying.

For a second time, his companion struggled to answer.

"No one has known my name since my parents. No one cared after I was abducted by the raiders who pillaged my home."

Caedus realized he had struck a private note but kept his stern face.

"Is that how you wound up working for one of Grimm's crew?" he asked.

A confirming nod grazed her crossed arms, and he sympathized with her.

"Killed your parents?" he said.

She nodded again. Caedus felt an urge to stretch his hand toward the girl to soothe her negatively nostalgic state of mind. His lack of experience in the art of comforting a woman clogged his decisions, however.

"What do you remember from your job before the Vaedorians found you?" he said to redirect.

The saddened guise of the soft-skinned girl shifted to a more neutral state as Caedus glanced at her. He then looked around to scan the room of drunkards and peasants while waiting for her to sum up the details. In the opposite corner, a shadowed, hooded figure with a covered face stuck out. The cautious captain met eyes with the stranger when he raised his head, but his sudden curiosity broke as the girl placed a finger on his forearm.

"All I was told is that the group I traveled with was hired by a noble to retrieve some artifact. I didn't know where we were going until we wound up in an abandoned temple in the middle of the mountains somewhere near here. One of the men I ran with said we were somewhere between Hostellus and Voluutia, somewhere not drawn on any map. I don't know much else, but we were lost for over a week before we stumbled upon the temple by sheer luck after one of the other thieves fell off a cliff and tumbled into the crater that protected the temple," she said. "I knew that it was an incredibly valuable job, however."

Caedus picked up the large stein that the barkeep dropped off and wet his throat with a hearty swig.

"And why is that?" he asked after swallowing.

"Because," the girl said, "Grimm's brother was our team leader."

The mention of any of Grimm's family collided with Caedus's knowledge of the bandit lord.

"That's impossible," the captain said. "Farricks was slain by King Matias after the Devil Twins attempted to overthrow the Hostellian government almost fifteen years ago."

"Well, that's a humorous story considering I saw Farricks alive and well about a week ago."

The captain looked at the girl with concern. Realizing that all leads on Grimm and his associates had drained through the sewers after their banishment from Hostellus, he deduced that Farricks's survival might not be too far fetched after all.

"Hmm. That's an interesting turn of events," Caedus said in a mutter. "What happened when you last saw him?"

"When we arrived at the temple, Farricks and a handful of others entered to find the artifact. After two days, the rest of the team followed them, but I lingered behind after losing myself in the forest that surrounded the grounds. With no one outside as my keeper, I left."

The bartender brought Caedus his food and the captain thanked him before digging around through the bowl of mystery ingredients.

"That's when you decided to head for Skulpos?" he asked while picking through the carrots and greens.

He watched the girl take her bowl of food from the server and slurp it down in a couple of gulps.

"Perhaps I should give you mine," Caedus said, lightly mocking her.

"It's been months since I've had a warm meal," she shyly said.

Again, Caedus made a fool of himself by underestimating the depth of the girl's harsh living conditions under Grimm's thumb.

"And yes, that's when I left for Skulpos," the girl said, continuing her story.

"Why there?" Caedus asked.

After a few slimy mouthfuls of vegetable and broth, the captain set his bowl aside.

"I'm about sick of soup," he said. "It's all I've had all winter."

"I wanted to sneak aboard a ship there," the girl said after a second.

Captain Redstone thought of the pirate-like culture of the coastal kingdom and grasped how easy it would be for her to slip aboard a vessel.

"For what?" he asked, trying to pry a more specific answer from her.

Suddenly, a strange feeling rose in him, as if another entity entered his mind.

"Zomed gorr, (He is gone,)" Osinian said to him in his head, like his own thought.

Caedus looked back up to the corner where the strange man sat and noticed that he was no longer there as the shade suggested. His wary instincts buzzed in the back of his skull, and he looked over to his three soldiers playing a game of cards and gambling away their gold. The captain's shifting eyes darted across the room again for any sign of the cloaked man, but he couldn't see through the low chaos among the peasants in the tavern. Caedus felt unwanted attention in his direction, so he sent a soft signal to his men by mimicking a bird's call, two short whistles repeated several times.

"I wanted to sail off to somewhere new," the girl explained, unaware of Caedus's call sign.

The captain met the eyes of his men as they recognized his call and stopped their game. Caedus signaled for his men to remain watchful for any suspicious activity. The girl to his right tried to continue, but Caedus stood from the table to fetch another drink.

"Hold on," the captain said. "Don't move."

"Caedus, where are you—"

"Shhh," Redstone said in a hushed voice while his eyes darted back and forth between each occupant of the inn. "Stay here."

Unable to detect the stranger, Captain Caedus relaxed his face and loosened his shoulders. He trusted his wary soldiers to warn him of danger, so he started to wander to the bar in a more leisurely manner. The cheers and laughs from the townsfolk clouded his perception. He passed by table after table, hand on the hilt of his sword once again underneath his winter cloak.

Figures moved in his peripheral vision that pulled his eyes from side to side. The uncertainty toyed with him; he hated being the prey. As he neared the bar, he brushed the back of his neck over his tattoo that marked his allegiance to the Black Legion, hoping his pursuer would notice and take the bait.

"Another drink, please," Caedus asked the bartender once he reached the counter.

Captain Redstone placed his palms on the edge of the wooden bar top. He studied a few warped faces that looked back at him with unfriendly expressions. Growing anxious, he tapped his fingers against the beer-stained oak. Shadows flickered against his observant gaze as the innocent drunks passed by. For a moment, his intuition deflated. Caedus tightened his lips out of disappointment. The barkeep returned with his drink, and he gripped the handle, lowered his head to pour the alcohol down his throat, and grazed his lips with the cup.

However, before Caedus could partake in his beverage, he twitched his ears once he heard two whistles of a mockingbird ring through the air, the signal from his soldiers watching over him. Suddenly, the captain felt a presence a few meters behind him after tuning his senses. He lowered his mug.

The figure behind approached, and Caedus faintly heard a soft metallic sound scrape against a sheath, a sound he could distinguish in any setting. The captain brought the cup to his mouth, chugged the contents, and set the cup on the counter with a firm grasp. After, the bartender glanced at him in confusion. Captain Redstone then raised the empty, dense cup to shoulder level and simply smiled.

"Cheers."

Caedus bolted from his stagnant position, violently swinging his right arm and torso to dodge the hidden thrust of a short dagger that collided with the bar, and crashed the empty mug into his attacker's head with such force that it tossed the hooded man over a table occupied by several townsfolk. A crowd of alarmed civilians formed as Caedus walked over to the disoriented man on the floor.

To his surprise, the cloaked assailant quickly rose to his feet and drew another dagger. Finding himself unarmed after dropping the shattered stein, Caedus reached to draw his sword, but the first strike from his attacker had cut his belt and dropped his blade onto the floor. The mysterious figure stepped to the side to cut the captain off from his weapon.

After a few moments of baiting each other, the assailant lunged with the second dagger, but the Caedus caught his arm by side stepping and clamping his elbow on the hilt. He then twisted his body away from the man, sending the short blade to the floor. Caedus stepped back and swung his fist at the covered face of his opponent before ducking his shoulder to tackle him to the floor. Meanwhile, he heard shouts and cries from the townsfolk around him. As he wrestled the man, Captain Caedus caught an elbow to the mouth. He tightened his arms around the attacker's chest from behind and covered the back of his opponent's neck with his hands, wrapping himself under the man's armpits.

Once Caedus strained enough to weaken his opponent, he shifted upward, kneed him in the ribs, and released his grip to stand up. Redstone frantically searched for the dagger hidden among trampling footsteps. As soon as he grabbed it, however, the assassin tackled him, forcing it out of his grip. Caedus's soldiers rushed over to aid.

"Watch the girl!" Redstone barked with blood in his mouth.

The attacker grabbed the curved knife out from Caedus's reach and attempted to thrust it into his neck, but he evaded death by grabbing the assassin's hand just before the tip of the blade reached his skin. He rolled on the ground until he laid on top of the man and placed the palms of his hands on the pommel of the dagger facing his attacker. Caedus struggled in a match of pure strength and bolstered all the might in his arms and shoulders to inch the steel closer to the man's unprotected neck.

Gritting his teeth as a trickle of crimson blood flowed from his lip to his chin, Captain Caedus shook as he forced the trembling dagger into his attacker's flesh under the bones of his jaw. The soft muscle tissue of the man's throat split open like underbaked bread. Caedus ruptured the critical parts of the neck with a solid jerk, causing a spray of blood to gush out. He then shoved the blade entirely through the man's neck until it punctured through the nape. His enemy's arms fell limp to the floor, a thick puddle spreading across the cobblestone.

Caedus stood victorious with arms, hands, and knees soaked in red. He grabbed the corpse by the shoulder armor and dragged it across the floor with a sneer, leaving a trail of thick blood in his wake. Once the captain approached the doorway, he heaved the body into the undisturbed snow outside. Stepping closer through the frozen air, he reached into the wet inner pocket of the man's cloak and pulled out a silver medallion molded with the Hostellian Eagle in the center, confirming his suspicion that a Vaedorian spy had caught his scent. Caedus nodded, took the medallion, shook the excess blood off his hands, and stood to return to the inn.

Before he could take another step, he faced a dozen crudely armed peasants pointing their farm weaponry toward him. Caedus paused in his tracks, unsure of how to respond to the defensiveness of the townsfolk. Thinking quickly on his feet, Captain Redstone held up the medallion.

"He's a Vaedorian," Caedus said, gesturing to the mutilated body in the snow with his other hand.

A harmonic wave of "ahs" came from the crowd. Once the peasants lowered their weaponry, Caedus shifted his way through the gathered people to find his men. He wiped the drying blood on his pants and grabbed a handful of clean snow to wash all that remained.

Inside, Caedus eyed his three soldiers surrounding the girl. Though ordered to keep her safe as his guide, the captain valued her more than that.

"Let's go," Caedus said, grabbing his gear from the table in the corner. "I need a bed."

"Are you all right, my lord?" one of his men asked.

Caedus cleaned the valuable medallion he'd removed from the assassin's body.

"I'm fine," Redstone said, brushing off any sign of weakness.

He neared the counter where the bartender stood and set the medallion down as payment for the disturbance.

"We were never here," Caedus said to bribe the innkeeper as he made eye contact with him.

After a confirming nod from the gentleman behind the bar, Captain Caedus ordered his men to follow. He eyed the stairs that led to the chambers above, climbed them, and longed for a chance to rest his exhausted body.

~ ~ ~

War drums pounded through the encampment as Zededia stood before his captains in the command tent. He opened a trunk near his cot and glanced over the armor it held inside. Before picking up one of the dark, metal gauntlets that would cover his entire forearm, he caressed its intricate design. He inhaled the fresh morning air; adrenaline started to build and he ached for action.

"Captain Ursa," Zededia said while studying his armor, "have all units assembled?"

"Yes, Commander," the head captain answered.

The prince slid each of his lightweight but sturdy gauntlets over his arms and fastened the straps. Next, he removed the greaves that covered his shins from mid knee to ankle. After Zededia sat on his bed, he fit the perfectly molded leg armor over the thick winter pants he wore to shield his skin from the cold.

"I trust everything is in order before we advance?" he said to his men.

"The Legonae awaits your command, sire," Captain Redding said. "Ready for war."

Zededia nodded in agreement as he tightened his shin plates.

"Good," he said before standing to his feet.

Shaking his lower legs to reach a comfortable feel for the newly added weight, Zededia grabbed his cloak from the bedpost and tossed it onto the silks he slept on.

"The Vaedorians?" he asked.

"Four thousand infantry, my prince," Captain Ammon said.

Zededia beamed his eyes at his dark-skinned captain that stood a head taller than him in shock.

"It seems the Hostellae are able to recover faster than I thought," Zededia said. "If Matticus is smart, he's held twice that many beyond the walls. Although, I wouldn't be surprised if he tried to throw everything he has at us right away. He's as eager for battle as I."

Heavily outnumbered, Zededia calmed the nervousness creeping up his spine. He gripped his thick, tanned leather cuirass that held several separated plates and inserted his arms through the holes on the sides. A large ceremonial 'Z' carved its way between the chest indentations, the mark of the Black Prince.

"That won't be an issue, however," the prince said as he tied the knots to secure his torso covering. "We're not here to kill them all or even face them all."

Zededia grasped the sheath of his infamous longsword and focused on the decorated hilt. Memories of its previous uses in battle flooded his brain, and he closed his eyes to channel that energy into the proper mindset.

"We are not here to win, gentlemen," Commander Zededia said to his captains. "As I've said before, we are simply here to buy Lord Redstone enough time to return with the Sword of Kings."

He placed his weapon on the left side of his belt before turning to his men.

"Nevertheless, I still expect perfection."

After Zededia met each of his soldiers' loyal eyes, the prince crossed his arms.

"Perfection does not mean the same thing here as it has before," he said. "Perfection means staying alive. We are not to take risks, we are not to pursue, and we are not to break formation unless it is ordered. Is that clear?"

"Yes, Commander," all Zededia's captains said.

The prince grabbed his cape off the bed and completed his uniform with the flowing fabric. He waved to tell his men to follow him outside into the snow. Walking through the rows of empty tents, he eyed the ridge that dipped into the white fields below. In the distance, Nyalis waited patiently for his arrival. Zededia patted the boy's head and then took his place a hundred yards away from the camp to command his army. Hundreds of soldiers filled his view, lined up in their formations, waiting for orders.

Commander Zededia looked beyond his men to the approaching enemy. An ocean of knights clad in silver armor and white and blue garments trudged toward him. He draped his hood over his head, crossed his arms, and studied the Vaedorian army's frontline soldiers. Like his own soldiers, his opponents marched in unison as standards bearing the Hostellian eagle waved high above them. The Vaedorians were ready; their ranks spread deep and wide over the plains.

"We are going to try something a little different today," Zededia said, scanning the vastness of Matticus's army.

"What did you have in mind, Commander?" Captain Redding asked.

The prince bit the insides of his lips and gathered his thoughts. The long, sturdy frontline of his enemy reminded him of a peculiar experience in his youth.

"Bloodletting."

Confused eyes glared back at him from his captains.

"When I was a young captain of the Hostellae," Zededia said, "my father sent me on a journey to learn and observe war strategies used by my cousins."

Pausing to remember his time on the road, he started to pace on the ridge.

"In Skulpos, I boarded King Neptabyss's fleet of ships to study naval warfare, but I paid more attention to his fishing vessels. When the Skulpins send out their whaling ships to harvest great beasts of the deep, they don't strike at their prey as hard as they can. They bleed it dry, stabbing and probing it when it breaches the surface repeatedly until it's too weak to swim. Then, they claim their haul."

He stopped walking, turned to his men, and waited for them to process his explanation.

"We will use a similar strategy today. We are the fishermen, and the Vaedorians are the whale. We will bleed them dry as much as we can."

"How are we to do that, sire?" Captain Ursa said. "This doesn't sound like something we've trained for."

Taking a glance at the defenders and their great shields standing next to the halberdiers, he hatched a plan.

"Orrso," Zededia called to Captain Ammon by using his first name, "merge your defenders with Sykas's men. A pike between every shield in the line."

"Yes, Commander," the massive captain said in a deep voice.

The Black Prince urged Captain Sykas to follow Ammon.

"Redding, Ursa, have your knights ready to relieve the front line," Zededia said, handing out orders down the line of his men. "Corso, patrol the perimeters. Turn the Vaedorians back into our wall should they try to flank."

One captain remained on the hill with him. Zededia turned back to the battlefield to examine it once more.

"Seether," the Black Prince said with a blank face.

"Sire," said the captain fully cloaked and wrapped in a black balaclava.

Zededia focused on the narrowing gap between his army and the Vaedorians. Too many approached for his men to handle all at once in too tight of a formation.

"How many of your riders are ready to engage?"

"All of them, Commander."

After a slight grin appeared on his face, the prince twisted to meet the bright yellow eyes of his cruelest soldier.

"Find the weak link," Zededia said. "Exploit it."

As Captain Seether jogged toward the group of his mounted archers, the prince slipped into a dark state. The ground under his boots lightly shook, his skin crawled with excitement, and the red glow in his veins appeared on the sides of his face fueled by his hate for Vaedor Sellos.

"Captain," Zededia said as his longbowman ran off.

Seether turned back. The prince paused.

"Release your malice."

Devious eyes stared back at him before Seether continued on, and Zededia longed for the chance to see the Legonae in battle. The pompous confidence Matticus waved around because of his massive forces was bloated and ready for a test. Savoring his moment to prove once again who dominated the battlefields in Hostellus, the prince put great effort into calming his raging adrenaline.

Zededia's blood boiled. The platoon of mad drummers behind him beat their instruments furiously, putting their whole bodies into their movements like wild animals. Under his armor, the prince's veins started to glow bright red with fury. All his soldiers looked to him for inspiration, and he took a deep breath of the stirring atmosphere. Scents of sweat and steel filled his nose.

He looked from side to side and met the gazes of his soldiers, ready in their stance to march through the snow to clash with the Hostellae in a glorious battle.

"The time has come upon us, sons of the Legonae!" Zededia shouted at the top of his lungs. "War! Is! Here!"

The deep, pounding beats of the drummers rang through the air as the Black Prince remained unmoved. Anger soured his expression, and his dogs of war started to clang their weaponry together at a slow pace.

"We serve as a reminder to the Vaedorians of who reigns supreme in these lands, who challenges their authority!"

All the Legonae raised their armaments in the air.

"Remember what they stole from you!" he shouted, referring to the night of their exile. "Remember your hate!"

Zededia darkened his tone as the redness in his blood filled the entirety of his eyes. Simultaneously, all his men twisted away from him to face the fields ahead. The drummers shifted to a faster pace of music, signaling an advance.

"Remember the *fear* we carry in the hearts of our enemies!" the Black Prince bellowed with a fist raised at shoulder level.

From the frontline, he heard Captain Ammon shout orders, and the rows of defenders drew their short swords, raised their right elbows to point their blades over the wall of shields, and marched as one cohesive unit toward battle. The Vaedorians neared, less than half a mile away. The ground shook like an earthquake had struck; the snow ached for fresh coats of red.

"Soldiers of the Black Legion!" the prince screamed, releasing all the cold air in his lungs. "Go forth in the spirit of darkness!"

Captain Seether and his horde of mounted bowmen trampled off the ridge around him.

"Bring damnation to the unjust!"

He regained his level position on the crest of the hill and glared at the enemy with a dead stare. Each of his units pressed on over the plains: Ammon and his defenders maintaining a steady wall with the halberdiers between them, the light cavalry patrolling the edges to maintain control, and Seether's horsemen screeching over the snow to make first contact.

"Nyalis," he said, calling to the boy standing behind him. "Come."

Shuffled footsteps sloshed through the snow. The red shine in Zededia's face reached his eyes and choked his pupils.

"Witness your commander at work."

Over the white horizon, Commander Osiris laid his eyes upon the marching mass of soldiers under his brother's command. Time slowed in his mind as the ice under his army's wake flurried into the air. He heard a faint, angelic hum as the pace quickened in the Vaedorian infantry's strides. Zededia glanced at his shield and spear men in front, ready to absorb the charge. Rage pumped through him. The battle arrived.

"Halt, infantry," Zededia said to the man on his left.

A low horn sounded off and signaled for the drummers to change their beats.

"Ready spears."

Another horn rang out after his second order, and his armies shifted into place.

The angelic hum in Zededia's ears grew in intensity once the enemy started to sprint from a short distance away. Captain Ammon clanged his short sword against his shield, signaling for the formation of defenders to brace themselves for an impact by hunkering down in their stance and using their gathered strength as an impenetrable wall, and Prince Zededia faintly heard the cries of the approaching Vaedorians. His disciplined soldiers remained unmoved and silent. The moment he had long waited for finally came to fruition; it surged upon him more than he had anticipated once the daunting atmosphere of battle barreled across the plains.

"Bolster shields," Commander Zededia barked to his messenger.

With relentless speed, the Hostellian professional army sprinted toward the Legonae while the spear men readied themselves to thrust their razor-sharp pikes out from the protection of the metallic shield wall. His captains shouted orders after the change of the frenzy-inducing music, his soldiers readied for the onslaught, and the prince himself found a fierce determination for victory. The back of his neck and arms crawled with goosebumps.

The Vaedorians neared Zededia's awaiting trap, only meters away as they carelessly threw themselves at the Black Legion's impenetrable frontline. The prince lowered his chin and sneering at the carnage to come.

Like a weak tide of the ocean crashing into a cliff, the Vaedorian infantry slammed into Zededia's defenders, spraying blood and torn flesh across the shield wall as they collided with the thick steel. The defenders remained strong and dug their heels into the earth. Broken and bleeding bodies bounded off and fell to the snow. The initial wave failed, and the defenders shifted their shields aside to allow the pikemen to skewer those who remained. Screams and wails of torment drowned him as his brother's army christened the trampled snow with their spewing viscera.

"Reform the line!" the prince shouted over the commotion. "Strike again!"

His hidden halberdiers soldiers thrust their weapons again, eviscerating the unsuspecting Vaedorian infantry like roasted pigs. Zededia widened his sneer while watching the defeated Hostellae retreat. A second wave of infantry made an advance to replace the dead and mangled, but this time they proceeded with caution rather than blindly sprint to their demise.

"Enter archers," Zededia said in a firm command, staying calm and stationary like a statue.

He heard the quick beats of the war drums followed by the flock of cavalry archers, led by Captain Seether, galloping in front of the defenders from the left side to join the action. The monstrous horses mutilated the corpses and poor souls bleeding out on the ground.

Zededia narrowed his eyes as Seether and company launched a volley of instant death at the second wave of Hostellae. The diversion created a perfect opportunity for the next phase.

"Advance, infantry."

The drums returned to their original beat, and the line of defenders marched over the dead Vaedorians. Hesitantly, the Hostellae tried their luck against the shield wall, hoping to find a crack to exploit. Dozens lunged in an attack, but they bounced off in pieces, the defenders hacking and slashing at all in their path. Time and time again, the Black Prince watched his brother's armies retreat and regroup only to fall in seconds. He hosted a sinister smile under his hood.

"Retreat, infantry," Zededia said with his arms still crossed once his soldiers reached the line he had pointed out in his meeting yesterday. "Regroup."

Hundreds of Vaedorian knights waited in the distance, and the prince started to wonder if Matticus would ever send them in. Familiar with his brother's tactics, Zededia expected an easy first day. He showed no mercy, nonetheless. Matticus's ranks fell apart and abandoned their position on the fields. Zededia had won the first skirmish with ease, and he reveled in the victory.

Blood-soaked and triumphant, his soldiers returned. While proud of his soldiers and their excellence, he knew more was to come in the following days. The fight was far from over, and he needed to steel himself for future engagements; no room to lower his guard, no room for a celebration.

Chapter 12

Fog of War

Day 18 in the Month of Snow

The first battle on the Hostellian plains reached a grisly end for Matticus. As the Osirian king led his band of guards through the ranks of his soldiers on the outskirts of their camp just outside the outer wall, he met a mixed bag of expressions. Those who returned covered themselves in salve and bandages, and the lucky few who remained unscathed kept quiet. The defeated faces of his men touched him. Before seeing any of the battle himself, he sensed fear and doubt spreading amongst his men.

A hazy fog started to roll in with the morning light, and one of the Hostellian flags detached from a standard into the wind. Like a plague, the dreadful silence dampened the king's spirits.

Once Matticus made his way to the front line of yesterday's battle where a fresh group of soldiers stood guard, he glanced ahead at the band of medics and clerics saving those that clung to life. Commander Nysis stood out from the figures ahead on his horse and the king steered his steed toward him.

The layers of snow meshed with rivers of blood seeping from the massed butchery ahead. As he trudged his horse over the ravaged bodies, he stared at their lifeless faces. Murders of crows grazed over the carrion, tearing eyes from their sockets and sinews from bone.

Though facing a heavy loss, Matticus held on to his courage, for he trusted his commander's strategy. He approached Nysis while keeping his eyes on the dead.

"How bad is it?" Matticus asked with a sigh as he glanced at the severed limbs and torn-open torsos on the frosty ground.

His commander looked up from a small leather book.

"It could be worse," Nysis said after counting the ticks in the journal. "It seems the Legonae's efficiency has not declined since I left it."

Matticus grunted.

"You have plans for tomorrow's battle? To ensure we don't meet a similar result?"

"Never fear, my liege," Nysis said. "Zededia's luck will run out."

Matticus raised an eyebrow.

"How can you be sure?"

"He's cocky. Overconfident," the commander said. "Believing that he has the upper hand plays more to our favor than his. Zededia is a psychologically gifted man just as he is a physical one, so we need to challenge him on multiple fronts. Test his patience, wither his resources. He'll break."

"I'm starting to see how you defeated the rebels in Korzeg so quickly," Matticus said, praising his highly intelligent officer.

As the king pulled the reins of his horse to ride next to the pile of corpses created by the gravediggers, a handful of soldiers of the Legonae approached on foot carrying a flag that bore the mark of a medical team. Cautious, Matticus studied the nearing enemy, and his guards drew their swords next to him. Upon further reflection and as they stopped for his response, he deemed them peaceful.

"Let them pass," Matticus said. "They're here collect their dead."

Matticus held ample respect for the ceremonies of the dead after battle, even for those involving his sworn enemy.

"Will the Hostellian king grant his hospitality to those who wish to retrieve their slain for a proper procession?"

"Aye," King Matticus said.

Although the soldiers before him had butchered his men and left many of Vaedor Sellos's children fatherless, Matticus harbored his aggression for another day.

"Sheathe your swords," he said. "Save your anger."

Matticus turned and rode back over to his commander counting the corpses in his book with a quill.

"What did you learn of Zededia's tactics?" the king asked as he watched the distant tree line and the columns of smoke that rose from the camp.

"Not much, I'm afraid. He relied on the strength of his defenders without showing much else," Commander Nysis said. "He did, however, incorporate his pikemen in manners I hadn't expected. We took heavier losses than we should have. It puzzles me how he holds his cavalry as the reserves, even when we present an easy target. He creates an opening with his ranged units, then engages on foot. I've struggled to understand Zededia's methods, but I have a feeling I know what he's up to."

Matticus watched the soldiers in black armor gather their fallen and noticed how they separated items such as swords and armor from the corpses and laid them on a large tarp like cloth.

"We shouldn't discuss this any further," the king said. "We'll formulate a plan when you return to camp."

"If Zededia wants to play mind games by hiding behind his shields," Nysis said, "then I've got something he'll not enjoy."

Eyeing the enemy soldiers near once again, Matticus decided to keep his lips tight.

Eventually, the mauled faces of his dead soldiers sickened him. Bloodied beaks cawed from the birds hopping from corpse to corpse. The king flicked his hand toward the barriered camp behind to signal his guards to change directions. With a stern face, he saluted Commander Nysis and spurred his horse over the bodies rotting below.

~ ~ ~

Inside the central barracks of the Vaedorian forward command post, King Matticus sat at a stone table where he had summoned all his generals alongside Commander Nysis. He frowned as he studied the map of the battlefield on the table.

"Nysis, present your report," the king said.

After his highest-ranking soldier stood from his chair, Matticus opened his ears with great interest in Nysis's explanation. Losing to Zededia so easily nearly sent him into a frenzy.

"Yesterday's defeat left us questioning our enemy's game," Nysis said. "Though the Legonae were able to cut down our infantry, their movements puzzled me. There's something strange about how Zededia ordered his men to fight."

The king watched his commander pace around the table.

"I've known the Black Prince for many years, as all of you have," the blond-haired officer said, "and I know of his strategies. However, he fought differently today than he ever has. He was more ... reserved ... than usual."

"What do you mean, Lord Nysis?" General Komm, the Vaedorian cavalry leader interrupted.

Matticus also held the same concern, remembering the years of scorched earth campaigns his brother architected against all Hostellus's enemies prior to his exile.

"What I mean is that Zededia has always had the same goal when entering a war: complete annihilation. He toys with his prey, finding soft spots, breaking their spirit, and gaining ground inch by inch until there is nowhere left to run," Nysis said, elaborating. "But the battle yesterday strayed from his reputation. After every engagement, Zededia pulled his troops back to their original frontline and waited for us to react. They didn't kill, march, and repeat like they have in almost every skirmish against us and every skirmish under King Matias's reign."

Matticus started to connect the dots on his commander's analysis of his brother's strange behavior.

"Zededia is playing a different game," Commander Nysis said, leaning over the stone table on his palms. "I think something else is driving him to make such a sudden appearance and fight the way he did, like he's the one defending us from something or someone else. Why would he suddenly march upon our doorstep, outnumbered ten-to-one, and challenge us in open combat to not even hold the ground he took? No. We're in the middle of one of his schemes."

Paranoia clawed its way up Matticus's throat.

"You're saying Zededia isn't here to what? Defeat us?" the king said as he placed his armored forearms on the table.

"I don't know exactly," Nysis said. "But I think that allowing Zededia to sit on whatever plan he has is a bad idea. He's waiting for something, which is why I think he's trying to box us in rather than push us back."

There's only one reason Zededia would go to such lengths to keep him occupied and Matticus circled it with anger brewing in his thoughts. His brother had found the Sword of Kings.

While Matticus's quest for his ancestor's mighty blade started with his desire to eliminate Zededia, his vision for a Hostellian empire depended on it the closer he came to invading his neighbors. Zededia's discovery of the sword placed his future for a united Osiria at risk, and that's something he couldn't allow. The premonition of his death at Zededia's hand lit his mind ablaze with rage and fear.

"We need to hit him. Now," Matticus said.

"Precisely," Commander Nysis said. "Your brother always has an angle. We just need to beat it out of him."

Zededia's deception pushed him over the edge. A plan to wipe the Legonae off the earth formed, and Matticus immediately grew tired of relying on the masses of his infantry. The time for a more dominant strategy surfaced. Matticus tightened his grip in his gloves.

"General Komm," Matticus said, "rally your knights. All of them. We're going to chase him down and end this once and for all."

The fiery strategy enlivened Matticus's worried mind with a powerful energy. So much so that he nearly forgot the embarrassing defeat in the morning. The king dismissed each of his generals, stood from the low table, and pulled Nysis to the side for a moment.

"No more waiting behind my men," Matticus said. "I will lead the charge. As my father would

"Sire, is that wise?" Commander Nysis asked.

Though the risk of death in battle fazed him, he expelled his worry with an obsession to murder his brother. Zededia might not be present on the front lines, but Matticus didn't care. He'd find him if he had to scour every inch of the Blackwood.

"Osirians are remembered for their glory in battle, for the blood of their enemies on their hands," Matticus said. "I will be no different."

The determination in his expression dissuaded Commander Nysis from any further argument.

"Very well, my liege."

Matticus placed a firm hand on his commander's shoulder. He signaled for Nysis to exit the barracks before taking his own leave. When he stepped outside, an eerie aura crept through the camp that chilled his bones. A brisk current of air brushed across his face, and a series of low clouds emerged over the forested rim of the mountain chain to the right. The brutal weather had hindered both armies' abilities to fight with freezing temperatures and thick snow.

"More punishment from winter," Commander Nysis said.

"Doesn't look like snow," Matticus said, scanning the landscape. "Something else...."

An hour passed and the cavalry of the Hostellae had amassed and formed a daunting presence. Six deep and a hundred wide, Matticus's knights wore thick armor, thicker than the infantry by nearly twice the amount. The king sat atop his horse behind his legion of riders and waited for any sign of enemy movement. Zededia's camp lay too far for an effective charge from this distance, but the front line where the Legonae had dug themselves in provided a perfect target. Commander Nysis rode up beside him, nodded for approval, and slid his plumed helmet over his head. Moments later, a squire jogged up to the king, struggling to traverse the icy ground, and held his helmet up to him. Matticus took a firm hold of the crown of the helm and hoisted it up. He stared into the inwardly slanted eye slits, saw the faint reflection of red from his glowing veins, and released a deep exhale.

Matticus put his helmet on and secured it against his head. He spurred his horse forward out of the command post surrounded by a shoddy palisade wall and toward his knights. Commander Nysis escorted him, and the Hostellae dispersed to let their king head the assault. At the front, Matticus's personal guards mounted towering horses; the white plumes on their helms fluttered in the breeze. General Komm joined on his left with Nysis on his right while he tipped the spear of his valiant army.

Veins pulsing with energy as he became frenzied at the sight of the Legonae rushing back and forth on the other side of the snow-covered field, Matticus wriggled his fingers and held tightly to the reins of his horse. The fog rolling in from the north thickened and dampened his view, but he cared not for the weather. Matticus savored the anticipation of battle, for his years of planning and waiting in his castle had finally ended. His hands would be soaked in blood by the end of the day, a feeling he had longed for in his early years as king.

The horses were restless, barely able to remain calm under their masters. Matticus glanced to his right and saw the Hostellian flag high in the sky, clear and present, just like it appeared during Matias's rule. Sensing his forefathers' eyes upon him from the heavens of Elysia, he swallowed his anxiety and steeled himself for war.

With pride and strength, King Matticus heaved his longsword from its sheath and held it in the air. The Hostellae followed suit; hundreds of blades stabbed at the sky. The wind blew hard, pushing the mist faster over the plains.

"On your lead, sire," General Komm said.

Matticus rallied his courage and centered his focus. The shining white-silver armor he wore gave him an intimidating appearance. Red eyes peered through the slits of his helmet, and he lowered his sword to point it at Zededia's encampment.

He spurred his horse forward at a slow walk at first. Each of his knights rode shortly behind, churning the snow under a thousand hooves. Horns of battle rang, and the soldiers in black in the distance scurried to their formations. Matticus's heart pounded through his thick armor. Quickening the pace of his horse, he started breathing heavier and faster. The slow march of the Hostellae shifted to a steady trot and then to a fearless gallop. Eyes narrowed on the frontline of the Legonae hardly visible through the fog, the king sprinted to the heart of battle.

Thunderous hooves beat against the ice, silver steel cut the mist as the knights held their arm high, and the Hostellian eagle soared through the air on dozens of flags. The Legonae's position grew closer, close enough to where he heard faint shouts of orders from his enemy.

A hundred yards stood between the two armies after the daunting advance, but Matticus lost sight of his target once the fog had cut his vision. The king slowed his horse back to a trot before stopping entirely. He looked back and Commander Nysis appeared through the haze moments later and rode next to him. General Komm ordered for the Hostellae to halt their charge. Suddenly, Matticus had led his army into the middle of the fog cloud, unaware and blind to his enemy's movements. Pausing to assess the situation, he peered through the mist with squinted eyes in search for any sign of the Legonae. He cautiously walked his horse forward with his men behind him. Eventually, he stumbled upon the edge of the fields where the ridge started to incline into the forest. Well beyond the frontline of yesterday's battle, Matticus sat in a daze as he looked upon half-carved wooden spikes and masterless weapons. Quickly realizing that the Legonae had abandoned their forward position with great haste, the king stopped.

"Something isn't right," Matticus said under his breath.

Commander Nysis caught up to him, creeping aside in a quite fashion.

"Your orders, sire?"

"I ... I don't know..."

Sinister sounds scraped Matticus's ears from the howling wind. His sanity tested, the king darted his eyes back and forth, and he blinked away the rapid hallucinations appearing in the fog. Images of soldiers in black played in his peripheral vision. At one point, a deep laughter followed the wind; raspy voices started to mumble and drowned his hearing.

A sudden urge to flee the field rushed down his spine. He hadn't encountered such a strong instinct of fear in many years. Before King Matticus had the chance to give a command of any kind, one of the knights from the pack lost control of his horse and galloped ahead, isolated from the rest and struggling to regain composure. Shortly after, the knight balanced himself and sat still several yards in front of King Matticus just within the range of his view through the heavy fog. An eerie silence fell over the field.

"Where are they?" the knight said.

Dozens of snaps sounded off from the murky depth of the fog followed by ear-gouging shrieks hurling through the air. Matticus watched stunned as black arrows struck the knight and his horse with such force that they knocked them both to the ground. The knight crashed into the snow, eight arrows protruding from his corpse from ankle to neck.

Seconds later, Matticus heard a faint shouting in the distance. Though unable to understand what his enemy yelled, he knew his position had been discovered, and more arrows surely came next. A shower of death rained upon the heavily armored paladins, causing panic to erupt throughout the ranks. Most of the black arrows collided with the riders' sturdy shields or the ground, but a few lucky shots managed to puncture the thick armor of the knights of the Hostellae. The king himself ducked out of instinct once he heard the arrows' flight. Order broke into chaos, but Matticus sneered in the presence of death.

"Forward!" Matticus yelled. "Advance!"

The blindly shot arrows struck a few of the horses under the king's riders, launching their masters to the ground before the bleeding beasts crushed them in a tumble. Completely thrown into the madness, King Matticus jerked his horse to the side to gallop straight into hell, hoping to catch the Legonae off guard.

Matticus steered his horse into one of his soldiers, causing both to stammer in place amidst the blind charge. An arrow skewered his soldier clean through the temple as the king made eye contact, spraying him with blood while lost on the shadowed battlefield. The gore staggered him; blood spewed from the slits of the eyes and mouth before the knight slipped off his horse. Matticus persisted, nonetheless. Wherever he found a gap through the stampede of the Hostellae, he surged forward.

Everywhere around him, Matticus heard his valiant knights screaming and choking on their own blood from the volley. One of the arrows grazed his helmet an inch away from his left eye and sent deep vibrations across his skull. He tore his headgear off his and threw it to the ground after the disorientation. Watchful eyes focused on any enemy he found, Matticus followed his men galloping ahead. His knights charged through the rain of arrows behind sturdy shields, giving him ample protection.

Eventually, the arrows stopped. Matticus's vision started to clear up as the fog dissipated and he eyed several of his men mangled in the snow. A ceasefire only meant one thing, though.

A wave of rushing cavalry in black armor burst through the fog, swords raised and swinging with fury.

"Attack!" Matticus shouted, rallying his men.

The Hostellae engaged the light cavalry sent in for a counterattack, and the heavy armor and sheer numbers of his knights gave him an overwhelming advantage. Matticus steered his horse in all directions, waiting for one of the Legonae to come his way. Prey arrived soon enough and rashly galloped toward him. King Matticus put all his strength into his shoulders and arms to slice at his target, cutting through the black knight's sword and chopping his head off. The severed head flew into the air and bounced across the ground, leaving a trail of blood melting the snow in its path. The true strength of his army barreled into the light, and the Legonae started to retreat.

Zededia sent in his heavy cavalry in response, and they clashed with Matticus's knights to even the fight. The king summoned his courage from deep within his heart, held his longsword with a firm grip, and galloped into the densest part of the fog to meet his enemy head on. He rode for a moment before engaging a knight of the Legonae on each side, missing his strikes as they dodged and deflected, but one galloped close enough to collide with the side of his horse, causing him to stagger. Slicing with empowered anger, King Matticus tore his opponent's neck open, showering his right arm in blood. Frenzied, he looked to the next contestant.

Most other encounters failed like before. When he managed to meet his steel with the flesh of his enemy, though, they died in an instant. The king lost all sense of direction on the bloodied plains; he craved more death, growing more enraged with each kill. After several minutes of warring with the Legonae, Matticus happened upon Commander Nysis with a wet blade and chipped armor. It took the king a moment to recognize his officer as red rivers ran down his exposed face.

"We need to order a retreat, my liege!" Nysis shouted over the fray as a new wave of the Legonae swarmed in like a hive. "We've lost control of the battle! This will end in death for everyone!"

"No!" Matticus bellowed, the veins in his neck bulging red. "This is our chance to strike at Zededia! We are nearing his camp!"

As the brave king started to turn to enter battle once more, Nysis rode in front of him.

"Matticus!" the commander yelled with a harsh tone. "We will not have an army to fight with at this rate! We may slay the Legonae, but at what cost?"

Against his rash desire to press forward, Matticus processed his officer's words. He stalled on his horse, fighting the internal struggle, and grunted through his teeth.

"Lead the men out of here, Commander," Matticus said. "I will remain."

Nysis glared at him for a moment, but Matticus had made his decision.

"Regroup!" Commander Nysis shouted. "Out of the fog! To the command post!"

The Hostellae around him followed orders, leaving him alone on the fields. Matticus wiped the blood out of his eyes, looked to the fog, and readied himself for another attack. The Legonae's elite cavalry danced around, calling out his position. Soon, he became surrounded. Matticus spurred forward, clashing with the nearest knight. A hint of steel shined in his sideview aimed directly at his head. With no time to duck, the king panicked and saw death approach. The sword fell to the earth, though, as Commander Nysis rejoined the battle and hacked down his assailant. Together, the two fought off the crowd of Legonae until they forced them to fall back.

"This way, sire!" Nysis said, pointing to where Zededia's camp should be.

Matticus tailed his soldier up the ridge, the presence of his brother drawing him in. During the commotion, though, the king lost sight of his commander, and his steed veered off course. A black rider intercepted his route and swung a low strike toward him, slicing his horse in the shoulder. Matticus's stallion tossed him to the ground after collapsing, crashing into the snow like a falling building. He rolled several times before finally stopping, face down. Matticus groaned, and a sweltering pain screamed at him from his left arm. Injured and grounded, the king kept his focus and searched for his enemy.

Once Matticus staggered to his feet, a sinister-looking knight dressed in shining charcoal-colored armor with a demonic helmet dismounted his horse, flipped his sword over his hand, and advanced toward him. Matticus sneered and gripped his blade, the bright glow shining down the length of his arms through his armor. Fighting the agonizing bruise in his shoulder, he stepped forward, took his *Igni* fighting stance, and engaged.

Striking at the center of his opponent with heavy blows, Matticus quickly gained ground. After the fourth swing, the king channeled all his god-like strength that his Osirian blood fueled into his right arm, ducked the Legonae soldier's counterattack, and smashed his steel-clad fist into the chest of his opponent, pounding a massive dent into the black metal cuirass.

The soldier tumbled to the ground and fought to balance himself on his knees. Matticus thundered forward, holding his sword with one hand, and ripped the helmet off his enemy with the other. He clasped his armored hand on top of the soldier's head, the metal gauntlets digging into skin, and his eyes burned with a furious crimson hue. A shrill cry escaped his victim as he firmly held him. The king savored the wail for help, squeezed with all his strength, and crushed the man's skull between his fingers, cracking bone and splattering his brain out on all side. Basking in his kill, Matticus kicked the carcass to the earth and shook his hand of the gore.

The mist settled after Matticus's savagery, and a herd of hooves rushed up behind him. He turned to face another attacker, but the sight of his commander leading his personal guards eased his worry.

"Are you all right, sire?" Nysis said.

With the sun's light finally shining as the fog faded away, Matticus scanned the battlefield. A sickening number of Vaedorians littered the ground once again, but plenty of the Legonae lay slain as well. Chest heaving from pounding lungs, Matticus surrendered to his exhaustion.

"Fetch me a bloody horse," the king said, shifting his shoulder in circles to disperse the pain. "I've grown tired of this battle."

Once he mounted a fresh steed, Matticus lowered his chin toward the battlefield, and the slaughter ceased. He signaled for his surviving riders to make their way to camp, ushered his beast forward, and made his way toward safety with a stern expression.

His eyes drifted to the fallen below. Guilt flooded his brain as he scanned more dead faces in the ice. Matticus thought of his youngest brother, Lucien, recalling how his father never allowed him to enter or even see combat. He quickly remembered why.

"Gather the survivors," Matticus said. "Prepare them for our next advance."

"Yes, Your Majesty," Nysis said.

Matticus tightened his lips and analyzed the corpse-filled fields one last time. Though he hadn't been able to reach Zededia's camp, he remained satisfied with the outcome of the battle. Both armies took heavy losses, but Matticus considered it a victory compared to yesterday. The day was won; the Legonae had retreated to the protection of the forest, and that was good enough for the king at this time.

~ ~ ~

Evening slowly darkened Vaedor Sellos as the red sun lowered behind the city. Prince Lucien, armed with his orders from Baeno, stood watchful on the balcony of the keep. With the war occurring between his brothers, he struggled to find his place in the world. A sense of helplessness plagued him; no matter how he thought to approach the situation, he feared he could do nothing to prevent the death of one of his brothers; both in the worst circumstance. The queen drowned in her loneliness, Matticus succumbed to his rage, and Zededia seemingly marched straight to his death. All the while, Lucien remained bound to guard duty for information he doubted would ever enter his presence.

Thancred had left him earlier in the day, off to act on behalf of the mysterious Order the doctor involved himself in. Lucien sighed. The warm aroma of the pipe in his hand defended his face from the cold, but he'd lost feeling in his toes surrounded by ice outside his leather boots. Taking a long draw of tobacco smoke, he held his breath, and it burned the back of his throat. Lucien exhaled after a few seconds and watched the plume of smoke disperse into the air. His mind raced with questions, and without the proper time to act upon them, boredom became increasingly tormenting.

In the distance, the vast camp of the Hostellae on the fields twinkled with lanterns and bonfires. Lucien's worry for his brothers' safety gnawed at him, for from even as far away as the keep, the bloodied frontline stuck out in his view. He knew neither Matticus nor Zededia would be able to stay away from the fight, and while he trusted his brothers' incredible skill in battle, he feared for them. For the longest time since Zededia's exile, Lucien failed to make the impossible decision of choosing which brother he'd rather lose.

For now, the prince waited. He filled his time with the herbs Thancred gave him to smoke and stared blankly at the courtyard two stories below his feet.

A disturbance caught his attention, though, as a messenger hawk fluttered into the guard tower on the inner wall that protected the upper city. Lucien squinted, watched one of the men on the wall approach the bird at its post, and tried to snuff out any suspicious activity. Upon further investigation, Lucien recognized the light armor and cloak of one of Rachtus's field spies. The hawk had soared in from the east, from Zededia's direction, and the spy reading the message tied in a capsule on its leg looked around frantically. The prince widened his eyes and leaned away from the stone railing.

The spy bolted from under the guard tower pavilion, sprinting along the top of the wall toward the bridge that connected it to the keep. Lucien froze. All this time waiting around and he had nearly forgotten his sole purpose for lingering in the upper city.

The spy raced into the keep, and Lucien shadowed him from a safe way away. He watched the young soldier run across the landing of the marble staircases on each side of the throne room and followed him to the higher floors where the grand spy chamber sat. Lucien approached the spy room with caution as the young spy burst through the door, leaving it cracked open as it swung back into its frame. Back against the wall, the prince inched toward the sliver of light beaming from a torch inside through the gap in the door, ears perked and eager to listen.

"Lord Rachtus!" he heard the soldier say. "We've received urgent news!"

"What is it? Who sent the message?"

Lucien recognized Rachtus's harsh voice from anywhere. Tiptoeing into the doorframe, he peered inside. The spy handed Rachtus a rolled piece of parchment, and the Spymaster unraveled it to study the message.

"Our agent near the Merrin checkpoint has spotted..." Rachtus said, "soldiers from ... the Legonae!"

An intense expression of shock washed over the spymaster's face.

"There's only one reason the Black Prince would send his men so far away from Anzagaar Nostir ... while marching to war with us in the opposite direction..."

"What reason is that, my lord?" the young soldier said.

Lucien raised an eyebrow from outside.

"Zededia Osiris," Rachtus said with deep voice, "has found the Sword of Kings."

"We must alert King Matticus at once!" the soldier said. "He'll want to know immediately!"

"Yes ... King Matticus would like to know," Rachtus said.

The prince watched intently, and his eyes focused on the Spymaster as he reached down to his belt. Rachtus removed a crude dagger from its sheath; Lucien became riddled with panic.

"But not yet."

Like a frightened child, Prince Lucien stood in horror as Rachtus thrust the dagger into the soldier's abdomen before he could react. Gurgling and choking on his blood, the young man staggered and fell to the floor. Lucien's heart raced. He struggled to make his next move.

"Forgive me, boy," Rachtus said, cleaning the dagger of thick, warm blood. "But this knowledge ... is sensitive."

An urge to erupt into the spy chamber compelled Lucien to act, strange mixes of anger and hesitance clashed with each other. He raised a trembling hand to the door, blinked several times, and wrestled with his rapid breathing.

His morals stepped aside; instinct took over. Lucien pushed open the door, fists clenched, and stepped inside.

"Prince Lucien?" Spymaster Rachtus said. "What are you doing here?"

Lucien looked down at the dead soldier gushing blood on the floor and then back at Rachtus.

"Now, just wait a—"

Rachtus started to step closer to Lucien with the dagger in hand, but the Spymaster stopped. Lucien's face glowed with pure Osirian energy in his veins, filling his eyes with a crimson shine. The prince lost control of his rational thought and he entered a trance of sheer hate. Rachtus froze in place as if someone were controlling him against his will ... and someone was. Flashes of rage overcame Lucien as he tapped into the godlike abilities of his dormant power. Soon, without so much as a spoken word to conjure

Osirian magic, the prince telepathically assumed complete control of Spymaster Rachtus. The same glow in Lucien's face appeared in Rachtus's, and the spy mirrored each of the prince's moves.

Lucien gritted his teeth and forced Rachtus to hold tight to the dagger in his hand. With a slow slice, the prince dragged his arm horizontally across his body at neck level. Rachtus gagged as he helplessly tore his own throat open at the will of the enraged Osirian.

The trance ended as quickly as it arrived, and Lucien descended from his high and returned to reality. His vision cleared from the blurry red haze, he regained control of his thoughts, and Rachtus's body slumped to the floor. He froze, standing in a deadlock.

"What have I done?"

Chapter 13
Hystatia's Rule

Day 19 in the Month of Snow

With a victory on each side, the Hostellian plains continued to bathe in the blood of both armies. The Black Prince maintained control of his position on ridge next to the forest, but the heavy losses from yesterday's battle crippled his foothold. Zededia accompanied some of his men near a large bonfire on the edge of camp where they lined their dead neatly on flat stacks of wood with oil thickly poured on them. A blank expression covered the prince's face; he remained still and composed, staring at the bodies of his men under the cloth that concealed them. The scent of smoke and burning flesh clogged his nose.

"We were lucky, Ursa" Zededia said to his captain. "If the fog hadn't hindered Matticus's charge, we'd be burning a funeral pyre for the next week."

He turned to his soldier.

"You have their names?"

"Yes, sire," Ursa said, "and their armor has been returned to the smithies for repair and redistribution."

The prince nodded and stood with crossed arms as he lost himself in the flames. His hood shielded his ears from the chilly air.

"My prince," Captain Ammon said, approaching from behind, "your food is ready."

"Thank you, my friend," Zededia said, taking another look at the fire.

He then dismissed his captains, wiped the pooling sweat from his palms, and turned away from the funeral procession. Several of his knights saluted him as he walked to a nearby campfire. Young Nyalis waited nearby, lingering to enter his presence once more after Zededia ordered him to stay away from the dead.

"Master Zededia!" Nyalis said impatiently. "Tell me! Tell me of yesterday's battle, you must!"

The prince chuckled as he sat on one of the flat boulders his army used for chairs outside the tents, the despair he felt from the loss of his soldiers fading in the boy's smile.

"Oh, I must, eh?" Zededia said, cracking a grin. "Didn't get a good enough view from the ridge?"

"I could see, yes, but not well."

Zededia looked down between his feet and interlocked his fingers. Memories of bloodshed taxed his somber heart.

"Those details are not to be discussed lightly, Nyalis," he said. "War stories are sacred, earned by those who fought. You'll have your own one day."

A squire approached the two with their meals. More stew warmed his hands.

"Our soldiers fought bravely against a powerful enemy," Zededia said through a mouthful. "That's all you need to know."

On the prince's left, opposite Nyalis, Captain Ammon took a seat as well. He looked up from his plate and noticed that his apprentice sent a cock-eyed gaze toward the massive man. The prince shifted his eyes to Ammon without moving his head and then returned to Nyalis. After a moment, Zededia realized how little time the boy had spent around his uniquely pigmented warrior.

"Never seen a Darkskin, hav'ya boy?" Captain Ammon said, joking.

"Wandering eyes will find you in trouble, Nyalis," Zededia said.

The boy dropped his gaze to the ground in shame.

"Although, I understand your wonder," the prince said.

A moment passed as Zededia shared a look with officer. He sifted through the meat and vegetables in his bowl before noticing the boy's sheepish expression.

"If you wish to inquire upon your curiosity, you may do so," the prince said.

Captain Ammon stood to his feet in Zededia's peripheral vision to fetch another plate of food to fuel his giant stature. The prince then twirled his right index finger in a circular motion to propel Nyalis out of his wordless stutter.

"Why does Captain Ammon look different than you or me?" the prince said, guessing for the boy.

After Nyalis nodded, Zededia gathered his thoughts to explain. He set his half-empty bowl on the snowy ground and cleaned his teeth with his tongue.

"In the sand-ridden deserts south of the lower Lunendar Mountain chains, the nomadic clans of a territory called Shee'Ra roam the barrens like swarms of locusts. They are in constant war with each other, damning their ability to build a foundation for advanced civilization, much like the clans of the Old World before the Aznogs took over," the prince said.

He stretched his hands toward the fire.

"Six years ago, roughly, on my twenty-first birthday on the twenty-fifth day in the Month of War, I ventured away from my home in Vaedor Sellos on a year-long journey to travel across the kingdoms of Osiria and the outlying lands to study war tactics," Zededia said. "My first destination took me to the heart of these clans as rumors of great warriors crept in from the south. I had heard stories in my childhood of towering, unbeatable soldiers with the strength of ten men, and so, naturally, I longed to meet these giants of the sands myself to see if they lived to up to their fearsome reputation."

Zededia paused to look around as an excuse to formulate the next chapter of his anecdote. He eyed Captain Ammon conversing with Captain Sykas, but they stood too far away for him to hear them. Looking back at the boy, he picked up his bowl of stew from the ice.

"When I arrived at the deserts, I saw nothing but dune after dune without a soul in sight. The emptiness overwhelmed me; I didn't see how anyone could live in such an area. After exploring the desert with my optimism, however, by the luck of the gods I stumbled across a traveling horde of mercenaries. My first encounter with them didn't go quite as I expected once they drew their swords and threatened to enslave me for their own amusement. 'Amusement' in this case meant armed duels against their other slaves in cages like rats," Zededia said. "Anyway, as soon as I brought my identity to the light and revealed my Osirian heritage, they quickly had a change of heart and invited me to participate in cage fights as an observer rather than a combatant. At that time, anyone I interacted with clad themselves head to toe in cloth to shield their skin from the sun, and so I hadn't yet realized what I was about to see. When I approached the fighting pit, I glued my eyes to two massive men brawling with each other inside an arena. The stories of the grand stature of the sand people proved more right than wrong. Most of my confusion was targeted at their skin, though, for the men in the cage wore lighter armor, showing a dark pigment, almost like charcoal. I became starstruck in wonder as I had never before seen someone who walked the earth in such an appearance. I was dazed, stuck in a pose of fascination, just as you were moments ago."

The squire returned to fetch Zededia's empty bowl once he finished his meal.

"I watched these majestic fighters beat upon each other like their survival depended on their victory, which I'm sure it did. Afterward, I sought out the victor to analyze him from a closer perspective. I found him, chained within the same cage he came from, and I struck a conversation with him, unsure if he even spoke Eldish, the tongue of the Old World and what we most commonly speak now. That is when I was told that he had never seen a 'Paleskin' before. It became apparent that the separation in our worlds resulted in complete ignorance and a need for further examination of each other," the prince said, elaborating on the severance of the two populations' connection. "And then, he introduced himself as Warchief Orrso Ammonladas, former leader of the Hirizhenzin tribe. I recognized that name from my storybooks as one of the most gifted groups of soldiers to ever roam the sands. I learned quickly that his skin color did nothing to hinder his status as a man or a warrior, nor any of the Darkskins that surrounded me. After seeing his ferocity, I was left with no choice but to offer him a place among my ranks in the Legonae; I had recently formed the Black Legion's army, and I needed men to lead it. That is when he explained that he was a slave in debt to his captors."

"What did you do?" Nyalis asked.

Zededia thought for a moment as the assessment of his largest captain's recruitment reminded him of the crueler aspects of the world.

"I 'purchased' him," Zededia said awkwardly. "More specifically, I purchased his freedom. He accompanied me for the remainder of my journey, the same one where I discovered Captain Seether robbing the emerald mines in Merrinine shortly after. The two promptly returned with me to Vaedor Sellos to serve in my army."

Zededia detected that his apprentice hadn't quite fully understood the message embedded in his story.

"Nyalis," Zededia said to regain his young soldier's attention, "when you see people who are different than you, such as Captain Ammonladas, it's foolish to measure their worth by those differences. Each man starts life with their own hand to play, with their own path to forge. We must be wary not to judge someone solely based on how they appear. On the outside, both Ammon and Seether seemed crude and unfit to serve a royal army, but once I saw their true nature, they proved to be some of the best soldiers I could ask for. People aren't always as they seem, do you understand?"

"Yes, Commander," Nyalis said.

"Remember this whenever you approach something outside your knowledge," the prince said, "or you will face a swift reminder that position and status do not grant you power over others."

"Listen to the commander, boy," Ammon said with a smile as he returned with a pile of food. "His wisdom carries weight."

Zededia grinned and shifted the course of his thoughts to Captain Ammon.

"Matticus will surely hit us with his cavalry again in his next advance," the Black Prince said. "He knows our riders are outmatched by his and he'll use that against us today. This time, though, we won't have the fog to bail us out."

Thinking of how to form his army to face the might of the Hostellae unhindered, Zededia filed through dozens of military strategies to find one that gave him the best chance of success.

"Are we going to match the Hostellae with our own cavalry?" Captain Ammon asked.

"No," the scheming prince said, a plan surfacing from the depths of his knowledge. "We're going to do ... something different."

~ ~ ~

Caedus's time dwindled as he led his team out of the snowy mountains and into the rocky terrain of the upper peaks. Loose gravel tumbled down the narrow road under the hooves of his horse. The captain leaned forward on his mount to balance himself, and he looked around into the steep valley to his right once the ocean of Merrinine's green grasslands came into view. He remembered voyages to the gem-rich kingdom in his early soldiering days and scanned the area as far as his eyes could see.

Once the road leveled to a flat opening, Captain Redstone noticed a series of paths descending deeper into the mountains' crevices. Up until now, the path ahead had steered Caedus in one direction with the help of the shade that Zededia had resurrected from Elysia. He paused for a moment to decide which road to take, knowing that the wrong choice might set him back at least half a day if not more. To aid his problem, the captain removed a thick, rolled cut of parchment from his satchel. Caedus unraveled the scroll and studied the map of the region that his commander gave him, but none of the routes through the Lunendar Mountains inscribed on the chart resembled his surroundings.

"Well, that's not good," Caedus said in a mumble as he surveyed the various paths. "Bloody useless now to sod around trying to find the right road."

The captain dismounted his horse, walked over the wide, circular clearing that sourced each of the roads, and examined their twisting routes. His inspection proved fruitless, though, and he grunted with frustration. Kicking a few stones around, Caedus found himself facing a difficult decision. The invisible clock ticked on his journey, and any sort of delay grew more dire with each minute. As Caedus's problem-solving skills started to reach a dead end, Osinian materialized next to him in the form of a black shadow.

"Which way?" Caedus asked with a defeated voice. "You've been here before, haven't you?"

The shade only looked at him for a moment, and the captain knew it didn't speak any Eldish as he feared. He held his open hand out to each of the paths, hoping to get his message across some other way.

"Bosch ekkedas ir porozne ed stetsed sett Xeprenagir Recsedas. (...???...)"

Caedus raised an eyebrow, unable to understand the thick dialect of Aznogsi that Osinian spoke.

"*Ech ir tozi sloholget mnonaag zant sen os klaestra lanpered, quurono lett densla aeno ter inagat gazsen lett struuma beresettos Hostellus. (... kingdom ... forest ... Hostellus.)*"

A few of the words that Osinian slithered out sounded familiar. Caedus recognized them from Zededia's meditation rituals. He glared at the beaming red eyes of the shadow. Knowing the phantom meant to inform him, the captain frowned as the foreign words bounced off his ears like rain on steel aside from those he had heard before around his commander.

"*Lett kaet therz omma lett densla spolerzhenag zant tellmek lett zonzet ipicrya ir bosch daesbej ozdi zot pekratram zezkos baused. (... fourth ... temple ...)*"

Redstone shook his head.

"I haven't a damn clue what you're saying."

Flat, irritated eyes peered back at Caedus, and he thought perhaps the shade could understand him after all. Perhaps Osinian merely inferred his body language.

"Which one of these leads to the temple?" he asked with an impatient tone, pointing to each path.

He watched the shade teleport to the fourth road and point its shadowy sword down the most crooked trail that lowered deeper into the mountains from the flat gathering point. Unsure if he should trust the spirit, Caedus remained skeptical, but he didn't have a choice. Turning back to his team, Caedus shrugged. The captain then mounted his horse, spurred the company forward down the craggy road, and kept an eye out for any landmarks he recognized from the map.

The descent pressured Caedus's ears, and they popped from time to time as he rode. He eyed the steep drop-off on his right once more. An eerie feeling sank in his stomach from the view.

After nearly an hour of careful travel through the perilous crevices of the no-man's-land portion of the Lunendar Mountains, the road flattened again and to Caedus's relief, the cliff ended as he strolled between two natural stone walls. The captain rounded the circular curve to the left and abruptly stopped.

Before his eyes, a seemingly man-made section of stone jutted from the ground and cut off the path. Caedus frowned, observing the weathered cuts on the corners and sides like those made by a stonemason's tools, marks he recognized as easy as any other. Riding near, he grazed his hand over the smooth rock.

"It seems you were wrong," Caedus said to the shade. "It's a dead end."

As he examined the wall, he squinted.

"But ... this is rather strange. This was placed here intentionally."

The intuitive captain ushered his horse back toward the rest of the company, slid off, and signaled for two of his soldiers to hoist him up. He stepped into the hands of his men, and once they heaved him into the air, he gripped the edge of the rock. Caedus struggled to pull himself up, but he managed to roll over the side after a few moments. Once he rose to his feet, his eyes widened at the view in the distance. A deep impression in the earth, similar to a sinkhole, carved a cone-shaped hole in the valley below. In the center, Caedus eyed a faint structure, and he knew what awaited the bottom of the crater after studying the golden aura shining through the trees that blanketed the valley.

"Finally," Captain Redstone said with a smile.

He observed the near perfect circular barrier of mountains that shielded the structure below, much like the Hostellian crater. Next, Caedus looked down to his feet and then to the horses. Another problem entered his path as he realized the impossible task of getting everyone and their gear over the rock.

"Now, we must travel ... on foot?" the captain said with a gripe.

After Caedus's complaint, the rock under his feet jolted to life and shook him. Slowly, the risen portion of the road sank back into the earth. Captain Redstone struggled to maintain his balance as a confused expression overcame him while he lowered. Once the wall of stone equaled the road, Caedus turned back toward his team and eyed the ghost of Osinian standing with an overturned palm in the air. It took a moment to realize what had happened.

"You ... you created this barrier?" Caedus asked while signaling his question by pointing to the shade and then to the cut section of road. "Why? To hide your father's temple?"

"Sett," (*Yes,*) Osinian said.

Caedus understood the simple Aznogsi word. He nodded, walked over to his horse, and then ushered his party to the next stage of their journey without any further delay. Captain Redstone knew the temple lay only a few miles away, and relief eased his tired body even though the most difficult part of his task awaited him in the day ahead. After scanning the forest, he caught a glimmer of the gold-inlaid structure in the center of the pit.

"Almost there," Caedus said to Osinian. "Let's see what your father has in store for us."

~ ~ ~

The Legonae stood waiting in the field for another battle as the Vaedorians presented their daunting cavalry. Behind Zededia, his captains stood by for orders. A mob of Vaedorian foot soldiers poured out from behind the regiment of cavalry in the distance and formed a wide perimeter around his camp, blocking any means of escape through the field. Though the odds were against him, Zededia knew the Vaedorians thought they had trapped him in with them, but *they* were trapped in with *him*.

"Captain Ammonladas," he said, "you have your orders. Is your army able to carry it out?"

"Yes, Commander."

"Good. The rest of you, on me."

Zededia knelt to the ground as the other captains neared. He tamped down a patch of snow and removed a dagger from his belt.

"This is what we are going to do," he said. "Assuming that Matticus will try to trample us with his horsemen, and from the looks of it, he will, given that the entire Hostellae has assembled."

The cold ice proved easy to cut as the prince created several 'V' shapes pointed toward the Vaedorian side of the field. He stabbed the area inside the 'V's and carved a straight line behind.

"Captain Ammon and his defenders will create a formation like this," he said while holding his dagger at the 'V's, "just before the Hostellae contact with the shield wall. They'll funnel the enemy cavalry into these choke points. The Hostellae will charge into these pockets, tripping over the hunkered defenders, and fall into the hands of the second line where they'll be met with swift steel."

Zededia pointed his dagger to the dots he'd created.

"The Slayers will wait inside the front formations," the prince said. "They'll dispatch any who find themselves behind the defenders. Sykas, your spearmen will create a border directly behind the Slayers to catch any riders who make it through. Gather your men at the choke points and it will act as a trap for Matticus's knights to fall into."

To the prince's right, young Nyalis stepped forth and placed a hand on his shoulder. Zededia kept his focus on the diorama, however.

"Seether, your longbowmen are to be scattered in between the wall of defenders," he said. "I know that's closer to the enemy than you're used to, but if Matticus plans to fire at us with his own archers, that's the safest point. Rain hell on them; Ammon will protect you."

Distant taunts rose from the Vaedorian front. Zededia looked up and peered over his armies.

"Redding, Corso, that leaves you to clean up," he said. "I won't have our riders collide with the Vaedorians head-on again, so the light cavalry will stand by to the left and right to puncture any weak points, and the heavy cavalry will stand guard to break a stalemate of infantry, should one arise. You will not engage the Hostellae's cavalry directly, is that clear?"

"Yes, sire," Captain Redding said.

The Black Prince rose to his feet, sheathed his dagger, and dusted off his hands.

"Listen for your call signs. Execute the plan. Survive."

Each of his captains bowed in a salute. Black Legion flags flowed against the breeze. The tension tightened between the two armies, each desperate to claim the upper hand, and Zededia released an icy breath.

"Keep your wits about you, my lords," he said. "Dismissed."

Five of Zededia's six war leaders departed for their respective areas.

"Where does that leave me, Commander?" Captain Ursa asked. "Am I to remain behind?"

Zededia bit the corner of his mouth and surveyed the marching enemy across the plains. He placed his palm on Nyalis's shoulder.

"No, my friend," he said, "you have a much greater task."

"What will that be?"

The prince grinned at Ursa.

"Leading the Legonae."

"Does that mean—"

"Yes," Zededia said. "We are going to operate under Hystatia's Rule today."

"Are you certain that's what you want?"

After careful thinking, the Black Prince nodded while squinting at the white and silver wave approaching.

"Yes. Go and bear my cloak. Bring me a Slayer's helmet and cuirass."

Ursa jogged off toward the command tent.

"What is Hystatia's Rule, Master? I've never heard of that before."

The war drums came alive and shattered the icy silence through the camp. Their beat infused the prince's body with a teeming blood rush.

"Hystatia's Rule, Nyalis," he said, "is a form of command where another soldier is granted control over the entire army and the leading officer takes a place among the ranks as a common soldier."

Nyalis's confused face amused him.

"Why on earth would you do such a thing?" the boy asked.

The prince grinned and removed the cloak that gave away his identity from far away.

"It's an ancient strategy," Zededia said, "meant to teach future generations of soldiers how to lead. Captain Ursa is whom I've selected to take command of the Black Legion and the Legonae should I ever be unable to. This gives him practice. That will be your place one day, so stand by him and learn as you did yesterday morning."

Captain Ursa returned with the black metal armor of the most feared soldier in all of Osiria. Zededia took the gear of his fabled two-handed swordsmen and gave Ursa a nod. He slid off his cuirass, set it on the ground, and replaced it with what Ursa gave him. The thin, metal chest piece fit around his broad chest perfectly, and a large, jawless skull insignia centered it.

"The straps, Nyalis," Zededia said.

His apprentice tightened the armor in a few quick seconds. The prince handed Captain Ursa his cuirass and wiggled his shoulders to acclimate to the feel.

"Are you sure you're ready for this, Commander?" Ursa asked.

"Of course," Zededia said with a smile. "It's been too long since I've been on the frontlines. Can't let Ammon have all the fun, can I?"

He took a firm grip of the horned helmet that struck terror in the hearts of all who gazed upon it. The upturned eye slits stared back at him, sending the prince into a mild trance that allowed him to bask in the glory of his former skirmishes.

"Stay with Captain Ursa, Nyalis," Zededia said, ordering the boy to remain on the ridge. "I will return to you once the day is won."

Ursa stretched a hand toward him, and the prince grasped his soldier's forearm before turning to join his army.

As the war drums increased in intensity with the advancing enemy, Zededia met the eyes of his army through their helmets. His heart raced, his muscles twitched, and he summoned his courage for the fight to come. He walked past his elite warriors, helmet in hand and sword at his side. The rest of the Legonae waited in front of him as commanded, and the knights of the Hostellae erupted into a charge across the white fields.

Moments later, a murder of crows flew overhead, sending their coarse caws echoing over the battlefield.

"Sire, the corvids," one of the Slayers to his left said. "They bring bad omens, do they not?"

Zededia took his place among his swordsmen, planted his feet, and gripped the top of his deviled helmet.

"Don't worry, boys," the commander said.

He slid the helmet over his head and peered through the frowning slots with reddened eyes.

"They're not here for us."

Zededia opened his palms to the sky at his waist, filled his lungs, and channeled the subdued ecstasy of murder bursting through him. The earth shook under his feet; the aroma of war drove him mad with ferocity.

Captain Ammon stood several meters ahead surrounded by other shieldmen. The giant soldier twisted back to salute, and Zededia nodded. Ursa's orders to the signal callers sounded off behind, and Zededia wrapped his left hand around the hilt of his longsword. The familiar grip hugged his fingers through his gloves, the cold leather sticking to the fabric.

Two Slayers stood to his right and left as he formed the head of the line. He kept his distance to make way for the acrobatic moves of their *Virtuo* fighting style. Each of them drew their blades around him and took their stance.

The Black Prince then heaved his sword from its sheath and listened to the ring as it sent chills down his spine. Shining like a star in the night sky, Zededia's weapon thirsted for blood in the arena of combat.

Waves of Vaedorian paladins barreled across the plains, kicking snow up behind them. Zededia's soldiers stood tall in the face of the onslaught, and he lowered in his stance identical to his soldiers nearby. He placed his left foot ahead, pointed the blade toward the enemy—holding it parallel to the ground and balancing it near the hilt—and stared along the razor-sharp edge.

Zededia felt his breath bounce off the inside of his helmet as he calmed it. He wriggled his fingers against the grip of his weapon. The enemy surged onward.

"'Heed me, O soldiers of death'," the prince said, quoting an ancient mantra toward all who could hear him. "'Have courage for your fellow man.'"

The swords of the Hostellae flailing through the air became clear and visible.

"'Have no mercy for your enemies.'"

The stampeding horses in his view crushed the earth. His abdomen tightened.

"'Know that your death, should it come in the glory of battle, will be remembered with goblets of blood ... and plates of bone.'"

Captain Ammon shouted new orders ahead of him from the war drums' shifted tune. The front line of defenders broke into the 'V' formations as the Vaedorians closed in.

"Brothers in arms!" Zededia shouted. "Do not falter in the face of death!"

Mere meters spaced the two armies. Zededia clenched his teeth.

"Reap your harvest!"

The monstrous horsemen in white and silver clashed into the heavy shields of his defenders, sending their riders over the front line and into the funnel of tumbling beasts. Horses squealed, armor shattered, and the ground quaked. Those caught under their steeds met a brutal end, but Zededia kept his gaze to the groaning Vaedorians crawling across the snow behind his defenders.

The Black Prince and the four Slayers in his row lunged in the same exact motion to skewer the wounded men in their reach. Zededia plunged his blade into another man's flesh through gaps in the silver plating. Blood gushed around his sword from the wound, and the enemy screamed into the sky.

He retreated, waiting for the next wave. A group of Vaedorians climbed to their feet and looked at him. Zededia took his original stance alongside his Slayers, stepped forth once again, and narrowed his vision on a target.

Slicing across his body, Zededia decapitated a soldier in white, kicked the corpse to the dirt, and thrust his sword toward the next challenger. The tip penetrated the weak neck armor of the second paladin and severed the spine through the man's nape. Zededia sneered and plucked his sword from the corpse. He parried an attack from another enemy rider, slashed upward, cleaving the third man's arm in two at the elbow, and hurled his steel back across through the abdomen. The paladin rolled over the ice in two clean pieces, steaming intestines spilling out under Zededia's feet. Black arrows hurled through the air, and the Legonae's heavy cavalry patrolled the backline for a breach in the shield wall.

Screams burst through the atmosphere; the Black Prince gnashed his teeth. After the initial attack, Zededia watched his enemy fall to ruin, the leading group of knights reduced to blood-soaked bodies on the ground.

In the distance, he saw the second phase of Matticus's attack: lines of infantry sprinting toward him. Ursa's commands resonated through the armies. Zededia obeyed and stood tall. Captain Ammon and his defenders grouped together in bunches to create gaps in the line while Seether's longbowmen rained hell upon the advancing units. The prince waited with his thundering lungs.

Arrows met their marks, but the Vaedorians produced archers of their own among their ranks. Zededia stood ready for action, trusting his captain upon the hill to act. To his relief, his squadrons of light cavalry soared into battle, pinching the exposed archers before they fired.

Once Captain Corso retreated and rode out of view, Zededia readied his sword for the next command.

And then, he heard it: the call of the Slayers. A wide, devious grin cracked across his face. The iconic horns of the Black Legion's elite swordsmen pulsed through his bones, shrieking over the plains like a screaming ghost.

He stepped forward, sword in hand, and marched over the dead men carrying his brother's insignia. Poised and prepared, the lines of Slayers spread out behind him and followed. Zededia halted after clearing the piled bodies and retook his stance. The Vaedorian infantry howled as they ran, but the prince remained silent, lying in wait for his prey to arrive.

He dug his feet deep into the snow. The next mass of enemy troops advanced. Zededia picked a victim from the crowd and emptied his lungs with a scream.

The sporadic charge met a hurricane of blades as Zededia and the Slayers whirled their swords. The prince struck a soldier across the neck, slicing through the chain mail like papyrus. A splotch of blood splattered on the mouth of his helmet, and he danced to the next enemy. One by one, Matticus's infantry collapsed to the ground, gashes spewing and eyes fading. The prince hacked through the waves of Vaedorians until no more stood against him.

Looking back at his soldiers, he saw that not a single Slayer lay dead in the snow. He raised his sword in the air and declared victory. All his men shouted and raised their weapons as well. The Black Prince felt invincible. Before returning to the forest, Zededia looked over his shoulder toward his brother's encampment, eyeing a particular figure standing atop a wooden tower.

~ ~ ~

King Matticus's fleeing soldiers sprinted away from the battle as he stood atop the watch tower to observe the fight. He struggled to contain his rage as his veins shined. The Legonae receded back to their camp, and Matticus's plans burned before his eyes once more.

When he rose to an upright position, he scanned the battlefield ahead and allowed his mind to wander. His eyes discovered an unusual sight, however, breaking his trance and shackling his attention. Matticus removed the seeing glass from his belt, extended it, and gazed out at the battlefield. A lone soldier stood in the snowy field as the rest marched back to the ridge. The king leaned forward and studied the dark, horned helmet magnified from the glass. Motionless, the figure stood sideways, peering at him like a phantom. From one angle, a faint crimson twinkle shone through the eye holes.

Matticus's lips parted as he stared. The man in the field haunted him. Time slowed, and knots swelled in his chest. His heart raced, pulsing down the lengths of his arms into his palms. A familiar connection arose in the king's thoughts. He looked to the incline above to scan for Zededia's unmistakable stature in command of the Legonae, but he found no one at the edge of the ridge.

A shiver shook across the king's shoulders. Matticus faltered. A warm tent waited for him below the tower. He struggled to leave the perch, however, the silent beckoning from the field buzzing through his memories. Commander Nysis stood below with the battle report, and the day waned. The king forced his vision away from the field, descended the tower, and tried to purge the strange feelings circling in his head.

Chapter 14

Requiem

Day 19 in the Month of Snow

The fourth night of Zededia's occupation in the Hostellian fields shadowed the edge of the forest. He studied the dark landscape of wheat poking through the melting snow with his piercing blue eyes upon the ridge, forever vigilant of Matticus's army. Young Nyalis accompanied him in the stakeout. With a deep exhale, Zededia revisited the events of the days before and scanned over each battle. The deaths of his soldiers burdened him less so than the times in his youth, but they weighed on him, nonetheless. Ever since the defeat at Appostal, each fallen soldier stung his soul. Time moved along with each victory and defeat, and the veteran prince coped with loss in the same manner as always: meditation and self-reflection.

He closed his eyes to align his inner spiritual entity with his active mind. Though proud of his victories, Zededia focused on the imperfections and the disaster of the second battle, where he could improve his commands, and how to save his men more efficiently.

After a long minute of contemplation, Zededia exposed his bright sapphire irises to the shaded terrain ahead. He fiddled with the steel ring that held an aquamarine, his birthstone, on his left index finger. Rubbing the smooth gem, Zededia reminisced over the memories of the day his father gifted the ring to him on his thirteenth birthday. The shining blue rock in the moonlight magnetized his apprentice's attention.

"What is that, my prince?" Nyalis asked, leaning over to observe.

The prince lifted his finger and moved the ring around.

"This was given to me by my father many years ago," the prince said with a voice of honey. "When I first discovered my sorceries, he presented it to me as a tool to enhance them, to channel it. Without it, the magic I wield will start to corrode my mind and run rampantly out of my control. An Osirian is a powerful mage, but he needs the proper equipment and guidance to use it responsibly."

A painful reminder of using Osiris's magics without his ring ran over the scar tissue on his right hand.

"I wish I could learn your magics, Commander," Nyalis said with a sigh. "The stories I heard as a boy told great tales of your powers."

"You are just a boy now," Zededia said, laughing. "You talk as if you are my age."

The warmth that Nyalis brought him distracted the prince's wandering mind. Their relationship had greatly strengthened over the past week, but Zededia's careful eye had watched the boy after his parents' death for years now. He sensed a developing attachment to Nyalis, something he had longed for in the absence of his own children.

"I wish I could teach you," Zededia softly said. "Having a son to carry on the Osirian name is a dream of mine."

His memory track shifted to his short yet passionate time with Queen Livia before Matticus stole her from him. The prince's salted soul ached in his chest as he lovingly held his dearest in mind. Fathering a child seemed silly in his current status, though. The blotched blood on his clothes, dirt on his hands, and distance from the one woman he had declared his love for barred him from any semblance of that future.

"Those days are fading, I fear," Zededia said, looking sadly to the ground and then to Nyalis. "That's why I'm instilling my wisdom into you. So that I may live vicariously through you even if you don't carry my name."

"I've enjoyed my time with you, Commander," the boy said. "You have given me hope."

Zededia smiled.

"Will you promise me that you'll stay by my side?" Nyalis asked.

Suddenly, the prince's inner core crumbled. The final act of his plan surged forward in his mind, the consequences of following through with it circling him like buzzards. Zededia hadn't given any thought to how his plan would affect Nyalis. Fighting back what ailed him, Zededia placed a hand on the boy.

"I promise," he said with a choked voice.

The words left a sour taste in his mouth. Of course, Zededia longed for the opportunity to mentor Nyalis all throughout his youth, but the possibility of doing so dwindled with the path he had set for himself.

"Perhaps you should get some sleep, my boy," he said. "There's nothing more for us on this day."

Nyalis stood as requested, and Zededia felt a light hand on his shoulder. He covered the boy's affection with his own hand and squeezed tightly. The prince stood himself and followed Nyalis through the camp back to the warmth of his tent. Finding his cot after the boy, he laid to rest.

A calming sensation washed over Zededia as his tired body thanked him for the comfort of his bed. He sealed his eyes, relaxed, and slipped into a meditative state as he slept.

In his sleep, his subconscious focused on what ailed him. The night sky loomed overhead, casting the light of the stars through the fabric of the tent. Zededia faced the hurtful reminders of his regrets in his dreams. Dead faces, some by his hand, passed him by along with his moments of immense rage and when he allowed his torment to run free.

The dream state soothed him, though, giving him a chance to confront what haunted him. His mind took him to the meadows of Elysia, the most peaceful place of all to him, and he sat with closed eyes and open hands. Guilt and grief gnashed at him, but the prince defeated his demons and tried his best to move on. Satisfied, he chose to wander in his dream to search the spiritual plane at his leisure. He focused his energy to transport him to the watery plains of Elysia where Bogrikrash dwelled, the same place he had traveled to days before.

Zededia opened his weary eyes. A daunting realization struck him, however, when he gazed upon the unearthly scene. Somehow, he had wandered into another spiritual realm, one that gave him a hellish sense of déjà vu. The cracked, cosmic atmosphere struck a familiar chord in the prince as he began to piece together the clues of his surroundings. A dark streak of red scattered across the sky, massive chunks of shattered roads, buildings, and earth floated in stasis, and a booming thunder echoed in the deepness. Terrified, the Black Prince stood to his feet on the slab of marble where his meditation took him.

"Oh no..." he said, mesmerized by the anti-ethereal plane.

From the corner of his eye, a shadowed mass seeped from a nearby section of stone that resembled the same material of Vaedor Sellos. The Vaedorian whiterock, as Caedus called it, hurled through the vacancy of the void after the engulfing mass of black formed a monstrous hand and tossed it aside. He froze, unable to command his legs to move, paralyzed with fear. Zededia hadn't ventured to this part of the spiritual plane in years, and for good reason. An inhuman roar clamored out of the approaching spirit's density and vibrated across his skin.

Zededia regained control of himself and bolted from his position. He leaped off the rock toward another, and as he soared through the empty air, a harrowing abyss appeared from below and rattled his already scattered thoughts. Roughly, he landed on the second chunk of stone. The prince eyed fragmented patches of road close enough to hop along and dashed across the weightless, floating rocks. As he sprinted with full intensity, a second shadowed entity spilled from a platform in the distance, took the shape of a nightmarish bird of prey, and screeched at him in an ear-piercing shriek.

Thrown into a state of chaos and dismay, Zededia panicked, and his heart pounded within his chest until his ribs ached. Though the prince's physical body remained behind in his tent on the Hostellian fields, the simulation of hell evoked powerful reactions as if he walked through Elysia as a human rather than a spirit. Zededia ran for his life with two dark entities hunting him from behind. A gap in the fractured road snuck upon him without warning, and he nearly slipped into the endless abyss below before slamming his chest into the next portion of rock. He winced and heaved himself back to his feet after a moment of struggle.

The Black Prince tuned his ears to the devilish beings behind him as one of them groaned his name with enough bass to topple the stone pillars in front of it.

Suddenly, the road ended, and Zededia dug his heels into the rock just before plummeting to the void. With nowhere else to run, the prince turned to face his assailants with a horrified expression, trembling legs, and a voiceless throat. A shrill, demonic laughter echoed through the hellscape. A third black mass appeared between the two monsters, an eerie white mouth gleaming in its center.

"Zededia..." the third shadow said in a higher pitched voice.

The prince tried to shout in panic as the shadow monsters swallowed him.

"Zededia!" Captain Ursa yelled, violently awakening him from his nightmare.

Quivering and hyperventilating, the prince jolted from his trance and flailed his arms like he remained in the spiritual plane with the demons around him. He looked at Ursa, who shook his shoulder, with a bewildered face and caught a glimpse of the morning's dim light through the crack in the tent flaps. Zededia spent the next several moments coming to his senses, but once he did, an entirely different type of chaos erupted though his camp.

"Zededia!" Ursa shouted once more. "The Hostellae are ambushing the camp! What are your orders?"

Cast into the next scene of horror, he jumped to his feet as quick as lightning and drew his longsword for battle. The prince's sense of hearing returned to its normal state as cries and shouts from his soldiers sang out from both sides of the camp. Sharp steel cracked against flesh and armor, arrows skewered tents and bodies on both sides, and pained wails of dying men plagued the air.

"Fight, soldiers of the Legonae!" Zededia screamed. "Fight to the last man!"

He sprinted toward the nearest fray with his longsword held vertically at his side. Once the prince dove into battle, he defended one of his defeated soldiers and dispatched the Vaedorian knight with one blow. A surge of other Hostellae burst through the forest line to engage the prince, but he sliced through them like butter with a cornered rage that broke free from its chains.

Zededia shouted a rallying cry and led his soldiers on a counteroffensive. Several mounted Vaedorian knights swooped in from his right; he ducked as a group of Seether's longbowmen came to his aid and showered the riders in a steel volley. He then charged his shoulder into a heavily armored Vaedorian and knocked him to the ground. Zededia took no pity in his fallen enemy and slashed the exposed neck of the knight without blinking an eye. With the Black Prince present and alert, the battle shifted to his favor.

Slowly, he and his scattered army regained the advantage and pushed Matticus's soldiers to the outskirts of the camp until they retreated toward their side of the battlefield. The Legonae formed a cohesive front, drove out the ambushers, and secured their hold of the ridge.

Looking around at his ransacked command post, Zededia frowned at the ruins of the slashed and torched tents. When he took the entire situation into account, he discovered that the damages weren't as bad as he thought. The prince paused, analyzed his brother's decision to send out such an attack, and wondered how the Hostellae managed to encircle him. The short skirmish struck Zededia in his side like a thorn, and it brought questions as to the integrity of his defensive line.

The ambush set the prince back in several ways, but his army stood alive and well, and that's all that mattered to him.

Zededia walked through the tents toward his and met the eyes of one of his Slayers lying dead on the ground. He glanced for a moment, silent in respect. Shifting his attention, he watched the Vaedorians flee across the fields in the distance.

Captains Seether and Sykas approached from the densest part of the base.

"Ambushed?" Zededia said toward his walking captains. "Not Matticus's style. Makes me wonder how bold he's become. The Hostellae are becoming more of a threat than a nuisance."

Ursa joined from the left of Zededia's view.

"Well, they didn't accomplish much. We lost few resources and even fewer men," Ursa said.

"I lost three," Seether said from behind his cloaked face.

Zededia expunged the air in his lungs through his nose.

"Matticus, you coward," the prince whispered to himself.

His command tent remained unscathed by some chance as the prince walked toward it with his captains behind.

"Nyalis," he said, wiping the tent flap aside. "Where are you?"

Zededia glanced at the small cot he had set up for his apprentice. The boy was nowhere to be found.

Suddenly, panic whirled through Zededia's skull. Though the Vaedorians had fought on the edges of the camp, he feared the boy had wandered off in the fray. Zededia sheathed his sword, quickly left the tent, and marched through camp. Eyes scanning each alley and hut in their rows, the prince frantically searched the ridge.

"Nyalis!" he shouted.

No response followed his summons. He became more frenzied. The fear deepened in his stomach when silence filled his ears.

"Nyalis!" the Black Prince yelled once more.

He waited for a moment once he veered off the path to the tree where Nyalis had set up his makeshift tent, but no one was home. Exhaling sharply, Zededia grazed his lips with his tongue to wet them. The pit in his abdomen burrowed a hole of dread, and his throat closed while his heart beat furiously.

Unsure of what to do, Zededia paced back and forth. A branch snapped from the woods, and he turned with hope. A small figure stumbled through the snow toward him with bright blond hair; Nyalis finally appeared.

A deep sigh of relief flew out of his mouth. He closed his eyes, developed a light grin, and stepped toward his apprentice.

"By the gods, Nyalis, you scared the hell out of—"

Horror struck the prince. A pained face emerged from the woods and staggered toward him. The grin on his face dropped to a gaping mouth. Nyalis held his hand behind his ribs and walked with half-open eyes, and Zededia saw a long, slender piece of wood sticking out of his apprentice. He sprinted toward Nyalis in terror, tripping through the snow as shock electrified him.

"No," he said under his breath. "No, no, no, no."

Nyalis fell to the ground on his knees as the prince's soul shattered into a thousand pieces. Sliding through the snow on his knees, he reached for the boy and took him in his arms. Zededia pulled the boy into his chest, looked over his shoulder, and studied him with shaky eyes. A sturdy, wooden arrow protruded from Nyalis's lower back.

Tears formed in the prince's eyes as he raised his head to glare off to his side. He slowly moved his hand around the base of the arrow, and his fingers drowned in blood. Nyalis whimpered from the pain, sending Zededia into a devastated frenzy. The prince raised his head again, the arrow in the boy's back too horrifying to look at any longer. Once he collected his misery, he swallowed the dryness of his mouth and met Nyalis's gaze.

Young, terrified eyes stabbed Zededia's heart once he turned the boy over. A tear pooled in his right eye, trickled down his nose, and dripped onto Nyalis's chest. Though the Legonae contained many skilled medics, he knew the boy's injuries pushed him beyond the point of saving. He pulled Nyalis into his left arm in a trembling embrace and gripped the Vaedorian arrow with his right. With a subtle snap, Zededia cracked it as close to the boy's body as possible. Nyalis yelped from the sudden jerk, and the prince held him tighter to comfort him.

"Shhhhhh," Zededia said with watery eyes.

Nyalis's blood doused the prince's pants and spread through the snow. Zededia tried with all his might to keep the boy's wound shut, but the pressure amounted to nothing. His cheeks trembled as he held back a cry of agony. Watching the boy's life fade into the void, he clung to the soldier he saw as a son. Nyalis curled his lips from his suffering and gripped Zededia's cloak with a weak hand, sending the prince further down the road of torment. He sniffed to clear the mucus from his nose and started to rock with the boy in his grasp.

"*Can you hear the waters calling?*" Zededia softly sang, reciting a nursery rhyme from his childhood to ease Nyalis's pain. "*Can you see the oceans blue?*"

As the prince progressed through the song, his voice fractured into a watery tone.

"*Ships are waiting, mice are crawling,*" he sang while staring into the boy's slowly blinking eyes. "*Run to join the sailing crew.*"

Zededia gripped Nyalis's hand and held it firmly against the gritty blood covering his own.

"*Sail to lands, grand and bold. Feel your feet amongst their sands.*"

A final exhale of stinging anguish burst from Nyalis's lips as Zededia watched the life wither from his apprentice's body.

"Build your home on rocks of gold," the prince sang, choking.

Nyalis's grip in his hand dissolved and slipped away, breaking Zededia's last line of defense for his tears. Several poured over his eyelids and trickled onto the boy's face.

"Walk the beaches of heaven's lands."

After finishing the nursery rhyme and Nyalis's head lay limp in the pit of his elbow, Zededia buried his face into the boy's shoulder.

Any joy left in his world burned to ash, and his heart darkened as it bled for young Nyalis.

Chapter 15
The Temple of Osiris

Day 20 in the Month of Snow

Captain Redstone peered through the coniferous plants that walled the ancient road under his horse's shoes. A pleasant aroma of the mystic atmosphere rose from the pit in the center of the crater. As Caedus and his five companions wove their way through the dense, uncharted areas of the hidden forest, the tired captain caught glimmers of gold and light that penetrated the concealing tree branches. Halfway into the descent, he looked up in the darkening sky and set aside his anxiety from the delays he had encountered. Day six quickly stretched over Caedus; the sunset crept along with a dark red hue over cragged ridges above.

Finally, after the meticulous journey, the grand sight he had ventured from Anzagaar Nostir to see sprouted into view as he turned a corner of the cracked road. He strolled under a weathered, collapsing stone arch and gathered his team in a clearing hidden by a row of boulders near the entrance of the lost golden cathedral. Caedus's eyes illuminated like two blazing stars once the entirety of the temple's magnificent architecture glowed into his sight. He scanned the two towers that speared from each corner of the front half before tracing the slanted sides of the base in a pyramid-shaped fashion. As Redstone dismounted his horse without removing his gaze from the temple's shimmering exterior, the architect inside his warrior's heart surfaced out of sheer respect for his childhood trade.

He stepped toward the temple, trapped in his own fascination. A rude awakening shook Caedus from his mild trance, however, when he heard a careless conversation of brutish voices from under the massive, rectangular doors that represented the temple's only noticeable opening.

An instant reminder that he lingered in neutral territory struck Caedus like a whip. He sank in his stance next to a large rock, scoured the direction of the raucous chattering for a sign of an enemy presence, and signaled for his men to sneak toward him for a better vantage point. The captain himself retreated into the foliage and sidestepped over roots and rocks to keep his shoulders square with the target area of interest.

From under a low-hanging branch of pine needles, Caedus climbed and inched over a smoothed rock on his stomach to investigate. The captain's eagle-like vision hovered over several men dressed as soldiers in front of the door to the temple. He inferred an atmosphere of frustration from the figures' flickering arms and barking tones. One of the men attempted to push on the solid gold gates, but as Caedus watched he realized the soldiers failed to budge the door by any means. He then noticed a sigil stitched into one of their tunics.

"Merrins," Caedus said to himself in disgust. "Bloody perfect."

On his left, the girl brushed against his shoulder with hers.

"How can you tell they are from Merrinine?" she asked in a low whisper.

Caedus pointed to the soldier that faced directly away from them.

"The emerald on his back. It's the Merrin symbol of authority like the eagle is for Hostellus," the captain said. "It seems that either Mythian knows of the sword's location, or his soldiers have strayed from their orders to find riches of their own."

Withdrawing from the scouting position, Caedus pondered whether to treat the Merrins with hostility or with peace.

"How should we proceed, my lord?" one of his soldiers asked.

"The treaty is still intact," Caedus said. "But ... the exiled don't abide by the treaty, do they?"

He received grins from his men, rose to his feet, and stepped out from the underbrush with a hand resting on the pommel of his sword. Their sudden appearance gained the attention of the Merrinine soldiers and Caedus bolstered his confidence. The Merrins drew their weapons as Caedus neared, but the captain kept his blade sheathed. One of them walked to the edge of the platform outside the golden doors where a lowly inclined ramp led down to the ground.

"Who the hell're you?" the soldier harshly asked. "What are you doin' 'ere?"

He eyed the other soldiers as they presented their arms, directing their attention away from the temple entirely.

"I could ask the same of you, soldier of Pyla Sellos," Caedus said, referring to the City of Gems, Merrinine's capital.

"That's none of your soddin' concern," the man said. "This is Merrinine territory. Everything here belongs to King Mythian and his estate. Best you be on your way, peasant."

Caedus smirked, given his true status as a lord of Monscarren, but he remembered the gear he wore knocked his social status down a few rungs to avoid detection from any wandering eyes.

"You can leave now and return with your lives spared," Caedus said. "There's no reason for you to die in such a holy place. There's plenty of gold elsewhere in the world."

The Merrins burst out laughing before descending the ramp to the stone road below.

"We're not here for gold, you soddin' moron," the leader said. "Don't you know anything about this place? What's inside? No, of course you don't. You're just a commoner, a petty thief. You're lucky we don't take you and your friends in for threatening guards of the crown."

"Guards of the crown?" Caedus said. "Shoddy pieces of filth, you are. You plague your kingdom like a disease, stealing from humble villages to fuel your crooked king's greed. The only thing you're good for is setting a proper example of how waste a life."

"I'll show you a waste of life," the soldier said, raising his sword to Caedus.

"Even if you managed to find the Sword of Kings," Captain Redstone said, "you are unfit to carry it, unworthy of everything it stands for."

The Merrin lowered his weapon slightly and paused.

"No one was told the sword's whereabouts but us," the man said. "How can you possibly know that? You're just—"

"A commoner," Caedus said, cutting the man off.

Rolling up his sleeves, the captain revealed a tattoo on his right wrist identical to the one on the back of his neck. His men stepped forward from behind him and drew their swords. Caedus approached.

"How could I possibly know?"

"Oh, shit," the Merrin said, slowly retreating. "They're-they're Black Legion!"

Captain Redstone narrowed his vision on the frightened Merrins, firmly gripped the hilt of his sword, and let a devious soft smile widen on his face.

"I suppose we are."

Like a bolt of lightning, Caedus tore his sword from the sheath, gutted the Merrin in his reach with a clean thrust to the lower abdomen, pulled it out, and forced his blade downward into his victim's mouth until the red-soaked steel ripped a hole in the enemy soldier's lower back, severing the spine and esophagus along the way. He yanked his weapon from the corpse and sneered at another Merrin running toward him with a reckless advance. Caedus ducked to avoid a savage strike and then drove his blade underneath the man's rib cage and out the opposite shoulder like a harpooned fish. He shoved the soldier to the ground, his sword fluidly scraping against flesh and bone as he removed it.

A frenzied image of red flooded the captain's vision after two executions, and the rest of the Merrins sprinted forward to engage. The three Legonae soldiers sprang to action in front of him, hacking down their enemies while Caedus regained his composure and flicked his short sword clean.

After the fray, the last Merrin fled for his life, stumbling over the loose rocks with cries of panic. Caedus took a step to pursue him, but a flash of black raced across the earth to his right. Osinian materialized in a dense stream of mist twisting its way to the soldier, constricted him like a snake, and plunged into his mouth before bursting out of all his pores moments later, popping the eyes out of their sockets. The shade then retracted and returned to his normal shape of a man in front of Caedus.

"*Ti bosch ozno ett mnesha zot landperedir? (Is ... become ... my kingdom?)*" Osinian asked in an angered voice, shaking the helmet of the Merrin in his hand. "*Poshtu, malakaz streya. (...???...)*"

Osinian tossed the helmet at Caedus's feet and then quickly faded into the air. The captain turned around and met the confused eyes of his men and the thief girl creeping out of the brush near the scene. Understanding the shadow's tone but ignorant to his rant, Caedus shrugged. More pressing matters awaited in the golden monastery.

Risen from earth upon a massive foundation of placed stone and mud, the Temple of Osiris shadowed the pit it rested in as Caedus stepped from the road onto the ramp inlaid with a carved image of a ceremonial priest. He admired the craftsmanship, inspired by the finesse of every segment of the structure. When Caedus reached the top of the shallow incline, he shifted his attention to the giant door that shielded the inside from the rest of the world. The captain's three soldiers approached the shining gate and attempted to push them open to no result.

As he waited behind, Caedus's tinkering mind sifted through possible solutions to the puzzle after noticing no exterior locking mechanism. He knew that the priests and designers of the temple had to have left a way in from the outside, so he scanned the ground and walls beside for some sort of clue.

Several minutes of critical thinking passed and Caedus grunted from frustration while his soldiers continued to try to muscle the door open. The girl walked up next to him and glanced around.

"Time for you to be useful," Caedus said. "You were here before. How did you open the doors?"

The girl shook her head.

"I'm not sure," she replied softly. "The temple was open when I was last here."

Faced with another challenge, Caedus brought his left hand to his mouth and pinched his lower lip as he scanned the ground outside. The raised platform held several dark stones in its complexion of decoration, and the captain then wondered if the key to the lock lay under the mosaic-style floor. Before testing his hypothesis, Osinian appeared in the center of the terrace.

"Sen hallasag lett zdraeno, zant ishkenang sen jeshirag olat lett sig sunzenir malakalas. (... open ... stones ... priests,)" he said, giving insight on the temple's secrets.

Caedus shook his head with an open mouth as if to respond, but the tongue-twisting words from the black mist confused the captain more than the locked door in front of him.

"Stones? Priests? What about them?" he said.

The spirit stood motionless except for its flickering edges.

"Show me," Caedus then said, pointing his finger to the ground.

He still struggled to determine if the shadow understood his language or not. However, something seemed to get across as Caedus watched it dissipate in an instant before reappearing upon one of the darker, rounded disks. Osinian pointed to the ground; an idea sparked in the captain's mind.

"Stand on these," Redstone said to his men while motioning to the igneous stones.

He heard a faint click from the rock the shadow pointed to, but as soon as the second soldier stepped onto the next one, the first disk jolted back into its original location. Puzzled, Captain Redstone suddenly realized that the levers required a precise order in which to press them.

"It's a sequence," he said, making his eyes dash back and forth between the rocks. "Step back onto this one."

Once his soldier reactivated the left-most disk in the circle of floor pieces, Caedus looked to the shadow, and it faded again before arriving to his right.

"And then here," the captain said to another soldier.

To his delight, a second click sounded from under the floor. Caedus and Osinian repeated the process until one stone remained, leaving the final notch for the captain himself. As he stepped onto the stone nearest to the solid gates, a jostling snap shook the gates followed by a low-pitched thud. Caedus smiled at the ingenious building design and walked up to the entrance. The doors left a small crack between them. He peered inside with his right eye, and a radiant view of gold and precious gems littering a vast lobby shined into view. Dazzled by the treasures inside, Caedus gathered his strength and heaved on the gate. Despite his efforts, the doors hardly budged until his soldiers caught up to him and pushed alongside him.

A quaking, rusted creak echoed through the open chamber of the temple as Captain Redstone broke its seal. Caedus wandered across the paved floor and piles of gold, and he glanced up at the murals painted on the arched supports and ceilings illustrated with scenes of Osiris's divinity. He stumbled over a loose mound of coins while distracted and scattered them in all directions. The sheer quantity of wealth just sitting in the temple astonished him, and he began to understand why raiders and bandits obsessively pillaged the other monuments to Zededia's holy ancestor.

"By the stars," Caedus whispered to himself, in awe of the alluring atmosphere. "No wonder nations went to war over this place."

Caedus bent down and picked up a sapphire the size of his knuckle. The gem twinkled against the golden light reflecting from the walls of the structure's interior. He rolled it in his palm before placing it back on the floor. A magnetic attraction pulled his eyes to another large piece of currency resting on the dusty floor. Shining as bright as the sun, a perfectly round coin that held a carving of a symbol that Caedus recognized as the sigil of the Monscarren Stonemasons, the elite builders of his native kingdom. The medallion plunged Caedus into his roots, and he guessed that the architects of his home had aided in the construction of the temple long ago. A sense of pride flushed through his heart, and he elected to keep this single piece of Osiris's wealth, hoping the all-seeing deity understood.

Quickly after the trip to his younger days, Captain Redstone shook off his euphoria and refocused on his purpose in the temple. The girl he had grown fond of wandered just as he had moments before, but he interrupted her trance with a straight-to-the-point question.

"All right, now what?" Caedus asked, allowing the girl to lead for a change. "Where's the sword in this labyrinth?"

A saddened face peered back at him with beaming eyes.

"Farricks's men made it to the tunnels in the heart of the temple, or at least that's what one of them said when they came back out to grab supplies," she said. "I suppose we just ... keep going."

Caedus tagged along behind the girl without any other option, but he worried about her gloomy expression, remembering how many of the people she had roamed with, whether she cared about them or not, had lost their lives in their attempt to pluck the Sword of Kings from the monastery.

His concern faded, however, when he noticed the rounded width of the girl's lower half under her rough clothes. A curious spark planted a seed in him as he walked. The temptation forced a frown on Caedus's face, reaching a part of him he gave little attention to. He shook off his lust and cleared his throat.

The gold on the floor continued to clutter the temple's open sanctuary, but once Caedus moved past a man-made waterfall that poured into a pool in the center of the chamber from an opening in the ceiling, he noticed a pile of bones sprawled across the edge of the bath with its torso submerged in the water. The decayed remains reminded the captain of the dangers that lurked in the temple, and so he scanned beyond the mounds of gold for any sign of danger. A calm silence washed over Caedus and his company, one that he disliked from his expectation of a threat.

He turned over his shoulder and peered at the door behind that seemed rather distant. The windowed walls decorated with tapestries and decaying oil paintings of Osiris drew his attention. Cautious still, he remembered what his commander had told him about the guardians of Osiris's holy grounds. As Caedus proceeded to the end of the worship chamber of the temple, he eyed a much smaller doorway than the gate outside. The arched entry point opened into a bathhouse behind the wooden doors that lay broken and unhinged on the floor. Amazed that water continued to run in the temple that likely hadn't seen maintenance in centuries, Caedus studied the spouts that poured into the bath.

"Thank Neshka," one of his soldiers said with a sigh from behind. "Fresh water."

"I ... I don't know if I would drink from that," Caedus said in a warning as he looked over the pool. "Though I doubt anyone has been here for a bath in quite some time."

Another corpse popped into view leaning against one of the support columns of the bathhouse. The body rested in an advanced state of deterioration, and Caedus noticed a large amount of flesh still attached to the bones he couldn't see. Realizing that this man had died much more recently, he turned to the girl.

"How long ago did you say you were here?" Caedus asked the thief girl.

"We left Beggar's Keep late in the Month of Decay, so I'll guess we arrived here around the end of the Month of Osiris."

Caedus deduced that the body in the bathhouse had to come from her company on their first voyage here almost forty days ago in the last month of the year. On the sides of the steam room, Caedus saw numerous hallways in between the pillars. He couldn't quite see the ends of the corridors, giving him an eerie feeling deep in his bones.

"Come on," Caedus said. "We need to keep moving."

On the opposite side of the pool, he halted in his steps and flinched at several other bodies on the floor, one skewered with an arrow in the back of the skull, one decapitated, and one without both arms. The thief girl gasped at the sight of them, and Caedus reached his arm out his arm for her to cling to.

"I-erm ... I'm sorry if they meant something to you," he said, trying to soothe her.

"They didn't," she said sharply. "But if everyone is dead, how long do you think it'll be before we join them?"

Captain Redstone frowned at the discomforting thought.

A heavy stone door with several phrases written in Aznogsi stood between Caedus and the next chamber. He moved past the corpses and brushed his hand over the symbols inscribed on the arched frame. As the captain stepped back in confusion, he darted his focus to the girl.

"Wait a moment," he said. "You said you never went into the temple and abandoned your group at first chance. How do you know this is the correct way?"

"Like I told you, when one of Farricks's men came out for more food, he told the rest of us the path he took when we were supposed to enter ourselves."

"Hmm."

Stuck in front of another obstacle after Caedus pushed on the door to no result, he curled his lips inward and thought of a plan of action. Breaking down the door with whatever tools he could find came to light, but the door's thickness remained a mystery. To aid yet again, the shade of Osinian emerged.

Caedus moved aside to let the first Son of Osiris work. He traced the black mist's hand touching several of the symbols in order and heard him mutter a few phrases he didn't recognize. After the shadow finished unveiling the magic barrier, the captain stretched out his hand to shove. Frowning, the captain heaved on the braced door back as it remained in place. Osinian pointed to the top of the frieze above the doorway where a globe of sand trickled through a small funnel.

"It'll open when the sand empties?" Caedus said.

The shade nodded.

"Great," he said sardonically.

Osinian vanished in his peripheral view, and Caedus then turned to the rest of his company.

"Well, I suppose we'll have to wait," he said with a sigh. "We should move these bodies. While I have little respect for them, I don't like breathing the same air as their rotting flesh."

"*I'm* going to take a bath," the girl said with a hint of defiance.

Though letting the girl leave his sight conflicted with his common sense, Caedus's curiosity urged him to let her bathe.

"Fine," he said.

Caedus pointed to his men to signal them to carry the decaying remains back outside.

After removing the corpses from Osiris's temple, the captain walked back through the main chamber and peered inside to make sure the girl hadn't run off. She stood near the water's edge, still clothed, and he nodded in contentment.

Caedus respected her privacy and waited in the sanctuary as his soldiers occupied themselves around the room with the limitless fortune of the monastery. His attraction to the girl in the other room elevated his temptation as he heard splashing water.

Checking on her well-being provided a decent excuse to watch her. Conflicted yet intrigued, Caedus bit his lower lip and stood from the rock he sat on. He made sure the gold on the floor distracted his men well enough before entering the short hall that opened into the bathhouse. The water whirled again, pulling him closer.

As he leaned his head inside, he fixed his attention on the girl, naked and beautiful in the water. Though she hid herself well facing away from him, he watched her wade through the pool. Caedus allowed his gaze to linger; he studied her soft curves and tanned skin with parted lips. A moment passed where she rose out of the water the hidden steps on the other side of the bath, revealing everything above her calves. A rushing warmth prompted him to pursue the sexual desire blooming within.

He adored the nameless thief girl, moving his tongue across the back of his teeth. Caedus understood the sinful nature enchanting him, but he desired her, nonetheless. Washing away the filth of the journey, the girl grazed her cushiony hips and thighs while Caedus's heart rose to his throat. She moved both of her hands to her wide, spherical buttocks, and a pair of inviting eyes underneath her dripping hair looked back at the enthralled captain, beckoning him to join her. She grinned at his presence, and Caedus slowly moved into the bathhouse corridor as she revealed the rest of her natural beauty to him.

She crossed through the pool toward him with her hair parted on each shoulder; nothing could pry Caedus's gaze from her as she swayed. Water dripped off her in small trickles, and the captain stood on the side of the bath glaring down at her. The girl wrapped her arms around his neck once she stepped out of the water, pulled him closer, and took the captain's hands and placed them on her hips. She then dug her teeth playfully into his neck. The coarseness of Caedus's skin kissed her delicate body. Her hand grazed down and traced the length of his abdomen all the way to just below his belt.

"Are soldiers allowed to have fun, Captain?" she whispered in his ear before weakly biting it.

Lost for words, Caedus delved into her elegant, amber eyes.

"You never told me your name," Captain Redstone said while exploring her neck with his mouth and tongue.

Caedus felt her hand tighten between his thighs as he sucked on her skin. She exhaled in his ear with a touch of pleasure, sending chills across his body.

"Raeza," the girl said with a satisfied murmur.

Moving both of his hands all over Raeza's legs, Caedus yanked her closer, feeling her embrace through his clothes against his strapping chest. The girl hastily unfastened his belt, and he became more aggressive as he pushed her against a pillar. As Caedus explored the malleability of her body, he thrust his hips into hers, forcing her legs open as she squealed. A powerful craving infected his brain. The spark he shared with Raeza since their first conversation exploded into an intimate affair.

Before too long after penetrating her, however, a crumbling vibration sounded from the stone door behind him. Short of breath with Raeza pinned against the wall and balancing herself on his waist with her legs, the captain glanced over his shoulder at the open archway. He turned back to the girl wrapped around him.

"Perhaps ... we should proceed farther into the temple," he said, heart pounding blood into his flushed face.

Raeza's disappointed sigh broke his heart, but he knew she understood after she kissed him extensively. Caedus pulled himself out of the girl, wiped himself clean with a handful of water from the pool, and buckled his belt. He struggled to set aside the intense lust overcoming him, but the Sword of Osiris called to him. Captain Redstone made himself decent, called for his soldiers in the sanctuary, and pressed on.

Chapter 16
Catharsis

Day 20 in the Month of Snow

Smoke pillared into the sky from the funeral pyre burning on the edge of camp, and Zededia stared into the cold abyss of the Hostellian plains from his place on the ridge with crossed arms. The valley warmed from the ice storm that swept over the land when he first arrived, melting the top layer of snow covering the wheat fields. Dead and hollow, his eyes moved to the Vaedorian camp in the distance. Nyalis's place in the prince's life had become void and desolate and drained him dry. His heart starved for revenge. Zededia shed himself of all emotion, only a wave of dormant anger bubbled under his skin. It torched him like wildfire.

Captain Redding approached in his side view, but the prince kept his focus on the fields. The image of Nyalis's lifeless face took a firm hold of him and planted its roots deep in his thoughts.

"The boy's procession is complete. He's moved onto the afterlife," Redding said.

Zededia remained silent.

"The men are uneasy, my prince. They've never seen you in such a state. How do you wish us to proceed in the next engagement?"

The prince heard his soldier's question, but the blistering reminder of his failure as Nyalis's guardian suffocated him. Numb, he slowly exhaled.

"You will not proceed," he said with a splintered voice. "Take the Legonae home."

"Sire?" Redding asked in confusion. "Are we not to continue the assault?"

Turning his head like a graveyard skeleton, Zededia peered over to Captain Redding. He resealed his lips, but the agony in his expression spoke for him well enough. The prince then took a step forward toward Vaedor Sellos, his boots sinking into the snow in his slow walk.

"Commander Zededia!" Captain Ursa shouted behind him. "Where are you going?"

Ignoring his soldiers, he dropped his hand from the pommel of his longsword. His weapon bounced off his hip with each step, weighing him down from his belt like a massive rock. With all joy vacant from his darkened soul, he marched.

"Commander, please," Redding said. "Let us fight for you."

Zededia stopped. He turned his head around to glare at his loyal soldiers, and a tear escaped from his bloodshot, weary eyes and flowed down the side of his nose.

"No more of you will die for a war I created."

The prince twisted back to face the fields. White, decorated flags rose high in the air at the center of the Vaedorian forward command post. Zededia's nostrils flared with rapid breaths. As he walked, the divinity in his blood shone bright, fueled by his rage. Zededia tapped into the deepest extent of his power, tiny red bolts of electricity scattering out from under his booming footsteps.

As time lulled in his aimless wandering, he allowed the darkness in his heart to take control. The Black Prince cared not for death, and if it found him in the fields, he ached to release the savage aggression luring him to his brother's army.

Soon, the Vaedorians took note of his presence once he had drifted over the battlefield of the previous skirmishes. The brutalized earth from the boots of soldiers caved to his footfalls. He heard a few faint shouts in the distance and saw several of the Hostellae rush to grab their weapons. Zededia slid his hand over the hilt of his longsword and freed it from its case with a firm heave. Passing the point of no return, the prince prepared himself for a slaughter. An icy stare beamed at the Vaedorians. The floodgates opened.

"Maelinag sen kar, prishkelezir zodanthris. (Fly to me, agents of darkness,)" Zededia whispered to himself, invoking his empowered sorcery. *"Haelag kar lett aantir zyentos. (Gift me the spirit of hate.)"*

The shine in his veins glowed brighter, and the ring on his index finger used to channel his magic emitted a faint red aura wisping around it. Probing his bleeding heart, the vision of Nyalis's death drove him to madness.

"Mealinag sen kar, prishkelezie zodanthris," he muttered in a louder voice. *"Haelag kar lett aantir zyentos."*

Zededia's mind raced between the painful memory of the boy's fading eyes and the malice he hadn't faced in years. He trudged his feet through the snow, leaving elongated footprints in his wake. The soldiers in white approached with swords drawn. Mercy long gone, the Black Prince sneered.

A black mist similar to Osinian's complexion seeped through multiple spots in the snow nearby and gathered in the palm of his open left hand. He turned his vision south, eyeing the phantoms from the abyss he called them from. The shadowed entities whirled around Zededia like a tornado. Beaming red eyes punctured through their transparency. With each spirit he conjured, more power channeled through his ring that shook violently on his finger.

Nearing his prey, Zededia quickened his strides. His brain buzzed with pent up emotion, and he revealed his teeth through a sinister frown. The infantry of the Hostellae continued their charge toward his location, unaware of the monster they were about to face. Vengeance lay meters away.

"*Maelinag sen kar, prishkelezir zodanthris!*" he shouted, buckling under the immense energy flowing through him. "Gift me the spirit of ... haaate!"

Zededia's power built to its greatest potential, the full might of Osiris coursing through every fiber of his being. Unable to endure such intensity, the gemstone of his ring exploded into fragmented shards. He shifted to a steady march surrounded by a veil of shadows.

The bloodthirsty predator at the loom of Zededia's mind erupted into action. He halted in his advance, planted his feet firmly in the snow, and jerked his open left palm toward the sky. Dozens of resurrected spirits taking the form of unnatural beings gushed from the earth. They sprinted, crawled, and screamed sounds of nightmares on their way to the first group of Vaedorians. They sliced the helpless men up like kitchen vegetables, drained their life forces, and reduced the remains to piles of dried skin and bones. Zededia callously stepped over the corpses and called his army of ghosts back to his hand. More enemies approached to sate his appetite for murder.

Not even the greatest of the Vaedorian soldiers stood a chance against the prince's rage as they fell to the dirt like butchered animals. Rather than utilizing the precision and discipline of his *Virtuo* stance, Zededia abandoned any fighting style and struck at the Hostellae with rash, barbaric attacks. Red flickers shone through the cracks in his armor and lined his skin.

A Vaedorian thrust at the prince in his blind spot, but Zededia quickly dodged out of the way and grasped the blade with his hand, the steel cutting through his glove. Zededia heaved his attacker's sword from his opponent with ease, strengthened his grip around the sharp edges, and slammed the hilt into the flesh between the collarbone and back muscle and drove it into the right lung with the tip of the crossguard. After shoving the body to the ground, he moved to the next challenger, plunging his longsword out through the back of the Vaedorian's helmet. Blood spurted from the faceplate as Zededia pried his weapon from the Vaedorian's skull with his foot firmly planted on the cuirass.

A larger group of soldiers circled him once he looked up from the carnage. He glared at them with hell in his eyes, spun between his foes, and hacked every limb that entered his range. Unmatched, Zededia slashed his way through the chaos without a scratch on him.

"Come on, you worms!" he bellowed in a demonic voice. "Present me with a fight!"

Finally, Zededia found a worthy opponent once he made his way through the entrance of the Vaedorian forward encampment. A knight in gleaming silver armor barreled toward him atop a great stallion with several others behind. The Black Prince hosted an evil smile, eager for the challenge. He ran through the rows of tents and palisade spikes, building incredible speed with each passing second.

The Vaedorian knight lowered the lance to strike, but Zededia stayed the course. As the horse veered slightly to his right, the prince lunged high in the air, aided by his godlike strength, swung his sword across his body, and sliced the knight's head clean off his shoulders. He landed back into the snow and cast his shaded minions forth with both hands pressed out in front of him to pluck the rest of the galloping soldiers from their mounts. The black phantoms burst into a whirling cloud and engulfed the riders, knocking them to the ground.

He roared at the staggered soldiers as the power of the shadows fused with his physical body and allowed his neck and jaw to stretch far beyond the limits of a regular man. Zededia leapt forward, stabbed his sword through the abdomen of the first who rose to his feet, yanked it out through the left side, and severed the head with a backswing through the spine. The rest of the platoon faltered as they stood up. Stomping on the mutilated body on his way to the rest, he squished and splattered viscera all over his boot. The Vaedorians back peddled and turned to run from his brutality, but a sense of ecstasy rushed through him from the opportunity of a chase. Zededia pursued the retreating soldiers with the aid of his conjured allies who surged over the bloodied snow.

A true nightmare haunted the Hostellian fields. The wrath of the Black Prince unleashed his torment upon the Vaedorians without hesitation; a wrath that rattled the cage in his soul every day, released in its unbridled form. As the shadows from the depths of hell clawed at the fleeing soldiers, towing them to their master, the prince cleaved with fury. One soldier at his feet desperately crawled on the ground to escape death, drawing Zededia's attention with a faint whimper.

No morsel of restraint prevented his cruelty. The prince stabbed his sword into the dirt, grabbed the soldier with both hands around the neck, hoisted him up, and squeezed until his victim's eyes bulged from the pressure. Gasping for a breath while dangling, the soldier pried at his hands, giving the prince flashbacks of the paladin he had thrown off the tower of his home a while back.

"You will suffer ... as he suffered," he said, the voices of spirits intertwined in his.

Without hesitation, he dropped the man to the ground, readjusted his grip around his skull, and plunged his thumbs into the soldier's sockets, rupturing the eyes and causing the gelatin-like matter to drizzle over his hands. A darker howl for help pleased Zededia and motivated his savagery. Dragging another Vaedorian, one of the shadows brought him a fresh prey grasping at the ground. The prince placed his heavy boot on the man's back and pressed.

"Cowardly and weak."

The prince ripped the cuirass off the squirming Vaedorian and forced his right hand into the flesh until he felt bone. He dug through the muscle tissue with his hand coated in the essence of the shadows around him and closed his fingers around the spine. A guttural scream shattered the air for the dozenth time as the soldier twitched with agony. Zededia heaved the backbone from his target and snapped the veins attached to it on the way out.

Dropping the spine, Zededia shook the blood from his hand. The remaining Vaedorians dispersed and fled back to the safety of the castle far away. Through his vermillion vision, a daunting figure stood out from the others. A prestigious paladin dressed in the armor he recognized as the symbol of the Hostellae's commanding officer waited for him in the distance.

"At last," he said, "the guilty arrives."

Zededia jerked his weapon from the earth and taunted his enemy. Carrying a long spear, the rider poised it overhead to hurl it toward him. The prince sank in his stance, and the knight's horse reeled back on its hind legs before galloping down the main path of the camp.

Thundering down the road, the horse trampled the snow and shook the ground. The rider cocked his arm, anticipating the prince to leap upward like before. Zededia altered his plan, however, and summoned all his might for impact. He exploded shoulder first into the armor-plated chest of the stallion, sending it flying over him. It tumbled across the earth with fragmented bones. The prince himself fell to his knees with a sharp pain under the dent in his pauldron.

After the dust settled, the horse wriggled and wailed, and Zededia stood, grasping his shoulder with an anguished face. He limped over to the knight on his back who struggled to move from his crippling injuries. The anger still surged through the prince despite his pain. Yanking the Vaedorian commander from under the horse with his good arm, he savored the revenge to come.

"You ... filth," he said darkly. "You stole him from me!"

The true torment from Nyalis's death emerged in his catharsis. He gripped the Vaedorian officer by the neck, hurled him in a circle around his body, and slammed him to the ground.

"He was just a boy!" the prince shouted, lifting the soldier above his head and tossing him several yards away. "A child!"

Through his rage, he heard the Vaedorian cough and wheeze under the helmet. As his opponent staggered to his knees, Zededia caught the weak punch sent his way and broke the man's elbow with a swift strike to the middle of the back of his arm. The muffled cough morphed into a groan as the knight fell over in agony.

"Get up!" the prince bellowed. "You will witness the hell you gave me!"

"Z-Zed..." the man faintly said.

He set his target upright on his knees and caved in the faceplate protecting his head with a bone-breaking punch. The Vaedorian's helmet flew off and bounced rolled in the snow. Zededia, at the height of his wrath, stared at the back of his opponent's head, and he readied his sword for the killing blow. Before the prince rained his bloodied steel upon the man, a familiar face peered back at him. Zededia widened his eyes in complete shock, losing all momentum and aggression.

As Zededia beamed at the blond hair and blue eyes of the Vaedorian officer with his mouth agape, the haunting memory of the soldier he lost years ago on the night of his exile shot ice into his veins. The man he once saw as his greatest friend, whose son he promised to look after and keep from harm, knelt before him, bearing the symbol of the enemy on his chest.

"Please ... please don't," Commander Nysis said.

Zededia dropped his sword. His eyes glued to Nyalis's father, presumed dead by Matticus's hand. As he glared at Nysis's face, the realization that his most revered captain in the Legonae had betrayed him collapsed his entire world.

A fresh suffering anchored him to the earth, filling his limbs with steel and his mouth with cotton. The sight of his former soldier forced all his aggression to wither and die, and he drowned in the fact that Nysis had orchestrated the death of his own son.

A parade of Vaedorian riders appeared, surrounded the prince, and drew their spears, aimed directly at him. He dropped to his knees and then on his backside, beaten with confusion and loss. The possibility of escape dwindled to zero. Zededia simply sat on the ground and surrendered.

He looked back at Nysis struggling to stand on his feet. Shackles and chains rattled to his left, and the wind chilled his exposed skin. Retreating into himself, Zededia masked his emotions behind a death stare forming in his eyes. One of the soldiers in white yanked him to his feet after securing metal braces around his wrists and feet.

"Cover his mouth," Nysis said. "Black magic has no place in Vaedor Sellos."

Zededia let his captors tie a rag around his neck and lips, having little care for his physical state of being.

The column of knights escorted him away from the red river flowing in the road behind. As the prince staggered along behind the horses faster than a comfortable walking speed, he glared at Nysis. The white walls of Vaedor Sellos beamed into view once the tents no longer blocked his vision, a sight that Zededia hadn't hated more than he did in this moment. The chains dug deep into his skin at the edges of his gauntlets, and he lowered his head in defeat.

The havoc he aimed to bring would have to wait; an advanced depression dampened his attitude. He hid his sorrow deep inside as the events of the last day crippled his will to press on. Darker days awaited him in the city. Abandoned, desolate, and void of all hope, the Black Prince closed himself off from the rest of the world, struggling to carry the daunting weight of his misery.

~ ~ ~

Earlier in the day, King Matticus returned to the upper city after growing tired of battle. He trusted Commander Nysis to protect Vaedor Sellos from Zededia and to notify him if something had changed. Away from the carnage, Matticus allowed the benevolent side of him to reemerge, and his chest ached at the absence of his wife and sons. The silence of his chambers elevated every little sound he made, from his rolling footsteps across the floor to his weathered hand grazing the bedposts jutting up to shoulder level. Peace came to him, and the distance he placed between him, and the controlled chaos of the city eased him. Pacing over to the window that overlooked the courtyard below, Matticus emptied his lungs and reflected over the worries on his mind: the return of his exiled brother, the Sword of Kings lying in secret somewhere just out of reach, and his crumbling relationship with Queen Livia. A melancholic mood seeped into his heart.

"Oh, Mother," he whispered to himself while leaning against the windowsill, "what would you have me do?"

"She would be proud of you," a familiar voice said from his right.

Matticus jumped from the unexpected company, but as soon as he turned, the grin waiting for him in the shadowy corner eased his tension.

"It's unwise to lurk, brother, even in my quarters. I came here to be alone."

He watched Lucien close the book in his hands and place it on a nearby table.

"I know. You seemed rather troubled when I saw you praying at Father's shrine when you returned."

Unaware that his keen brother had seen him kneel, Matticus thought back to where he might have missed Lucien's presence.

"When I told you to be vigilant of the people in our home, I didn't exactly mean me."

Lucien walked toward him while eying the table to his left. The game of chess that had collected dust over the past few months sparked pleasant nostalgia. Matticus traced his fingers across the back of the chair closest to him.

"It's been years since we've played, hasn't it?" Lucien said as he sat down on the opposite side.

Matticus raised an eyebrow.

"With everything that's stirring outside our city's walls, you expect me to amuse you in a game of chess?"

"That's exactly what I expect you to do," Lucien said with a bright grin. "We've not spent time just you and I in ages, and I miss that. Now, sit and play the damn game."

Matticus hesitated for a moment, not completely having bought into Lucien's distractive plan. Nevertheless, a break from his concerns sounded quite soothing to his pounding head. He pulled the chair out from under the table and squared his shoulders toward Lucien, who leaned over on his elbows like a child. Matticus couldn't remember the last time he and Lucien spent any time alone together that didn't involve politics or war as his brother had pointed out.

"Zededia would slaughter me at this game when we were boys," he said. "I threw one of these figurines at him almost every time."

He felt Lucien's gaze on him but decided to keep his focus on the board. The realization that he had spoken of his worst enemy as if war had never occurred struck him and a sickening feeling climbed in his throat. The cracks of Matticus's hard shell splintered; he didn't understand the sudden sentiment blooming inside.

Lucien moved his left center pawn forward one space to initiate the game as Matticus recollected his strategies from the past. He opened the space in front of his right knight to allow the bishop to move freely.

"I know things are troubling you, Matticus," Lucien said as he took his turn. "You worry about too much."

Matticus moved his next piece.

"I can't hide that from you it seems."

"Just like I can't hide my emotions from you, no, you cannot. Not while I'm here to watch over you."

Matticus chuckled at his brother's tenderheartedness.

"I wasn't aware you tend to anything other than Thancred's tobacco and Father's liquor," Matticus said in a joke.

Lucien captured one of his pawns with a knight, which triggered a chain reaction that removed his right knight from play after falling for Lucien's trap. He frowned, disappointed at his lack of vision.

"Damn you, Lucy," he said. "I remember now why I stopped playing this game."

A quiet laugh came from his brother.

"I watch over your family, Matticus," Lucien said after a calm moment. "I watch for those who seek to weaken you with one hand and a dagger in the other."

If Matticus ever suspected Lucien as a traitor to the Black Prince, he removed it after the touching statement. In the back of his mind, however, he remained skeptical of everyone. Including his closest ally across the table.

"And, uh ... have you noticed anything ... suspicious ... lately?" the king asked. "Disturbing events took place while I walked among the armies outside the castle walls."

"What events?" Lucien asked.

Matticus detected a hint of nervousness in his voice. The tap of Lucien's chess piece rang in his ears.

"Spymaster Rachtus has disappeared."

"Disappeared? As in he just vanished?"

Matticus focused on the evidence at hand of the dried blood found in his war room.

"I don't know," he said. "Rachtus is nowhere to be found, and I fear that someone who ranks highly at my side is responsible for that somehow. The guards have told me that no one distrustful has been in or out of the keep, but..."

"That's not what you believe, is it?" Lucien said.

Matticus nodded as he looked up to his brother.

"I don't know what to believe, Lucien. Rachtus wasn't the type to lead a successful life as his and to take leave at the most crucial time of the plan we've been putting into action for years now. The circumstances force me to consider the possibility that there's a defector in the keep. Rachtus knew something, and someone made sure he'd never share it."

The king noticed a subtle fright emanating from Lucien's eyes, a look he knew well enough to detect.

"Do you know anything about this, Lucien?" he asked.

"I do not, brother. I only fear because I have many friends here in the keep."

"You speak of Thancred?"

"Yes," Lucien said, "he is a great mentor and has shown nothing but devotion to the crown his entire life. It troubles me to think he could commit such treason."

His suspicion of Lucien's secrecy faded from his brother's answer, and a wave of relief washed through him.

"I know of his importance to you and to the people of Vaedor Sellos as a physician. And I agree with you, I do not think he could ever devise such a scheme to rid the world of a man like Rachtus, even if he wanted to. So perhaps I should close that door altogether."

Watching Lucien's tension fade, Matticus slid his left rook across the board, capturing his brother's queen.

"However, there's something you can do for me that would ease my worry," he said. "You are nearly the last person I can trust."

"What's that?"

Matticus remained silent for a moment, careful of how to tread.

"I need eyes in the city, Lucien. In the last day, I was so fixated on defeating Zededia outside the castle that someone inside struck at me from the shadows. I need you and your perception to look after Vaedor Sellos, our home, in my absence."

"What about Commander Nysis?" his brother asked. "I didn't even know that Zededia's former right-hand man served the crown until his return from Korzeg."

As Lucien closed in on his king piece, almost ending the game, Matticus risked his queen to save himself. He saw Lucien frown for a moment.

"Nysis is a soldier," Matticus said in a mutter. "Soldiers only look after power. Money. Land. He's invaluable as an officer, but I've yet to feel as if I can trust him with more important things. He betrayed Zededia in a heartbeat. What's to say he won't do the same to me one day?"

He kept his focus on the board game and heard his brother lean back.

"So why the hell do you keep him around, Matticus?" Lucien asked, opposing the king's decision to promote Nysis to Zededia's previous rank of Commander of the Hostellae.

Matticus sighed, digesting the complexity of the situation.

"Like I said," he said, "he's an invaluable soldier. Someone who can match Zededia's skill on the battlefield is too great an asset to forfeit."

A silence dampened the air for a moment. Matticus felt a chill from the breeze blowing in through the window. While Lucien took his turn, Matticus tapped the table. The distraction of the game with his brother withered, forcing the issues deep in his mind to reemerge.

"I've made countless mistakes, Lucien," he said, delving into the chaos he attempted to obscure. "My decisions as king have affected people for better and for worse, and I live with them fairly easily."

Matticus swung the momentum of the game in his favor by removing Lucien's last rook and placing the king piece in check.

"My decisions as a man, however," he continued, "have left me..."

The words that rolled on his tongue didn't feel right.

"Distraught?" Lucien said.

Matticus smiled.

"I suppose you could say that. I am winning a war on one front but losing one on the other," he explained.

"Perhaps you should focus on one front at a time, then," Lucien said, suggesting a change of strategy.

The king looked up to his brother with a shocked gaze from the simplicity of Lucien's thought process.

"If only it were that easy, my young brother. I wish the world worked like you think it does."

"Well, on what front are you winning?"

Matticus thought for a moment on how to elucidate.

"Zededia has been the root cause of my defeats and humiliation for my entire life. I am finally within reach of the weapon that will eliminate him for good."

"And the front you are losing?"

Matticus moved his bishop to corner Lucien's king.

"For reasons I can't explain, I find myself unwilling to follow through on my ambitions. I think my guilt and regrets are catching up to me."

Right under his nose, Matticus's king piece became trapped by Lucien's pawns and bishop, effectively ending the game. He scowled at his younger brother's maneuver. Lucien grinned back at him, and he exhaled in defeat.

"Is that why you were praying at Father's shrine earlier? To ask for forgiveness for whatever you seem to think you've done?" his brother said.

"Yes," the king said after a moment.

"Well ... forgiveness will come. But you need to release your hold of what ails you. It'll eat you alive."

Matticus sighed with subtle delight, finding himself in a state of mind that reminded him of his childhood and that healed his wounded heart.

"Now you're starting to sound like him," he said, jeering. "Where has this wisdom come from exactly?"

Lucien's eyes wandered to the sky outside as Matticus waited for an answer.

"When you spend your days looking after those you care for, no matter their transgressions, you tend to learn a bit from their actions. Thancred is also a good mentor."

"Then it seems removing him from your side would be most injudicious."

Lucien stood from the table, and Matticus felt a sturdy hand on his shoulder. He watched his brother head for the door before looking over at the book on the bed. His curiosity soared, so Matticus stood and walked over to read the title.

"I will do as you ask, brother," Matticus heard from his right as his fingers touched the cover.

He turned his head to Lucien.

"I will watch over what you hold dear," the prince said, "for no other reason than that I hold you dear as well, and I cannot bear to watch you decay."

The warmth that Lucien brought branded his heart. Though he appreciated the company, he found himself unable to respond to compassion.

"Better days are ahead of you, Matticus," Lucien said. "Focus on the small things. You'll survive."

The king received a light bow from his brother, and he looked down at the book in his hand. He scanned the title and recognized it from his childhood when his mother had gathered all three of the Osirian boys to read to them. It was a book he had latched on to, one that penetrated the angered exterior he flaunted so frequently.

For the first time in months, a true smile appeared on his face. He then longed for his wife and sons, whom he hadn't seen in days. Their embrace eluded him, replacing the worry in his heart with sorrow. For an instant, he wondered if he hadn't let his ambition guide him to the fields to face the Black Prince, perhaps he could have spent that time with them.

Yet another regret piled onto the king's plate, but the time to dwell on it dwindled. A faint trampling alerted him from the window. Matticus hastened over to observe. He peered into the courtyard and witnessed dozens of people running to the main gate. Horns sounded in the distance and communicated the signal of victory.

"Lord Nysis is returning to the city!" one of the guards shouted to the crowd. "The Black Prince has been captured!"

"Zededia," the king said to himself, flushing away all positivity. "Finally."

Matticus set the book on the windowsill and made his way toward the door to exit the keep. He longed to see his exiled brother in chains for himself and to revel in his defeat. The three yearlong chase for his most hated enemy drew to a close, and King Matticus fell back into a vengeance-seeking state of mind.

Chapter 17

Osirisigniros

Day 20 in the Month of Snow

    Caedus stepped through the mystical door leading deeper into Osiris's great temple after waiting out the time lock placed by the priests living on the grounds before its desertion. Dust and musk clouded him like a fog, and he looked around to study his surroundings. A long corridor stretched perpendicular to the doorway in both directions, the wall opposite of it twenty feet away. The interior of the temple hid them from the last strands of sunlight beaming through from above, creating an eerie darkness through the hall. Captain Redstone, faced with a decision to make, turned to Raeza for assistance.

    "Now where?" he asked.

    She shrugged and remained silent, but Caedus had expected nothing less.

    "I'm beginning to question your use as a guide," he said with a grunt. "We'd better just choose a path to follow."

    Caedus slid his foot onto a metallic object that scraped against the stone floor. He glanced down at the rusted blade under his boot. After he kicked it out of his way, he squinted his eyes to scan for any other remnants of past travelers. The captain flinched once he discovered a pile of bones through the darkness. Some of the remains appeared intact, others lay broken and slashed to pieces. Upon closer inspection, he recognized a few of the armor segments from warriors under the flags of Osiris's first heirs, the Eight Sons. The tale of a great war over the temple's riches validated itself in Caedus's eyes, leaving thoughts of speculation behind. Just as he stepped closer, the shade of Osinian formed in front of him.

    "*Bosch nalazan esli nox ir zot praetoraei gualiri sen cesin. Zot mirzshagai draeimegs sen ullmaz zot pekratram ell prozem dorzgo. (... temple ... soldiers' ... rest ... father ... destroy it ...)*" the specter said. "*Za sicirnegi lett nalazan poromengraziri sen ballas lett lelinsloti ish collei aenost, sen daelegace dorzgo. (We ... temple ... artifact ... destruction ...)"*

Caedus struggled to understand the full message, but deep inside, he felt the sentiment from Osinian's story. He understood that the ancient king standing before him valued his men enough to take a moment of respect for them, a decision that most others would carelessly overlook.

The shade looked up from the dust-collecting bones under weathered iron and met his gaze.

"Za rogtanteg cod voni sola sen threshzni lett pekratramenros ish zomaos berrides ter zanto morisa zerkizen. (We fought ... honor ... father ... legacy ...)"

The captain nodded.

"My condolences for your men," he said. "I'm sure they served you well and died the same."

The shade hesitated for a moment, looked back to the bones on the ground, and faded.

Caedus reflected over the importance of Osinian's past with the temple and ushered his team into the hallway.

After several minutes of wading through the thick aura of the inner corridor, Caedus caught a scent of foul decay that burned in his nostrils. He held his cloth shirt over his lower face and searched for the source of the smell. Lighting a torch with his flint, the culprit came into view with a wicked entrance.

"By all that is holy," Caedus said, "what the hell happened here?"

The odor forced his eyes to water and his stomach to wretch as he glared at scattered pieces of rotting remains strewn about from wall to wall. An arm hung to the left, skewered by a spear, and the upper half of a headless torso spilled its innards across the floor, attracting all sorts of scavenging creatures. Behind him, Raeza lost all control of her nausea and vomited a trail of greenish-yellow bile. Caedus nearly hurled himself, but his stout resilience prevented such a reaction.

"If these belong to your crew, they've been here a month," he said to Raeza.

Her frightened eyes looked at him. Caedus stretched his arm out to hold her hand, and she clung to him in an instant. While he enjoyed the embrace, his focus remained fixed on to the severed body parts and torn flesh that littered the hall for as far as he could see with the scarce light. Only one fully complete corpse separated itself from the lot with a sword struck through the abdomen, pinning it to the brittle stone as rotten intestines hung out of an open wound. Rats and insects scattered in between the carcasses to devour their rancid meal.

"No rest for the damned, I suppose," Caedus said.

After bolstering his courage, the captain tiptoed over the putrefying remains and proceeded. His sense of caution lit in his brain, reminding him that the dead men at his feet met their end in a grisly fashion right where he stood. Caedus looked over his shoulders at his men, and they carried worried faces just as he did.

He grabbed Raeza with his left hand, his other firmly around the hilt of his short sword ready to act in the face of danger. The darkness blurred more than it already did.

An archway to an adjacent corridor emerged on the left and gave Captain Caedus another choice to make. His attention shifted to a large seal on the ground engraved with Aznogsi symbols on the floor where the hallways met. As soon as he moved closer, a current of air rushed from the opening and knocked away the cobwebs in the corners of the walls. The hum of the wind echoed throughout the hollow temple and Caedus's skin crawled and stiffened the hair on the back of his neck.

"Something isn't right," he whispered.

Caedus drew his short sword from the scabbard. The air stilled.

"Lett hororizezkos enve stliltos!" Osinian yelled incomprehensively from behind.

In the confusion, Caedus studied the black doorway. The piercing sound of metal scraping together blistered his ears as the rounded seal sank into the floor, slid open, allowing a monstrous beast to jump from the hole in the floor, and closed underneath it. A humanoid figure made of solid gold looked down upon Caedus after twisting its head completely around as if its neck melted to a fluid for a brief second, and the captain faltered backward while it swung four arms like a whirlwind before stopping to point at him, wielding a blade in each hand. Caedus's eyes widened with panic, for such an adversary had never crossed his path before. The mouthless colossus squinted at him in anger. Frozen, the captain stared at the golem and struggled to find a plan of action.

"Run," he said under his breath.

"My lord?" one of his men asked.

"Run. Run now!"

He released his grip of Raeza's hand and heard his four companions dart off behind. The golden giant diverted his eyes away from the captain, giving him an opportunity to strike. He frantically tumbled between its legs to buy time. All four of the swords' blades crashed to the stone floor with enough force to shatter it. Caedus scrambled to his feet, scanned the golem's back, and noticed a small sigil on the crest of its spine

The colossus, standing at nearly twice his height, wriggled, turned its head around again, and spun its arms around its torso, pushing the emblem to its new back. It writhed as Caedus readied himself for another advance. The giant sliced its left two arms horizontally at him, but the agile captain sidestepped to the other side. A similar attack came from the right arms and sliced deep into his left shoulder. Caedus's fresh blood splattered on the floor, and he cursed in pain.

He swapped his sword to his cut arm to hold the wound with the other along with the torch. His fingers became soaked with warm blood. Caedus noticed that the golem's arms wedged in the cracks of the stone wall from its rash attack. The captain heaved his blade into its arm and dashed back to reset his stance as the golem freed the two stuck blades.

A fresh dent appeared in the golem's wrist. He wondered if the blow would be enough to give him a chance at a fair fight. The golem wound up its arms to swing again, but this time the impact of the attack and the crack in its wrists combined to snap its hands off. With a muffled roar, it staggered backwards and turned away, and Caedus utilized the moment to jump onto its back, driving his sword into the sigil on the nape of the giant's neck with both hands, dropping the torch and delving through the soft gold.

The colossus twitched before falling to its knees, and Caedus rolled off onto the dusty floor. He looked back as the temple guardian collapsed, sending a thunderous boom through the halls. Taking a breather, he relaxed on his back and fought the pain in his lungs. After a moment of peace, the captain stood, weary and wounded. His three soldiers with weapons drawn walked back into view with Raeza behind. She picked up the torch and walked up to him, tracing the outline of the hemorrhaging wound on his outer deltoid. Caedus flinched as her finger touched the sliced flesh.

"You need to stop the bleeding," she said with a worried face.

"I'll be fine."

Captain Redstone then heard a low-pitched scrape from the other end of the hall behind his soldiers. Heavy footsteps followed.

"Besides," he muttered with a fixed gaze at the other direction of the hall, "we've got another friend."

Caedus stepped forward to study the massive figure approaching. A shimmering gold head emerged from the shadows. An identical golem of the one he had slayed stomped forward, raised its four arms to strike, and aimed its lapis lazuli eyes toward him.

"It moves with haste," Caedus said. "Weaken its arms."

A deep hum resonated from the golem, a wicked call that chilled the air.

"Move quickly. Wear it down."

The golem then flicked all four of its swords across the backs of its hands and slashed with its left two. Caedus pulled the collar of the closest soldier to save him from evisceration.

The other two soldiers next to him pinned one of the arms by interlocking their swords with the giant's, and Caedus sliced at its wrist like before. A similar dent appeared in the malleable metal. It swiped at Caedus again, who ducked just in time, and lodged one of the swords in the wall as the first colossus had done. However, unlike before, the golem released its grip of the stuck sword and heaved its fist into the chest of one of Caedus's men who held the lock on its pinned arm. The soldier crashed into the floor with a thud, but Caedus kept his resolve. He analyzed his mythical opponent, realizing it adapted a strategy from the other's fight. A hypothesis formed in his brain that suggested the two beings shared a common mind, perhaps because of the divine power in the temple.

With only one man holding its arm, the giant broke free and aimed its three swords at the nearest target. Caedus avoided the slice as the sharp swords crashed into the wall, but his soldier wasn't so lucky. When the captain looked over after regaining his balance, his eyes flickered with horror as his knight slid down the wall in three segments, slowed by the gushing blood sticking to the stone wall.

Death had plagued Caedus before, but seeing a man he had trained and fought with for years fall to the floor like chopped pork damaged his composure. He staggered back as the time to grieve expired in seconds. The metal guardian lunged to strike again, but the other two soldiers of the Legonae conjured their strength and leaped into action before him. He watched them parry, deflect, and cut at the golem with a vengeance for their friend. Eager to join them, he tightened the grip on his sword.

With three opponents, the colossus struggled to endure. The dents carved in its appendages caved under the pressure, and each of its arms dropped to the floor. Disarmed, the golem fell to its knees. Caedus approached it, summoned all his strength in a slash, and hacked the golem's head off.

The captain caged his ferocity after reducing the two colossi to pieces. His heart beat furiously, and he exhaled through his flaring nostrils. Once he found his composure, he turned to Raeza and his men. Caedus's adrenaline coursed through him, and he looked back at his dead soldier as the remaining members of his party stood by. Time waned as he delayed.

"Come on," he said. "We need to keep moving."

"Is there something we should do, my lord?" one of his men asked. "For Brakkas?"

"No," he said after a moment. "We keep moving."

He took a torch from his soldier and trudged further into the temple. The path where he had met the first golem led to another series of corridors that shifted his course like a maze. Acting as the only method of direction, a damp moss growing in the cracks of the stones caught his attention. The captain's high intellect told him that a water source must be nearby.

He stretched his hand out to meet the cold stone and found it quite soothing. With some investigation, Caedus discovered that the moss thickened as he progressed down the hall. His dirty fingers brushed the rootless plant off the wall in a search for any sign of a door.

"This way," he said.

"You're trusting the moss to guide you?" Raeza asked.

Captain Redstone stopped to peer through the darkness that thickened as he explored the temple's deep infrastructure.

"Moss only grows where the air is damp. There wasn't this much in the other rooms, not even the bathhouse. We must be heading in the right direction or at least somewhere different."

Soon after, Caedus's perception served him well as a faint, flowing sound trickled in his ears from a short distance away. He quickened his pace, eager to find the artifact he had been sent to claim. A blueish glow appeared from the shadows, and Caedus made out the outline of a doorway on his left. Once he stepped close enough to peer inside, the luminescent beauty of the next chamber lulled him. His eyes marveled the sight of a man-made, circulating pool in the center of the rounded room that cast a bright shine across the fallen pillars. More piles of gold shimmered as well, and several votive statues resembling Osiris poked their heads out of the wealth.

Caedus loosened his grip on his sword and started to lose sight of his quest. A small river flowed into the pool on one side and exited from the other, creating an alluring current around the marble statue in the middle. Wandering through the heavenly chamber, he looked up to the ceiling and studied the gems that provided the dim, celestial light. The pattern of the inlaid stones fascinated him.

"It's a man-made ... illumination chamber..." Captain Redstone said as he swiveled around with his attention glued to the starry mosaic.

"What's an illumination chamber?" Raeza asked with the same bewilderment. "Looks like just a bunch of shiny stones."

Caedus felt her head on his outer arm and her hand on his wrist.

"An illumination chamber," he said, "is a type of sanctum where Osirians are able to connect with the beings that dwell outside this plane. They can mend the bond between themselves and a divine entity ... or worse."

"Worse?" the girl asked, clinging to his arm.

Caedus traced back to the memory of Zededia's fascination with the illumination chamber deep within Anzagaar Nostir.

"There are places like this spread all throughout Osiria. I know someone who obsesses over it, always sifting through the cosmic energy to find someone he lost," Caedus said as he walked toward the pool.

He glared into the blue water, knelt on one knee, and cupped a handful to wet his face. The cold liquid refreshed his weary eyes, and Caedus wiped his face with his hand and returned to his feet.

"He found something much darker waiting for him. An entity that haunts him to this day. It drove him mad in the first few weeks; I can still hear the laugh he imitated trying to explain his torment."

Raeza's beautiful face grabbed his attention as he turned back to her. His eyes moved over every feature, growing more attached the longer he stared, until he gazed into her eyes that twinkled.

"The darkness spread to you, didn't it?"

The bold question caught him off guard, but he knew that he couldn't lie to her. Not in this moment, when truth and history blinded all else.

"Yes."

Caedus felt a bit of pity from her but chose to ignore it.

"Is that why you are so loyal to him?"

He nodded, restraining his words.

"I know what plagues my commander, Zededia. I know that what he carries cannot be endured alone. He needs someone to aid him, even if he doesn't admit it."

"But why? Why do you serve him if he has done nothing for you?"

Caedus grinned, thinking back to the hundreds of times when Zededia had saved his life or career as a soldier.

"Because he is my friend, and he's done more for me than I can ever repay him for. Without him, I would be back in Monscarren with a rock hammer in my hands. Zededia holds the purest heart of any man I've ever met. He's the rightful king of Hostellus, the only Osirian I've met who places his people before himself."

He thought over his friendship with Zededia and quickly remembered the task at hand.

"I am lucky to march under his flag. Even luckier to act as his second."

While he took delight in the banter, he knew of the urgency that pressured him.

"Let's find the sword," he said, leading her back toward his two soldiers digging through the riches.

The moving water sparkled over the gold, revealing a figure in the background near the wall of the room. It appeared to take the form of a long, rope-like structure. Caedus thought nothing of it as he scanned his surroundings, but he heard something slither across the floor after a moment. The captain paused. He watched his soldiers carry on, admiring the perfection of the coins as they skimmed. The slithering continued.

The scarce light of the illumination chamber played tricks on his eyes, deceiving them and casting shadows in his peripheral vision. He stretched out his hand and signaled for Raeza to stop walking. Suddenly, a grim feeling crawled down Caedus's spine.

"There's something in here with us," he whispered.

"My lord?" one of his soldiers asked.

Caedus shushed his men. The slithering ceased. He kept a keen sight on the dim perimeter of the chamber. A few gold coins toppled off a pile nearby, and an eerie silence screamed at him to flee.

In the vastness of the shadows, the captain happened upon two orbs of yellow floating ten feet above his eye level near the chamber door. It took a moment to put the pieces together, but before he could send out a warning, the being exploded from the darkness and crushed the nearest soldier in its jaws, revealing two massive fangs as it lunged. It thrashed, coiled, and swallowed Caedus's soldier near the gold pile in seconds. Thousands of coins exploded from the commotion, and the temple shook like an earthquake had struck.

Caedus backed away, haunted by the serpent's swift strike. There was no time for his soldier to escape death, even as one of the most elite warriors across the Osirian territories. Captain Redstone retreated further and watched the massive snake retreat behind the pillars into the darkness.

"It's going to come back," he said, searching for a plan with his arm guarding the girl.

The captain frantically searched for an exit, but none stuck out other than the one he entered from. While the snake slunk around the chamber, Caedus listened to his instincts. He took the girl's hand in a firm hold and bolted toward the door. Before reaching the tunnels, however, the serpent flicked its heavy tail and smashed the stone above, blocking the exit with crumbling debris. Caedus fell to the floor with a hard impact.

"Shit," he said in a panic.

After rising to his feet with the aid of his last remaining soldier, Caedus held his sword toward the yellow eyes that hunted him from the shadows. He caught on to the snake's game.

"Find cover," Captain Redstone said. "It's after me."

Once Raeza and the soldier scurried away, Caedus planted his feet to gain a proper foundation. Two porous nostrils emerged from the beast's upper lip over a mound of gold. Caedus kept his focus on the coiled length of its body, calculating the right moment to jump to safety. A pause of nerve-fraying tension rose between Caedus and his hunter, and then, like a lightning bolt thrown from the gods, the snake retracted, bared its fangs, and exploded into an advance. Around halfway through its lunge, Caedus dove to his left, missing the snapping jaws by an arm's length.

He pounced upright to make the most of his opportunity and slashed his sword from overhead with both hands, but the sharp steel bounced off the thick scales as hard as diamond. Caedus's weapon shook in his hands, hindering his ability to maintain a firm grip.

The serpent hissed at him and rose above him to strike again. Seeing that his option to wound his target had vanished, Caedus retreated to his backup plan: running for dear life.

Like a rabbit, the captain beat his boots on the stone as fast as he could, ordering the other two to do the same. The predator chased with relentless aggression, giving him almost more than he could handle. He toppled to the floor repeatedly as the leviathan pursuing him chomped at his ankles. Finally, the captain found a solid footing and slid behind a stone column on his stomach.

Sniffs from the giant snake sent terror through him. Crawling next to the pillar to avoid detection, the sharp pain reminded him of the deep gash on his shoulder. He pressed on the bloodied cloth around his shoulder and gritted his teeth to disperse his agony. A golden crown skimmed over the sea of coins and brushed his boot after the beast wriggled through the room.

Raeza and his last soldier gleamed at him from behind another column, but the sound of the snake's tongue slurped between him and his party members. Caedus closed his eyes and tried to calm his beating heart. As quiet as possible, he leaned toward his foot and scraped the cusp of the crown with his fingertips. The serpent drew closer, rounding the corner and turning toward his position with black scales casting tiny reflections from the twinkling rocks above. Like a message from death itself, a wave of warmth from its breath brushed his right shoulder.

Caedus trembled in the struggle to reach the object at his feet, pushing it farther away with each tap, but he managed to take a firm hold of it after a risky move. Without hesitation, he launched the crown over the barrier of gold to his left, sending a crashing echo through the chamber followed by a rain of coins. The snake pulled back to investigate, and the exhausted captain leaned his head against the column to rest. His body begged him for peace. As he twisted around and peered over the other side of the column, he eyed a winding tail.

"This is the last bloody thing I do for Zededia," he said.

With the beast distracted, Caedus beckoned for Raeza and his soldier to make their way over to him.

"We need to find a way out," he said. "Fast."

Before the captain could decide how to lead his team, a strange sound resonated from the center of the room. Caedus frowned in confusion. He stood to his feet and rounded the column with his sword drawn. The serpent's body lay sprawled out across the illumination chamber and Caedus flinched once it came into view. However, he noticed that the beast had focused on something else completely, and he stepped away from cover. The snake hummed a deep growl, pacified by whatever it sensed.

A strange voice spoke in the distance. After pacing forward, Caedus saw an outstretched hand of black mist touching the snake's snout. Osinian's red eyes glanced over to him as he watched the shade soothe the great serpent into a stasis.

"Nal gaz zlotha, xensi sen lett hollodras, zot soor kell. (...???...)" Osinian said like he spoke to a pet.

It slid away and climbed into a hole in the ceiling from one of the support columns after the shadow lowered its hand; Captain Redstone approached and lowered his sword.

"Where the hell have you been?" he said.

The shade kept his attention on the beast retracting into the void above and Caedus waited for a reply that he knew he wouldn't understand.

"Zoam nest forza mensh zanto promos nesla sen dismli ozno zant drace. (I ... language ... you ...)"

Caedus grunted. He turned to Raeza behind him to discuss the next path forward now that the threat was gone.

"They didn't tell you about this place when the survivors came back out, did they?"

She shook her head. With nowhere left to turn but the dark tunnels in hope of finding another chamber, Caedus sat down on a pillar that had toppled over long before he entered the temple. He brushed his hands over his face and massaged his eyes.

"Well ... Farricks did mention that we were supposed to find a hidden door ... the entrance to the inner shrine," Raeza said.

Caedus looked around, defeated and tired from his mission. He scanned past the column supports and across the curved wall of the room.

"We could be searching for days and never find it," he said.

As the captain dropped his head with a sigh, he noticed the shade walking by. Raeza continued to mumble to his left, but her words trailed off while he studied his guide. Osinian's spirit phased through the gold piles as if they weren't there until he faded from his view. The captain stood to his feet, followed the trail of murky shadows left behind in the phantom's footsteps, and waited. Osinian paced around the edge of the room with an outstretched hand until a faint blue glow sparked from a gemstone lighting up in the wall.

"Actually," he said, studying the outline of a door activated by Osinian's presence, "we may be in luck."

Captain Redstone jogged around the ruins of the chamber and jumped over the narrow stream to stand next to the shade. A sudden jolt shook the dust off the stones slightly raised from the wall, and a faint crack appeared down the center of the doorway. Caedus pressed his hand against the wall and pushed to reveal an aura of golden rays seeping through the gap. Once the hidden entrance opened to the gleaming light of the inner shrine, the dark illumination chamber shone to reveal the hidden patterns in the mosaic walls. Caedus looked back to admire the craftsmanship one more time and then squinted his eyes after turning back to the brightness ahead.

"Tanz ene don klessisha rezk sont," the first Son of Osiris said. *"Zant lilli ishken sen porg lett moorsla aeno. Ili oolso os quirazen staall. (You ... right ...)"*

Osinian's shadow remained after it spoke instead of fading like before, giving an inference that Caedus tread close to his prize. The captain focused on the center of the room where a grand staircase ascended toward an altar pulsing with energy.

Before his eyes, the blurred outline of the Sword of Kings gleamed like a diamond among sand. All the glory of Osiris waited just yards away from him. However, before the captain took another step toward the golden artifact, a scattered lot of corpses caught his attention. He studied them to determine their deaths, for the flesh remained in a decaying state.

"Do these look like your company members?" Caedus asked Raeza.

He felt her presence to his left but kept his eyes on the bodies.

"Yes," she said. "Farricks led over thirty of his men into the temple, and I suppose the last of them wound up here."

"And where is Farricks now?" Caedus continued, analyzing the layout of the squared chamber.

"There."

He glanced over toward where Raeza pointed and noticed the Ehthilian helmet. The tales of Grimm's thievery in the kingdom north of Hostellus seemed to fall into place as the captain recognized the prestige carried by the head armor. No matter, it had failed to aid the bandit leader here as Caedus took note of the open chest cavity with all sorts of scavengers crawling around the edges.

"At least he made it this far," Caedus said.

Advancing toward the ascending staircase, the dead men at his feet disturbed him more than those he had previously seen. Something about the gaping holes right where their hearts should be made his skin crawl. They stared at him with empty eye sockets. Osinian passed him on his right, walking straight at *Osirisigniros* hovering above the altar.

Caedus paused for a moment, his instincts raising red flags at every chance. Raeza and his last soldier followed close behind.

He looked to the other side of the chamber and saw similar doors to the one he had traveled through and realized that there must have been half a dozen paths that led to the sword's resting place. As the captain continued toward that altar with slow, careful footsteps, he took another look at the corpses and the wounds too large and circular for a spear or a sword to have made. The edges of the injuries appeared charred on the surface, as if something had burrowed into them with extreme heat. Additionally, each of the dead bandits held the wound in the same place.

"They all died the same way," he said. "Facing ... the altar...."

Caedus halted again, keeping a firm hold of the pulse atop the cone-shaped pedestal in sight. The blurred mass of energy gushing up and surrounding the sword puzzled him, and a low, booming sound came from deep in the ground lasting several seconds.

"Lett signiros ti sont! Moonsla ozdi zo densla gad! (The sword ... I ... it!)" Osinian said, getting closer.

The concentrated energy shifted in the shadow's direction.

"Wait!" Caedus shouted.

The warning failed, however, as a bright, fiery beam of light shot from the altar and vaporized Osinian, scattering black mist across the room. Caedus's heart rose to his throat, a feeling he'd grown rather tired of. He froze as the swirling essence turned its attention to his party members.

Another loud hum buzzed, the light brightened, and Caedus feared it had selected its next target. He jumped from his stance toward the nearest cover and high-stepped over the bandit's bodies. Grabbing Raeza's hand on the way, he stumbled as she tripped from the frantic movements. The swarm of light released another bolt of hellfire just after Caedus yanked on her arm to pull her from death's grasp. Like a missile, the ray screeched toward her heart in the blink of an eye. It fired again and the captain turned his horrified gaze to see his last remaining soldier standing with hands twitching at the hollow, singed hole in his chest. The man dropped to the floor a second later.

Caedus staggered at his soldier's demise for a moment, but he picked Raeza off the floor, carried her behind a low stone wall, and crashed to the floor with her on his lap. She cried softly in his arms and quivered with fear. Though equally terrified, Caedus contained his emotions.

The ethereal being charged for another attack, and it fired at the wall. Loose dust trickled down from above as the building shook, and Caedus flinched with each strike, not knowing which one would penetrate the stone and turn his heart to ash. His resources ran dry with his soldiers claimed by the guardians of the guardian and Osinian nowhere to be found. Caedus's prayers for success ran unanswered. The sword's protector fired twice more, chipping away at the only thing standing between the captain and a swift end.

"There has to be a way around this," Caedus whispered to himself. "How did the priests pass through without turning to dust?"

A shimmering image caught his eye on the wall he faced. Another mosaic similar to the ones in the previous chamber depicted a ritual of the clerics who dwelled here. However, Caedus focused on one of them in front of the others, for a unique feature kept him intrigued. The figure held a rectangular, bright object up at the depiction of the altar; he quickly understood. He searched the area around in hope that the priests had left their gift nearby. After a few moments, Caedus stared at the decorative frame of a mirror upside down on the ground covered in debris and pebbles. Setting Raeza down beside him, he crawled over, plucked the mirror from the pile, and scooted back to the wall. A thick layer of dirt coated the glass, but he managed to clean it of the grime.

"Hmm," he said, scanning over the mirror and comparing it to the artwork on the wall.

His common sense frowned at him as a daring thought entered his brain. He ignored it, however, wiped the last bits of dust away, and held the mirror out. Shortly after, the guardian sent a hasty shot, but the powerful ray of light bounced off the old mirror like a weak punch, only causing Caedus a moment's struggle from the recoil. He pulled the shining glass back and looked for a massive hole like that in his soldier's chest.

"Incredible," he said, rubbing the unscathed smooth surface.

The daring thought evolved to insanity as he held a tight grip on the frame with a hand on each side.

"What on earth are you doing?" Raeza asked.

"Stay here."

"You're mad! You don't stand a chance!"

Caedus glared at Raeza with disappointment. Though, he didn't completely believe in the plan either. He slid out from behind the wall regardless, keeping the mirror covering his torso and pointed toward the guardian. The sweat on his palms itched, causing the mirror to slowly slip.

The energy pool erupted once more, beaming at the captain too fast for any reaction. Standing his ground, Caedus closed his eyes and braced for impact. He staggered for a second, and the mirror shuddered in his hands. Captain Redstone took a moment to ensure his safety and glanced at the back of the mirror. The reflective glass had protected him and cast the light beam to the far stretches of the chamber. A large smile cracked on his face. Placing his right foot forward, he proceeded with caution. Another ray of death bounced off just as ineffective as the first. The captain grew confident and walked his way to the base of the stairs. As soon as he made contact with the first step, the low hum in his ears withered to a silence. He watched in awe as the energy field surrounding the altar funneled through a drain just below it. Caedus Redstone had outsmarted the gods.

"Come on," he said, calling back to Raeza.

Osinian's shade appeared in the same spot where it had dispersed, and Caedus sensed its worry as it searched around the room.

"Seems your father added a bit of security since you've been here," he said with a snarky tone.

The shadow's flat eyes stared back before he scaled the steep stairs. Once he reached the top platform, he investigated a pool of gelatinous fluid wriggling in the center of the stone pedestal. The clear jelly pulsed with shimmers emanating from the artifact inside. Unsure of what to do, Caedus reached out and touched it.

Suddenly, the blurry liquid shivered, sending waves of itself rippling out from where his finger had grazed it. A blurry, slender object appeared and moved closer to him. The viscous barrier formed an opening, and Caedus stood in fascination. Like a gift from the gods, a golden hilt bearing a large ruby in the pommel emerged. He held out his hand, and then a blade unlike any weapon he had ever seen was uncovered from its protective veil. Three razor-sharp edges of solid gold spiraled to a tip, merging with each other in the center. Caedus raised an eyebrow at the peculiar weapon, but he knew a blade of this caliber could only be the Sword of Kings.

The captain wrapped his hand around the hilt and plucked it from the aura that held it above the altar. Shifting like a sentient, fluid material, the grip fit to his hold perfectly. Caedus scoffed with a half grin and flicked it over the back of his hand.

"Light as air."

He tested the blade's tip.

"And sharp as obsidian," Caedus said as a drop of blood swelled up on the tip of his finger.

Stories about *Osirisigniros's* abilities told by Zededia and others raced through his thoughts. Hundreds of years of war and death circled the artifact in his grasp like a constant storm of sins committed by the Osirian bloodline. Its elegance matched its incredible power. As he swung the blade from side to side, however, he frowned.

"What makes you so worthy of all of this, hmm?" he said to himself. "What makes you so special?"

Osinian's shadow walked up the steps of the altar to his right. It stretched a hand toward him, and though he trusted the shade, he hesitated to release the Sword of Kings from his possession, remembering what it cost to obtain it. After a moment, Osinian pointed to his short sword instead. Confused, Caedus drew his blade and handed it to the shadow. A spectacle overwhelmed him, forcing his jaw to drop once he realized that Osinian unlocked the artifact's sly potential, morphing the Sword of Kings into a copy of his in mere seconds.

"So that's how it's been able to hide," Caedus whispered. "But how did it end up here?"

Osinian's action threw a series of questions toward him, but he tossed them aside for the sake of time. He tested the grip of the disguised Sword of Kings in one hand and his short sword in the other, unable to distinguish a difference other than the weight. Then, the ancient Osirian shifted both swords to take the appearance of *Osirisigniros*, informing him that he could disguise his own.

The time to return to his commander had arrived. Caedus sheathed his weapon and wrapped *Osirisigniros* in a cloth from his pack once he descended the stairs.

Hints of grief pressed against him from his three dead soldiers as thoughts of the voyage home sprouted. As he processed the loss, Raeza approached him.

"I'm sorry for your men, Captain Redstone," she said.

"Don't be," Caedus said, eyes on the corpse in black armor. "They did their job."

"Now what do we do?" Raeza said, Osinian approaching.

He looked into his soldiers' lifeless eyes on the floor once more and mourned. Each death under his command chipped away at his resilience, but Caedus understood the consequences of the path set before him better than any other. The captain sighed. Raeza reached out to hold his fingers, and he faced the situation with his chin high.

"Now," Caedus said, "we go home."

Chapter 18
Welcome Home, Zededia

Day 20 in the Month of Snow

Steel chains weighed heavily on the Black Prince's hands and dragged them to the earth where his sullen gaze remained. His tattered cape fluttered through the gusts of wind as shadows of the white walls of Vaedor Sellos blotted out the sun. Defeat spiraled through him, dissolving any desire to resist the hell that awaited within the city. His body ached, bones and muscles shivering in the cold.

"Call forth to the gatekeepers!" Zededia heard from Commander Nysis in front of him. "Inform His Majesty, King Matticus!"

Zededia gnawed on the cloth wrapped around his mouth, and his weary eyes transformed to bitter pools of hatred. He looked at Commander Nysis, the man he once saw as an ally, a brother, and nearly chewed straight through the fabric between his grinding teeth. Nysis twisted his head around with a devilish smile.

"Tell him ... the Black Prince has come home."

Struggling to control the thoughts racing through him, he became numb from the memories of Nysis as his most beloved friend. For four years, he had mourned his death and sworn to guard Nyalis as the boy's interim father. The torment of his apprentice's death stung even more.

Zededia winced at the sound of the city's gates opening to a crowd of cheering Vaedorians. The icy slush under his boots shifted to weathered cobblestone. When his toes dug into the rock, his mind surged back to the agonizing reminder of his exile. He hadn't touched Vaedor Sellos's roads since that night.

Shouts from the gathered ocean of civilians forced his bloodshot eyes to look ahead. Zededia knew humiliation. He knew the sensation of shame. The lashes from his father after the annihilation of Konkour traumatized his image of the courtyard behind the outer walls. Matticus's sneering face haunted his eyelids as he resealed them;

he knew his brother lurked somewhere nearby. The coolness from the shadows vanished, unleashing the sun's scorching light onto the pavement and into his hooded face.

"Traitor!" he heard from the crowd. "Fiend!"

Slurs crashed into him like boulders, but the Black Prince shielded himself with a tense chest and tight shoulders.

"Death to the snake!"

Zededia grinned after hearing his nickname from the common folk. He waited for the column of soldiers to disperse for his brother, who assuredly would make an appearance for his long-awaited return. The prince looked to the fabled statue of his father that centered the courtyard. The lifeless marble eyes cast a solemn glare.

Eventually, his captors brought him to the square arena that stood between the rest of the courtyard and the city behind. In the impression of the arena floor, he strengthened his defensive front and channeled his will to endure the day.

Zededia fell to his knees when Nysis dismounted and yanked on the chain. Vaedorian soldiers rushed toward him from every direction and stripped him of his armor along with his cape.

"Theatrics won't aid your status," the prince said with a muffled voice from the gag, "nor does it prove your worth."

He met eyes with Nysis and received a dull stare.

"That's all your presence brings, Zededia," Nysis said. "Theatrics."

Zededia softly chuckled. Nysis yanked the chains once more, ushering the prince toward the center of the column-lined arena.

"Matticus will want to see you before we throw you into the darkest pit we can find," the Vaedorian commander said.

The prince's tired arms flew above his head after Nysis threw the chains over a hook at the top of a tall wooden post. He faced the pole and rested his forehead on the rough texture. Hardly able to hold himself upright, Zededia trembled from exhaustion. While he wanted to fall to the ground, the shackles around his wrists gave little slack. The shouts from the crowd faded in his ears after concentrating to tune them out.

Several minutes passed, and Zededia felt a presence among the crowd that cooked his Osirian blood.

"Make way for the king!" a Vaedorian knight said. "His Majesty arrives!"

"Finally," the Black Prince said, complaining in near gibberish.

Zededia summoned his strength and hoisted himself up from the slouched position. He turned his head toward the people on the street side and watched a battalion of heavily armed soldiers with white plumed helmets clear a path. Clenching his teeth, he gripped the chains as the mighty King Matticus emerged from the protection of his bodyguards. His brother's angered face sparked a flame in his heart, but he controlled it and stored it away to use later. The shining white-silver armor Matticus wore gleamed with disgust.

Against the deafening shouts, Zededia heard his brother's footsteps descend the small staircase to his level. The red glow under his skin coursed throughout his face. Matticus stopped behind him, and the Black Prince cast his defiant personality with a smirk.

"It's about damn time," he sharply said through the cloth. "What's the matter, Matticus? Hesitant to see me after four years?"

"Silence, devil," the king said. "Your silver tongue is powerless here."

"Come to give me a proper welcome?"

Matticus walked over to him, and the king's heavy breath from flared nostrils wet the side of his face. Zededia looked around his arm and glared.

"I will show you a hell not even you are capable of imagining."

"Don't make promises you can't keep, dear brother," he said, chuckling through his staggered breaths.

The cloth began to tear from his dampened gnawing.

"Can you at least let me address you properly?"

His brother stepped forward with a scowl in his side glance and Zededia noticed how the king kept a hand on his father's sword. From Zededia's blood-encrusted finger, Matticus removed the ring that he had destroyed from his extensive use of magic on the snow-covered fields. He opened his mouth to let Matticus remove the cloth. The king aggressively tore it off.

"That's more like it," Zededia said, continuing to flaunt. "And here I thought you didn't miss my silver tongue."

He started to smile but flinched as Matticus swiftly seized his jaw, nearly chipping his teeth. The Black Prince soured his expression and struggled against his brother's immense strength, his enraged eyes beaming at Matticus. Zededia heaved against the tight chains as his brother leaned closer.

"The only thing I missed," Matticus said with a growl, "were opportunities to rip your skull from your shoulders."

Zededia's chest pounded with adrenaline pumping anger to every corner of his body. Matticus released him, and he shifted his jaw around to regain feeling. Zededia's dark nature stepped forth after his smile faded.

"Behold your enemy, citizens of Vaedor Sellos!" Matticus shouted at the top of his lungs. "Behold the evil of this world in the chains of your valiant heroes!"

Watching his brother parade around the arena like a beast tamer, Zededia's urge to break free peaked. Even if he managed to escape his bonds, however, he knew he couldn't face Matticus in his current condition. Dozens of duels with his brother in their past had always ended in a draw, and he had needed every ounce of his power just to reach a stalemate. Though the temptation barked at him, Zededia remembered his mission to occupy the Vaedorians until Caedus's return.

"No more shall the Black Snake hide in the shadows!" the king yelled. "No more will Hostellus fear this parasite!"

His brother turned back, and Zededia bolstered himself for the punishment to come. He stared at the king's fist. Matticus's armored feet marched closer as the prince tried to hold himself away from the post.

Without any means to defend himself, Zededia fell victim to the gut-wrenching bash from Matticus's steel fist. He groaned and coughed, his ribcage rattling like a bull had charged straight into him. Before he could raise his head to meet Matticus's glowing eyes, the king threw a haymaker across the left side of his face, hurling him off his balance.

A taste of copper covered his tongue, and he gathered some behind his teeth. As Matticus reared back for another blow, Zededia leaned forward and sprayed him with a mist of blood and spit. The prince burst into laughter as Matticus wiped his face. His act of defiance managed to quiet the crowd, enabling his hysterical cries to echo against the columns of the arena.

"Come on, Matticus!" Zededia shouted with a psychotic smile. "You can do better than that!"

Zededia's taunt triggered a subdued rage in the king as his brother launched an assault of punches at his torso and face. The prince tried his best to shield himself against Matticus's armored blows, but his low energy drained to zero as his ribs cracked. He struggled to see through the red haze that blurred his vision. The skin under his tattered tunic bruised a dark purple and his legs failed underneath him. A high-pitched ring flooded the prince's ears as he hung from the chains like a hooked carcass. Consciousness fading, Zededia hardly sensed Matticus kneeling to his level.

"Now the world will see you for what you really are," the king said as he gripped Zededia's short hair and held his head up. "Broken. Empty. Vile."

Zededia allowed his chin to slam into his chest after Matticus let go. The blood in his throat clogged the airflow, dampening his breaths into a wheeze.

"Drag him to the Felling Pit," he heard his brother announce against the muffled shouts of the public. "Toss him in. Let him rot."

Though Zededia couldn't stand on his own two feet, he smiled internally at Matticus's decision to hold him a while longer rather than execute him right away. Though he anticipated Caedus's arrival with *Osirisigniros* in a matter of days, he prayed to whoever listened that relief came soon.

"Your greed will lead to ruin, Matticus," Zededia muttered through his bleeding lips. "You'll never see the sword as long as I'm alive."

His brother stopped in his footsteps and turned around, falling for Zededia's lure. The prince flinched as Matticus wrapped a metal hand around his neck.

"Luckily for me, that won't be much longer. You will die a disgrace to the Osirian name. A reminder of Father's failures, void of any purpose or worth."

Zededia deflected his older brother's jeers with ease, resorting to the countless times Matticus had tried to puncture his mental toughness. The king's words waned in comparison to the beating he had endured that left his body screeching for mercy. As he swayed back and forth, he raised his head to the roaring crowd. Familiar faces sneered at him. One caught his eye with a face hiding under a blue hood.

Matticus walked away and the soldiers guarding Zededia departed as well. The hooded figure approached from the parade of people following the king's wake and stood with his back turned to him.

"After all this time apart, I thought we'd meet on better terms," the man said.

"Lucien..." Zededia said between breaths, "listen ... to me."

Zededia pulled his strength together to open his lungs enough to speak. Two guards unhooked the chains the held him upright, allowing him to crash to the ground. Zededia leaned up and lunged his arms over Lucien's broad shoulders once his brother took a knee. He turned his head inward.

"Find ... my ring ..." the Black Prince whispered.

Though he wished to reconnect with his dearest brother, Zededia knew that Lucien might be his only chance to make it out of Vaedor Sellos alive if he couldn't contact any of his hidden agents. Rekindling the bond between them would have to wait.

"Find it," he whispered once more.

The guards heaved on the chains to yank him back. They dragged him across the ground toward the street that led to the keep on the hill ahead. As he slid and scraped his shoulder blades on the stony ground, Zededia looked back to his hooded brother in the scattering mass of people, forced to place all his trust within him.

~ ~ ~

Lucien stood amid the ensemble that escorted his captured brother to the dungeon in the inner sector of the city. He kept his hood firm over his head and tightened his cloak around his arms. Though the guards looked at him for a moment before Zededia's departure, the prince concealed his identity with ease and turned away. A hurricane of questions rattled in his mind.

"Not how I thought our reintroduction would play out," he whispered to himself. "How the hell does he think I can help him find his ring if it isn't already on his finger?"

Unsure of his next move, Lucien meshed with the commoners to seek counsel elsewhere. He followed the path of Matticus's entourage up the main street of the city and maintained a steady distance from any high-ranking officials. Thancred might know what to do. The prince veered off into a side street once he traveled near the Merchant's District where he and the old doctor frequently met.

The tall, connected buildings gave him the perfect chance to slip away and lose himself. Most of the workers of the area had taken a hiatus from their crafts to celebrate the king's victory over their sworn enemy, leaving him in solitude for much of his journey to Thancred's office in the lower city. Though his friend spent most of his time in the upper ring, he elected to search the city from the ground up.

Lucien rounded a corner in a lesser traveled section of the Merchant's District that cut a quicker path to his destination, but when he started to make his way down the shaded alley, a suspicious looking figure dressed in a cloak quite like his leaned against the wall about halfway down. The prince stopped for a moment until the man peered his hooded head at him from afar. An eerie chill shivered through him, so he shifted course and turned around. Another cloaked man appeared in the entrance to the alley, cutting him off. Lucien then understood this was no random encounter; they knew who he was. A third hooded figure stepped out next to the one in front of him in much shorter stature.

"Forgive us, Your Highness," the man said, "but you'll be coming with us."

"And if I say no?"

"I'm afraid we must insist."

The strange men presented no immediate threat, but he didn't like the idea of being ushered around like a foreigner. Lucien surrendered, though, and paced forward to follow. As he neared, he caught a glimpse of one of the emblems on their inner shirt and recognized it as a mark of the Black Legion. Zededia's agents had sought him out for some reason, raising Lucien's curiosity.

They escorted him through the city and a series of back alleys until he saw an unmarked door in the side of a random building. The Black Legion spies stood in a triangle around him in front of the door, and the front man knocked in a particular rhythm. A slot at eye level slid open.

"Midnight callsign," the doorman said.

"Star. Marble. Zero. Sword. Marker."

A second later, a metal thud sounded from behind the dense wood. Lucien glanced down a dimly lit hall as the iron hinges swung open. The spy on his right pressed a firm hand on his back, pushing him inside. Ducking his head to clear the low corridor, the prince arrived at the backroom of a tavern, one he didn't recognize despite his frequent trips to the bars of the lower city. He walked in, noticed an elderly woman sitting a small round table, and removed his hood.

"Ah, welcome, young prince," she said, lighting the burnt wick of a candle below her. "Thank you for accepting my invitation."

"You didn't exactly give me a choice," Lucien said.

"Dire times require a bit more ... coercion ... than usual. Today is no exception."

Lucien squinted.

"What need do you have of me?" he said. "It's quite risky to lure an Osirian to a dark room in unfamiliar surroundings."

The old woman started to chuckle.

"Oh, all three of you have that same streak of arrogance," she said. "Your mother tried to wash that out of you for years."

More questions flooded the prince's thoughts.

"So ... you knew our mother as well?" he asked, taking a seat across from the woman. "Who are you?"

"That's right, my dear. My name is Eudoria. I was one of the queen's handmaidens. Helped raise all three of you boys at some point or another."

Lucien faltered for a moment, another layer of his past unveiling itself to him for the first time.

"But, my prince," the woman said with a calm respect, "we haven't the time to discuss Her Majesty, do we?"

Lucien nodded in slight disappointment.

"Right," he said. "Zededia is being hauled to a dungeon deep underground. I'll assume you and your associates, whoever you are, are planning to free him somehow? And you need my help?"

"We aren't going to free the grandmaster from anything, Prince Lucien," the woman said.

Astonished at her reply, he stiffened his shoulders and frowned.

"But ... Matticus will torture him. He's planning an execution as we speak. How are we to sit here and let that happen?" he said, confused.

The stale air grew silent as the woman leaned forward, sending Lucien a stern set of eyes. He looked for an explanation in each of the guards' expressions, but their white helmets acting as disguises in Matticus's army concealed their faces.

"My prince, I admire your steadfastness to act on Zededia's behalf. Matias would be proud," Eudoria said. "But your brother will be fine."

Lucien crossed his arms.

"So why am I here?"

Two of the guards standing in the shadows behind the woman stepped forward. One of them placed a silver pendant on the table covered in dried blood.

"It seems you took Baeno's rash advice to heart," the woman said.

The prince stared at the emblem of the eagle he last saw hanging from the Hostellian Spymaster's neck.

"So, it was you who moved his body? Matticus seems to think he's simply gone missing."

"Yes, and you're welcome for doing so. If we hadn't happened to be on the watch for the Spymaster ourselves, his murder would have been discovered. However, regardless of the mess you made, I must thank you for eliminating him."

"Rachtus was a problem for you, then?" he asked.

"The Spymaster made life quite … difficult for us. Now that he's gone, we will be able to aid you much more efficiently with your problem."

A frown appeared in the prince's eyebrows.

"What problem?"

The woman waved a finger and beckoned the other guard behind her.

"We saw you talking to Zededia," the man said. "What did he say to you? What did he ask of you?"

The prince hesitated, still puzzled by his brother's request.

"We were not able to have an exchange with the grandmaster," Eudoria said. "But you were. He needs something, and he asked you to do it for him, didn't he? From the look on your face, it's not a task easily done."

Dancing around the top of the candle, the orange flame on the table flickered across Lucien's face. He lowered his gaze in deep thought.

"Zededia asked me … for his ring?" he said. "But that doesn't make much sense."

"Why?" the woman asked.

"Well," Lucien said, "at first I thought he was talking about the ring that Matticus pried from his finger, but when I looked at it after he threw it to the ground, it was destroyed, nearly cracked down the middle."

Lucien studied the concentrated look on the woman's face as she processed the information he had given her.

"He means his second ring," she said.

"Second ring? I wasn't aware he had a second ring. In fact, I seem to remember my father forbidding the use of multiple rings."

"Your brother kept one in secret," Eudoria said with a sigh, "in case he ever needed it to channel greater powers."

"What?" Lucien said. "What powers?"

"Powers no man should ever possess."

Eudoria sent his wonder to a dead end. Trying to piece together the rapidly evolving events between his brothers, the prince lightly shook his head.

"All right, well, where is this ring? How do I get it?"

"Let us worry about the grandmaster's ring, my dear," Eudoria said. "You just be ready to give it to him."

"Give it to him?" Lucien said. "How in the world can you expect me to reach Zededia once he's locked away in the most secure prison in all of Hostellus?"

The woman gave him a sly smile.

"Because," she said, "we're going to sneak you in."

~ ~ ~

Zededia cast his weary, defeated eyes upon the keep he had grown up in as a column of soldiers escorted him across the courtyard. The entrance to the underground dungeon lay behind embedded in the mountain, and the gleaming glass windows of his former home twinkled in the sunlight. A tear rested on the roots of his eyelash as he stared, agonizing memories of his childhood lighting his mind ablaze. His bleeding heart fell into a void, and the frigid wind frosted the edges of his ears.

Eventually, the Vaedorians dragged him around to the clearing to the left of the keep. The prince kept his vision low to the ground, dreading a painstaking sight that he only visited in his dreams. Zededia lowered his head to hide, but reflections of yellow and purple shined through his slowed eyelids. Fresh, sweet scents filled his nose. The prince opened his eyes after a moment, the temptation of the agony calling him to look.

Even in the peak of winter, the Vaedorian Gardens bloomed brightly with colorful tulips. Zededia restrained his torment. With the memory of his mother so closely attached to the gardens, he damned their beauty. The stone pavilion that centered the grounds hadn't changed at all. He stared at the path leading into it, picturing the late Queen Niike carrying him inside just like the vision he saw while exploring the planes of Elysia on his journey to find Osinian.

The pooling tears spilled over and streamed down his cheek. He had forced all notions of his past into the bottle submerged deep in his heart, but seeing the source of his anguish once again foiled his efforts. Reminders of his exile, his loss, and his failures lingered in the rows of immaculate flowers like needles against his skin.

Usually a man of words and wisdom, the Black Prince walked in silence until Commander Nysis stopped the convoy outside the edge of the mountain. Zededia sighed and steeled himself, for he knew of what lay in store in the dungeon. After aiding his father in the construction of the prison he named the Felling Pits, the sour irony of his current situation blistered his tongue. The cruel, torturing design of the winding cave awaited its creator.

"Torches," Nysis said as he struggled to dismount his horse, wounded from the beating he took earlier in the day.

Zededia sealed his eyes shut once more, taking every chance to prepare for the hell beneath his feet. Two soldiers grabbed his arms and heaved him toward the iron gate ahead. Standing at the entrance, with several Vaedorians surrounding him, he eyed their swords drawn and ready to strike at the first sign of resistance. A lone set of footsteps sounded off to his left. He traced the heavy armor up Nysis's body and eerily twisted his head to glare.

"I suppose your surprise might be well placed," Nysis said, holding his broken arm in a sling. "Almost four years since you left me at the gates and fled to the forest."

The Black Prince shuddered with a mixture of anger and self-hatred, reliving the night of his exile in his mind as if it happened yesterday. Flickers of the chaos sparked across his eyes, and the faces of his dead followers on the cobblestone streets of his father's city haunted him.

"Why, Nysis?" Zededia said chokingly. "After years ... of friendship ... and service...."

His eyes watered more with a blink.

"Why align yourself with Matticus?"

"As much as I would enjoy reminiscing about the past, I would much rather see you thrown to the misery you brought to Hostellus, my home."

Zededia's knees vibrated, his feet numb from the long march to the inner city. He wriggled his fingers across his damp palms.

"Take him inside," Commander Nysis said with a groan of discomfort. "No food. No water. No contact."

The wicked metal doors to the prison below mocked the prince, seeing hundreds of his father's enemies over the years. A clang sounded off from the dense lock outside, and the jawless skull insignia carved into the steel stretched toward him, splitting in the center to reveal the blackness within. Zededia's resilience bolstered, summoning all the strength of his spirit to endure imprisonment. A sharp pain in his lower back forced him to wince as one of the Vaedorians jabbed him with the hilt of a sword to shove him forward.

He stepped onto the wooden platform held over a deep chasm held by a series of ropes and turned to face his captor. Two guards stood on each side with dim torches in their hands. The sway sickened him. Nysis stood in the doorway, and the Black Prince looked up at the shadowed silhouette in the blazing sun. A jolt released the holding mechanism from underneath the wooden floor, slowly lowering him into the mountain. As he descended, he kept his fiery gaze latched on to Nysis.

"Welcome home, Zededia," the Vaedorian commander said in a deep voice. "Enjoy damnation."

The depth of the cave consumed his view. His composure melted at the seams. Trapped inside the most infamous dungeon in all Osiria, Zededia remained isolated from any allies, any aid, and any hope.

Chapter 19

Reunion

Day 24 in the Month of Snow

Three days after Matticus's soldiers imprisoned the Black Prince in the Felling Pits, Lucien leaned himself against the outer wall on the second story of the keep. Facing the entrance to the prison in the mountain, he held his pipe to his mouth, casually inhaling the bitter fumes of burning tobacco. Thancred sat on a marble bench to his left, just inside his peripheral vision. His friend's presence had eased his nerves over the last few days. Forced to wait for the signal from the agents of the Black Legion, Lucien convinced himself to remain calm. Livia had become more frantic as well, begging him to do something. He kept himself at bay, though, waiting for the right moment to make a move.

The prince fixated his eyes on the skull on the metal doors, endlessly filing through every possible method to gain access to his brother. Each route met a dead end, resulting in detection and worse. Lucien tightened his lips out of mild frustration.

"I don't think there's a way in, Thancred," he muttered in defeat. "A dozen armed guards surely lie between us and Zededia, and there's only one way in."

He heard Thancred inhale another puff of smoke. Silence followed.

"Do you have any ideas?" he asked with a raised eyebrow.

"Patience, my prince," the old medic said.

Lucien scoffed to himself.

"And how is patience going to help us when he's sitting under our feet in a cage?"

"Baeno will be here soon," Thancred said. "He'll have a way."

Without any other option, Lucien sighed.

"Livia will want to see him," he said, changing the subject. "She came to me a week ago, longing for some sort of connection to him."

"Then you had better find Her Majesty before we enter the darkness of the Felling Pits. We may only have one chance."

Lucien looked at Thancred.

"What is Baeno planning?"

He drew a lungful of smoke.

"We'll know soon enough. You just need to be sure to play your part and avoid getting caught."

"Easier said than done."

The metal gates screeched open below, catching Lucien's attention enough to pull him away from the wall. He noticed three figures approaching the gate captain with a citizen in chains. Their conversation bounced off his ears, but he understood the general topic. The guards ushered the enslaved man into the cave behind the gates, and they closed them as quickly as they opened.

"That's our way in," Thancred said softly.

Lucien turned with a bewildered expression.

"As prisoners?" he asked through a whisper. "Are you mad? Who's going to escort us? How are we going to get out?"

"The same way you went in. Baeno will take you down into the cave, and you can traverse from there. The only guards on post are at the top; moving amongst the inside of the dungeon is the easy part."

"Baeno agreed to this?" Lucien asked.

"Eudoria didn't give him a choice."

Lucien hunched over the guardrail of the walkway and interlocked his fingers around his pipe. The name Thancred mentioned fluttered through his thoughts.

"Wait a moment," he said, connecting the dots. "That's who I spoke to earlier, isn't it?"

"I don't know who you spoke to, my prince," Thancred said.

Lucien caught a faint smile from his friend that told a different story. He decided to let it rest despite the urge to pry. The dungeon gate jarred his nerves when he cast his eyes on it once more.

"Have you ever been inside, Thancred?" Lucien asked.

"Fortunately not," the doctor said. "I only remember the traumatized miners who returned from the wretched depths of those caves."

"Father told us never to go down there when we were young. I never knew why."

Lucien reminisced upon the time when both of his older brothers attempted to sneak into the mines when he was eight years old, roughly fifteen years ago.

"Zed and Matticus followed a crew in one day before any thought was given to convert it to a prison."

"Ah, yes," Thancred said between puffs of his pipe. "I will never forget that. Your father nearly tore their backs to pieces when they returned."

The prince chuckled, feeling a twisted sense of pride in the fear that had saved him from punishment.

"Oh, how they tried to lure me inside. To scare me, no doubt."

As the happier memories of his family surfaced, his heart sank.

"I do miss those times, though," he whispered to himself. "Life felt so ... simple."

"Life for young princes is meant to be simple, Lucien," he heard over his shoulder.

He tightened his lips and released the warm air from his lungs through his nose.

"Times have changed, though. What I wouldn't give for the three of us to be together again."

Just as Lucien thought over what his life might have been like in different circumstances, a pair of footsteps approached from around the corner. He pivoted to meet them with his left hand resting on the hilt of his sword.

"We don't have much time, Thancred," the first man said.

Lucien recognized the voice and small stature to be his brother's runner, Baeno. The larger man behind stared at him, sending a wave of caution across the prince's skin.

"It's Teodrid, my prince, the runner you met under the city. You needn't worry."

"Why haven't we much time, Baeno," Thancred said.

"Matticus has planned Zededia's execution for tomorrow morning," the runner said. "Whatever we're going to do, we need to do it now."

The thought of his brother's death nauseated Lucien.

"So, where do we go from here?" the prince asked urgently.

A pause broke out between the men as Lucien looked around.

"Teodrid will act as the guard change to come slightly ahead of schedule," the smaller man said. "Lucien, you will enter with me to find Commander Zededia so that I can give him this."

Baeno held out a darkened ring with a bright red gemstone. While he wondered where the runner had found Zededia's secret secondary ring, Lucien knew he lacked the time for a proper walkthrough.

"And where will you be?" the prince asked Thancred.

"Right where I am, watching the entrance to make sure no one goes in while you're looking for Zededia."

"You think you can prevent anyone from entering? You're a healer, not a soldier."

On a rare occasion during his friendship with the old man, Lucien caught a glimpse of uncertainty between two gray eyebrows.

"Worry about yourself, my prince. We need to act while we have time."

Lucien curled his lips inward from stress.

"I need to find the queen. She should be close by in the keep."

"Be quick about it," Thancred said. "Baeno will wait for your arrival to move toward the gate."

"Change your clothes, Your Highness," the runner said. "Put these on. The queen should do the same."

Baeno tossed him a raggedy shirt and pair of pants.

"You'll make a fine prisoner yet."

~ ~ ~

A few minutes later, Lucien wound his way to the fifth floor of the keep where his brothers' chambers lay. At the end of the hall, Zededia's old room caught his eye for the first time since the Black Prince's exile. The empty chamber stuck out in his view more than normal now that Zededia lingered in the city. Lucien wrapped his fingers across the metal handrail and focused on the cracked door of the king's bedchamber to his left where a glimmer of light from the stained-glass windows colored the hall.

He pressed the back of his hand against the treated wood and sent a creak echoing under the jovial conversations. Queen Livia looked up to him with a genuine smile, holding Ender in her arms while Mattox sat beside her. Tempted not to disturb the peace, Lucien hesitated. He knew taking her to Zededia would sacrifice her immediate joy for closure that would hurt worse than she imagined. With a comforting smile, the prince remained in the doorway to hide.

Livia stood from the floor and handed Ender over to one of the girls at her side. Lucien admired the family life for a moment as he watched her kiss Mattox on the cheek before walking toward the exit. The prince stepped back, and Queen Livia shut the door behind her.

"You're going to see him, aren't you?"

Livia's shift in attitude caught him off guard, but he knew that type of change from how his father did the same in his youth to spare him from the harsher aspects of life in the castle.

"Yes," he said. "I've come to see if you would like to accompany me."

"I've been waiting for you to say that for three days now. I'm worried sick about him."

Lucien grinned.

"We don't have much time, but we can take you down."

"We?" Livia asked.

"It's quite difficult to explain, my queen," Lucien said, trying to figure out how to inform her of the plan. "You had better just let me worry about it. Oh, and you'll need to dress more ... peasanty. If you can manage."

Livia cast him a puzzled look.

"If you insist," she said with an annoyed look. "Take this."

She handed him a bundled wrap. Feeling it around, he felt a strangely soft object in the cloth.

"Don't squish it," she said, turning away to change her attire.

"The hell is this?"

"Bread," she said. "And water. For Zededia."

"Hmm. All right, I'll wait here for you."

After allowing the queen her moment of privacy, she rejoined him in the hall of the keep. Lucien then led her down to the balcony where Thancred said he would stand watch. He stuck his head out of the archway onto the patio and made sure no one had seen him. After the doctor gave the all clear, the prince made his way to meet him.

"Are you ready, Your Grace?" Thancred asked. "Will you manage?"

"I am," Livia said. "Lucien will protect me."

Thancred brought forth a set of chains.

"Here," he said. "Put these on. I know shackles have no place on members of the royal family, but we must do everything we can to sell your disguises."

Lucien nodded. Outfitted just like a prisoner, he waited. Baeno approached from the keep in a guard's armor.

"Slight change of plans," the runner said.

Lucien raised his eyebrows, already on edge from the task at hand.

"The prison guard schedule shows that two guards are supposed to relieve the captain already stationed outside the gates. Matticus seems to have doubled the security given the new prisoner.

"Where are we going to find another guard willing to aid us at this time?" the prince lightly shouted.

"I don't know," Baeno said. "You're going to have to traverse through the Felling Pits without me. I'm needed to stand watch with Teodrid outside."

The prince blinked and widened his eyes.

"Well, all right, then," he said. "If we have no other choice."

"You'll be fine once we get inside. I'll lower you down to the dungeon, and I'll pull you back out once you've met with the grandmaster."

Lucien held a firm hold of Zededia's ring in the pocket of his tunic and looked at Livia.

"Okay," Baeno said. "Let's go."

The runner dressed as a Vaedorian soldier escorted him and the queen off the balcony and across the grounds behind the keep. The day's fading light aided their secrecy, and Lucien dropped his head to hide his face from the guard standing in front of the thick metal gates. Teodrid had already reached the dungeon entrance, adding to Lucien's anxiety. The fear of something going wrong caused him to nervously perspire. Baeno stepped forward once they approached.

"Took you bloody long enough," the real guard said. "I've got better things to do."

"Oh, sod off," Baeno said from under his helmet. "More prisoners means more coin in your pockets. You'll be fine."

The Vaedorian grunted and walked off, Lucien keeping a side eye on him as he did. The four of them stood alone, and the prince raised his head, wiped the cold sweat from his forehead, and took a deep breath.

"Easy enough," Baeno said.

"I suppose," the prince said.

Teodrid unlatched the lock as Lucien allowed the queen to go ahead of him. Still as creepy as it was fifteen years ago, the skull carved in the metal doors glared at him like it knew of his scheme. The blackness of the Felling Pits daunted him after Zededia's spies revealed the endless cave system inside.

"Head inside," Teodrid said through the rounded steel helmet that only revealed his eyes. "We'll stay here and await your return."

"One second," Baeno said, grabbing a key from the loop on his belt.

Lucien held out his hands and allowed the runner to unchain him after the queen.

"That should be better," Baeno said. "Be quick if you can, Prince Lucien. I've got an eerie feeling that Matticus will send another round of guards unexpectedly. Or worse, he'll appear himself."

Understanding the situation, Lucien took Queen Livia's hand to guide her into the prison.

Steam rose from natural air vents in the rock that hovered over the natural river within the cave, and the prince studied the cracked, chipped cave walls where miners had gathered iron ore from the mountain's vault of plenty. As he glanced back at the guards in disguise, Lucien took one last look at the outside world for the time being.

"Take care of that ring," Baeno said. "Zededia's survival depends on it."

Lucien nodded, and the queen's hold on his hand tightened. The creaky platform lowered into the old mine, and the light faded as Lucien's allies sealed the gates. He quickly encountered the terror that the caves sprouted in their inhabitants and why Zededia had chosen to convert such a place into a dungeon. Pitch black darkness suffocated his view and a pungent musk of damp earth filled his nostrils. Dripping water turned to explosions in the harrowing silence of the descent.

"Lucien?" the queen whispered.

"Yes?"

"You've been down here before, haven't you? You know what to expect?"

The prince's eyes darted back and forth, clinging to dancing shadows against the jagged walls of the shaft.

"I'm afraid not, my queen," he said. "Father forbade the three of us to enter, now I see why. Although, I fear we've yet to see the worst by far. Zededia's imagination tends to linger in the ... darker ... places of this world."

The hair on Lucien's neck stood straight up as panic set in. A mixture of claustrophobia and uncertainty swept over him. Below, demonic cries that sounded like tortured souls burning alive clawed at his eardrums. Lucien shivered and blinked rapidly. Though unsure of what lay under his feet, he remembered stories that passed from the miners to the keep's guards and recalled the insanity-inducing air passages that chanted symphonies of sorrow every time a breeze blew through. Lucien couldn't distinguish the rushing wind from shrieks of men.

"What madness has been under us all this time?" Lucien whispered.

The wooden platform clanked against the bottom of the cave, tossing him off balance. He maintained his grip on the queen's hand despite falling to his knee. When he stood, a faint lantern flickered in the distance.

"I guess that's where we are supposed to go," Lucien said, his eyes wide open to absorb as much light as he could.

The dripping water increased in intensity, and the prince stretched out his hand to run his fingers across the rough, damp rock wall. He traced the gritty stone to guide him along the natural tunnel. The orange flame neared, revealing his bright irises expanding like tiny, green galaxies.

At the mouth of the tunnel, he realized it opened into a massive crater. Lucien halted in the archway and scanned the chamber, eyeing the holes in the jagged ceiling that revealed several rays from the sun above ground. He looked down and saw a series of carved ramps circling the inside of the crater. Cages and iron bars lined the craggy path.

"This is where they keep them, the prisoners," Lucien said. "Zededia must be in here somewhere."

He searched for other lights where Vaedorian soldiers stood at their posts, but none came into view. A gust of wind whistled through the holes in the cave and echoed through the chamber. The air howled, mimicking the horrific cries he heard earlier, and he staggered from the knives stabbing at his ears. Several moans of agony followed from the captured criminals below as the wind died.

"How can the earth produce such a monstrous sound?"

"Lucien," the queen said to his left.

The prince turned and squinted at Livia's dark outline.

"Yes, my queen?"

"Have you noticed the lack of security here?"

He nodded in agreement.

"This atmosphere promotes lunacy," Lucien replied, gesturing to the imprisoned men and women below. "Too much even for Hostellus's finest."

Lucien took a step toward the ramp without looking, and a skewered skeleton jumped from the shadows in his peripheral vision.

"Shit!" Lucien shouted, cursing as he stumbled.

Livia yelped as well. With a grunt, he regained his composure and frowned at the decrepit set of bones, realizing it hadn't moved at all. After standing upright, the prince proceeded down the ramp while keeping his eyes glued to the skull.

"Come on," he said. "Let's find Zededia."

~ ~ ~

After an hour of searching through the crude cells of the rocky prison, Prince Lucien approached the final holding block with Queen Livia behind him. Defeated, he walked up to the bars, grabbed them, and peered inside at the body lying on the ground.

"He isn't here," Lucien sighed, observing the older man in rags barely clinging to life.

He tightened his grip on the iron door, whitening his knuckles, and leaned his forehead on the cold metal.

"There has to be another area where they keep more prisoners, maybe more dangerous ones," Livia said.

Lucien glanced around the chamber and to the ceiling stretched three stories above his head.

"There is no other route that I can see. It just ends down here on the bottom level."

"Look deep ... beyond the archway," a hoarse voice muttered from behind the prince, startling his aggravated nerves.

He turned to face the prisoner, who'd sat himself upright and revealed a face of wrinkles and white hair. An outstretched hand missing two of its fingers pointed toward the distant wall on the other side of the dungeon. Lucien followed the path laid before him and scanned over the curved doorway blocked by a boulder.

"There?" Lucien asked. "Where does that lead?"

"I ... I don't know," the man said, struggling to speak from severe starvation. "But they brought a man down here some time ago.... He was in shackles ... and dripping with blood."

"Zededia," the prince whispered.

"Hurry, Lucien," Livia said as the prince felt a swift tug at his cape.

Before setting off, he eyed the old man once more out of pity.

"Thank you," Lucien said. "May you find a better life ... in Elysia."

He pivoted toward the door and jogged to where the man had guided. When he approached the cave wall, he traced the outline of the doorway with his hand. A large stone rested against it, and Lucien heaved on it with all the might of his young, muscular body. Despite his strength, the rock wouldn't budge.

"Seems like an adequate way to keep someone inside," Lucien said, stepping away. "There has to be a lever somewhere."

Lucien's mind raced as a bead of anxious sweat crawled down his face.

"Come on, Zed," he whispered. "Where did you put the switch?"

After a moment, Lucien's eyes sparked as they moved over a metal crank hidden behind the curvature of the wall. He yanked on the lever, sending a vibration deep in the stone. To his relief, the rock in his way sank into the floor, and another tunnel opened on the other side. He thought the cave couldn't contain any more darkness than the previous hall, but the blackness of the corridor gave a new meaning to the word.

"Further in we go," Lucien said, unsure of his decision to proceed.

He slowly explored the dark of the deeper section of the prison with a deep sense of caution.

"Further into madness, perhaps," he said under his breath.

At the end of the tunnel that stretched for what seemed like miles in the ocean of shadows, Lucien rounded a corner and gasped at the sight of a towering metal door. He stopped to analyze the skull insignia that matched the gate on the surface, guessing that this was where the most threatening personnel were kept. Another gust of wind swept through the cave, sending the haunted shrieks into the hall and scraping Lucien's skin like a blunt blade.

The prince walked over to the wooden pulley system in place in front of the gate and released the locking mechanism. Low-pitched moans squealed from the hinges, and a crack of light escaped from the gap between the two sides. In the distance, Lucien stared at a figure sitting on the ground with his head lowered to his chest.

"There he is," he whispered.

Lucien turned to Livia, who stared at her love with watery eyes.

"My queen," he said, beckoning, "perhaps it would be best to remain here until I can talk to him. I can't imagine what state of mind he's in, and I don't want his first words to you to be groggy and ill-spoken."

He sensed the pain in her gaze and hated making her wait just outside Zededia's reach. Livia understood, though, as he loosened his grip on her hand.

"You'll see him soon," Lucien said with a soft voice.

Turning to the wide-open room stretching far above his head, Lucien focused on his brother's slumped position and moved into the gateway. Though his eyes remained on Zededia, he scanned every detail and crevice of the cave wall in his peripheral vision, including the large hole in the ceiling where a sliver of light shone through like a natural spotlight. Pebbles crunched under the hardened leather soles of his boots.

"Finally coming to see me, Matticus?" Zededia said in a dark, ragged voice.

Lucien guessed that his brother mistook him for the king due to the intensely harsh conditions of the prison. He paced closer and watched Zededia lift his head from his chest, receiving a glare of death and despair. As Lucien stepped into the light, however, his brother's stern, squinted eyes melted and allowed bright blue pools to glimmer.

"Lucien?" Zededia asked, sitting up for a closer look.

The prince smiled and started to open his arms.

"It's me, brother."

After he spoke, he stopped in front of Zededia as he scrambled to his feet within the constraints of his chained wrists. Lucien couldn't help but notice his brother's staggered movements.

He spread his hands out wide and closed in for a proper embrace. Zededia fell into his chest, revealing the extreme exhaustion that plagued him. The prince wrapped his brother in his arms and squeezed, chuckling in his throat.

"Oh, how it warms my heart to see you," Zededia said in his ear. "Friends are few and far between down here."

Lucien released his hold and leaned back to meet him eye-to-eye. After nearly four years apart, his mind blanked for a greeting.

"I wish I could explain to you the misery your absence has brought me," Lucien said.

The chains around Zededia's wrists clanked against each other, drawing the prince's attention to his brother's state of being once again. Zededia rested on the edge of death, clothes torn, cuts bleeding, and bruises forming, all on top of the darkness, frost, and hunger gnawing at him from all sides.

"Seems Matticus saved the red carpet for you."

His brother scoffed with a grin.

"The sun hasn't set on me quite yet," Zededia said, retaking his seat on the cold floor. "But ... I've been given my mortal reminders. I don't have much time here, so, please, let's just ... hold off ... on catching up."

Lucien studied his brother's face and how it fell to the floor, blank and joyless. A deeper note of agony struck him. The last time he had seen his brother, Zededia had a proud smile on his face, glaring back at him in his memory on the day before his exile.

"Your eyes were once oceans, vibrant and teaming with life," Lucien said. "There's a darkness within them now."

The Black Prince opened his mouth, but Lucien heard no reply. Gusts of air whirled once more around him, and the cold musk of the cave gave him chills.

"If my eyes were the oceans that gave you hope in our youth," Zededia said after a moment, keeping a dead gaze on the distant wall, "then there is none left for you to have, dear brother."

Lucien took in the reality of Zededia's brokenness surfaced, punching Lucien in his gut. The once lively, dreaming older brother he had looked up to as a child had withered to a dying shell of a man. Cracks formed at Zededia's seams; his lifelong hero started to break. As his brother remained motionless in shackles, Lucien's throat swelled and his nose flared. To comfort his exiled sibling, Lucien took a seat next to him, touching shoulder to shoulder and looking out into the shadows.

"If only we could revisit those days, huh?" Lucien said. "Now, it seems our fate has caught up to us."

"Your fate has yet to come, brother," Zededia said. "Your life remains here in the safety of our walls."

Lucien turned his head, Zededia's depressed face staring away from him. "And yours?"

A deep sigh left his brother's body. Lucien traced the frosted breath as it dispersed into the vastness of the prison cell.

"My fate ..." The Black Prince's voice started to weaken, "... lies ... elsewhere."

Lucien witnessed a tear leaving his brother's eye as his began to dampen, nearly leaking themselves. Livia peered around the corner, but the prince shook his head. Zededia's hollowness stuck him like sharp spines.

"My torch is fading, Lucien," Zededia said, condemning himself. "There are ... so many things I wanted to show you, to teach you, but ... life decided otherwise. Perhaps if things were different, if there was no madness in the world, I could have shared more with you."

Lucien choked for words. Thoughts of his Osirian sorcery surfaced, knowing how excited Zededia might be to discover that he had finally tapped into it, but he elected not to bring it up. Not at this moment.

"There is nothing left for me here."

"There are the people who love you, Zededia," Lucien said, grasping his brother's forearm with a firm hand. "The people who need you here."

As best he could, the prince comforted Zededia's trembling hands.

"Livia has forgotten me, Lucien. I've been away from Her Grace for far too long. My presence left her years ago."

Lucien smiled, thinking of the queen eagerly waiting in the distance.

"Your brothers love you," Lucien said.

"Matticus doesn't love anything," Zededia said, chuckling. "Certainly not me."

Droplets of water leaked from above, and Lucien held out his hand to catch them.

"Is my love not worth your efforts, then?" he asked.

He heard Zededia sniff and clear his nostrils.

"Lucy," Zededia said, "you cannot heal my wounds. You cannot fix me."

Lucien stood from the cold rock and looked down at his decaying brother.

"I know," he said. "That's why I brought someone who can."

~ ~ ~

Zededia frowned at his brother's remark, curious to see who else came to visit him. His younger brother walked toward the gate, leaving him to wonder. The Black Prince stared out into the darkened archway ahead. Time stalled as his eyes washed over the flowing brown hair emerging from the shadows. He recognized those silky strands. Rising to his feet, Zededia lowered his jaw and stepped forward.

Speechless as Livia's pleasantly curved figure stepped into view, Zededia stood in shock. A tidal flood of anxiety and swirling blood rushed through his body. The prince focused on her perfect skin revealed by the gaps on the sides of her garment, almost feeling her legs in his hands once again. Two big, loving eyes rose to meet his as his breath quickened, pushing the dampness of his esophagus into his mouth.

No words formed while she walked toward him. He ignored Lucien leaning against the cave wall, but he could see him in his side view. The queen's full beauty cascaded over her soft edges covered in common rags. Zededia scanned her every detail from her beautiful, perfect nose to her lush hips, the sunlight above creating a glowing aura around her like an angel. She neared him, heightening his urge to break free from his chains to hold her. Testing the slack of his restraints, he stood a few feet away from her for a moment. His eyes watered again, but for a different reason. Four years of separation tore at his heart as the flame he had shared with Queen Livia raged once more.

"Oh, darling," Livia said softly as she lifted her clean hand to Zededia's filthy cheek. "What have they done to you?"

Zededia did all he could to resist falling to his knees. He stared into Livia's eyes, feeling the redness in his veins crawl toward his pupils. At the end of his limits, Zededia reached his hand to hers on his face and wrapped his fingers over the back of her palm. Words clogged his mouth, but none escaped.

"Why are you here?" Livia asked.

He concentrated on the tear streaming down the edge of her nose.

"I..." Zededia said. "I'm ... buying time."

"Is what you delay for worth this much misery? Locked away in the darkest part of the world? What on earth could drive you to such insanity?"

Zededia smiled and admired the queen's concern. It touched his heart and sewed a few of the bleeding cracks together.

"As Caedus always says, I long for misery and cannot live without it."

"You silly boy," Livia said with a grin. "You carry too much weight on your shoulders to be chasing misery."

Livia dropped her hands, and Zededia held them both. He leaned forward, closed his eyes, and met the queen's forehead with his own. The tender moment alleviated all his pain in an instant.

"I feared your love had long abandoned me," he said, lips lightly trembling.

She raised her head, and he opened his eyes.

"Nothing can take you from me, not even time," Livia said.

As much as he longed for the queen's embrace once more, he knew her touch would leave him soon enough. Zededia's spirit cried out. Livia's affection complicated his plans.

"Unfortunately, my love," the prince said, "time is something I'm rather poor in."

The sadness in her eyes shattered him.

"Please, Zededia," Livia begged, clutching his hand with a firmer hold, "please tell me you have a plan to escape this execution."

Zededia looked over Livia's shoulder at his brother.

"I need help from a few allies," Zededia said. "But do not worry. I always have a plan. Surely you haven't forgotten all those nights sneaking around the keep?"

The shared moments of their past evoked a light chuckle from the queen, a sound that soothed his aching ears like a potent cure for his internal afflictions. Conflicted, Zededia knew the sand in the hourglass of his campaign neared the final grains. He closed his eyes and squeezed the queen's hands.

"You needn't linger, Livia. Matticus's guards change more frequently than ever, and they will check on me soon."

As Livia nodded, he brushed his finger over her cheek. The Black Prince longed for just one more moment to caress her, but everything he had set in motion defied the idea. Zededia fought back a mild shake.

She kept a firm hold on him until he let go.

"Please, just a few more minutes."

The prince shook his head and forced himself to deny her request. He kissed her hand and released it.

"We cannot ... I'm afraid."

The sentence poisoned his tongue, taking his last strand of hope with it.

"Goodbye, my queen," he whispered in broken words. "Until our reunion."

"Take this," she said, setting a wrapped fold of cloth on the ground. "Eat it when you can."

He warred against the hell in her eyes, thankful for the loving gesture she had gone through great trouble to bring him. After placing the food at his feet, Livia turned her back, and Zededia glued his eyes to her once more, clinging to her beauty for as long as possible. A life with her soared above all other desires, but he knew the path before him forbade such happiness.

His attention shifted to Lucien approaching in the distance and turned his thoughts toward the task at hand. The Black Prince retracted his hemorrhaging emotions and stiffened his posture.

"Did you find my ring?" Zededia asked once his brother neared.

"A thank-you could be in order. Mother would hate to see her well taught manners wasted in such moments," his brother said.

"I think my current position justifies the absence of manners, Prince Lucien," he said with a sharp tongue.

He opened his palm under Lucien's fist and caught the cold metal ring. The red glare of the gem stuck out to him.

"What are you doing with two rings of sorcery?" Lucien asked.

"Nothing you should concern yourself with," he said.

"Hmph."

Zededia held the remarkable piece of jewelry for a moment longer, staring into the shining rock held in place in the middle.

"You have a plan, right?" Lucien asked. "Or have I risked my life for nothing?"

Zededia slipped the ring into the pocket of his pants as dozens of options raced through his thoughts.

"More or less," he said.

"That's not exactly convincing."

The sun's rays inside the cave dwindled as the day expired. Zededia looked to the ceiling and clenched his fists.

"Then you'll have to trust me. My end will not come through a disgraced ceremony plastering me as Hostellus's villain, I can assure you of that."

He understood Lucien's skepticism, however, and patted his shoulder.

"We will meet once more before this war is over," Zededia said. "Search for that opportunity when it presents itself to you."

Zededia turned away from his brother, fearing the expression on Lucien's face. A loud bang clamored through the prison from the gates at the surface, signaling his brother to return.

"Go," Zededia said. "You will see me tomorrow morning, but you are not to intervene with whatever Matticus has planned. Is that understood?"

A firm hand grabbed his sore shoulder.

"Fearing I'll do something to ruin your scheme?"

He twisted his head around with a half-smile.

"Exactly. Now, leave while you can."

Lucien's eyes beamed at him before he faced the cave wall. As if they were children again, the Black Prince looked after his brother and wished for nothing but his safety. Lucien departed, and Zededia trusted him to escort Livia back to the open city without any trouble. Leather footsteps rolled off the rocks and faded away.

"Keep a watchful eye, Lucien," Zededia said.

Once he heard the inner gate reseal and knew he remained alone, he sighed. The absence of company stung him once more.

He inhaled the moldy air and released it shortly after, channeling his spirit. The dark one he had resurrected called for him in the shadows.

"Traasela xensi sen kar, zot kell, (Come back to me, my friend,)" the Black Prince said.

Several moments later, a set of crimson eyes peered at Zededia aside a black cloud. The shroud wisped, bending the tiny beams of light that remained. At the cusp of his vision, Osinian stood before him, ready to act on his command.

"Por Caedus dask lett signiros? (Did Caedus find the sword?)"

"Sett. (Yes.)"

Zededia's sacrifice proved worth the reward. A different manner of smile from the one he showed to Livia and Lucien appeared between his cheeks. Each piece of his grand plot moved closer together.

"Aeleda. Nok, zoam aelosteus sen ishken zanto grazeki mensh zealadet. (Good. Now, I'm going to need your help with something.)"

Chapter 20
Smoke and Shadows

Day 25 in the Month of Snow

After the long, tiresome journey back to the Hostellian Valley, Captain Redstone spurred his horse to the edge of the crater that overlooked the Blackwood. Eyeing the white city in the distance, he squinted. Anzagaar Nostir's tallest tower rose over the tree topped hills to the right. Caedus kept a firm grip on the Sword of Kings, keeping it at an arm's length since he left the temple. Raeza rode next to him, and he faced a difficult conversation.

"Well," Caedus said, "your contract is fulfilled."

He kept his focus on the landscape.

"You are free of my service."

Raeza's disappointed glare burned the side of his cheek, but Caedus knew taking her to the center of the war between Zededia and Matticus would slow him down and bring unwanted misery to her.

"I ... am not to join?" she asked.

"I'm afraid not," the captain said. "My path ahead is one I must travel alone."

"What path is that exactly?"

A hint of regret rose in him, and he wondered if maintaining a life as a mason instead of a soldier would have led to more pleasant circumstances. He grinned.

"Your freedom awaits you, Raeza," Caedus said. "Take it. Before someone else does."

The dull air carried a windy silence in his ears.

"And what if I liked giving it to you?" Raeza asked in a sad voice. "What if I choose to stay at your side?"

Caedus picked his teeth with his tongue and surveyed the crater of Hostellus.

"There's nothing but death and decay in this land. You should find peace elsewhere."

Raeza's pause nauseated him.

"Very well," she eventually said. "If you think it's best I leave, then I will burden you no longer."

"Where will you go?" Caedus asked, still unable to meet her eyes.

His eyes fell to the forest edge and the several smoke columns ascending from his commander's camp on the Hostellian Plains.

"Back to Skulpos, I think."

"Going to sail away after all?"

"I suppose," Raeza said. "That was the original plan."

Caedus thought of half a dozen reasons never to explore the coastal kingdom that smelled of nothing but fish and piracy.

"To find a home?" he asked.

"If I'm lucky."

His heart longed to give her the protection she deserved, elevating the sickening sensation in his abdomen.

"Well, then ... may you find it beyond the reach of Osiris's descendants."

Caedus offered as a makeshift farewell.

"Will your campaign here ever end, Captain Redstone?" she asked.

The question hit a little too close to home for a reply. His mouth dropped open for a moment.

"Hopefully," he said. "One way or another."

The sun breached the mountain range and cast its orange hue across the kingdom. Caedus followed the bumpy horizon as far as he could see.

"I, uh ... I wish you well," Raeza said, "and that the future you strive for finds its way to you."

He focused on her horse's footsteps turning away from the mountain's edge. As he listened, the lingering desire for the thief girl he had met several days ago yearned for him to stop her.

"Caedus?" Raeza said from a good bit down the rocky road.

The captain twisted around, the features of her beautiful face still visible.

"If I should want to see you again, after your trials end," she said, "where can I look?"

Caedus caved to the joy branching out from her question, allowing a smile to form. The unknown road in front of him dampened his spirit, but holding the end goal in mind warmed him.

"Seek the Order of the Black Legion," he said. "You'll find me among them."

Caedus shared a grin with Raeza before she turned back to the steep incline of the mountains. He watched her until she shrank in the distance.

With a shift of heart, Captain Redstone geared his thoughts toward his nearly completed mission. Zededia's time dwindled. He spurred his horse down the path that emptied into the forest below. Every minute mattered on the final day of his journey, and the fate of Hostellus rested upon the golden sword in his possession.

~ ~ ~

Deep inside Vaedor Sellos's underground prison, Prince Zededia reserved his strength in a powerful meditation as he rested against the cave wall. Years of practice enabled him to blot out the unbearable environment and find tranquility.

The calming waters of Elysia trickled over his bare feet in his vision. He waded around and lost himself in the infinite expanse of the stars overhead. Peace flowed through him. The silence served as an escape from reality, his personal paradise. Time faltered, giving the prince a sense of immortality as he wandered without care.

"I was worried you weren't going to come here again," a manly voice echoed from above.

Zededia ceased his meandering and searched for his father's spirit. Matias's figure appeared in his view, taking the shape of a humble man rather than the glorious king Zededia always saw him as.

"Father?" the Black Prince asked, never having seen another spirit besides Bogrikrash walk through Elysia's neutral plane. "What are you doing here?"

"I could ask the same of you, given your position locked away in your own home."

"*Your* home. Matticus and Lucien's home."

The prince churned the shallow pool of his dream.

"It pains me that you think that, Zededia. Have you never felt safe in the walls I built for you?"

He scoffed at his father's question.

"You and I both know those walls were to seal our losses in, not keep others out."

"I built them to protect you! All my sons!" his father said with a raised voice.

A grimace crawled across Zededia's face.

"Hmph. A fine job you did of that," he said. "Your eldest descends into madness, seeking a weapon of mass war; your middle sits enslaved a hundred feet below your keep; and your youngest stands alone between the two, constantly trying to find his place. Lucien is lost in this world, Father, he always has been."

He turned his back to Matias.

"He'll receive most of the fallout between Matticus and me. Even before my exile, I sensed his distance from the life created for him."

To his surprise, the late king didn't return with any sort of prideful remark. The silence dissolved his frustration and cleared his mind.

"You didn't come here for me to tell you of your failures as a father," he said. "So why have you come? To offer advice in my darkest hour?"

"I have come to plead with you, my son," Matias said. "Once again."

Instantly, the prince discovered his father's ploy and took a firm stance against whatever argument may follow.

"Please reconsider your intentions, Zededia."

"You know nothing of my intentions," the Black Prince said. "Even if you did, you cannot stop them."

Ethereal footsteps neared from behind him.

"I know enough to recognize the look on your face when you're alone, when you remove the mask you hide behind."

Zededia frowned, realizing how much his father saw through his emotional disguise.

"You are my son. I know you better than anyone else. I've shared the plans rolling around in your head once before."

"Then you know what must be done. What I must do."

He looked down at the coursing water, following it to the edge of his sight. For a moment, his reflection peered back at him, but he avoided it in disgust.

"I cannot live your life for you. I can only offer guidance."

Zededia's concentration broke as noises from the physical world stirred him. His meditation ended without his consent, and the child in his heart surfaced for a moment, longing to reach out for his father's affection while Matias faded away.

"Your mother and I love you, Zededia," Matias said as the vision blurred.

When he woke, the prince shook his head to gain full consciousness. The metal gates of his prison cell cracked open, and he watched Commander Nysis appear from the abyss in his prestigious armor plus the cloth sling that held his broken arm. Zededia's heart raced as his plan for the execution catalyzed toward its climax. More chains rattled in the distance.

As the guards closed in, Osinian's essence seeped into his skin from all corners of the room. He summoned the shadow back into his mind and linked with him. As the power of his ancestor aligned with him, Zededia emptied the frost in his lungs.

"Oded elezkoren. (It's time.)"

~ ~ ~

Hours passed as Caedus grew bored of the endless trees and dead leaves around him. For a moment, he wondered if he had been traveling in circles. Eventually, a clearing neared, exposing a ray of sunlight reflecting from the golden fields ahead. With the adventure closing to an end, Caedus spurred his horse to quicken the pace. He galloped out of the forest directectly toward the group of soldiers gathered on the snowy ridge.

"Almost there," he said to himself as he bounced on the saddle.

When he reached the camp in a barreling approach, he noticed the ruin that plagued it, torn tents and abandoned campfires all around. Caedus searched for his commander, scanning the area for any sign of him. The only men in his sight turned their attention to him from the edge of the hilltop. A familiar face jogged closer.

"Lord Redstone!" Captain Ursa shouted. "You're back!"

"Where's the commander?" he asked, glancing around at the empty camp. "Where's the army?"

"The commander isn't here," Ursa said. "We were instructed to return to Anzagaar Nostir; Captain Corso led the march back home two days ago. A few of us decided to stay behind."

Caedus frowned.

"So, he's in the city, then?"

"Yes," Captain Ursa said. "How did you know?"

With a deep exhale, Caedus tried to wrap his mind around the situation.

"Because that's where he said he'd be," he said with a sigh.

As quickly as he arrived at the Legonae's former base, Captain Redstone flicked the reins of his horse to leave.

"Where are you going, Caedus?" Ammon asked while the rest of the captains gathered around.

He paused, hesitant to tell them the fullness of Zededia's plan. The oath he had made to protect his commander's secret seemed difficult to keep.

"When Zededia first laid out his scheme to seek the sword," Caedus said, "he told me that becoming Matticus's prisoner was necessary. He wanted to see the city one last time before ... never mind. I'm to meet him with *Osirisigniros* far on the south edge of the crater where the caverns empty into the lower lands beyond Osiria. He's going to Talion's Tomb."

"What the hell is he going to do there?"

"I don't know," Caedus said after a moment, lying to his fellow officers. "But I promised him I would be there."

As the captain started to ride off toward his next destination, Ursa ran beside him.

"Wait a moment, Caedus!" he said. "We're coming with you."

Captain Redstone slowed his steed, thought hard on whether Ursa's decision complicated things, and scanned the distant forest.

"Commander Osiris has counted on us before," Captain Seether said from under his wrapped face. "He'll need us now."

The others agreed, denying Caedus's request to set out alone. He curled his lips inward and saw no other option.

"Fine," he said. "Arm yourselves. The Vaedorians won't be far behind."

~ ~ ~

As the sun beamed down on his glistening silver crown, Prince Lucien shifted in his armor atop a massive horse in the parade of Vaedorians. Hundreds of citizens lined the streets, tossing flowers in the fanfare. He looked to Matticus in front of him with his long blue cape and then to Queen Livia to his left. Her uneasy expression matched his as they rode toward the central courtyard where the grand ceremony awaited. The shouts of joy from the gathered city folk sickened him; they all cheered for Zededia's execution.

Lucien met the faces of several commoners, forcing him to host a fake smile. Matticus waved to the people of Vaedor Sellos, and Lucien eyed little Mattox's hand stretched out in front of the king at certain angles.

"I don't suppose you have anything left in your flask?" Livia asked under the commotion.

Lucien smirked with a scrunched forehead.

"How do you know I have it on me?" he said.

"When do you not?"

The prince scoffed.

"Fair enough," Lucien said. "I don't have much, I'm afraid."

"I'm going to need it before this day retires. My mind is frayed."

Thankful that Matticus seemed too preoccupied to notice him, Lucien allowed his worry to sink in. He knew Zededia had an escape plan, but not knowing the details ate at him.

The columns of the arena in Vaedor Sellos's main courtyard rose high in the sky as Lucien and the royal ensemble rode close enough. Thousands of people pushed their way forward for a clear line of sight. When Matticus stopped the procession, Lucien dismounted, keeping the false happiness spread across his face. The king hit the ground with a thud, his massive stature and heavy armor shaking the stones under Lucien's feet. The prince watched him saunter through the crowd with his eldest son in his arms.

Lucien followed behind the queen through the madness toward the platform where his throne sat. The wooden staircase creaked under his steps, and he took his seat to the right of Livia with Matticus another seat down.

"Where is Ender, my queen?" Lucien asked.

"He's being cared for in the keep. Such a boisterous occasion isn't the place for an infant's ears."

The crowd calmed, but Lucien sensed hundreds of eyes on him.

"You're going to allow Mattox to watch an execution?" he said

With his focus on Matticus as the king stood from his decorated chair and walked up to the edge of the stage, Lucien wriggled his fingers from anxiety.

"Hopefully, there won't be one," Livia said under her breath. "But Matticus insisted, saying how his son needs to experience death to understand the reality of his life as a royal."

"Well ... Father made the three of us attend many ceremonies like this when we were children, so I don't suppose that's too out of the ordinary."

The commoners erupted again in cries of excitement, catching Lucien's attention. Chains clanked against the stone ground, and the prince assumed that the Vaedorian guards were hauling Zededia through the parting crowd. However, to his dreadful surprise, two other faces emerged from the gap of people. Baeno and Teodrid trudged among the group of soldiers with blank expressions and shackles around their wrists and ankles.

"What the hell?" Lucien whispered, a blaring stare aimed at the spies he colluded with yesterday.

Stunned, the prince's thoughts raced back to Thancred, and he wondered if Matticus's men would present him in the arena next.

"Welcome, citizens of Vaedor Sellos," King Matticus shouted with his right hand raised, "to the hour of victory!"

A rock sank in the prince's stomach.

"Welcome to the beginning of a new era! One free of the blight of these lands!" Matticus said. "One free of the scourge we call the Black Prince!"

Lucien scooted to the edge of his seat.

"The men shackled before you are criminals! Guilty of treason by aiding an exiled enemy in illegal affairs across the city! For their heinous actions, these traitorous agents have been brought forth before you ... for execution!"

The prince darted his eyes around as Matticus turned to retake his place. Anxiety plagued him, forcing a thick sweat to layer his skin despite the cold of winter.

"Don't look so green, Lucy," Matticus said with a smile. "This shouldn't be unfamiliar to you."

Given Matticus's eerily happy mood toward him, Lucien guessed the spies in chains hadn't given him away. A wave of relief calmed his nerves, but he waited in paranoia for Vaedorian soldiers to take him by surprise and haul him to the center of the courtyard. He caught a nervous side-glance from the queen; he knew she shared his fear.

From the other end of the arena, the prince eyed a gigantic man standing with a black metal mask with a demonic face plate. The man held a flat-tipped sword upside down at the ground, the blade wide enough to match half of Lucien's torso.

"And so, the face of justice arrives," Queen Livia said, referring to the executioner. "Seems more like cruelty if you ask me."

"Death will come swiftly," Lucien said. "If death comes at all. Wherever Zededia is waiting, his men need him."

The guards shoved the two spies up to the chopping blocks spread out in the center of the arena. Harshly, they swiped at Baeno's and Teodrid's knees, knocking them down to a kneel. Lucien dug his fingers into the armrests of his throne and slightly pulled himself forward. A crier walked forward to address the crowd of people eager to see the blood of the Legonae spill across the ground.

"As chartered under King Obedeus in the five hundred twenty-seventh year in the Age of Steel, all condemned persons found guilty of crimes committed against the crown that pertain to murder, treason, extortion, smuggling, dealing of illegal substances, and all other deeds deemed unjust in the eyes of the law are subject to a fair and equal punishment dictated by the current magistrate of the kingdom," the man read from a scroll, laying the foundation for the execution. "His Royal Majesty, King Matticus Osiris, son of Matias, has concluded that the prisoners before him are to be met with no other punishment than death at the hands of the executioner."

Deep drums rhythmically beat across the city square. Lucien's heartbeat matched their quickened pace.

"Gentlemen," the announcer said, directing his attention to Baeno and Teodrid, "may your blood, shed and spilt, cleanse your sins and carry you to the planes of Elysia."

Lucien sat up in his chair as the executioner stood to Baeno's left and hauled the decorated blade into the air. The time to act sprang into maturity; the prince's scattered mind weighed the consequences of an intervention. Nearly rising out of his chair, he stopped, though, as Baeno met eyes with him and subtly shook his head.

"This is all my fault," Lucien whispered.

The executioner kept his masked face pointed high before sending the blade hurling toward the earth. Lucien flinched, and his spine crawled as the heavy sword hacked through Baeno's neck in a clean strike, spilling a river of crimson through the cracks in the stones below. The prince bit his tongue and watched the spy's head roll around like a marble. He paid no attention to the praises singing in the air from the people of his home.

Lucien shakingly rose to his feet and walked toward the back of the platform. A quiet pause doused the people behind him followed by the haunting sound of Teodrid's head dropping to the pavement moments later.

The prince turned back, hardly able to look in Matticus's direction. When he returned, he stood behind his throne and stared at the dead bodies of Zededia's spies. Commander Nysis climbed the stairs of the royal platform shortly after, raising an eyebrow at him. Lucien locked his glare at Matticus's most decorated soldier whom he knew was responsible for discovering Baeno and Teodrid.

"Be wary, humble citizens!" Nysis shouted, quieting the crowd once again. "There are other enemies among us!"

Feeling the target grow on his back, Lucien swallowed his saliva.

"As evident by the criminals gathered here, the Order of the Black Legion is still alive within our walls. Keep a watchful gaze. These traitors must be discovered for the safety of Hostellus!"

As Nysis finished his sermon, the prince walked back around and retook his place on his throne.

"How are you faring, my queen?" Lucien heard Nysis say as he kissed Livia's hand.

"Fine," she bluntly said with a weak grin.

Lucien leaned back as far from Nysis as he could.

"Smile, Lucien," Hostellus's commander said. "With Zededia out of the way, nothing will stand between us and a future of glory."

Though the prince hadn't spent much time around Matticus's elected military leader, he knew of Nysis's slimy personality well enough to detect the hidden plot laced in his words. Lucien returned his gaze to the streets and the guards who held the bystanders at bay as they yelled, threw chunks of vegetables, and rushed to break through the line of soldiers. The Black Prince had arrived.

Zededia's sneer emerged as Lucien tried to think of what his brother had in mind for an escape. More than a hundred Vaedorian knights patrolled the area. Lucien struggled to control his breathing, his chest shaking the ceremonial armor he wore. The crown on his head sunk lower as the sweat in his hair pooled.

"Come on, Zed," he whispered to himself. "Get yourself out of this mess."

As the next platoon of soldiers took Zededia's shackles and shoved him along the arena floor, Lucien waited patiently for his brother to break free and slaughter them all.

However, the prince studied his brother's state of being; several bruises and cuts covered his body.

The guards exchanged a few unsavory words that Lucien failed to decipher, but his brother's defiant smirk widened, giving him an idea of what they said. Zededia neared the chopping block already soaked in blood. Lucien zoomed his focus in on his brother in chains and noticed him subtly shifting his hands.

"All right," Lucien whispered once again, "anytime now."

For a moment, his nerves calmed after seeing the faint outline of the red gemmed ring on the Black Prince's finger. Whatever Zededia had planned surely followed, Lucien assumed.

"Zededia Osiris!" the crier on the stage yelled. "You have been deemed guilty of villainous activity against his majesty and the public of Hostellus. The crimes you are hereby charged with consist of murder, terrorism, theft, treason, leading a criminal organization, and general menacing. By the laws of this land, His Majesty, King Matticus, has sentenced you to death by execution."

"Kill the snake!" one of the commoners shouted over the others, sending the rest into a higher state of frenzy.

"At long last," Matticus said, "the thorn in my side is removed."

A lump of spit clogged Lucien's throat and he shared a worried side glance with the queen. Without further delay, the executioner kicked Zededia down to a kneel. His brother lifted his head with shoulders resting on the bloody wood and stared at him with a blank face. The queen clutched his hand. Lucien compared the terror of Livia's expression to the creepy delight of Matticus's. His eldest brother troubled him; Lucien saw a spiraling darkness leak from the cracks, the sight of death and destruction becoming something the king longed for.

The executioner lifted his heavy blade above his head. Lucien's panic climaxed. Lucien dropped his jaw, staring at his brother as sweat began to seep into his eyes. His brother seemed too calm to be mere moments away from death. The conflicting signals nearly caused Lucien to retch.

And then, in the height of chaos, Zededia smiled, throwing Lucien off guard. He frowned, confusion drowning his thoughts. Before lowering his head to the block, his brother winked at him. Lucien shot up to his feet.

With a low grunt, the executioner broke the stagnant hold of the broadsword and heaved it at the bare skin of the Black Prince's neck. Lucien contracted his abdomen, nearly leaping off the stage.

As soon as the steel met Zededia's flesh to cast him into damnation, Lucien gasped. Instead of a head tumbling across the arena floor, a black mist exploded from his brother's body, taking the shape of a ghastly figure with red eyes. Zededia faded into the wind like a shadow, and a maniacal laughter bellowed across the arena, forcing Lucien to cover his ears. The entire square of citizens fled in terror. When the black mist dispersed, Zededia was gone. Lucien's heart nearly beat out of his chest, the people of Vaedor Sellos erupting further into horrified hysteria.

"What the hell," Lucien whispered in complete shock.

To his left, King Matticus crashed into a meltdown of rage, blood vessels bulging and glowing red.

"Where is he?" Lucien heard the king shout while using his empowered strength to grab his throne and hurl it into the vacant arena.

The decorated wood shattered into splintered fragments.

"Find him!"

Guards and soldiers alike scurried under the king's orders, preventing Lucien from making a proper escape. Jumping down to ground level, he shoved people out of his way and sought any opening he could take. He regained his bearings and spotted Thancred's gray beard under a thick hood. Lucien frantically sifted through the rushing citizens over to him.

"Did you know that was going to happen?" the prince asked in a raised voice.

"No," Thancred said, looking around, "and it seems whatever your brother wanted to achieve here, he did."

Low-pitched horns blared through the city, guards atop the castle's outer walls shouted down below, and Lucien recognized the signals of war from his youth.

"Zededia's stirred the rats' nest now," he said.

Vaedor Sellos opened her gates, giving Lucien a peek of the outside world for the first time in a while. He recoiled as dozens of mounted stallions stomped through the courtyard, swords drawn and ready for battle. King Matticus followed shortly after, leaving Lucien behind in a storm of chaos.

"They're going after him, Thancred," the prince said. "We need to follow."

"Why on earth would we do that?" the older man questioned amid the commotion. "My warring days are far behind me."

Lucien paused, rethinking his options.

"In the caves, Zededia told me to look for an opportunity to see him again," he said. "I think this is what he meant."

As Prince Lucien pushed his way to the stables several blocks away, the city emptied, sending hundreds of soldiers past his position. The conclusion of his brothers' feud neared, and he feared the worst was yet to come. Something in Matticus's shift of character told him that he'd pursue Zededia to the ends of the earth after being so close. Whatever lay ahead of him, Lucien knew he needed to be there to see its end.

Chapter 21
The Duel of Sinners

Day 25 in the Month of Snow

After a daring escape from the clutches of the Vaedorians, the Black Prince raced across the Hostellian fields on horseback with the wind in his face. A wide smile spread across his face, and he leaned down to the saddle to minimize resistance. Shouts and battle cries sounded off behind him in the forward camp outside the city where scattered groups of the Hostellae stood guard. He focused on the vast forest to the south, his eyes narrowed on the overgrown road that led to Talion's Tomb deep in the crevices of the mountains.

"May fate have been on your side, Captain Redstone," he said to himself, his breath bouncing with the horse's pace.

All the parts of Zededia's plan had fallen together with one final act remaining. He knew Matticus would hunt him in a blind fury; he counted on it. His father's words from his last encounter with him echoed in his thoughts, but he cast them aside

Once he neared the edge of the woods after nearly an hour's ride, Zededia slowed to glance behind him. A wave of white and silver surged over the snowy grounds.

There was no turning back now; he had to press on. Zededia took a moment to collect himself and stared at his kingdom's capital. Seeing his childhood home dampened his eyes, and Livia's cruel reminder that she still held him in her heart stung deep in his chest.

He sighed, flaring his nostrils with the warm air in his lungs. The forest called to him, fate shone overhead, and the Osirian prince turned to meet both with fierce determination.

The winding tree roots sprang out at his horse's feet, creating a crooked path to follow. Zededia remembered exploring Talion's Tomb in his adventures as an adolescent, but some parts of the route faded from his memory. He watched for the overgrown stones on the decayed path that acted as guide markers. Every so often, he paused to gather his surroundings to ensure that he maintained the right course. Midday came faster than he realized, the sun shining over him through the jagged cracks in the tree branches.

"Alright, Caedus," Zededia said while rubbing his horse's neck, "you'd better maintain your impeccable timing."

Zededia trotted his horse up to the tomb's entrance, the shadows of the woods covering the dead leaves on the ground with crooked patterns. He scanned the ancient, runic archway inscribed with Aznogsi words.

"Here lie the sinners of the Eldish kings," Zededia said, "put to rest by the Holy Uniter."

The prince recognized the words from texts he read from his ancestor's days. Zededia appreciated the care Osiris gave to the dead, even those who had served different masters. Before heading into the crypt, Osinian's shade rose out of the ground next to him.

"*Eeslas zanto flayesa cresso gornnang, (Seems your escape plan worked,)*" the spirit said.

"*Gad ozesk nes ed izizen menshinni zant, zot kell. (It wouldn't have been possible without you, my friend.)*"

"*Ozno ene zant chiszna ter volesir Talion nlazgos? (What are you planning that involves Talion's Tomb?)*" Osinian asked.

Zededia sat in studied thought for a moment, rethinking how to carry out the finale of his desires.

"*Matticus flaelideshir eg am ir tsen sen zomae sont, (Matticus's numbers will be of no use to him here,)*" the Black Prince said. "*Zoam aelosteus sen rogetag zomae ish drownae bosch zolloda cod snega. (I'm going to duel him and end this war for good.)*"

"*Oldeki prayest zanto igneer sen cost lett Osirisigniros sont? Ozno da zant folst? (Why tell your captain to bring the Sword of Kings here? What if you fall?)*"

The prince smiled.

"Zo zagergae zant sen provnoles lett sigiros naalae. Ter'si ozno zo mogolag zant sen ra. (I resurrected you to keep the sword safe. That's what I expect you to do.)"

"Uruz oznet? (Until when?)" Osinian asked.

Zededia looked to the entrance of the cave and then back to the spirit.

"Ozesk zant polos prost? (Would you ever stop?)"

Osinian shook his head at him.

"Traasela ola, (Come on,)" Zededia said with the grin still stretched across his face.

After dismounting his horse, Zededia entered the darkness of Talion's Tomb and conjured a green orb of fire in the palm of his hand to light his way. He passed by dozens of stone sarcophagi containing the remains of Osiris's enemies from nearly a millennium ago. The moldy dust clogged his nose, smelling of decayed bone and damnation. Shaded corridors played with his vision, but a faint glow in the distance caught his attention as he wove through the maze of archways and makeshift holes in the earth.

"Caedus is already here," the prince said under his breath.

Cobwebs and skeletons littered the ground; he basked in their decrepit nature. Knowing Matticus maintained a special fear for the dead, Zededia knew Talion's Tomb provided him with an advantage to outweigh the damages of his injuries. He stretched his hand and rubbed the dry, crumbling stone. He coughed every so often from the unclean air.

"Let's see if I remember how to find Talion himself," Zededia whispered.

"Zo oolso tieren oeleedance ir Talion ish zomaos morisa, lett soor Hostellus prinisecir, (I've heard stories of Talion, the old Hostellian regent, and his people,)" Osinian said as he walked beside the prince.

Zededia stopped to analyze an inscribed mark on the archway.

"Zom nento osi sazborosen gaarl. Os morros gaarl, (He was given an honorable death. A soldier's death,)" he said. *"Haelisi lett kiil sazborosen inni ir laena lett Prinisec. (Perhaps the most honorable of all the regents.)"*

The ancient map on the wall pointed toward a steep staircase that stretched into the murky crypt below. Zededia planted his foot on the first step and squinted. As he descended, a wide clearing appeared, visible from the torches hanging from the columns inside. At the base of the stairs, Zededia observed the great stone casket on a pedestal. He looked around for his captain and paced toward Talion's resting place. When he reached the coffer, he brushed his hands over the weathered carvings.

"So, seems your plan worked," a voice said from ahead.

Zededia peered forward as Captain Caedus emerged from behind the tunnel leading farther into the cave system. The sight of his closest friend soothed him.

"And it seems my faith in you has not gone to waste," he said, walking over to the captain to give him a sturdy embrace. "It's good to see you, my friend."

He leaned away after a moment.

"I was worried I hadn't given you enough time," Zededia said.

Several footsteps sounded off from Caedus's origin, alerting Zededia of a possible threat. However, when he glanced over familiar faces and war-torn black armor, he relaxed his grip on his sword.

"Our accord stated that you alone would meet me here, Caedus," the Black Princes said out of range of his soldiers.

"Yes, well," Caedus said, turning to the others, "I wasn't exactly given that choice."

"Commander!" Captain Ursa said.

The prince nodded as he approached. The rest followed behind as Zededia advanced to greet them.

"I hadn't expected to see you all here," he said, "but it warms me, nonetheless."

"My prince," Captain Seether said. "Why have you come to such a place?"

Zededia paused, hesitant to reveal every detail.

"The Vaedorians are in pursuit. Matticus has surely learned by now that we've been chasing the Sword of Kings," Zededia said, shifting his attention to Caedus.

The Black Prince then looked into his friends' eyes, feeling a sense of guilt for dragging them into his scheme.

"We can no longer defend ourselves against his armies. The walls of Anzagaar Nostir are not enough to protect our people from Matticus's rage. With *Osirisigniros* in his grasp, we are doomed."

Zededia walked over to Caedus as the captain pulled a bundle of cloth from inside his cloak. The prince brought a slow hand to the sheathed blade of his ancestor's weapon, avoiding the red ruby of the hilt sticking out of the fabric to prevent himself from tapping into the blade's nearly limitless power.

"I've spent four years orchestrating this moment. All that points to one goal: keeping the Sword of Kings out of Matticus's hands."

He turned back to his captains.

"To ensure that my brother never sees this weapon, I'm going to face him and put an end to the hunt of our people."

"With all respect, Commander, what if you are bested?" Captain Ammon asked. "Your injuries are severe and your past duels with King Matticus have rarely ended with either of you standing over the other."

Zededia took a deep breath.

"Let me worry about Matticus. Just keep yourselves alive. The Vaedorians will bring great forces."

From the staircase, several echoing voices bounced into the catacombs.

"Our time fades," Zededia said with a firm tone. "Keep the Hostellae away until Matticus arrives. Give him a wide berth; he's here for me."

"Yes, my prince," Captain Ursa said, ushering the others to prepare for battle.

He waited until they scurried off into the various tunnels branching from the primary crypt and turned to face the staircase rising from the entrance.

"Are you ready to proceed, Captain Redstone?" the Black Prince asked, his cold glare beaming at the archway where King Matticus would appear.

"Are you, Commander Osiris?"

Zededia inhaled the stale air and nodded, the anticipation of a duel crawling across his skin. His armor lay elsewhere, out of reach, and his body trembled from his broken ribs and bruised muscles.

"Yes," he said softly as the dormant anger in his heart surfaced once last time. "Yes, I am."

Footsteps shuffled in the distance.

"Well, if you're going to follow through with your duel," Captain Redstone said behind him, "you're going to need this."

Zededia glanced over his shoulder.

The shining, blood-caked handle of his longsword stretched out to him from Caedus's hand. Surprise overcame him as he ran his fingers along his weapon in its sheath.

"You found my sword?" Zededia asked.

"Captain Ursa retrieved it from the plains after your capture," Caedus said. "He seemed to think you would need it again soon."

Zededia locked his fingers around the hilt, savoring the feeling firm in his palm, and yanked it free. The signature shriek of the blade echoed through the chamber. Holding it upright, he traced the silver shine up to the tip.

Sounds of metal clashing rang in his ears from the shallower sections of the tomb. Zededia filled his lungs, closed his eyes, and held the sword close to his face, nearly grazing his nose with the flat part of the blade. Dust from the ceiling fell to his feet as his soldiers battled above. The fabled moment he waited for neared.

"Go, Caedus," the Black Prince said in a deep voice as he channeled his vigor. "Join the others...."

Falling men screamed with their dying last words. The Black Prince shifted his feet against the paved path, grinding loose pebbles. Heavy metal boots pounded in the distance, separated from the others by a slower pace. His captain hurried off through the rear tunnel, leaving Zededia alone with Osinian watching from the shadows.

The prince's heartbeat quickened. He longed for another match against Matticus. More dust floated down; he opened himself to the fury of his ancestors, allowing the shine in his blood to appear. The redness flowed like rivers across his forearms and hands. War drums of the Legonae beat in his ears as audible hallucinations. Even in their absence, the prince used their rhythm to drive his aggression. The crimson power rose to his eyes, choking his blue irises.

As the Black Prince stood at his full might, he caught a glimpse of thick, silver greaves descending the staircase. A massive set of armor followed, preceding his brother's stern face and shining crown. Zededia contained the savagery barking at him to engage, saving it for the first strike. Seeing Matticus stand before him with an opportunity in hand ignited his passion for violence. The king stopped just inside the entrance to the chamber, and the prince eyed the two hulking guards behind.

"This ends here, Matticus," Zededia said with a light scowl. "After all this time chasing each other in our little game, everything has led to this moment."

"There is no end for you here, snake," King Matticus said in a bellow. "Slaying you is only the beginning of your torment."

Zededia's sinister laugh slithered from his throat.

"I've spent years trying to think of how to kill you," the Black Prince said. "But everything paled in comparison to throwing your corpse to the worms that fed on the damned who opposed the Osirian legacy."

Itching to make the first move, Zededia forced his feet to remain still.

"I must confess," the king said, unsheathing Matias's famous longsword and taking a long look at it, "driving our father's sword through you has become a mild obsession of mine."

Zededia scanned the decorated hilt and steel blade.

"And after I kill you," Matticus said. "I will find Caedus Redstone. I will find the Sword of Kings you so charitably retrieved for me."

"You will never see *Osirisigniros*. Not while I stand here to defy you," Zededia said.

His brother bore a wicked smile.

"That won't be much longer."

Zededia took one step forward, planting his dominant foot while flicking his longsword over the back of his hand.

"Remove your guards or I will remove them for you," the Black Prince said. "This duel is between you and I alone."

The prince received a cocky sneer from his brother, and the massive Vaedorian soldiers drew their swords. Zededia whistled after Matticus disregarded him, and a mist of blackness surged to the guard on the right, burrowing into the chest plate before erupting outwards in a bloody rain. Osinian moved on to the other guard, siphoned his soul out through the mouth, and reduced him to a pile of skin and bone in the dense armor. The dead Vaedorian collapsed, and the prince grimaced.

"This *will* be a fair fight," Zededia said.

"Fair?" Matticus said. "What do you know of fair?"

"Hmph. Still clinging to the past, are we? Still thinking of your failures, of how I defeated you for the whole city to see?"

"You didn't defeat me!" the king yelled. "You cheated! *I* deserved your glory! *I* deserved Father's love!"

Weary of bickering, Zededia slid into his *Virtuo* stance with great hostility, sword aimed at Matticus's throat over the top of his forearm.

"This is your only warning, brother," the prince said. "Submit to me. Abandon your campaign for the sword and your hunt for my people."

Matticus took his *Igni* stance twenty feet away.

"You will not sway me from my ambitions."

Zededia lowered his head, strengthened his grip on his blade, and clenched his shoulders.

"Then become the dirt I walk upon."

Pulled from the depths of his rage, Zededia's voice echoed through the quiet chamber with a demonic tone.

He accelerated from his stance to a brisk walk, gaining speed as he neared Matticus. His red vision narrowed on his brother's scowl. After cocking his arms for a full swing, Zededia Osiris brought hell with his sword and clashed with the Vaedorian king with such fury that sparks flickered to the floor.

His attack fell to the wayside, the momentum sacrificing accuracy for power. Zededia charged for another swipe from the left and met Matticus's steel with the same effect. The two Osirian brothers traded blows before the prince allowed his nimbleness to take over after brutality opened the duel. Dancing around Matticus's sides, Zededia pushed his brother across the arena of Talion's Tomb and glared at him.

"Surely that's not all the fabled King Matticus has to offer!" Zededia shouted while crossing blades with his brother, their hilts nearly touching.

He lunged backwards as the king shoved him away, and his lungs ignited with quick, rapid breaths to fuel his aching muscles. Zededia allowed his brother to gain ground and match his aggression that longed for a worthy fight. Now on the defensive side, he dodged, spun, and cast Matticus's brutish hacks aside until he stood in the center of the chamber over the sigil that marked the tomb. Like a taunted bull, the king's chest heaved.

"That's more like it," Zededia said with a sick smile.

The prince hurled himself back to battle, shouting just before he crashed into Matticus's horizontal block. Over two decades of training, blade discipline, and sheer desire to dominate his brother surged through Zededia's body. On several occasions, Matticus's blows at his torso slashed too close for comfort. Sweat trickled down his forehead and hands.

Zededia swung his blade in an arch from side to side as he held the king in a deadlock. When he broke free, he charged with his shoulder and struck Matticus in the chest, knocking his opponent back a few feet. The prince winced after crashing into the heavy armor, forgetting the massive bruise blooming from his trapezius to his lower deltoid.

Though crippled from his wounds and depleted energy for magic, Zededia had Matticus exactly where he wanted him. The king launched forward with a violent thrust, but the prince sidestepped the piercing steel, ducked around Matticus's overextended arms, and pressed his heel sharply into his side.

Toppled over on the ground, a new flame awakened in his brother. Zededia knew he only angered him further. With his back now to the staircase, the prince shuffled his feet and deflected Matticus's explosive strikes from overhead. For a moment, Zededia thought he'd dug himself too deep into a hole and dropped his sneer. He dropped down to a squat to miss a stone-splitting swing, feeling the air rush over his hair. When he rose, however, Matticus's heavy fist struck him in the jaw. The prince staggered backward and bent over to recover.

His ears rang, black dots clouded his vision, and the time for toying with Matticus had expired. Zededia gathered the blood drowning his tongue and sprayed it across the floor.

"For years," King Matticus said in the eye of the hurricane, "I've dreamt of your death, for your answer for your sins."

"*My* sins?" Zededia said, rising up. "What of yours?"

Nearly cornered, the prince's nostrils nearly froze from the cold air constantly coursing through it. Exhaustion started to take its toll on both Osirians, sweat and raspy breaths escaping each of them. The pause repelled Zededia from advancing.

"You have no grasp of your effect on me, do you?" the prince said. "You have no idea what you did, the pain you've caused me? And what about the hundreds of young men you've sent to their doom in your attempt for the Sword of Kings? What about Father, Matticus? What about the man who *raised* you? I know his end came too early. I know you played a part in his death."

"We've all made mistakes, brother," Matticus said in a strangely calm tone, "but you will pay for yours here."

"You condemned me to exile! Your own family! What more must I pay?"

As he waited for an answer, he thought he saw a bit of remorse in his brother's eyes. The sentiment faded, though, as Matticus's scowl reappeared.

"Father would have chosen you to take his place had he had the chance," the king said. "You stole my birthright from me ... and I will ensure my kingdom is safe from your wrath ... for good."

The prince clenched his teeth and tightened the grip on his longsword with both hands. He panted from the fight and took advantage of the break before jumping back into the fray with his gathered strength. Favor changed hands again with Zededia's relentless assault. Challenging Matticus's reaction speed, he alternated targeting the king's ankles and neck. The prince cleaved at his brother's foot, met with a sturdy block, and then twirled completely around on one foot, sliced at Matticus with a backhanded strike, and clashed with a hasty, off-balance deflection. The king fell back onto the ground, tripping over the loose rubble; Zededia advanced.

"Get up!" the Black Prince shouted. "It shall be I who kills you, not a stone!"

Matticus's sword skidded toward the cave wall, but Zededia found no desire to bar his opponent from a weapon.

"You see?" Zededia said. "It wasn't magic that allowed me to beat you years ago. I didn't need it then, nor do I need it now."

Matticus climbed to his feet and pulled a dagger from his gauntlet. The prince then tossed his sword away to even the odds.

"You will not die because I am a better god than you," Zededia said, inching closer with his hands raised ready to engage in close combat, "but because I am a better man."

In a flash, the king propelled toward him and jabbed the dagger at his abdomen. Zededia, light on his feet, evaded his brother's rash thrusts with little trouble. The short blade prevented him from closing the distance, though. He needed to remove it from play however he could. On the king's next attack, Zededia shot his hands to Matticus's wrists, arms trembling as his brother started to overpower him the longer he held on. The dagger tipped in his direction at the bare skin of his throat. No matter how much force he applied, he couldn't outmatch the king's barbaric strength.

To break the standoff, Zededia rocketed his knee into Matticus's right oblique muscles at the weakest point of the armor protecting them. Though it barely fazed his brother, Zededia distracted him well enough to pry the dagger from his loosened grip. He staggered back and stared at Matticus like a crazed hunter, dipping into the extreme reserves of his stamina.

The prince attempted the killing blow to bring an end to the fight, but his brother sidestepped, bashed his fist into his stomach, and halted his attack. Zededia's staggered, dropping the weapon to the ground. He knelt over, coughing from the heavy impact to his guts. Matticus swung once more, forcing him to retreat. Another jab clocked him across the jaw. Zededia's vision faded in and out, and he stumbled a few feet away, back turned to the king.

As best he could, he collected himself, spun around in preparation, and threw a sloppily calculated punch. His strike missed by a wide margin, and his brother heaved an uppercut directly under his chin. Nearly knocked off his feet, the prince sluggishly fell back into position, but his entire body seized once the sharp edge of cold steel penetrated his lower torso.

Eyes wide and in shock, Zededia wobbled backward, peered down at the Vaedorian dagger protruding from his abdomen, and held trembling hands around the hilt. Blood spurted out from all sides. Weak and hemorrhaging, he stumbled across the arena until he slammed his back against one of the stone columns of the tomb and slid down to its base. Violently coughing, blood and bile filled his throat. He became blind to all else in the haze, unaware of his brother approaching. Matticus ripped the weapon out of his flesh, reopening the wound.

The prince gasped once more, face pale and mouth agape. Out of the corner of his vision, Captain Caedus appeared into view. Zededia looked to his friend with a shaking expression.

Memories of his life flew through his panicking mind. All the loved ones he was attached to, the places he had come to call home, and the happiness just outside his reach washed over him.

"Ah, Lord Redstone," Zededia heard from his older brother. "I believe you have something that belongs to me."

Several sets of metal boots trudged into the chamber, cutting off all exits as he lay dying on the floor of the catacomb. He focused his blurry vision on King Matticus taking the wrapped cloth that concealed the Sword of Kings from Caedus by force. His brother looked at him as he held Osiris's great weapon. Matticus's stern frown glared at him, and Zededia watched his older brother turn away from him and march for the exit of Talion's Tomb.

"Let's go," Zededia heard. "We're done here."

~ ~ ~

"Hurry, Thancred!" Prince Lucien shouted as he wove through the southern forest's crooked path.

He ducked from the branches and followed the faint white blips through the trees. After tailing the Vaedorian hunting party all morning, Lucien came into a clearing where the towering archway of Talion's Tomb rested embedded into the mountain's crevice. He scanned the various soldiers in white and silver gathering their belongings and saddling their horses. The blood and bandages among them showed signs of battle, and they carried their dead across the prince's path.

Thancred caught up to him on his right. Lucien dismounted, held a hand on his sword hilt, and jogged toward the tomb entrance.

"Where is the king!" Lucien asked the nearest soldier.

Before his question met an answer, a bulky figure emerged from the shadowed tunnel. King Matticus walked toward him, head low, hands to his side. Lucien glued his eyes to the bundle of cloth in his grasp and the red jewel poking out. He then scanned the dripping dagger in Matticus's other hand, his heart skipping a beat as he read between the lines. Jaw dropping, he squeezed his eyebrows together in worry. Matticus gave him a sideways glance as the prince stood motionless and stared in horror.

A stone dropped in Lucien's stomach. His chest nearly caved in on itself, and he sprang from his position, sprinting into Talion's Tomb to search for Zededia.

The maze of the underground cemetery escalated Lucien's anxiety, time ticking away with every wrong turn.

Finally, the prince caught a glimpse of one of Zededia's soldiers at the bottom of a long staircase. He tumbled down the stone steps, tripping over his own feet.

When Lucien stomped into the main chamber, he darted his eyes to several familiar faces all crowding around one of the columns. He pushed his way through and saw his brother leaning against the support column, soaked in blood.

"No," Lucien sporadically said, rushing to Zededia's side.

His brother's bright blue eyes looked at him with a waning strength. Lucien carefully grabbed Zededia's right hand with his own and pressed his other on the gaping wound to stop it.

"Lucien..." Zededia said with a weak grin. "You found ... the opportunity."

Lucien's eyes watered at the sight of the Black Prince slipping away.

"Come on, Zed," Lucien said, acting as if everything were all right. "We need to find you a surgeon."

He tried to keep his focus away from Zededia's fatal injury.

"No..." Zededia said, slowly shaking his head. "It's ... it's too late for me."

The pooling tears streamed down Lucien's cheek.

"Not yet," he said. "I'm getting you out of here."

"Brother, stop."

The prince fell into the crooked reality that Zededia lay inches away from death's heartless embrace.

"My light ... is fading," Zededia said. "Elysia ... has opened its gates."

Lucien couldn't contain his anguish; his face became flushed, and tears dripped off his nose. Shuddering, he gazed at Zededia. He tried to speak once more, but his throat tightened to a close. Lucien felt his brother's free hand graze his bearded face, leaving a trail of blood in his dense black hair.

"It's all right," Zededia said. "You can let me go."

"No," the prince said with a broken voice, "I can't. I can't lose you again."

"You ... you never lost me, Lucien."

His brother wheezed a fluid cough.

"Promise me something, Lucien," Zededia said.

He nodded with crumpled cheeks.

"Promise me ... to find your light. Protect it ... against all evil. Against the darkness of this world."

"I–I don't understand," Lucien said.

"You will. Just keep your heart where it should be, and ... and you'll find it."

Lucien desperately clung to his brother's hands, squeezing far tighter than he realized.

"Caedus," the Black Prince said.

Lucien slid over to allow Lord Redstone to kneel. He heard Zededia whisper something to the captain, but he couldn't make out what he said. When Caedus stood and moved out of the way, Lucien inched closer. His breath pulsed out of control through his nose that dangled a tear on its edges.

"It's okay, Lucien. Let me go," Zededia said in a softer voice.

Hell lit his mind ablaze.

"It's okay ... Lucien ... it's ... okay...."

Zededia's words trailed off in Lucien's ears. His brother's grip faded completely. A storm of agony filled the prince's heart after his brother slipped into the void. Looking into Zededia's lifeless, glassy eyes, he wept.

As he mourned with shivering cries, he pulled his brother's corpse to him and embraced it. Lucien's world fell to pieces, shattering to fragments from the death of the Black Prince.

Chapter 22
Fool's Gold

Day 25 in the Month of Snow

The battalions of the Hostellae gathered on the sides of the road leading to Vaedor Sellos as King Matticus triumphantly strolled by. He held his chin high with pride to set a shining example for each of his men. The cheers fueled his ego, furthering his success in slaying the infamous Black Prince. The gates to his home opened to thousands of citizens erupting with joyous commotion. Matticus basked in the splendor of his great victory, and the weight from his feud with Zededia slipped off his shoulders.

The king took the afternoon to saunter through his city's streets, absorbing all the praise he could. In the upper city, the councilmen, politicians, and the clergy celebrated him as well but with a softer, gentler tune. As he walked along the center of the stone path to the keep, Matticus looked over his grand fortress with a new perspective, one absent of the darkness that plagued him.

For the first time in years, he felt free. He glided past the welcome party on the marble steps and turned his horse back to them. A wide grin took control of his face. With great energy, Matticus shot his fist into the air while holding the cloaked Sword of Kings.

"Glory to Hostellus!" he shouted at the tops of his lungs. "Glory to Vaedor Sellos!"

The masses roared. When they settled, the king inhaled a cold breath of air.

"With this ... this gift from Osiris," he said, "we will march into a future worthy of the gods themselves! No longer will the neighboring kingdoms sit idly by, wasting away, putting my family's legacy to shame!"

Darker thoughts sprinted through the king's mind, giving him a slight buzz in the base of his skull. The united nation he sought to create waited at his fingertips.

"A new era begins," he bellowed. "The era ... of the Hostellian Empire!"

A wave of excitement crawled across the back of his neck.

"Go, now. Go back to your homes. Rest peacefully, for the snake has been slain! Hostellus's sons have returned, ready to bring peace and order to Osiria."

Matticus waved to the crowd once more before retiring inside. When he pushed the large doors open to the keep, Matias's towering statue stared at him from the center of the throne room. A pained sense of guilt struck his heart as he looked over the stern expression carved into the marble. He dismissed it after a moment, pushing any sentiment toward his father far away.

From every room in the keep, his massive guards flocked to him as he walked by. Once Matticus reached the upper floors, he briefly scanned for his wife and sons. The laughter that had once filled the halls had fallen silent. He missed their warm presence, leaving him with an empty feeling. More pressing matters persisted, nevertheless.

The king entered his war room on the top floor and eyed Commander Nysis peering out the large window on the opposite wall. Matticus fixed his attention on the map hanging like a tapestry where he and Spymaster Rachtus had once plotted. The disappearance of his tactician still puzzled him; Nysis had assumed Rachtus's responsibilities in his absence.

"Leave us," Matticus said to his soldiers.

Muffled thuds bounced through the chamber, and the scurrying footsteps faded.

"Congratulations, my liege," Commander Nysis said, pivoting away from the window. "Everything we've worked toward has fallen into place."

"Our conquest is far from over," he said, standing next to the table in the center of the room while glaring at the rough sketch of Ehthilia's terrain.

Matticus pushed the metal figurines that resembled his armies over the parchment, moving them across the Nekroa River outside Hostellus's borders.

"Ambrose has allowed his kingdom to falter for too long," Nysis said with his gaze pouring down into the courtyard below. "With a clear path south of Monscarren, Korzeg's forces will meet us for our assault on Voluutia. From there, things are much simpler."

All signs pointed to Hostellus's primary military rival, Voluutia, and Matticus's desire to conquer King Raed's territory soared above all.

"You're sure King Holthiem will hold his end of the deal?"

"Even if he doesn't," Nysis said. "The Hostellae are strong enough to force his allegiance as well as the others. Monscarren can be left alone. King Taalpin would sooner attack Voluutia than rush to its defense."

"And now," Matticus said, shifting his gaze to the mighty weapon wrapped in his hand, "we have the power ... of the gods."

Matticus looked at the golden hilt peeking from underneath the cloth in his hand. The greed and lust for power that the Sword of Kings brought with it took control. He paused with his fingers dug into the wrapping, savoring the fact that the treasured blade he had sought for years sat in his grasp.

"I haven't seen it in its full glory," Matticus slowly said.

Gripping the cloth, he yanked it off to reveal *Osirisigniros* inches away from his face, its golden hue gleaming in his eyes. A wicked smile cracked his lips as he studied the triple-bladed corkscrew spiraling from the hilt. Though smaller than he imagined, his ancestor's artifact sent the king into a light frenzy, the empowered blood coursing through him faster and faster. Matticus flipped it upside down and peered through the red gemstone embedded into the pommel.

"It's more beautiful than I could have ever imagined," he said in a murmur. "All of Osiris's power ... finally in my grasp."

Gripping the sword tighter, he held it right-side up again and waited for a surge of energy to flow through him. Matticus frowned after a moment as *Osirisigniros* remained dormant. The stories of red lightning shooting in all directions once an Osirian took hold of the weapon had given him higher expectations, but nothing happened as he glanced over it.

"Why isn't it..." Matticus said in a whisper. "It's ... not working."

Flustered, he swung it through the air to try and force the stored magic out of it. Matticus grew angrier by the second as the Sword of Kings felt identical to a regular weapon in his hands. He glanced at it, scanning it from top to bottom, and frowned.

Suddenly, the sword shivered like a pool of liquid metal. The king blinked, barely able to perceive what was happening. Osiris's fabled source of power morphed into an ordinary short sword in mere seconds.

Matticus couldn't believe his eyes. The key to Hostellus's unification of the other kingdoms had fallen into oblivion. Fierce anger cooked his blood, pumping a red shine into his face up to his eyes.

"Damn you, Zededia," the king spat under his breath.

Matticus's enhanced strength crushed the hilt of the imposter sword. The sheer heat and channeled rage seeping from his hand splintered through the length of the blade with cracks of fire. He unleashed a deep roar, threw the last piece of it at the nearby wall, and began destroying everything he could get his hands on. The keep rang with Matticus's temper let loose like a ravenous beast, and the Sword of Kings lay out of his reach once again.

Chapter 23

Procession

Day 28 in the Month of Snow

Heavy rain soaked through Prince Lucien's hood as he stood under the leafless canopies of the Blackwood. Alongside Captain Redstone in the back of his brother's funeral procession, he kept his arms crossed and his lips sealed. Horns hummed a low tone throughout the forest, echoing through the hundreds of soldiers standing between him and Zededia's body ahead on a high stack of logs and twigs under a ceremonial cloth. Lucien stared off into the mountainside, his mind wandering through everything the previous couple of weeks had thrown at him.

The icy water chilled his skin. As groups of Legonae soldiers walked over to pay their respects to their fallen commander, Lucien's guilt suffocated him. His eyes produced no tears with his spirit dead and gone, withered from Zededia's passing.

"I'm sorry, Lucien," Caedus said through the rain.

The prince kept quiet. His brother's lifeless face in Talion's Tomb disturbed his thoughts. Images of the horror he had endured punctured him like flying arrows. Several minutes passed before he mustered any courage to speak.

"I don't understand, Caedus," he said, thunder booming in the distance. "He told me he had a plan. He told me he had a way out. But, in the end, he seemed so ... hopeless. Like he wanted me to let him die."

"Hmm," Captain Redstone said with a grunt.

The years of happiness between him and both of his brothers replaced the agonizing memories of Zededia's death, but they haunted him far more. His youth, before the three of them fell apart, stabbed at him.

"When we were children," Lucien said, "we thought nothing could stand in our way. We thought we'd conquer it all and stay together until the end."

Lucien sniffed, shaking the cold from his nose.

"We ... believed.... we believed we were united."

The prince shifted his feet in the loose dirt. As the rose of his heart shed its final petal, he glanced up to the sky and embraced the rain on his face.

He sighed.

"All along ... all these years ... we doomed ourselves."

Lucien lowered his head down and shivered.

"It seems like yesterday that Zededia still lived at home and looked after me. Now, I find myself saying ... goodbye."

Lucien's voice started to crack. He watched the passing soldiers with a loose focus.

"Free the heart that longs for silence," Caedus said. "Let it rest as it desires."

As Caedus spoke, Lucien looked over to him, recognizing the quote.

"Your brother used to say that whenever something troubled him," Captain Redstone said. "Though, I don't really know what it means."

The ceremony drew to its conclusion as a squad of men poured oil over Zededia's corpse, and Lucien glanced over the weathered marble archway that circled overhead. Torches met wood and the funeral pyre erupted despite the torrential weather.

Dead, trampled leaves littered the forest clearing in the mud after the soldiers who had gathered to mourn Zededia dispersed. Once the smoke rose high, Captain Redstone shifted in his side view.

"Caedus?" Lucien said while keeping his gaze on the flames.

After he noticed that the captain had turned back to him, he scanned over Zededia's final moments once more.

"What did my brother whisper to you?" he asked. "As he lay dying? What did he say to you that he didn't say to me?"

He waited for a reply, but a long pause kept him anxious. Captain Redstone exhaled to his left after another moment.

"Keep it safe."

Lucien twisted his head and peered at his brother's second in command with a confused frown. He received a subtle nod. Soon after, Caedus left him alone under the descending sun behind the dense clouds above.

Grief and uncertainty clawed at him. The thought of carrying on without his brother tortured him. Lucien sighed, finally deciding to leave Zededia's floating ashes behind. He trudged over to his horse tied to a nearby branch, loosened the ropes, and mounted it. Checking his pack to confirm its contents, he pondered which path ahead to take.

The winding forest offered many routes back to Vaedor Sellos, and Prince Lucien struggled to stray anywhere away from his home. On the other hand, the wastes outside Hostellus called to him. His heart sank. With the feud between his brothers settled, more or less, Lucien's mind split apart at an impossible decision. He closed his eyes, and though he sat unsure of which path to take, he knew his days as an Osirian prince had forever changed.

- Epilogue -

Day 27 in the Month of Iron

King Matticus stood alone with a firm stance in the center of his throne room as he gazed upon the painting of his family. Zededia's youthful face stung his eyes, seemingly darkened since the last time he had looked. Over a month had passed since the Black Prince's death, and each day widened the growing vacancy in his heart that his rival had once occupied. He had lost sight of his purpose in life without a clear enemy to challenge.

The approaching spring gave life to his ambitions, however, and he turned his attention to a new opponent. Years of warring with his brother had sharpened his armies.

Matticus inhaled the keep's stagnant air and traced over his parent's faces on the oil painting. Footfalls echoed off the marble staircase behind him as he glared.

"What news of Lord Redstone?"

The footsteps grew louder.

"None, my liege," Commander Nysis said. "Caedus hasn't been spotted at any of the border checkpoints. We have scoured all Hostellus's cities, and there's no activity from Anzagaar Nostir. It's unlikely he's storing it there."

Matticus wriggled his knuckles in his metal gauntlets and diffused his accumulating anger.

"Yet he remains lost to us," the king said. "Thousands of soldiers are roaming the crater and we can't find one man. Caedus is too smart to take *Osirisigniros* into Merrinine. He's sought the protection of the Ehthilians."

"Which gives us all the more reason to initiate the invasion. Your armies are growing restless along the banks of the Nekroa."

Unification of the neighboring kingdoms remained his primary goal, but without the Sword of Kings, conquering his relatives' lands forced his hesitation.

"Ambrose won't be able to resist our occupation and deal with Grimm at the same time," Nysis said.

King Matticus turned, paced over to his throne, and studied the shining design.

"Very well," he said, hands held behind his back. "We've delayed long enough. You may give the order, Commander."

Nysis stepped into view from his right, and he noticed the silk sling keeping his soldier's elbow in place.

"Are you sure you will be able to make the journey? Your arm hasn't fully healed."

A half grin beamed back towards him.

"We've been dreaming of this day for years, Your Majesty. Nothing will keep me from the front lines."

At the cusp of the campaign before him, Matticus struggled to maintain his hold on the gravity of future events. As daunting as the task ahead remained, the thought of Ehthilia's flag under his boots sent a numbing chill down his spine.

"Yes..." Matticus whispered, "our empire awaits."

The keep's emptiness bored him. With the majority of his soldiers standing near the northern river, Matticus dissolved his worry and set his focus upon the long march between Vaedor Sellos and King Ambrose's castles.

"Ready your horse, Commander Nysis," the king said in a dark voice. "We ride for Ehthilia."

Osinian Osiris, the first of the Eight Sons

- Acknowledgements -

    This book is dedicated to my mother, who is arguably the reason I became an author in the first place. From her, I received my motivation, my voice, and my passion for this craft. My mother was a linguist masterfully skilled in both French and English, so I've always guessed that's where half of my abilities as a wordsmith originates.

    There's quite a bit of anguish laced in the lines of this book. Like many writers, I've chosen to express my anguish in an artistic form and to combine it with imagination, fantasy, and heroism. My mother is most remembered by the lives she improved and the people she loved, but I have hopes that with this book, she will also be remembered for her impact on her only son.

    I love you, mom.

The Sons of Osiris series continues with

Book 2: Regicide

Look for the second installment of Michael Westmoreland's Epic Fantasy series coming late fall/early winter of 2024

Sign up for the reading list for the most up-to-date details!

www.michaelwestmoreland.com

A Tennessee native, Michael Westmoreland grew up in the foothills of the Appalachian Mountains where roving hills and vast forests sat in view from his backyard. This upcoming inspired the setting for the Sons of Osiris universe.

Before pursuing a career in publishing, Michael began his writing journey from the early age of nine when he wrote a short fiction story for his English class. His love for literature and the more artistic aspects of life blossomed in the support of his parents, who both studied language intensively and implemented it in his youth.

Michael takes great pride in his ability to shape a world with his experiences, but none of his achievements would be possible without the overwhelming amount of support he received from his friends, family, and colleagues in the publishing field. As a self-published author, he's building his brand from the ground up, learning how to better master his skills as a writer and entrepreneur on the way.

Join him on his publishing journey at www.michaelwestmoreland.com. Sign up for the reading list, check out his other works coming soon, or simply leave him a message with your thoughts. He takes great delight in talking about any topic related to writing and language (and Tennessee sports.) Be sure to keep an eye out for *Sons of Osiris: Regicide* to come out sometime in late 2024!

Printed in the USA
CPSIA information can be obtained
at www.ICGtesting.com
JSHW021018111024
71251JS00006B/2